FROM THE SKY

FROM THE SKY

J.M. ANTONY

Valorum Books

Published by Valorum Books

First Edition

J.M. Antony asserts the moral right
to be identified as the author of this work

A catalogue record for this book is available from the
National Library of New Zealand

ISBN: 978-0-473-60535-3

FICTION

From The Sky

is for Heleine, Romano and Adrijana

Foreword

The *Natui* people as described in this fiction are a design of my imagination. I created them as a reflection of a unique civilisation who may have lived in the early nineteenth century and during a time of upheaval amongst the peoples of the South Pacific. The Pacific Island nations at the time did not have enormous populations, and there were vast distances between those nations, making contact difficult and often dangerous. However, sizable empires, such as those ruled over by the Tu'i Tonga lineage of the Tongan Islands, conquered many parts of what is now known as Fiji, Samoa and the surrounding ocean. This was an impressive feat given the enormous stretches of ocean between land masses.

By the early 1800s trading vessels from many competing and sometimes warring European powers had become frequent visitors to the South Pacific. This created a power imbalance with some Pacific Island peoples who eventually recognised the new technology and trade could be used to great advantage, not only to create wealth but also to overpower their ancestral rivals. Arriving on one such voyage, William Mariner was one of the first Europeans to live amongst the Tongan people of Ha'apai and Vava'u, at first as a captive and later as a trusted young ally to

Chief Finau, a great warrior and cunning leader ruling over the expansive island of Vava'u and Ha'apai.

The legend of Mariner and my several years living in the South Pacific were an inspiration to me in creating this fiction. My experiences as a husband to my beloved wife who was born in Tonga and our children who share her Tongan lineage have given me a unique perspective on the Pacific people. For ease and familiarity, most of the language and names of the 'Natui' people are derived from the Tongan dialect. Some of the traditions and practices described relate to several Pacific cultures. This is in an attempt to build a unique people and not to reflect one that already exists.

Perspective is important in telling any story. I have been told by many of my extended family in the Tongan community that sometimes what is heard or seen does not do justice to what is truly meant when one is witness to Pacific traditions. You may describe a cultural practice and never truly understand its true purpose unless it is explained with historical context and metaphorical meaning. Traditional dances, kava circles, legendary stories and the deference to one's place in society are all subject to this complexity in providing perspective.

My journey in writing this novel provided me with as many questions as answers about the psyche of the Pacific people at that historical juncture and what the first interaction with Europeans may have been like. We know from the recordings of European explorers and the oral history of Pacific people the first encounters were sometimes chaotic affairs. Four of Abel Tasman's crew were killed by warriors of the Ngāti Tumatakōkiri tribe during their first contact with New Zealand Māori in 1642.

Tasman had been attempting to communicate with the residents of Mohua. However, Ngāti Tumatakōkiri may have believed the Europeans were wicked spirits, or an enemy attempting to raid their ripe harvest of kūmara (sweet potato) and sought to protect themselves. Warriors attacked a small boat carrying Dutch sailors, resulting in several deaths. Other early explorers, such as Captain James Cook, approached the Māori in 1769 with benevolent intentions, but the first attempts were fraught with tense encounters. Further loss of life, this time on the side of the Māori, resulted from a lack of mutual understanding. Conversely, the encounters between the Tahitians and Cook were friendly and marked with generally favourable relations.

However, rather than a history book, what lies ahead of you is a story of adventure and passion at a time of political conflict.

The South Pacific nations are places of idyllic beauty and rich traditions. If you travel to that part of the world and experience their cultures, you will find an enriching experience. You will never, ever grow tired of a flawless sunset suspended over the sandy beaches of an island nation like Tonga, its many outer islands and its wonderfully warm, generous people.

ONE

The first of Abel's senses awoke. A tremendous ache in his head overwhelmed all other worldly concerns. His lungs screamed for air. Someone was pressing on his chest and relief came as a gush of briny water erupted from his mouth. He spluttered and coughed, drawing a laboured breath. Then the rest of Abel's sensations stirred in an overwhelming cacophony. There was the distinct sound of breaking waves. A rising sea wind. The desperate voices of men. Terrible screams. His heart beat at an alarming speed.

A sharp blow to his cheek woke him fully. He squinted as raindrops battered his face. There was little more than a blur at first, but he recognised the silhouette of a thin-faced man whose hair was dripping with water. A hand rose above him and came down, again striking him hard on the face.

"Stop hitting me." He meant to shout, but the plea was barely audible.

The man above him sighed loudly.

"Young Kinkade, can you move?" It was the ship's surgeon, Robert Wickman.

"I can't breathe, Doctor ..."

"Aha, the lad's alive! By God, if you weren't breathing, you wouldn't be eyeing me up with that stupid look on your face. I need to get you out of the surf. Are you able to stand, boy?"

Wickman was shaking. He strained his voice when he squealed the question. Abel sat up with a helping hand from the doctor. He looked down at his stiff legs and shivered. The edge of a frothy ocean tide lapped over his body.

The white sandy beach was a blur, with salt water obscuring his vision. Despite the rain and grey skies, the mid-afternoon sun found a small patch of clear sky to brighten the day. When he had strength again enough to wipe away the sand and sea spray from his face, he gasped at the sight of the rising flames erupting from their wrecked two-masted sloop. The *HMS Viritus* was in jeopardy. Smoke flooded the seashore with wave upon wave of nauseating grey billows. He had spent the last year on that ship. Now it was grounded on a vast coral reef, listing steeply on its stern. There were more shrill screams from the water and sandy beach, with the smell of burning timber filling his nostrils. He dry retched and coughed up more putrid sea water before collapsing on his back again.

"Now, lad, I'm going to help the others, but I need you to stand. I don't have the strength to drag you any further. You almost drowned when you knocked your head. The tides coming in so you'll soon drown a second time if we don't move quickly."

Abel took a breath. He sat up and took Wickman's outstretched hands, allowing himself to be pulled up to his feet. The world spun around him as if he was still on deck of *Viritus* during a storm, but with the help of the surgeon he walked twenty-five yards to a dryer patch of land between the upper beach and the grassy dunes.

"Remain here while I help the others. Don't move, lad. You have a head injury and you will only do yourself harm if you exert yourself further."

"Where's Lieutenant? Did he survive?" Abel said.

Wickman nodded. "There's nothing to fear. I've seen your cousin reach shore already. He was one of the last to leave the ship."

The doctor helped him to sit against the bank of a steep sand dune before rushing away towards a group of men. They were dragging the limp body of a fellow shipmate with them. Some of the men were burned and covered in blood, and as they reached the safety of land they fell in tired heaps.

"Help me, please ..."

Abel heard a familiar voice emerge from the water's edge. It was Mathew Stough. Abel was only seventeen, and Mathew was only one year his elder, so they had become natural friends. The ensign was struggling out of the shallow tide and was holding his blood-soaked stomach, his face screwed up. His features were ghastly white, entirely drained of colour, whilst the sand and water beneath him had become crimson with his blood. Before he could reach the dry sand, Mathew fell forward. His face buried in a shallow estuary.

Abel didn't hesitate.

I'm not just going to sit here. I need to save my friend. Vincent would want me to.

With as much effort as he could muster, Abel stood and tried to run towards the fallen shipmate. However, he fell when his legs gave way to weakness after only a few harrowed steps.

He could barely move his limbs. Nothing seemed corporeal, and he knew he was close to losing consciousness again. His eyelids edged closed; the pain mercifully overcame him. Only the cool breeze and thick rain drops rushing over his body brought him to his senses, if only briefly. He turned and dug his fists into the soft ground and tried to reach Mathew. He was still so far away. For all his efforts, the torturous movement only sought to make the pain so unbearable that no amount of resolve would move him any further. Abel heard an agonising scream that seemed to last forever. He wept silently, turning on his back with his last effort of strength. He wept for his friend. Mathew needed him, but there was nothing he could do in this broken state.

Above, the palms of a tall coconut tree provided some shelter. A loud squawk of frightened seagulls captured his attention as they passed overhead. He watched them catch the wind, then swoop back out to sea, before he lapsed again into unconsciousness.

Though the sun had warmed the ocean the weeks before the grounding, when he eventually awoke, the warm tropical heat had turned into a maelstrom of wind and crashing waves. His eyes stuck together with grit, and it was difficult to prise them open. As he sat up, Abel wiped his eyelids of the salty grime before trying to surmise his surroundings. It was dark, with only a small wavering campfire to provide light. There were men. He couldn't tell how many, but they were all cramped into a small cave. Most of his fellow sailors huddled together and tried in vain to keep sheltered from the entrance. Outside, a gale and torrential rain threatened to consume the entire world. Those closest to the entrance were drenched, trying unsuccessfully to use some paddle shaped leaves to keep the water from their heads. Abel had been laid asleep nearer other sick and infirm sailors at the very far end of this rocky space. Now that he had awoken, a thirst gripped him so terribly that he forced himself to his feet and towards a spout of water, splashing from the cave's mouth. He caught the drops on his tongue as it fell. A great relief spread throughout his body as he drank; however, the pleasure ended when a heavy hand pulled him away. It was Doctor Wickman again.

"Bloody hell, boy, have you no sense at all? Drink slowly. You've had nothing but drips of water for days." He furrowed his brow as he took Abel by the arm and pulled him back into a dryer corner. Wickman had always been kind to him on the journey, even when others bullied him for his lowly rank as ship's boy.

"Keep yourself free of wet clothes. Dry your boots. The wet will surely curse you with eventual sickness. Keep away from the entrance … Abel, are you listening?"

Abel nodded and looked outwards into the howling darkness. "What happened, Doctor?"

"What happened? A bloody typhoon happened, that's what. You've been sleeping for two days. After we ran aground, the weather turned nasty. We had to seek shelter. Barely had time to stitch up these bloodied lot and salvage what we could from *Viritus* before we had to find a place to keep ourselves dry." He shook his head. "Vincent led men to put out the flames … but some perished before the rains leant a hand in the task. It's bad enough we were forced to abandon *Viritus*, only to have to endure another of the Lord's storms. What element has not betrayed our endeavour?" The doctor's frequent melodramatic speeches were expected. But this time Wickman wasn't exaggerating. They had recently been plagued with an unusual run of bad luck. He wiped raindrops from his face and ran his hand through his grey beard before pulling his jacket collar higher to cover his face from the cold.

Some men looked at Abel and gave a forced smile. "Well done, lad," a few of them murmured, though he could barely hear them through the roaring typhoon that encompassed the world outside. He counted his fellows and viewed a few dozen survivors but could not see the captain in the group. The first mate, Master Titus Larkin, was alive. He had been cut across his left temple with a deep gash and was languishing at the far end of the cave. With some great relief, Abel could also see Lieutenant Vincent Luther, who had taken command of the marines after his own superior had perished of dysentery some weeks beforehand.

Luther took the blanket he was wearing and draped it around a wounded man's shoulders before kneeling and speaking to him up close. Abel couldn't hear what was being said, but he could see the blood-soaked marine stiffen and his head held a little higher after a few moments. The lieutenant clasped his shoulders firmly, and with a pat on the back, he moved to the next man. Luther had become a popular leader amongst all ranks of the crew, even if he was a marine and a highborn gentleman. Most importantly, Luther was his family.

After the misery they all endured, Abel blinked back tears as Luther started to sing. It began slowly but powerfully, and he watched as the huddled men stirred at his baritone voice.

"Farewell an' adieu to you fair Spanish ladies,
Farewell an' adieu to you ladies of Spain,
For we've received orders for to sail for old England,
An' hope very shortly to see you again."

After the first verse, the rest of the crew joined in. Even the doctor sang. The voices raised their spirits despite the thunderous typhoon and gales that swept salt and rain into their eyes, causing many to blink uncontrollably. The presence of the lieutenant made all around him sit up a little straighter with pride and hope that all was not lost. Abel had not met a man as virtuous. He dreamed he would one day be just like his cousin. Chivalrous and honourable.

"We'll rant an' we'll roar, like true British sailors,
We'll rant an' we'll rave across the salt seas,
'Till we strike soundings in the Channel of Old England,
From Ushant to Scilly is thirty-four leagues."

Every man who had sailed on an English ship knew this old shanty. They sang it on a journey home to the motherland, and its lyrics seemed strange given their current predicament. Abel felt warmed by the powerful voices. Beside him sat Timothy Millstone, the ship's cook. During the last verse of the song, he wept but covered his face when he saw Abel had noticed.

"Let every man here drink up his full bumper,
Let every man here drink up his full bowl,
And let us be jolly and drown melancholy,
Drink a health to each jovial an' true-hearted soul."

The mirth was fleeting, and there was silence for the rest of the night. The irony of the shanty was likely not lost on Abel's comrades given they had spent their days being pursued by a French man-o'-war prior to running aground. In the end it was fire which sealed the fate of *Viritus*; a fire which the others now spoke about only in whispers.

Luther approached and crouched beside him. Abel smiled and tried to stand, but his cousin motioned him to remain resting.

"Wickman told me you would recover in time. I had no doubt, cousin," Luther said as he felt the back of Abel's head. "No stitches needed, thank God. Are you well, otherwise?"

"Aye, sir. I will live."

"I'm glad to see you mostly unharmed. Keep as warm as possible and rest. You'll need your strength in the days ahead. A good Englishman never surrenders to despair, correct?"

"I'll be right. You can rely on me."

"I've no doubt,' said Luther. 'This storm will end soon enough."

"Sir. At the beach. I saw Mathew. I tried to help."

Luther's face fell but he stayed silent.

"I was wondering, where is he?"

The lieutenant sighed and looked at the cave entrance. "I'm sorry, Abel."

The young man understood, and his heart dropped.

Luther shook his head and moved away, speaking briefly to Doctor Wickman before returning to see after another injured marine.

He knew his friend was no more. There was nothing he could do except hold back more tears.

Abel's muscles ached, and his legs were cramped, making his attempt to sleep fitful and uncomfortable. Eventually he became so tired that even the stony ground could not keep him awake, and he drifted into slumber.

Before he closed his eyes, he watched as the doctor remained fixated on the entrance of the cave where the light of the fire was at its meagre range. A faint white patch of chalky water was dripping away from the wall where rain was splashing and further spreading a thick white resin. Before it had become unrecognisable in the wet, it had been a distinctly drawn shape; the impression of an albatross.

The first men arose from the mouth of the cave, pushing aside the branches they had bundled together at the entrance to keep the rain from their clothes. Sunshine beat down on the exhausted faces of each hungry sailor while they stretched and wiped the sleep from their faces. Abel stepped into the light to find that the entrance was not on the beach, but somewhere inland and surrounded by tall coconut trees and leafy palms. A strange stick insect moved away from Abel's hand as he brushed by, and he watched it camouflage itself against a winding tree truck. It turned soil brown and almost faded away completely.

"How far away are we from the water, Lieutenant Luther? I'm well enough to help on a search if you have orders."

The tall marine had his back turned as he addressed his men. He had already given them orders to scout the bush for a flowing water source. He turned and eyed Abel up and down. Abel often felt that Luther and the other officers still regarded him as little more than a growing boy. He certainly didn't feel that way. A fortnight beforehand he had turned seventeen years of age and was turning into a strong young man from the labours aboard *Viritus*. The other sailors had told him he was a handsome lad, though only during jest when they lamented over the lack of female company. The many months at sea had turned his skin olive and his hair a light blonde. Although his facial hair was growing, he had kept himself shaven, complaining that he didn't like the feel of a scratchy beard. Many other men on board playfully mocked him for his boyish looks.

"Why don't you come down to the beach with me, my young ensign. You too, Doctor. I have some matters to discuss if you don't mind."

Abel looked at the doctor and then over to the cave where Master Larkin was huddling and cradling his head. They walked away from the others, following the lieutenant to the shore. As the heat of the day struck them, Luther wiped away sweat from his brow and unbuttoned his red marine jacket. The colour was striking against the backdrop of the white sand. It made Luther and his fellow marines stand out from the rest of the crew, who wore blue reefer jackets and white trousers. Most had discarded their jackets in the heat but would don them again at night as the air became cooler.

Their refuge was almost two hundred steps from the shore. When they exited the bush, they could feel the warm breeze of the ocean blowing eastward, folding the long beach grass in its wake. The sand was golden yellow and strewn with shells. Crab holes punctured the surface all along the beach, which was both wide and long, curving away at the edge of Abel's vision. Their black and stricken ship had garnered the attention of a flock of seabirds that perched lazily on its stern. It was a partially charred hulk now.

The sight of their vessel pained Abel. He remembered first stepping onto *Viritus* almost one year ago, soon after his mother had died of consumption in London. It had meant an escape from the deep sorrow of his loss, and his father had recognised the need for Abel to find focus and strength in a long sojourn. Born to Jonathan and Mary Kinkade, his father had been a sailor himself and had always talked about his journeys on tall-masted ships just like this one. His father had taught him the basics of knots and rigging as a child, but Abel had not had the chance to board a proper vessel until he signed up with the British Royal Navy, not knowing where they were sailing until they left port. Lieutenant Luther was his mother's nephew, an officer of the vessel who had recommended him to the ship's captain and had now taken Abel under his wing. From first sight he was in awe of *Viritus* and perhaps even nervous about his decision to join the crew, but after a few days at sea he had grown to love the ship and the freedom of the ocean.

"It's hard to believe we survived the French guns, let alone made shore before the ship burned." Doctor Wickman shook his head and placed his hands on his hips.

The lieutenant spotted something in the surf and strode into the water up to the knees of his blue trousers. He bent down and picked up an object, examining it up close. Looking out to sea, he scanned the horizon for a while and then walked back to the two, turning the object over in his hands. It was the half shell of a coconut without its husk or flesh. Doctor Wickman scratched his beard and took the shell, examining it for himself.

"Polished and marked. We might not be alone, sir. I also saw some tribal markings in the cave. They might even be on this island." Wickman's breath became quick and shallow. "This situation is getting worse."

"Leave that for me to worry about. Calm yourself. The cup could've come from anywhere, and the drawings could've been there years before we arrived. Abel here is going to walk the length of the coast for us. Assuming he's fit for duty and recovered? I've also sent men inland to scout and search for supplies." Luther turned to the doctor. "What's the condition of the men?"

The simple object found in the water had bothered the lieutenant. He was listening as the doctor spoke, but he fixed his gaze on the other islands. In particular, a sizable expanse of shore some three miles to the northeast. It was hard to tell from here how large any of the islands were, and he was sure that the crew was unfamiliar with waters this far from their intended route. Last night he overheard the men whispering that the maps had been lost when they abandoned the ship and not even Master Larkin was sure where they were.

"Ahem." The doctor cleared his throat. "We had already lost a host of men even before we landed. Fifty-eight men were still alive when we struck the reef. One, whose belly was torn amid the evacuation, died just hours before the storm struck. Two men died last night of burns from the fire that engulfed much of the upper deck. Another man developed a strange sickness which has left him paralysed. The poor soul ate some strange fruit. Devoured the whole thing soon after landing. He died last night. I've let the others know to keep a distance from that fruit, of course. Of the men who are left we have present company, Master Larkin, fifteen of your marines, the master at arms, our boatswain, Midshipman Andrew Smith, Mr Millstone, a few mates and twenty-nine seamen – most of them able. That's fifty-five men alive."

"What of Master Larkin?" the lieutenant questioned.

"Well, sir, the cut on his scalp was deep but didn't reach the bone. He sustained it during the attack some days ago and I had stitched it. Unfortunately, they've come undone and I've lost my medical bag. Your men didn't happen to procure my baggage when they were looting the ship?"

"Doctor, it's not looting when it's your own ship." The lieutenant raised his voice as he continued. "And, no, we weren't bloody looking for your personal baggage when we were emptying the ship of powder and supplies. Such would be your own damned responsibility, would it not?"

Wickman looked down at his scuffed boots.

Abel liked the handsome young lieutenant who always had a kind word and smile for him, occasionally sharing a mug of rum even after he had drunk his own ration. He was also wary of the lieutenant's temper, which could often cause even the hardiest of men to step back in fear.

"I'm sorry for my tone, Robert, but these events have not done well for my demeanour." He placed his hand on the doctor's shoulder. "As for my question, I realise Larkin's wounds are not life threatening. It's not his wounds that I'm curious about."

The doctor frowned and swallowed. His lips were dry. Abel could see sweat pouring down his face with heat and exhaustion. His own breath was laboured as he swatted away mosquitos from his brow.

"Sir, I don't know what to say. He hasn't spoken to any of the men since we disembarked and has hardly moved in all that time. At first, I thought it was the wound, but now I believe it is some terrible melancholy that has struck. I've seen this before on long voyages."

"Bollocks. Not from a second in command, Doctor Wickman. He's alive and should be thankful. The men need guidance. As it is, I've overstepped my bounds by taking control when we landed, but he'll need to pull out of whatever rut that now enslaves him. These men require leadership. He simply idled off the longboat and lazily sauntered onto the beach whilst the rest of us pulled dying men from the water!"

"Vincent, please. He needs time."

"To be a coward?"

"No, Vincent, of course not." The doctor gestured his hand calmly towards him as he spoke. "Just time to heal and gather his mind. We've all been through an ordeal."

"Did we save the powder and muskets, sir?" Abel interrupted the two.

Luther looked at him with a puzzled expression, and then his face relaxed.

"Of course, young Abel. You were off with the fairies when we arrived and didn't see us flailing like lunatics, trying to save the dry goods before the weather turned. We were lucky, to be honest. The rain doused the fire well before it ever threatened the magazine, fortuitously by drenching through the French damage to the main deck. We have some bags of wet flour and some dried meat that survived. Cookie can make something of that. We managed to save three crates of muskets and six barrels of powder and ammunition."

"The cannon is still intact?"

"It's possible almost all, though it's not my greatest concern at this very moment." The lieutenant laughed. "You seem more interested in the cannon than the news that you may have another meal tonight, young lad. I presume the cannon is still intact on the ship, and when we have half a chance, I intend to retrieve whatever else I can from the wreck at low tide. The reef is very shallow so we can walk the distance if the tide is low enough. For now, we need to scout the island, find water and build proper shelter." Luther paused for a moment, narrowing his brow.

"We also need to consider from what direction we're vulnerable. I'll have the men hide our long boats away from sight. If we're truly lucky, the ship may be salvageable enough for us to repair or with enough time and effort, we could strip it down to build a smaller seaworthy vessel."

The sun burned their skin as it rose higher in the sky, and they retreated to the shade of a young coconut grove.

Luther pulled out his sabre and started drawing small round objects in the sand. He marked an "X" in the southernmost circle. "That's us."

"Are those the islands surrounding our beach?" Abel said.

"Aye, well spotted." He pointed to the middle of several shapes he had drawn. "That small island there is where we landed. Those two islands are the ones you can see to our immediate north. The one to the east is small and low. The western island appears much larger. I'm not sure how large it is, though I've seen great flocks of birds emerge from its direction. I don't think our own island is inhabited. I'd say that if any peoples live close to our shore, it'll be from the westernmost island to our north. It's part of the reason Master Larkin settled us here to repair the vessel, if that's even possible. All the other land sighted from our eastern approach were too small for our numbers, and we couldn't chance an encounter with potentially unfriendly natives."

Luther stuck his blade into a batch of circles to the far east of his drawings. "These are the Tonga Islands, where we had intended to intercept the whalers. We're possibly three or four hundred miles from there and in relatively uncharted waters."

Wickman shook his head. "Bloody hell-sent French pushed us that far?"

"Captain didn't think we could fairly match the enemy frigate. Before he was wounded, he honestly thought that if he led them to dangerous waters that they would eventually give up the chase. We kept a distance for four days before they caught up and barely had half a day to find refuge after the encounter," Luther said.

Abel winced as he remembered the moment the two ships unleashed their cannon. He had watched the horror unfold from behind the bulwarks. Then below decks he was called upon for much of the battle. The doctor conscripted him to restrain wounded men while the physician sawed off bloodied limbs. The French ship had been slowly gaining on *Viritus* for days until they turned to face the inevitable clash. The French cannon had greater range than their own, forcing *Viritus* to manoeuvre closer to the enemy's flank. When the battle was done, both vessels became so badly damaged and had lost such a host of crew that they were both forced to retreat. Struck in the chest and stomach by pieces of an exploding deck, Captain Barker was in incredible pain. Imbedded as deep as it was, Doctor Wickman wasn't able to remove all the shrapnel. Despite this, the captain refused to remain infirmed and forced members of the crew to help him throughout the ship while he continued to give orders, becoming more aggressive and unpredictable in the final hours before they struck the reef. The fire started just prior to its grounding. In the rush to escape *Viritus*, Abel had fallen from the deck and struck his temple on the bow of a longboat.

"Sir, what happened to Captain Barker?" Even though Abel knew the captain had been injured, he had hoped that he had survived their arrival.

Luther frowned again, clenching his teeth. "He perished as we approached the reef."

"How did the fire begin?" Abel had seen the flames, and the ensuing chaos, but not the source of ignition.

The lieutenant, stared straight ahead, his eyes hard and cold while he answered. "Barker became convinced the French would take the ship. So rather than let them, he tossed a bucket of pitch onto the main deck and broke a lantern on the whole damned mess. Lit up like a bonfire. Then he shot himself in the head with his own pistol. Perhaps if the Master and Commander was still alive, he could've told us all about it," Luther answered with a pinch of sarcasm.

Before Abel could ask more questions, Doctor Wickman examined his head wound with concern.

"You're bleeding again. We'll need to find some clean cloth to wrap that wound tightly. Come with me."

Luther stopped Abel before he left. "Come back as soon as you're done. I have duties for you. Prepare some rations for a journey on the morrow."

TWO

Timothy Millstone held the container above his mouth and took a long drink. It had rained heavily the evening before, but they had few vessels to catch the precious liquid. The morning sun had dried much of what remained. Thankfully for the crew, their island was host to thousands of coconut trees, and the water inside those life-sustaining fruits was a welcome substitute.

Sweat poured down his puffy cheeks, and his stomach rumbled loudly. As ship's cook, he had plentiful access to food, and over the past year his ever-widening hips and belly had become the daily joke of the rest of the crew. His left arm was weakened from an old musket shot wound that almost destroyed his left shoulder. These days, his services were mostly only of use in the galley. But he never complained, and had become skilled in his new profession. Abel liked him. Millstone's pudgy face had a perpetual smile wrapped across it, and he always had time for a friendly chat over a tea and hot bun.

Millstone and Abel had been assigned a mission to scout the length of the shore. When the cook had learned they were to be joined by Petty Officer Grigory Worthstead, his perpetual grin almost disappeared.

"You stinking fat twat. You're gonna drink all the bloody water before we ev'n get 'alf way." Worthstead chuckled. "Will you look at this young Abel? The fatso 'ere goes a few days without pickled pork and looks like he's about to croak."

Worthstead laughed at his own joke as they continued their journey around the outskirts of the island. The three had begun their journey at first light and were almost two hours into the walk. Abel figured that they may have already travelled a full half length of the shoreline.

Twisted rocky outcrops extended from the beach and into the rising tide. The water halted their journey across the beach. Worthstead, a sailor known more for his love of rum more than his discipline, lay down on the beach with his feet dipped into the cool sea. He was a rascal, but Abel knew him to be loyal to the lieutenant and a capable watch captain.

"What say we just relax in the sun for a spell? Ol' fatty jollocks 'ere can whip up some greasy muck and pour a mug of ale for us weary souls."

Millstone grimaced at the insult and casually kicked a clump of sand, recently made wet by the incoming waves. A small crab popped its head out of a sandy hole, remained still for a moment, and burrowed its way back under the sand as another rush of water swept a wreath of seaweed across its hiding place.

Millstone took most jokes at his expense in good humour but didn't enjoy insults regarding his cooking.

"If I could catch enough crabs, I could make a good stew. Just ain't got no stinkin' pot." He looked over at Abel, who had picked up a handful of stones and was skimming them across the incoming waves. "What about you, young man? If you could 'ave anything to eat from old mother England, what would you 'ave?

"Fat bastard talking about food again. Likely this island's as poor as Job's turkey and we starve in less than a fortnight," Worthstead said.

"Wasn't talking to you at all. Not one little bit I say."

Worthstead was still laughing, eyes closed and basking in the sun.

"The doc told me it was the turn of the new year a couple of nights back," Millstone said. "Eighteen hundred and seven it is now. We had a bonfire but no whiskey to see it pass proper. Christmas wasn't much better, either. No Chrissy pudding. Well, Master Abel? What would you wish for if you had your choice? A pot of lamb stew? Pork pie? Steak and kidney pudding? I miss steak and kidney pudding. My mother and father would make a pudding—"

"I try not to think about it, Tim." Abel cut off the cook mid-sentence. "It helps the days pass by faster when I don't think of the food I miss. Or England for that matter."

Abel was only mildly paying attention to the conversation as he was now focused on the thick foliage that marked the edge of the island's tree line. A light breeze caused palm fronds to sway ever so slightly and the fine dry sand to drift over his feet. He walked away from the surf and stepped into the shade of the jungle canopy. The ground beneath him crunched under his weight as he stopped and looked at the broken vegetation.

Millstone looked on curiously and wiped several beads of dripping sweat from his face. "What do you see Abel?"

"A trail of broken twigs and shrubbery, Cookie. Something's been running through here."

"Not a chance ..." Millstone approached and looked into the shadowy edge of the thick greenery. "Dunno, lad. Maybe. Could be a boar. Could be the storm. I ain't seen no pigs in this part of the world where people ain't livin'."

He patted Abel on the shoulder and walked back to the edge of the water to cool his feet. Abel remained standing and bit his lip, staring as deeply into the tree line as he could. A branch snapped somewhere ahead, and he held his breath. For a moment he thought he could see some movement further into the foliage.

"Hello."

The leaves and long grass swept across his vision with a persistent rustle in the wind. There was no answer.

After some time, he saw and heard no further disturbances, so returned to the water's edge.

"You 'ad nuff of conversing with that chatty bush?" Worthstead poked towards Abel with a stick.

The young man narrowed his brow and continued on his way down to the beach.

"He's an impatient young man now, ain't he?" Worthstead brushed himself off from the wet sand, and the three continued their journey.

They climbed carefully around a narrow ledge of rocks where the beach had turned into jagged reef. It perched against a hard outcrop of cliff face rising over forty feet. The men were grateful when the rocks ended, with a narrow strip of sand widening to a beach and a sharp turn to the west. From here they saw some smaller islands in the distance, and the tops of swaying coconut branches were visible from their vantage point.

There was beauty here. Abel had grown to love the sea and the mysterious places far from home. The South Pacific was always warm to his skin, and he had become accustomed to the endless world of tropical islands they had encountered along the way. He was not so sure how he felt now that he couldn't leave. There was no doubt that he had grown and learned so much more under the guidance of Lieutenant Luther. The whole voyage felt like some great adventure but it wasn't all sea shanties and tropical islands. The lieutenant had asked the doctor to continue his schooling in arithmetic, geography and literature. In his own time, Luther reinforced the importance of duty and obedience in Abel.

"One day, and with God's help you may turn into a gentleman, make something of yourself and escape this bloody widower of an ocean."

But Abel didn't want to leave the ocean. He felt at peace at sea, surrounded by well-travelled men, each who had more than a few stories to tell of their exploits across the waters of the world. One day he would make it to the Americas and see the colonies for himself.

"What we got 'ere then?" Worthstead said.

He motioned for his companions to stop. He was the first to see movement further up the beach where the smoke of a small fire drifted lazily on the breeze. Around one hundred paces ahead, two figures sat beside each other. A small boat resting closer to the water.

Worthstead's eyes widened. "It's a lad and I think the other is a young lass." He pushed Millstone and Abel behind a large log of driftwood and out of sight.

The three kept hidden, peering over the flotsam to spy.

"What do we do now? Go back to camp?" Millstone said.

"Bloody 'ell I don't know. Maybe. Or maybe we just keep our peepers on the blighters up ahead and see what 'appens?"

Abel shook his head. "I want to get closer. We need to know who they are. Lieutenant Luther sent us on a scouting mission, and he wouldn't want to us to turn back without knowing more."

He stooped low and ran into the brush beside the beach.

"Wait … Abel. They might see you. It's dangerous," Millstone said.

Abel pretended he hadn't heard and became excited by the chance to get closer. He would gather a better description if he could close the distance. If he recognised a language or any markings on the equipment they carried, he could relay this to Lieutenant Luther and the doctor. It was an important mission. He would not fail his cousin. Abel moved further inland. He would be able to circle back towards the beach and closer to the edge of the forest where he could keep hidden and watch the strangers. However, halfway to his destination he heard brittle leaves breaking underfoot, followed by the sounds of men. He slowed and crouched low again, moving forward until he saw an area of sparse vegetation. Two sailors of the *Viritus* stood ahead of him and were conversing. Their voices were distinct. He recognised them as Midshipman Andrew Smith and his lackey, Seaman Caleb Buxley.

"Damn, it had to be these two," he said to himself in a whisper.

Smith was an officer, and though he had little to do with Abel, the young man despised him. He was a bully and unusually hard task master. Luther had been clear with Abel that he needed to respect the rank, if not the man, but he didn't have to like him.

The two crewmen had trekked their way through the centre of the island, penetrating the jungle before Abel had crossed their path and had found themselves in a strange clearing.

He watched and listened as Midshipman Andrew Smith crouched amongst an evenly planted crop and plucked a green, heart-shaped leaf from one long stem. The man crushed the leaf between his fingers and held it to his nose, smelling the earthy scent. With his knife, he levered up the root to extract the plant from the soil. Turning it over in his hands, he inspected the long and sinewy tendrils of the unknown plant.

Seaman Caleb Buxley, a towering giant of a man, stood close and watched as Smith scattered soil from the mass of tangled roots. "What you got, sir?" He gestured with his musket which otherwise he kept trained warily on the undergrowth. "Can we eat it?"

"Not sure, Mr Buxley. Not sure."

Buxley swatted away a buzzing mosquito with his hand. "Are we going to stand here all day, sir?"

Luther had sent the two men on a mission inland to find a source of water. Smith would have likely resented the task, as it was beneath him as a ship's officer to be scouting. However, they had earlier discovered a small freshwater pool near the centre of the island, and Luther had ordered them to press on in search of food. It had become apparent the island was unusually bountiful, and they had come across evidence of wild pigs, breadfruit and yams.

Smith surveyed his surroundings. "It's a crop. They've grown in patterns. You see? Over there … and there. I don't know what it is, but someone's tending this field. There's a clump of soil on the other side which has been dug up. Recently too."

"That's good news, sir. Lots of food. We can't eat stale bread and coconuts forever."

"Not necessarily, Buxley. It's a cultivated crop. Its evidence of farming. That means there are people nearby and we don't need the trouble." He drew his pistol and stepped forward, sniffing the air. "I smell smoke. Come with me."

Abel followed as closely as he could without being seen. At a short distance from behind a copse of banyan trees, he watched the two run onto the beach.

Smith hurried through the bush and emerged onto a wide beach on the edge of a calm lagoon. The sudden brightness of sun and white sand made him squint. He blinked his eyes and rubbed them, straining to see. A haze of smoke drifted across the beach. He spotted the campfire, but it had been doused with water and sand, leaving smoke pouring from the remaining hot ashes. A roughly constructed spit made of sharpened sticks still held aloft a half-cooked piglet. Further down the beach a boy and girl were fleeing towards their narrow boat perched on its side.

"I knew there were islanders nearby," Smith said.

He watched the boy reach the boat first and pushed it towards to the water. The weight of the craft was clearly too much for the boy alone to move with much speed, and once the girl arrived, she pulled with as much strength as she could muster.

"We can't let those little bastards go."

Smith dashed towards the pair with Buxley in tow. Their boots slammed into the sand and slowed their run. Abel saw the girl's eyes flash as she witnessed the two men barrelling towards them. The boat slid into the water too late as Smith reached the boy. Raising his pistol, Smith slammed the butt of the weapon against the back of the boy's head. A burst of bright red emerged, and he slumped face first into the wet sand. Seeing him fall, the young girl screamed and took a rough-cut paddle from the boat. She let out a guttural roar, then threw the paddle towards Smith. It hurtled towards his head, but with a jerk, he tumbled backwards to avoid the weapon. It spun awkwardly beyond him and squarely into the face of Buxley. There was a loud crack, and a jet of blood spurted onto Buxley's white shirt. He bellowed in pain, clutching at his nose.

"The little whore broke my nose. I'm going to fuckin' gut that trollop!"

Smith rushed towards the girl. She saw the danger and turned to run. He reached out to grab her by her arm, but the knee-deep water slowed his momentum enough for the girl to break past his grapple.

"Buxley. Grab her!"

The seaman was still dazed from the heavy blow to his face, but the sound of splashing beside him and the shouts of his superior caught his attention. Before she could run past him to freedom, he kicked out his with his tree trunk legs, making her trip and fall into the shallow water. The girl was quick to scramble up to her feet again, but not before a large hand wrapped around her hair and yanked her backwards. The two men were upon her, and for a moment the frothy water covered her face completely. Buxley grabbed her by her slender neck and pulled her out of the sea, dragging her onto the sand. Lying her on her back while she spluttered and struggled to escape, he twice brought down a heavy fist to the side of her head. On the second blow, she stopped struggling and groaned in a dazed whimper.

"Little bitch. How's that nose of yours, Mr. Buxley?"

"Damn right, she's a little bitch." Buxley wiped away the blood that was pouring freely from his injured nose. "I think she broke it with that paddle."

The two looked her over and glared at her partially clothed body. In a style they had seen commonly amongst the native peoples of the south Pacific, the girl appeared to be in her mid-teens and was bare-breasted. Apart from a thick necklace of polished shells and stones around her neck, she wore nothing above her waist. Her long black hair plummeted to a skirt of shredded bark cloth, which came down to her knees. With his pistol, Smith parted the skirt's many strips of cloth, and he smirked as he gazed between her thighs.

"I'll make sure she can't run away again," he said.

With a swift movement he raised his pistol to her chest and pulled the trigger. The hammer sprung with a *clink*, but it failed to fire.

"It's wet, sir. The powder's wet. It's not—"

"I can fucking see that." Pulling out the long blade from his sheath, Smith knelt over the girl who was now stirring. She opened her eyes. Pressing the sharp blade against her neck, the first trickle of blood appeared, glistening with a brilliant ruby glow in the bright sun. Smith's work was short-lived as an angry yell caught his attention, followed by a sudden blow. He was lifted from his feet by a running tackle from his right. The knife flew from his hands, and he landed painfully on his back, his attacker still tumbling past him from the barge.

"What the … Buxley, why weren't you watching the boy!" Smith scrambled to find his knife. The hilt was sticking from the sand, and he easily picked it up and turned back to strike. He stopped when he saw it was Abel who had interrupted his sport.

"Get the hell away from her." Abel came to his feet and faced the larger and more experienced midshipman.

Smith's face became red and was etched with deep lines. Abel knew the men of *Viritus* took care in his physical treatment as Luther's cousin. The seamen would often tread lightly dealing with him. But he knew he had gone too far this time with his superior.

"Why you little shite. How dare you strike an officer. I'll have you whipped."

He dealt a quick blow to Abel's face, followed by a backhand across the right side of Abel's temple. Abel fell back and covered his face to fend off any further blows.

Behind them, Millstone and Worthstead caught up to the fracas.

"I see more interfering wastrels have arrived," Smith said.

Millstone, exhausted from the short sprint, was still able to find his voice. "Sir, if you will, please stop it. He's just a young lad."

Smith's brow scrunched. Abel could almost see the heat move from his neck to his head. It was all he could do to stop himself from bursting. His anger was rarely restrained. "You'll be next, Cookie. Shut your fat face." He picked up the discarded paddle and strode towards Abel. The boy would not avoid his discipline this time.

"But, sir, Lieutenant Luther would take exception to the beating. You know how he's taken favour on young Abel here."

Smith looked down at the paddle and back to the ship's cook. The eyes of the other men were upon him.

"Also, if we kill the girl, someone's going to come looking for her. I don't suppose they'd be pleased with finding her with a slit gullet and all."

Smith took a few deep breaths. They would need to report all of this back to camp. Luther's strongly held opinions on the proper and decent treatment of the people they encountered was well understood. Abel knew this would prove troublesome for Smith who was clearly hesitating at the thought.

He dropped the paddle. "We'll take them all to Larkin for a decision."

"The first mate's not feeling so good. Maybe Lieu—"

"I *said* we'll take this to Larkin to decide. Buxley, the boy is still alive, so pick 'em up and take 'em with you. The girl can walk once she's on her feet. As for you, little turd," Smith said, looking at Abel, "this isn't over. Come on. Time to get back to camp."

Abel kept to the rear of the march. The men spoke very few words on the journey back. The boy struck down by Smith's musket had stirred awake and the midshipman had ordered that the two captives be bound by strips of cloth. Angrily, he tore strips from Abel's shirt for the task and made him carry the half-cooked piglet over his shoulder as punishment. Millstone eyed the carcass with a hungry glare and considered how he might have prepared the beast as a fine feed if given the right spices.

"She's a beauty." Millstone chuckled, licking his lips and looking to Worthstead for agreement. However, he frowned when he saw that his fellow shipman was not paying attention and was instead glaring lustily at the slender body of their female captive.

With a grimace, Worthstead nodded slowly. "Aye, she is. We might 'ave to keep a sharp eye on some of the itchy fellas if we wanna keep that one unsullied."

Abel looked over at the boy and girl. Compared to his own, their skin was the colour of the ashen bark, and although they were both slender, there was a healthy strength in their bodies. The girl was slightly taller than the younger looking male, who was clutching his head in pain now that a large bloody welt had formed at the back of his head. He guessed the boy was about fifteen and the girl a similar age to himself.

Buxley was herding the captives forward. The girl was breathing heavily and was clearly scared. She looked back and met Abel's gaze, but as the sailor roughly pushed her forward, their stare was broken.

Using their sabres, the group hacked away at the thick branches and ferns to clear the path the scouts had already traversed across the centre of the island. Their tense journey contrasted against a scene of idyllic beauty. Luscious ferns and foliage wrapped the landscape in a blanket of vines and canopies from the harsh sun above. Half way back, Smith pointed to a high ridge where a stream emerged from cracks in the stony formations. The water flowed out from behind a high, sloping wall of vegetation and rocky debris.

"Some kind of aquifer? An underground freshwater stream perhaps." Millstone eyed up the water source. "That'll do for our thirsty lot. I know I'll be the first one to take the wrath of all of you seething buggers when the heat makes your throats parched. We'll need to tell Luther 'bout that, aye?"

They took their fill of water and filled their canteens with a fresh supply. Abel took his shirt off and kneeled at the edge of the clear stream. The water tasted fresh. In the reflection, he could see his bloodied and swollen face. A colourful bruise was forming on his cheek, which he rubbed tenderly. Dousing his face and body to wash himself, he noticed Smith had kneeled beside him, away from the others.

His hand gripped Abel's shoulder. Smith's expression was as calm and cold as the island stream.

"Abel, I want you to know that everything is different now. We're going to be here for a very long time. Perhaps forever. For whatever perverted reason the crew has shown you favour is meaningless here. Your cousin can't be watching you all night. When the men realise we aren't going home, there won't be any more favourites. When the time comes, Abel, I'm going to remember your slight against me, and I'm going to eat you like that stinking pig over there."

Smith leaned in further and his voice closed to a whisper. He motioned to the girl. "That little fishy over there's going to die. The first officer will see things my way. But before she gets her due, I'm going to persuade sir to hand her over to the crew for a bit of fun. We have to maintain a sense of morale for as long as possible, don't we?" He smiled and leaned in closer. "You're a young, good-looking boy, too. Who knows what we might do with you once the men get desperate and lonely, aye?"

"Get away from me." Abel stood and backed away from him.

The midshipman laughed loudly, capturing the attention of the others. "As I said, no hard feelings, boy. Let's just get back to camp before dark."

Abel had little to do with the officer on *Viritus* but had known him to be a strict and ambitious leech who had always attempted to curry favour with his superior officers. Now Abel hated him and the thought of what he might incite the others to do. He would need to tell Luther. The hair on the back of Abel's neck rose. He found his hands shaking. If he were to be a target of the officer, he would need to defend himself. In combat he only had rudimentary training from the lieutenant in the art of swordsmanship, and Smith was an experienced soldier a decade his senior. Abel knew how to load and fire a musket. For a moment he considered snatching a pistol from Buxley. The burly seaman's back was turned as he shuffled through his satchel a few yards from the stream.

Smith watched him with a look of disgust, but then stood, stretched his arms behind his head and yawned. "Get your arses up and start moving. It's a long trek back to camp," he ordered the group.

Abel kept his distance. His thoughts swirled and his heart beat furiously.

Calm yourself. You have a duty. Luther would expect you to keep a level head. Don't let that bastard scare you.

Resisting the urge to panic, he looked at the boy and girl who were bound and being forcibly marched backed to camp. They were innocent. They had done nothing wrong except have the misfortune of crossing paths with that sadist, Andrew Smith. Abel was resolved to do everything he could to keep them from harm. However, he knew that the presence of an indigenous people changed everything. For better or worse, the knowledge would cause conflict amongst the crew of *Viritus*. If they were to escape this remote paradise, they might have to contend with more bloodshed, but leave they must.

Luther would know exactly what to do. He always knew what to do.

THREE

It was not until late-afternoon that the group emerged from the dense foliage and the campsite came into view. The ship's boatswain, Jack Horton, was directing a work crew to construct shelters. Horton was an adept carpenter, a much-needed skill at present. Rope and scorched timber from their ship's hull and from wooden crates which had washed onto shore were drying in the blistering sun. Any dry material was being hastily patched together to form barriers from the elements. Ferns and tree bark had to be gathered to make roofing. Horton's task ahead was to build a liveable village for the fifty-five men who would, for the foreseeable future, have to irk out a living on this small island.

Three of Luther's marines greeted the group with muskets raised. As they were recognised, they lowered their weapons but gasped when they saw the two young captives. It took no time for the rest of the crew to surround Smith with questions and curious stares.

Lieutenant Luther and Doctor Wickman emerged from the cave and pushed through the throng of men.

Doctor Wickman frowned as he looked over at the girl and boy. They were both wide eyed with fear, holding on to each other tightly at the sight of so many sailors.

"Oh, dear, what have you found? And what have you done to them?"

The doctor approached the girl. When he reached out to touch her bruised face, she snapped out with her teeth, and he quickly withdrew his hand. The crew scoffed with laughter at the sight of the doctor's rebuff.

"Everyone quiet!" Luther looked Abel up and down. His jaw clenched tightly when he noticed his beaten face. "Report."

Abel stepped forward. "Lieutenant, they've done nothing wrong. They—"

"I didn't ask for a report from a cabin boy when there is an officer clearly present." Luther's features darkened.

Abel lowered his eyes.

"Midshipman Smith, step forward and report. What is this? I asked you to scout but you bring me back captives instead."

Smith considered his superior officer for a moment before he spoke. "Ah, sir, with respect ..."

"Yes, Midshipman. Speak."

"I would request that I present my report to the first mate."

There was a tense moment amongst the crew, and more than one quiet murmur of disbelief was heard amongst them.

He's testing Luther. Thinks that he can undermine him already, Abel thought.

The crew were watching this exchange with bated breath. The midshipman was the next officer in command and the men may have seen this as the start of an early power play. Both officers would already know that men marooned so far from home would need strong leadership and that the first days stranded would make or break them. If discipline broke down so early on, their days would be numbered, and they might not last in such a hostile environment.

Luther spoke slowly but clearly so that all could hear him. "I deny your request. The first mate is not in a healthy condition. When he is well, you may address him then. For now, I await your report. If you are not capable of following my request, you may resign your commission, leave the camp, and I will promote another in your place."

Smith smiled and bowed slightly. "No, sir, that will not be necessary."

He grabbed the boy and yanked him forward roughly, holding onto the cloth bindings around his wrist.

"'Oua teke puke pehe'i au," the boy protested.

Buxley answered him with a slap to the side of the head. The midshipman pushed the boy to his knees.

"We encountered these two spies on the southern shore. When we approached, they both made a dash for it. When we tried to stop them from reporting back to their people, they viciously attacked us with their primitive weapons. Look at Buxley's face." Smith gestured to the girl. "The both of them have the look of killers. I say we rid ourselves of these savages and cast their bodies adrift. We don't have the resources or ability to house them. If they escape, we may risk being exposed to the locals before we have a chance to defend ourselves."

A few members of the crew grunted their agreement.

"My God, is there a Christian soul amongst you? Why would you condemn two young lives for the crime of standing on their own beach?" Doctor Wickman shook his head.

Smith continued. "And another thing, sir. That little turd cabin boy assaulted me when I was trying to put the waif down. I demand some justice for the insubordination."

The lieutenant held his hand up. "Quiet, all of you. There will be no killing."

Abel stared down his accuser. He refused to be intimidated.

"If this is true," Luther said. "I will personally see to his punishment at a later time."

"Bollocks, sir. You won't lift a finger over your dandy cousin here. I demand—"

The midshipman found himself stopped mid-sentence with a backhand to the face from his superior.

"Smith, are you questioning my judgement and rank? If you are, make your intentions clear and we can solve this issue without further time wasting."

Luther drew his pistol and pressed the tip of the barrel firmly against the man's forehead. A gasp from the crew was audible, and Doctor Wickman placed his hand on the lieutenant's arm.

"Vincent, please, is this necessary?"

"Let go of me, Doctor."

Wickman pulled away and stepped back.

Smith licked and then pursed his lips. "No, sir. I yield. Forgive me. You are in command, sir."

"Actually, I am in command." A deep but strained voice emerged from the mouth of the cave. The first mate clutched his bandaged head and walked out into the sunlight.

Luther lowered his pistol. "Attention men. Master Larkin," he said.

The crew snapped to attention and saluted their superior officer.

The injured officer had presented himself in full dress uniform with a long blue coat adorned with gold buttons and a white waistcoat underneath. His white breeches were remarkably clean, though Abel noticed the decorative epaulette on his right shoulder was torn and frayed.

"I see that we have some visitors. Ensure they are under guard at all times, Luther. I will decide what to do with them later, but for now they'll be secured in the cave, fed and watered. Once done, I want to see you, Smith, Doctor Wickman and the master of arms in a private counsel immediately. The rest of you are dismissed."

Luther's posture was upright and stern. "Aye, sir."

Everyone returned to their duties in building the campsite, collecting wood for the night's fire and foraging for food. A party of men were sent to a spot where the scouts had seen a small crop of yams, and another group returned to the shore to collect shellfish from the water.

"Looks as though we've got our first mate back again, aye porky? Best you be putting that piggy on to roast before the bitin' flies have their share of the grub." Worthstead swatted some flies away from the carcass now dumped on the sand at Millstone's feet before walking away.

Now their superior officer had reasserted himself, the politics of the camp had altered once again, and Abel wondered what would become of the prisoners who were now being pushed into the cave entrance. He was exhausted from the trek, so he sat on the outskirts of the camp and felt his stomach rumble. Two marines with muskets stood at attention at the cave's entrance and whispered quietly to each other whilst glancing over to the officers holding talks under the shade of a large swaying palm. The doctor reapplied a bandage to Master Larkin's wounded temple, which made him wince and grit his teeth before leaning forward and speaking to his officers. Even from this distance Abel could see that the meeting was sombre, and on occasion a raised voice would gather the attention of the crew before falling silent again.

Larkin held a reputation as a lofty and hard taskmaster. An experienced career officer, he had been hardened by his voyages to the new Australian and New Zealand colonies during the first settlements after 1788. Abel had heard talk amongst the crew that he had never held enough favour amongst his superiors to gain captaincy of his own ship. As first mate, he hoped to take the helm of his own vessel one day. He was respected but showed little personality or emotion in the year since Abel had joined *Viritus*. This has earned him a reputation for being by the book and strict, which the lieutenant had said was a good trait for an officer. The lieutenant had also told him that an officer should be both tough and compassionate, that the crew would respect a man who held a high standard but was willing to muck in with his subordinates and share a round of ale or two. Master Larkin only held one of these two traits.

By the time the sun was ready to fall, a meal of yams, twice roasted piglet and a shellfish broth had been prepared for the famished men of their camp. They used the half shells of split coconuts as bowls, drank the nutritious water inside and filled the remainder with the bitter soup. Millstone sliced off a small chunk of pork for Abel and handed it to him while he sat beside the now raging campfire. Small sparks crackled from the blaze around which dozens of men slurped and ate hungrily. Abel wolfed down the meat and drank the broth in barely a few gulps.

Millstone watched him in awe. "Slow down. You'll spew up good grub from that famished belly."

"Cookie, what do you think they've decided?" Abel asked.

"What? Oh, the officers? Dunno, lad."

Abel sipped from an opening on the top of another coconut shell. "They're innocent. We can't kill them."

"Aye, lad." Millstone looked at Abel with piteous eyes. "I saw you eyeing up that pretty girl. You can't cry for the world. Some smart alec once said that I think. And they're probably right."

"Smith hates me."

"He's a nasty one, he is. I wouldn't worry too much."

"He wants to give her to the men before they kill her."

Stirring the broth, Millstone took a sip of the concoction and watched as a log rolled from the fire and red sparks burst against the large, encompassing stones.

"Are you listening, Cookie? I said—"

"I know what you said, but ain't nothing you or I can do. My advice is that you pocket that anger for the right time. Just to let you know, now is not that time, aye?"

Abel was worried. Most of his fellow crew had come to respect the peoples of the Pacific they had encountered, especially when trade and hospitality were successful. Others took a superior view and looked down at the natives. Master Larkin's attitude seemed mostly indifferent. But now, Larkin was unwell and under pressure.

The two peered over at the cave where their captives were being guarded. Millstone gathered some palm fronds and coconut shells. He scooped some broth and pieces of white yam into the leaves and shells before handing them on to Abel. "Go on. At least we can treat 'em well for the time being."

"God bless you, Cookie." Abel took the small meals and approached the two marines. They grinned at Abel as he approached. One of them nodded his head. "Good lad, bringing us some grub. You'll go to heaven for this."

"It's for them, Private Moore." Abel pointed his chin towards the cave.

The marine's face dropped, and his companion laughed. "Spoke too soon, soldier. This one wants to go courting in yonder cave. Well, go on then, *Saint Abel.*"

They shoved Abel inside, and he squinted his eyes in the dim light. A few small burning torches had been wedged into cracks lining the walls of the cave, and this provided some dull light to guide the way to the rear where the two captives were being kept.

In a large crevice, crates of Brown Bess muskets were stacked high, and beside them carefully arranged barrels of gunpowder had been placed in the cool cave to ensure they were kept as dry as possible. Other supplies gathered from the remains of the ship were also roughly placed at different points in the crevices and nooks of the cave, wherever the sailors could store any of their precious goods.

The cave was only fifty feet long, and Abel could see the two figures ahead of him as he approached. The boy was sleeping, his head in the girl's lap, but when she saw him, the girl woke her companion and they scurried backwards as far as they could hide.

"It's fine. I'm here to … Here's some food."

Pushing the small amount of fare towards the two, they hesitated at first before giving in to their hunger and devouring the paltry offerings. With their hands bound, they were still able to grasp the bowls and drink the warm liquid in a few gulps. Abel passed them a half coconut shell which had been filled with water, which they also drank heartily. The girl gave her offering to the boy, and when he had drunk half, he passed the remainder to her and she finished the rest, wiping her mouth with the back of her hand. She breathed deeply and looked at Abel with tears forming in her eyes before throwing the bowl back at him indignantly.

Pointing to himself and crouching, he spoke his name. "Abel. My name is Abel. A–bel."

"Epeli?" she said and nodded as if she understood.

"That's close enough, I guess. You?" He pointed his finger.

"Mahina."

"Your name is Mahina? Very well, Mahina. And him. Who is he?" Abel motioned to the boy, who was now covering his face with his hands and groaning in pain and exhaustion.

"Afah."

"Well then, it's a pleasure to meet you, Mahina and Afah. I'm sorry that you—" Abel didn't get a chance to finish his words before Mahina lashed out with her tied hands and hit him over the head with a balled fist. He stumbled backwards and was assaulted by a tirade of words.

"Tukuange kimaua na'a ha'u 'emau tamai 'o 'ave kimoutolu 'o fafanga 'aki 'ae fanga 'anga." She stood and continued to scream at him.

The two marines ran into the narrow cave, guns raised to see what the commotion was about.

"Your lover girl didn't like the food?" One marine joked as he came across Abel backing away from the pair.

"I'm sorry …" Abel gestured with his hands raised.

"Don't fret, Abel. This's what marriage is like back in old England too."

The sailors laughed loudly while he rubbed his scalp.

"Just a little longer, if you gentlemen don't mind?"

"It's up to you, lad. But I would seek a divorce from the magistrate before you get her knocked up." The marines chuckled but shrugged at his request and left him with the captives.

The girl had stopped shouting and had retreated to her brother, where they huddled together. Abel reached into his pocket and brought out a small notebook. It had a brown leather cover and as he opened the pages, he realised some of them were stuck together.

"Water damaged it is. But I had it with me when I jumped ship and I dried it in the sun."

Mahina looked curiously at the book but otherwise didn't react to what he was holding.

"Doctor Wickman gave me this book and told me to write simple words from languages in the South Pacific. I've learned greetings in six different tongues. Other common sayings too. When we stop places to trade for supplies, I record what I learn from the people we meet. People are friendlier when you try to speak their language."

Abel opened to a page filled with several phrases he had recorded. "The doctor thinks that if we can speak to people like your own, we might be able to avoid fighting and misunderstandings and things like that. I've discovered I have a knack for languages."

Abel turned the book around so that the girl and boy could see the writing, but they looked at each other blankly and shook their heads. He read each phrase as he had written them down and watched to see their reaction.

"Talofa." He read the first greeting. They didn't understand him, so he continued, hoping they would eventually know at least one language he had been scribing. "Ni sa bula vinaka … No? How about. Aloha … La ora na … Malo e lelei …" As Abel uttered the last phrase, the young girl's eyes lit up.

"''Io. Ko 'eku lea ia," she said. "Malo e lelei. Mahino."

"That's the language of the Tongan people. You're Tongan?" Abel asked excitedly.

"Tonga? 'Ikai. Ko 'emau ha'u mei Natuini," Mahina said. She shook her head.

Confused, Abel thumbed through his book to see what other phrases he had in Tongan, but stopped when he recognised her phrase.

"You speak the Tongan language but you're not Tongan? I heard that language when we sailed through Tongatapu." His fingers turned the pages until he found more phrases, but he was interrupted when Afah shouted at him.

"Tukuange kimaua ke ma foki ki 'api." The boy spoke angrily and pointed to the entrance of their stony prison.

Abel didn't need to find the words to understand his meaning, and shook his head sadly.

"Fakamolemole." He spoke the word for sorry, a phrase he had committed to memory for several languages he had heard. If he should learn any part of any language, Doctor Wickman had told him, an apology is the most likely phrase to keep a man alive.

Before they could speak further, he felt the tug at his collar and saw that the marines had come to retrieve him.

"You being here is a distraction to our duties, so bugger off, boy."

They pulled him outside and resumed their post, watching as he walked away still nursing the blow to his head.

Returning to the campfire as the day's light faded, he saw the four officers had completed their discussion and were now talking amongst the men, except Master Larkin, who had claimed the first makeshift shelter for himself. Lieutenant Luther sat with a few of his marines on the opposite side of the circle, but when he saw Abel, he motioned him over. He sat beside his mentor, and Luther smiled.

"I got the truth out of Millstone. He tells me you were quite the chivalrous hero today?"

Abel blushed and cleared his throat. "I considered what you would have wanted me to do."

"Really, Abel. You struck a petty officer and broke your oath of obedience as a seaman?"

"Yes, but …"

"But what?"

"He deserved it, sir."

There was a brief silence. Luther sent the surrounding marines to make ready for patrol and guard duty. When they were alone, Luther spoke.

"I've told you I served with Admiral Nelson on the *HMS Captain*, correct?"

Abel was surprised. His cousin rarely spoke of his own naval exploits and travels. "Yes, sir. Everyone in our family speaks of it with pride. My father spoke of it too when he told me I was to voyage with you. Did you know the admiral?"

"Know him? Ha-ha, I held Smith's rank on his vessel during the battle of Cape St. Vincent some years now passed. He used to jest that the Portuguese named the Cape after me in anticipation of the battle."

Luther threw another log on the fire. The warmth was welcome as the evening's air cooled. "I heard him once say that 'you must always obey orders without any opinion of your own'. He meant that it is the very foundation of order in the military for discipline to be respected and adhered to. Absolutely."

"I see, sir. I understand they must punish me for what I did to Midshipman Smith."

"Yes, I suppose you must." He stroked his short blond beard in contemplation. "Of course, Nelson only won himself an admiralty after disobeying his superior officer, Admiral Jervis, during that battle. Without his quick thinking and measured disobedience in our fight against the Spanish, we may not have claimed victory that day. It's an irony to be sure."

Abel turned his head. He looked at the tanned faced of Luther beside him, whose eyes had glazed and whose face seemed contemplative of days long passed. Although the night obscured Luther's features, the occasional flicker of light from the fire betrayed his feelings. His frown lines were deep, and shadows had formed under his eyes from a lack of sleep.

"Much blood that day …"

"Is that where you received your pin?" Abel asked, admiring the metal award Luther wore on the lapel of his shirt.

"Aye," his cousin murmured in reply, touching the decorative piece lightly.

To Abel, his cousin was the epitome of valour and honour in his role as a marine. Vincent Luther had come highly recommended from the captain's peers and was an obvious choice for *Viritus* in its charter to protect British whalers harassed by French and Spanish vessels. Some months ago, they sailed north of the Tongan Islands, where a small fleet of whaling ships were preparing to return north after a successful hunt. The captain expected that the precious oils coveted in civilised ports would catch the attention of enemy privateers seeking to disrupt this rich trade.

Both men sat quietly again. Luther's face had become dark.

"First mate Larkin will contemplate on our situation and provide us with his orders tomorrow." He spoke in a matter-of-fact tone.

"Will he kill the boy and girl? Their names are Mahina and Afah. They're no older than I am."

"He will decide on their fates tomorrow. You know their names?"

Abel nodded. "And they seem to speak the same language as the people of the Tonga Isles. The girl says that she's from Natuini, so that must be where we are?"

Luther shrugged. "I've not heard of these lands but good on you, boy, for keeping a good head about you." He patted Abel on the back proudly. "Your mother was just like you. A bright and generous soul. A good Christian too. But she did not judge imperfection or difference like others would."

Luther looked warily at his sabre beside him before unsheathing it and placing it into the hand of his cousin. "Take one of these. You have much to learn but I've taught you how to use it at least to a middling standard." He lowered his voice further so only Abel could hear him. "At first light, you are to keep this by your side. Do not put it down for any reason. Keep away from others and remain at the edge of camp at all times. Do you understand?"

Abel blinked. A chill ran through his blood at the lieutenant's warning. "What's going to happen tomorrow?"

"I asked you if you understood, cousin."

"Yes …" Abel didn't have the opportunity to respond further as the lieutenant stood and walked away suddenly. At the edge of the firelight, he could see Doctor Wickman, deep in thought. The worry lines on his forehead were a dark contrast to the orange glow of embers and fire.

Abel found it difficult to sleep that night. His fitful slumber ended as he awoke to an ugly birdsong. A flock of large gulls squawked loudly above the camp as if to signal the break of day to the camp's inhabitants. Some had already begun their day. A blurry eyed seaman finished the last dregs of rum from a glass bottle he and some of his fellow compatriots had found washed ashore the day beforehand.

After a quick bite of some hardened bread to ease his hunger, Abel made a loop in his rope belt and slipped the sabre inside. It dangled from his hip and tapped the back of his ankles as he walked. Abel had been trained with some rudimentary skills to use the blade, but had not worn a sword by his side before in battle.

"Expecting an invasion, mighty conquistador?" The grizzled and bearded seaman mocked Abel as he walked by.

At the edge of camp, he watched as marines changed shift at the entrance of the cave. Other crewmen went about their daily camp chores. Two of Luther's most skilled scouts, Cambridge and Rowe, were preparing to hike towards a boar trail further south, where they would lay traps.

John Horton was studying the planks of timber he had been drying in the sun, wondering how he was going to construct decent shelters with a limited supply of nails, saws or hammers, all of which were still on the ship. He shook his head and spat at the ground. This would be no easy task.

Before long, dozens of men were busy preparing what little food they had gathered for a morning meal. Cookie had no pots, but had found a large strangely-shaped stone with a deep indentation. Filling it with water, he had built a fire around the rock and heated it enough to cook their meals. He had found other thin sheets of stone and heated them in the same method, making hot plates for frying. Looking very pleased with his makeshift ingenuity, he boasted of his cooking utensils until the men grew tired of his gloating and threatened to throw him onto the hot plates.

The bustle of camp did nothing to hide the obvious worried stares and whispering from the marines who remained around camp. The two men who were preparing to lay traps for the day had already left in a hurry. Abel didn't even notice them eating with the others before they departed.

As most men had finished their meagre meals, Midshipman Smith walked with haste from the first mate's shelter to the centre of camp and addressed the men. "All crew at attention. Master Larkin wishes to address the camp."

Luther and Doctor Wickman, who had been conversing with some men, stood to attention before the gathering group. Smith joined them. A few stragglers emerged from the beach after being summoned, and they were reprimanded for their tardiness before the first mate emerged from his roughly constructed quarters.

Larkin straightened his ripped uniform and adjusted the military sabre he wore. The man was mostly bald but maintained a thick horseshoe of hair around the side of his head. He looked in stronger spirits and was making a fast recovery. A mosquito buzzed by his forehead, and he swept it away along with a few drops of sweat which splashed on his blood-stained collar.

Standing before the men and beside his officers, Larkin addressed the waiting crowd. "Gentleman, I have been unwell. However, with God's mercy and Doctor Wickman's fine work, I stand before you strong and healthy. In the days after our arrival, I was not of proper mind, due to a blow to the temple. That has passed and shall not be pondered upon." He nodded to himself reassuringly and smoothed down his moustache, gauging the mood of the men.

"I have spoken to my officers, and they have made me aware of our current situation, including the state of our supplies. You'll be aware of our violent encounter with the natives." His words were cut by a sudden wave of dry coughs which wracked his body. When Smith reached out to hold his shoulder, he pushed it away before regaining his composure and continuing.

"Believe me, men, when I say that we will make it home to mother England. We will post watch for any ships that may pass, and we will explore to see if another, better area for a short-term encampment is possible." He peered over to the cave.

"I've considered the two captives. I have been asked to consider their fate and Lieutenant Luther has requested that we let them free and perhaps even use them to make contact with their people. This may favour the trading of resources and peaceful relations. Midshipman Smith has argued that we kill the two and keep from making ourselves known to any potentially hostile people. I have considered our options."

Abel narrowed his gaze to meet Luther's, but his cousin was staring directly forward. He gave nothing away as to his thoughts.

"I have taken advice from my officers, and it is my decision that we do not attempt any contact with any local tribesmen, wherever they may be. Since we can't allow the potential for the two captives to escape and report our position, we cannot suffer them to live." He turned to his second in command and spoke deliberately with a deep command to his voice. "Lieutenant Luther, you are ordered to take the two from the cave. Your marines will execute them without delay, as your colleague attempted so upon their first discovery. Use bayonets. Powder and ammunition are not to be wasted."

Smith cocked his head to the side and did not hide his pleasure at his vindication. He smiled broadly at the other officers, baring his teeth.

The lieutenant's jaw clenched. His cheeks turned a shade of red. However, he did not move from his spot, keeping his eyes facing forward.

"Did you not hear my command? I believe I was entirely clear. Order your marines to execute the prisoners." Larkin snorted like a roaring bull.

"Sir, I heard your order. However, I respectfully decline." Luther remained unmoving.

Larkin's face turned bright red and his eyed widened. "You fucking dog. This is an *order* Lieutenant. See to it or I'll have you face the bayonets yourself!" Larkin fingered his own sabre. A trickle of blood appeared from underneath his bandage and spilled down his rigid cheeks.

"No, I will not, sir." Luther turned to face him. "I ask you to rescind your order, and we will discuss the situation further between us. There are alternatives to what you are suggesting which can be explored, without the shedding of innocent blood."

His request was met by an incredulous gaze from his superior. Not one man amongst the crew uttered a sound.

"There is no discussion, soldier. Your insubordination is—"

"You've gone as mad as the captain," Luther said, interrupting his commanding officer, no longer able to control himself. He stepped in closer. "I will not let this happen again. Someone is going to come looking for these two and when they find us, they're going to guess that we slaughtered their young ones. Children, they're bloody children. I joined *Viritus* to fight the enemies of England, not to butcher boys and girls at your whim."

At this outrage, Larkin's eyes lit up like a volcano. He turned to Midshipman Smith and barked the same order at him. "I order you to dispose of the prisoners. The lieutenant is to be arrested and detained for his mutinous actions."

Smith nodded enthusiastically but was interrupted by Luther.

"Andrew, please. You and I are not friends, but I know you're capable of reason. Don't do this."

Smith paused only for a moment to consider Luther's words. Then he jabbed his finger to a group of astonished sailors. "We all have our duties to follow. You men, secure the lieutenant. Buxley, you and some of your people are with me." With a swift action, he drew his pistol and headed towards the cave. Buxley and three other men stepped in stride beside him.

The two marines at the mouth of the cave snapped their rifles up in unison and pointed them directly at the five men, stopping them short. The remainder of Luther's men rushed forward to protect their lieutenant. Each of them unsheathed swords towards the other crew who were shouting profanities in a loud chorus of panic.

Luther drew his own sabre. "If any man takes a further step towards the boy or girl, open fire. Master Titus Larkin, I am relieving you of command. You can't be trusted to lead us through this, sir. Please give up peacefully so that no one is needlessly hurt."

Arguments broke out amongst the men as they realised they may have to take sides, and weapons were drawn. Most muskets were safely locked away in their timber crates, but the majority of men had at least a knife and if they didn't, they gathered up rocks or branches within reach. Some pushed and shoved, but most of the hostilities were directed towards the marines and their lieutenant, who was attempting to overthrow their superior.

The two marines holding muskets trained on the party of executioners shouted at their fellows to stand back. However, several others were joining their ranks, and the camp had become a mob of swift confusion. A rock was thrown at Private Moore, and he flinched as the small object struck his shoulder. This was all Smith needed to take advantage of the sudden lack of concentration. He straightened his arm and, with a quick squeeze of the trigger, fired his pistol into the private's chest. Moore gasped in horrific pain, but still standing, he instinctively fired back. His musket blasted a torrent of smoke at the crowd. The shot struck a man in the face, obliterating his jaw and blowing a large hole in the back of his head as the ball carried on through. Both men fell. The second marine fired his musket, and the camp turned into a bloody ruckus of combat.

Abel was safe from his position at the edge of the forest clearing. He drew his sabre and stood motionless as the drama around unfolded. Doctor Wickman was running towards him shouting something inaudibly. He could see the men with Buxley had rushed towards the marine and were now engaged in a physical struggle. A man screamed. Another seaman held his arm in pain as blood poured from a knife wound. The other members of the crew who had not been involved were scattering into the trees or onto the beach, fighting each other or paralysed with indecision, uncertain which side they should join. Amongst the fighting, Smith had retreated to Master Larkin and was pulling him towards the shore and away from the carnage.

Doctor Wickman was now upon him. "Get out of here, Abel. Come with me. We must run." He tried to pull Abel away with him and into the trees, but he wouldn't budge. Instead, he stood motionless, watching the crew turn on each other while holding tightly onto his sabre.

"What are you doing? We must retreat now lest we be killed."

Abel wasn't listening. He could only hear his own quick and shallow breathing as he tried to decide how best to get to the other side of the camp and into the cave. Moments later, Cambridge and Rowe entered the clearing from beside Abel. They aimed their muskets and fired at crew who were joining the attack on Luther and their fellow marines. The trap laying expedition had been a cover.

Another man fell. Another clutched his shoulder in agony. Abel saw his opportunity when a few of the men facing the lieutenant retreated and the marines started pushing forward with their heavy sabres. The snipers who emerged from beside Abel were reloading frantically but were noticed by another marauding crewman who rushed to stop them before they could fire another volley. With some space between the cave and the ever-widening brawl, Abel dashed across the camp and behind the fight, avoiding a stray rock being thrown by a man retreating onto the beach.

With sabre still in hand, he was unsurprised to see Mahina and Afah standing and ready to defend themselves. Gesturing towards their hands, Abel made a sawing motion and pointed hurriedly to the entrance.

"I know you don't understand me, but you have to come with me right now. I'm going to cut those bindings. See? I'm going to cut them. I'm not going to hurt you."

Mahina looked nervously at his blade and her bindings. He sensed that she understood his meaning and spoke to Afah beside her. They both held out their hands with some hesitation. He stepped forward and slipped the blade carefully over the cloth around her wrists and with a swift cutting motion, set her free. Afah was next. He touched his raw wrists gingerly where the cloth had been wrapped too tightly.

"Follow me. Keep close." He moved away, but the two did not move. "You need to hurry. Come, come."

"We … run?" Mahina's words were clumsy and heavily accented, but unmistakably English.

"Yes …"

Abel gazed at her in surprise, but without time to question how she learned these words, he grabbed their wrists and pulled them towards the entrance. Once they started moving, he let go, and they ran with him. At the entrance, Private Moore's lifeless body stared blankly up at them.

The frenzy of battle in the campsite had moved further down the slope to the shore. This created a sizable gap between them and the riotous seamen. The trio ran across the centre of the camp towards Doctor Wickman, who was still standing alone and hopelessly in danger. Another close musket shot distracted Abel. He turned towards the noise to see the lieutenant fending off a blow from a thick branch wielded by one of Smith's men. With a skilful step backwards to avoid the strike, Luther parried the club and kicked his boot into his attacker's chest.

Mahina screamed. Abel was still moving forward but not watching his path, and he was abruptly halted in his stride. Mahina had tried to warn him when he ran headfirst into the chest of an older seaman who had blocked his passage. He collapsed on the ground but quickly scrambled to regain his footing. The seaman thrust at him with the tip of his rifle.

"Sorry, boy. Master says they're supposed to die. Get out the way, so I can do the business."

Abel avoided the first blow from the rifle the seaman had clearly taken off from one of the fallen marines. He jabbed again from above, but this time, Abel brought his sabre up to block the attack and was now fully on his feet. Thrusting forward mercilessly, the seaman gritted his teeth and marched towards him with a grunt, aiming to stab Abel in the stomach. With his inexperience, the seaman struggled to fend off the thrusts. From his side, Mahina appeared with a large stone, hurtling the object into the seaman's legs. He didn't flinch or stop, but Afah threw another and this one hit the man squarely in the neck. He gagged at the force of the strike, momentarily lowering his musket. Seeing his chance, Abel stepped in with his right foot and swung the sabre in a wide arc, digging the blade into the seaman's waist. He growled and clutched his side in pain, but Abel could see much of the strike had been dulled by a thick leather belt holding up the man's breeches.

However, it was enough to drive his opponent back, and the three darted past him, shouting at the doctor as they ran. Doctor. Wickman followed. Suddenly they were surrounded not by men, but by a mass of endless bush and trees which slowed their run until they crossed into the path trekked by scouts during the first days of exploration. They ran as a group for several minutes before Wickman called out for them to stop in the middle of a vine strewn clearing. The doctor was puffing furiously and bent over with his hands on his knees for support. "I can't go on. I'm too old to run, and I need to tend to the wounded once this is done, anyway. I'm sorry Abel, but I can't continue."

Abel stopped and dashed back to the doctor. "Doc, if you return, they might kill you. I'll go back with you and help Luther. I want to fight."

"No. That's not what he would've wanted. Let him do what he has to do without having to worry about your safety. Take these two and get as far away as possible. We don't know who will win the day, but I know there will be plenty of injured who will need my help when the wet work is done." He caught his breath and looked Abel in the eye. "Don't stay on this path. If Larkin and Smith are the victors, they'll know you would've taken the easiest path to flee. Make a new one."

"And go where?"

"I don't know, son. There must be places to hide."

"I'll let them go. I'll take them to their boat. We beached the vessel on the dunes where we found them."

The doctor shook his head. "And if they return with their people, telling a tale of invaders and kidnappers? What then?"

"I'm sorry, Doctor. Please be careful when you return. I'll come back as soon as I can."

Mahina and Afah had watched the doctor and Abel talk but were eager to keep moving. As soon as Abel turned, he tapped the two on their arms and they began their run again, leaving Wickman behind. Taking Wickman's advice, Abel ventured off the path and headed south. The sounds of battle were now well behind them, and Abel's heart slowed down to a steady beat. Again, they were slowed by the thick foliage. His arms quickly became tired from cutting down bush and plants to make a passage. It was difficult to see the position of the sun through the high canopy of trees above him. A colourful bird on a branch rained down a cackle of mocking songs. Looking behind, he wasn't sure what direction the camp was in, or even if they were still heading south. Exasperated and tired, he slumped onto a fallen log and looked at Mahina, who had stopped behind him.

"I don't know where we are. I'm afraid I have us lost."

She shrugged her shoulders and turned the palms of her hand in a questioning manner. "Ko 'etau 'alu ki fe?"

He looked at her posture and decided she was asking him where they were going, or perhaps what his plan was. "I want to get you back to your boat ... or ... I don't know how to explain it, Mahina." Picking up a stick, he cleared a swath of leaves from the ground, uncovering the rich dark soil below. A centipede, disturbed by the intrusion, scuttled away. In the soil, he drew a crude series of waves and a boat. Inside the boat he drew two stick figures. One with long hair and one with short hair to show his companions.

"Yaah. I know you say … canoe." Mahina nodded her head furiously, pointing to a patch of trees behind them.

How does she know English? Abel thought. *She couldn't have learned it after just one day.*

"Look, if you know where to go can you take us there?" Abel asked.

"'Oku 'iai 'emau popao. Muimui mai koe hala 'eni." She nodded again.

This time it was Abel who followed Mahina. She seemed to know how to navigate the thick trees of the island. He guessed she knew he didn't want to follow the beaten path, so took them on a longer and rougher journey. At one point she took them to a spring of fresh water where they drank their fill and rested again before moving on. In just over an hour, they emerged from the shadowy canopy of trees and onto a sandy beach. Abel guessed they were probably west of where they had beached the vessel, and he knew he was correct when Mahina started leading them east and across the sand. It was a short journey before they saw the boat's hull sticking out from the undergrowth. Buxley had hidden the vessel from anyone who might come looking.

Mahina pointed and smiled for the first time since he had found her. "Vaka, vaka."

"That's what you call your canoe? It's a vaka?"

Mahina nodded and together the trio pulled the boat across the sand and towards the smooth surface of the lagoon. Before it entered the ocean, Mahina's smile disappeared and she stopped, peered towards the tree line and turned to Afah speaking hurriedly.

"He 'ikai te tau 'alu he kuo pau keu foki 'o 'omai e kava." Afah grimaced and shook his head. "Ikai."

She dashed away from the boat and back towards the trees, disappearing into the bushes beyond.

"What? Wait. Where in hell is she going? You both need to leave. There's no time for this, for God's sake." Abel considered going after her, but sensing his worry, Afah waved him down and motioned in her direction with two fingers, making the action of legs walking away and then returning to the boat.

"Fine, but when will she return?" His question was answered when Mahina emerged from the bush moments later with a bunch of strange, twisted roots in her hand. Running swiftly down the beach, she grasped the roots tightly and carefully placed them into the hull of the boat.

"Kava." She spoke proudly.

"Are you kidding me? That's what that dirty root is? You went back for a *kava* root?"

He had heard the crew of *Viritus* talk of the earthy and bitter root that was crushed and made into a drink by many peoples of the South Pacific islands. It held some kind of drug-like quality and although some of the more well-travelled men had tried it, Abel had neither seen nor tasted the kava root for himself. Kava was not uncommon in this part of the world, so he was at a loss to explain why the young girl would risk their escape on returning to dig out one of the musty smelling plants.

Abel and Afah pushed the boat into water. Mahina and Afah gripped the sides and, one by one, jumped into the narrow boat while Abel held it steady.

Abel took a breath before pushing the vaka into the water. He looked at Mahina and considered the look of relief on her face. A glimmer of a smile settled on her lips, and as he pushed them even further into the lagoon with a heave, he could see her fear subsiding.

"Fai mo 'ai ke tau 'alu, vave." Mahina spoke forcefully at the boy who fished out two short paddles from the hull, passing one to her. They began paddling away from shore almost immediately.

"Good luck," Abel said.

Mahina's eyes settled on the tree line further up the beach and for a moment Abel thought she might spring from the boat and retrieve more kava for the journey. When she began frantically pointing and screaming, Abel knew something was wrong. Turning, he saw they had been found. Buxley and three other men loyal to Smith were emerging from the scout's trail and had already spotted the boat. Abel knew they couldn't catch up with the boat now that they were on the water, so when they started their sprint across the sand, he understood it was him they were after. Smith would have his vengeance. His pursuers already had their knives drawn.

"Come, come!" Mahina called to him.

There was no other choice. Nowhere else to run. The only option was to leave the island, so he dived into the water, frantically swimming the short distance to the boat. When he reached the vaka, Mahina held out her hand and helped him on board. There was little room for all three of them and the boat sat low in the water, but as they paddled further away from shore, he was relieved they were now out of harm's way. Peering towards the island which grew further with distance in every stroke, he could see that Buxley and the others were standing at the water's edge. They hurled curses at Abel, kicking the sand and water in frustration.

He was safe, but suddenly he felt very alone. Where were they going? If Buxley and his men had made it this far across the island so quickly, did that mean that Smith was the victor and had killed his friends? Sitting up straight, he positioned himself backwards and faced Mahina. There was a scowl running the length of her face. She grunted angrily, pointing at the timber hull below him. He was sitting on her precious kava root.

FOUR

Cool water lapped over Hiva's firm thighs as she ventured into the surf. It was a welcome feeling she drew pleasure from in the day's sweltering heat, and a pleasure equally shared by her two servants. Moving slowly and watching her footing through the clear water, she was careful to avoid the sting of sharp coral hidden by the light-coloured sand below. Beside her, a young male warrior kept a close eye on the movements in the water and was ready to defend the first wife of the chief with his life. In his hand, he held a long spear and kept his gaze on any potential threats. All Natui were taught the saying 'Nothing on the land could kill a fierce warrior'. However, it was not meant to bolster the pride of the Natui men. Instead, the expression held greater meaning for what dangers lay in the sea around the many islands of their home. Many a fellow villager had died painfully from the bite of a sea snake or hungry shark, which had ventured close to shore. He flicked his eyes up to another servant girl, who splashed playfully in the light waves around her as she waded. When she met his angry gaze, she stopped disturbing the surface and turned her eyes downwards in reticence.

Now up to their waists in water, they reached a stretch of lo'akau leaves. They were bleached to a colour of fine sand in the ocean's salty brine. Harvested and carefully cut to narrow strips many days beforehand, it would not be long before weavers would take them from the sea for drying. They would weave a fine mat from the many flowing lengths. Hiva felt one leaf between her fingers and rubbed the rough material to measure its thickness and durability. No ordinary mat would be weaved from these lo'akau leaves, and she would oversee every aspect of its laborious creation. She would handpick the dyes, decide upon the patterns and ensure only the most skilled weavers would touch this beautiful craft. One of many. After all, once married, her only daughter would need many fine things to take with her to her new husband's village. As Mahina's mother, she was responsible for keeping the dignity and reputation of her daughter from birth to bride. Now, at sixteen years of age, Mahina would soon leave her mother's protection. Once her beloved child was carried away from their home by her husband to be, Hiva's responsibilities ended. But for now, she was preparing for the last duties she would need to perform for her daughter, and she knew how important the marriage would be for the future harmony and safety of all her people.

A warm hand touched her forearm gently, and she looked into the eyes of the young warrior beside her.

"Hiva, we should go back. Yellow bellied snakes come far into shore after a mighty storm. It is dangerous here."

It was taboo to touch a chief's wife, but she did not flinch or pull away with surprise. Instead, she nodded and smiled at him, noticing his eyes stopped in lustful gaze over her now wet and glistening body. She had married as a child, and even though her body held the marks of giving a child to her husband, she was beautiful and often attracted the gaze of men. Something she still desired since her husband had not touched her once their daughter was born or since he had taken two other wives. She had not given him a boy and could not bear children again after her daughter was born. Nor had the second wife Tihani, whom had been deemed to have a barren womb herself after many miscarriages. The chief had banished the girl to a remote village called Hule on the northern tip of the main island. The third, a young girl called Becca, no older than sixteen years of age, had swiftly fallen with child soon after the marriage. That the child was to be born a boy had become an obsession for Lokai, so much so that he had demanded all holy men from every village in Natuini to sacrifice a bird each morning to the god Tangaloa, deity of the sky and fertility. Many whispered that this union was blessed above all others. The matapule, the trusted seer of her people, had predicted a boy child. She knew her husband had produced boys after liaisons with common women, but none of those illegitimate children could take a noble title. All were sent elsewhere after they were born, along with their mothers.

For ten years, her sleeping fale had not been visited by her husband, and although she held a position of trust with the chief and respect amongst her people, she had become increasingly lonely. Which was why, after many years, her attentions fell on a younger man assigned to her personal guard. They had become lovers, and now he held her arm with a tenderness she had rarely felt in her marriage.

Realising they were being studiously observed by her handmaiden, she blushed and pulled away from his grasp, starting the walk back to shore. A betrayal of Hou'eiki Lokai would mean certain death, and her heartbeat quickly at the lapse in judgement; allowing the touch to linger so long may have caused suspicion at the familiarity shown. She took a step away as if to examine the lo'akau leaves further.

"Ono Hiva." The young handmaiden addressed her by the noble title. "Look out to the sea. A vaka approaches … maybe it's your daughter?"

Hiva blinked. The glistening water shone in her eyes, but she could see the approaching craft. It was still distant and slow moving. She felt her heart leap.

"Come, if it is my Mahina we'll greet them at the meeting house along with my 'beloved' husband. We must summon the faifekau to witness the crop."

Hiva flashed her eyes at her servant girl, who understood the command was for her to leave. When she ran up the beach and into the shadows of the tree line, the noble woman turned to her male protector and spoke with a low growl as soon as she was certain no one was there to see them. "You must be careful, Ruaka. You cannot touch me like that in front of Pua. She's young and naïve, but I know her to be a teller of tales amongst the other girls."

The tall warrior turned fully and cocked his head to the side, smiling. The anger in Hiva's face subsided. He had always been able to disarm her so quickly, and she longed to wrap her arms around him even now.

Once a slave, captured long ago as a young man during her husband's skirmishes with the people of Tui-tonga, he had since been set free. The Natui elders recognised his talents in warfare, and he quickly gained status as a leader amongst the fierce fighters of Natuini. He was a handsome man and well-muscled. To ensure his enemy had no advantage in a close struggle, he had shaved his hair close to the skin with a shark tooth blade. No warrior could now pull upon it in a fight and his close peers would occasionally call him "Boko" meaning the "Bald One". Hiva loved the feeling of running her hand over his smooth scalp; a rare pleasure made more intense by the few meetings they had shared since they had first lain together many seasons ago.

"But, lady, you know I can't help myself. When I watch you, it's all I can do to keep my hands away." He looked down at her neck, where she wore a necklace of freshwater pearls. Their black and polished surfaces sparkled against the blue water. He touched the largest of the pearls, which sat at the centre of the necklace. "This one. The most beautiful of all. This is the same I gifted you, yes?"

Hiva nodded. His hands lingered too long, and he was so close that she could feel his warm breath.

"And what of my maidens? You know some of them spy for Lokai," she said.

Hiva dismissed him with a wave of her hand, moving away from him once more.

"Lady, maybe next time we lie together, the young girl Pua can join in? That way she will not tell your husband."

Hiva's eyebrows raised high, and she appeared to be enraged. He feigned a serious look on his face, but just as quickly burst into laughter.

"You're right about the sea snakes. They're all around. The ugliest of them all stands here before me," Hiva said.

"Haha! A snake? A snake who pleases you much, I think. Anyway, my friend Seletute has eyes for the girl. He thinks he will take her as wife one day."

She smiled, giving him a playful slap on the arm. She loved him. Though she would not admit it. He was one of the few things in her life that gave her joy, aside from her daughter. A daughter who would soon be married and then taken away. Her heart ached at the feeling as they made their way back to shore, remembering her own marriage to the chief. There had been little occasion for laughter or happiness since then, and now that her daughter was close to her own time, a great dark cloud encompassed her thoughts. For now, there was a duty to be done, and she would need to receive her daughter at her husband's meeting house. When the most important families of the village, the holy faikekau and Chief Lokai himself, had gathered together, the strange circumstance of her daughter's arrival was not what she had expected.

❋

A throng of people gathered on the beach after the vaka was spotted by an elderly group of ladies picking cockles amongst coral. By the time they reached the shallows, over one hundred men and women had hurried to the beach. They had swiftly arranged themselves in a corridor of bodies leading from the water and back into the treeline beyond. A group of women and girls of Mahina's age were busy laying down palm fronds on the sand, creating a soft green pathway to walk upon. Abel had seen the commotion on shore and worried about his own fate when the inhabitants of these people finally saw him, particularly now that he suspected his companions were likely of importance.

Who are you? he thought. *You've been welcomed home by the whole village.*

He could see half a dozen older bare-chested men standing tall in front. Each of them grey-haired and holding a wreath of colourful flowers interwoven with large spiral seashells. The crowd ahead was clearly excited. He could even see some younger men and women clapping hands and singing heartily as they stomped rhythmically on the soft sand. They were clothed similarly to the siblings; most were bare chested, and many wore either a skirt of pounded bark skin or layers of dried lo'akau leaves around their waists. The sound of strong voices drifted in the easterly breeze and grew louder the nearer they paddled. However, as they approached, the look of excitement turned to one of curiosity and confusion as several saw him and pointing furiously. The dancing stopped. Their attention turned to the faired haired visitor accompanying Mahina and Afah.

Mahina's face grew dark as she looked at Abel and spoke to the other boy in their unfamiliar language. By the time they reached shore, Abel decided he had made a dreadful mistake coming here. In his voyages aboard *Viritus* he had seen some interactions between the crew and people of the South Pacific which had been a mix of both friendly and unwelcome encounters. There was a need to trade for fresh water and food with the people of these many islands, despite the danger. However, some of the dark-skinned peoples were wary of the strange pale-skinned strangers who sailed around their islands, or had faced the muskets of unfriendly whalers who cared less about diplomacy and more about greed and the lust for women so far from home.

Until the incident with Smith, the men of *Viritus* had traded fairly, and the crew had acted with honour during their voyage. But that had not stopped the occasional misunderstanding resulting in bloody noses and broken bones.

Luther had told him the story of Captain James Cook's death by the Hawaiians some years beforehand after a period of friendly relations, and he now considered that his own death might be at hand – by club or dagger, as the life of the great explorer had been taken.

Abel studied the shore, calculating where he might escape, but saw no obvious path. He gripped the side of the boat and stopped paddling. There was nowhere to run. Even if he could get past the ever-growing mass of people, he was unfamiliar with the territory and was a long way from home. There was nowhere he could go and his heart beat faster, his breath shallow and quick. He gripped the paddle in his hands with such strength that his knuckles went white with the strain.

Get a grip on yourself. Don't be a coward.

Afah leapt from the bow of the tiny vessel. Abel could already see several warriors rushing down the beach with large wide-headed clubs raised high, shouting with high-pitched rage at the newcomer. They were all warriors. The eyes of the five men holding wreaths who were nearest to the three darted back and forth from Abel to Mahina, who was sitting close to the young mariner. One man motioned for her to leave the vaka and was shouting frantically at the two, waving his arms about at the surrounding crowd to force them back. Most simply looked on speechlessly and made way for the armed men who had now reached the boat and who were arguing with Afah. He pointed at Abel, speaking rapidly and attempting to have the men lower their clubs.

At the forefront of the warriors was a giant of a man with a broad face and a large, jutting chin. He was tattooed with rigid patterns around his muscular stomach and arms, and although many other men around him were also tattooed, the extent of his inked skin was much more impressive than the others. He wielded a paddle-like weapon with two hands, swinging it above his head in preparation to strike. It was a distinct weapon from the others. The terrifying object was ashen black, with an elaborate motif of a soaring bird upon the blade. Afah grabbed its shaft and tried to pull it away. It was a futile attempt. The lead warrior towered over him, took him by the arm and tossed him easily to the side, striding forward towards Abel with teeth bared.

There was nowhere to go. Abel was not well trained as a swordsman, and his sabre might not hold back even one of these angry men, but he jumped from the boat and unsheathed the weapon. With only the length of a boat between him and his challenger, Abel was preparing himself to die. To his surprise, Mahina interposed between him and the approaching men. She pushed Abel backwards. In the shallow surf, he almost lost his footing and felt a sharp pain in his right calf as he sliced his flesh on the hidden coral. Blood flooded around his feet. A spill of red burst against the crystal-clear water. He grimaced at the pain but tried his best to ignore the cut in what might be his last moments.

"'Ikai, Kalafa, 'ikai." Mahina stopped the quickly approaching mob in their stride. She was pleading with them, her voice becoming quick and shrill.

An argument ensued which ended in a frustrated look upon the face of the warrior. Finally, she placed her hand on his chest in a familiar way and he seemed to calm down, his face softening slightly. Even so, he kept his eyes on the intruder. Weapons were lowered and Afah nodded towards the sabre Abel was holding in his right hand. He was certain he was expected to drop it and seeing that Mahina may have prevented his death at the hands of her people, he dropped it into the vaka and allowed several of the warriors to pull him from the water and into the tree line beyond.

FIVE

The stone structure which formed the entrance to the sprawling village was etched with numerous markings and pictograms. It was an ancient trilithon made of two tall upright stones supporting a third across the top. Abel was naturally curious about what these might mean. He was also in awe of the enormous scale of this structure and wondered how it could have been constructed without a crane or pulleys that he had seen in operation in London's ports. In a more favourable situation, he may have stopped and examined the wonder, but he spent little time on the thought. His fate was still yet to be determined. The group passed under the large stone cross bar reaching as high as two men. Beyond, there were dozens of structures hoisted upon heavy poles that lifted them off the ground by several feet. A great swath of the forest had been cleared to accommodate the village with a large, open space directly in the centre. A series of cooking fires were lit and were burning with billows of white smoke. There were many low buildings made from sturdy constructions of flax, timber and coir rope. With the thick poles underneath, none but a few touched the ground except for the bases of the shafts and short stairs that led up to the entrances.

From the flames of the cooking pits, a dusty haze filled his nostrils. Men and women of all ages emerged from their homes, and while there were few children upon the beach, many were now appearing and rushing forward in wide-eyed curiosity. The heavily tattooed warrior who stood vanguard to the others made a low growl at some of the younger boys and girls who were brave enough to run forward, making them step back fearfully. Some ran back to their shelters or hid behind their parents whilst the other inhabitants present gave a wide berth for the group to pass. The warrior paced quickly towards the largest structure in the village – an enormous walled building with a flax rooftop and massive supporting poles spaced evenly to increase its height and presence over all the other buildings. Outside, many villagers had gathered. At least a dozen armed males stood at attention, moving to the side only to allow the warrior to walk upon the raised wooden entrance and through a high beamed opening. He disappeared for several minutes before appearing again to usher the group in.

Inside, the building housed just one spacious chamber. The room was elaborately adorned by large mulberry cloth mats laid side by side on the timber floor. Spaces between the high ceiling and the thick woven walls provided for ample sunlight to stream through and onto the faces of the inhabitants within. Around forty men and women were sitting cross-legged upon the ground. At first, they were smiling, and some were chatting mirthfully. As they saw Abel emerge, the bright faces around him changed instantly to bewildered frowns, the whispers now muted. Mahina and Afah were close behind, and he looked back at both of them as his stomach churned. One of his captors hustled him roughly forward. He stumbled on the edge of one of the thick mats but caught himself before he fell onto one man sitting close by.

Surrounding the edges of the large hut, people of both sexes sat silently and watched him with wide-eyed fascination. An elderly lady reached out, touching his leg. She rubbed it ever so slightly as if to see if he was real and retracted her hand after one of her female companions rebuked her with some swiftly muttered word. Taken to the centre of the structure, he was pushed to his knees, and two men on either side grabbed his shoulders, turning Abel to the very end of the space where a singular figure sat above all others.

Upon a large stone block covered in several layers of thick woven flax, an enormous man was perched in a high cross-legged position and peered down at him silently while scratching a motley white beard. A bead of sweat rolled from his neck, which was wrapped in a necklace of shark teeth, and down onto his chest and belly. Apart from a tanned bark skin skirt, he was unclothed, showing his many rings of faded tribal tattoos around his arms and legs. Beside him stooped another man. A frightening being whose face and long braided hair was painted entirely in white. In his hair, twisted green vines were folded into the braids, giving the appearance of hanging snakes. He wore a large flax mat dyed entirely charcoal black, with several thick folds in the back of the mat, delivering the appearance of a winged creature. The man clenched together razor-sharp teeth in disgust at Abel. The sight of this horrific winged beast made his throat dry. He could feel the moisture build on his palms as his breath became shallow.

The rotund figure seated on the stone block considered Abel for several more moments before noticing Mahina was standing close by. His face lit up with a brilliant smile, and he stood up, motioning her to approach.

"Hoku 'ofefine talangofua. 'Oku ou feifia 'aupito ho'o hao mai. 'Oku ou sio kuo ke ha'u mo ho kaume'a?" he bellowed before embracing Mahina, lifting her in the air as if she were a rag doll and settling her back down gently.

Her cheeks turned red and as he took his seat upon the carved stone chair, Mahina kneeled to the ground before presenting him with the small bundle of kava root. He took the root in his hands and beamed with pride. His expression slowly darkened, however, when he looked back over at Abel and leaned in to speak to the young girl in low, gruff tones.

As they spoke, both Mahina and the man would look back at him occasionally. He could hear a deepening tone in the man's voice. Tears welled up in Mahina's eyes, but she remained composed and continued the exchange.

"I'm going to die here," Abel whispered. With some resolve, he decided he would not spend his final hours in fear, so raised his eyes in defiance. The painted figure standing beside the stone chair had not averted his gaze from the boy since his arrival. The figure met Abel's eye and clenched his jaw.

"I'll not live my last moments as a captive. I'll die fighting you," Abel mouthed from across the room.

Another person approached and kneeled beside Abel without making a sound. Abel thought he was going to be pushed down by another rough handed warrior. Instead, and to his amazement, he looked into the face of another European dressed in brown priestly robes, holding a gnarled wooden staff.

"Buongiorno, young man. I suggest you don't make trouble with that one. Masila is one very dangerous *amigo*. Also, don't look the chief directly in the eye. Don't touch him for any reason and if you have taken his daughter's virginity, be prepared to be cooked alive in the village roasting pits. Also, my name is Father Marcello." He wiped away moisture from his brow and smoothed down his clothes.

"What?" Abel said. "Who … what are you doing here?"

"Never mind about that, my son. You just need to get through the next few minutes with his majesty, and I can answer all of your questions later."

Father Marcello looked over at the white-haired figure and nodded with a polite smile. In return, the man spat at the ground with gusto, and his face twisted like he had eaten a bitter fruit.

"That one. He looks like an angry seagull," said Abel.

"Si. I have not heard that before about my friend, Masila. But yes. Seagull is an apt description.

"You're not English. You have an accent."

"Venetian. I am Venetian, but I have had the opportunity to live in England. Listen, forget about me for now. Just tell me, did you penetrate the poor girl?" Marcello raised his eyebrows in anticipation of the answer.

"No … no. Of course not. I didn't pen — I didn't touch her, I swear."

Marcello sighed and nodded.

He appeared to be in his forties. Despite his long black hair, his face was clean shaven but had several cuts and small scars. The robes he wore had seen better days; they were old but intact, with rough stitching.

"Hmm. In my time I have known many a young man in confession to lie about such things, followed soon after by a young lady with a swollen belly. Anyway, it seems that the young princess saved you at the beach, so I'm thinking you helped her somehow. That might be enough to keep you alive. Now remember, address him as 'Hou'eiki Lokai'. 'Hou'eiki' means lord, or high chief. The lesser noblemen here are called 'eiki. He will speak to you directly, but only speak when he addresses you. And start thinking of some way you can be of use. I can't keep you alive if you are of no worth to Lokai." Marcello emphasised the last part of his advice with a wag of his finger.

"That's truly his daughter?" Abel said.

"Yes. And the lovely lady seated to the right is her mother, Ono Hiva. A very important lady."

Mahina's mother was sitting with her legs resting to her side upon layers of soft cloth mats. She had no expression on her face and had remained stoic since his arrival. She was currently watching Mahina, her gaze unwavering.

"What are they saying?"

Before his new companion could speak, they were interrupted by a hand gesture from Hou'eiki Lokai, and Abel was pushed by two warriors further towards the foot of the stone seat.

The narrow eyes of the enormously girthed figure looked him up and down. "'Oku ke fiekaia? 'Oku ou sio ki a koe 'oku ke holo?" he said.

The room remained silent as they awaited Abel's response.

"Ah, I don't understand." His voice trembled slightly, but he stood a little taller to exhibit some courage.

"I said, are you hungry?" This time the chief spoke in heavily accented but unmistakable English.

Again, Abel's mind raced with questions. "How do you know my language?" He looked around at Father Marcello, who had his eyes trained ahead but below Lokai's gaze.

"Language is not yours. Words go from mouth and become belongings to other men. So now your language is my language. Here I am chief. I own all you can see and all you can hear."

With a grunt, he stood up from his throne and took Mahina's hand. She stood with him, and the chief led her towards Abel. It startled him how close the burly man stood and he involuntarily stepped back a pace.

"God-Man teach me words. Teach my pretty daughter too, but she no like your strange words so only I know well. Is that not right God-Man? He say my English is still broken, but getting better every day." Chief Lokai gestured towards Father Marcello.

"Ah yes, mighty Hou'eiki. That is absolutely right. His majesty is one of the greatest warriors and scholars of his people. He has even learned to write our language and his own."

"God-Man from Venice teach me well so he is living still. So I keep him here and he teaches me about the mighty god in the sky. He tell me great story about the son of the mighty god. He say that if I believe in his mighty god that I live forever and gods will make me great king and win many wars. Young man, tell me truth? Will your god make me a great warrior if I make many gift to him?"

Abel looked back again to Father Marcello, who was sweating profusely. He had his eyes closed as if praying and was breathing heavily in the humid air.

"Lokai leaned forward and spoke in a quieter voice. "Is true?"

Abel considered the questions and decided that there was only one answer to safely give. "Yes, Hou'eiki. It is true. This man speaks the truth. Great kings in Europe pray and are faithful to God. They build mighty churches for God and fight in his name."

"Mighty churches? I know you speak of meeting house for speaking to your god. God-Man tells me that the meeting house is much bigger than mine and made of gold and stone." He smiled and looked around at his own structure in which they stood. "So I am generous. I ask Marcello to build church in the Mala'e kula."

Abel looked at the priest, unsure of what Lokai had said.

"El me scuxa. Ah, excuse me," Marcello said. "I sometimes forget the English. It means, 'sacred red grove'. Hou'eiki Lokai has been so benevolent as to allow me to build a place of worship in the very fields the Natui people have been praying to their own gods for millennia. It is a great honour. I am almost finished."

"God-Man makes many, many promise about his god. He say the Natui people will never die if we become Christian."

Marcello bowed. "Si. La Biblia la promete che nel futuro 'no ghen sarà pi la morte. This is true. The bible tells us that one day there will be no death."

The chief laughed as he continued. "But my matapule tell me this is palangi lie and I should put the church to the axe and burn. He also say that you will bring more palangi and my people will suffer." Lokai gestured over to the white-haired figure, now looking with even greater disgust at Abel. He twirled a long shark tooth from his necklace and ran it across his own neck, as if in warning.

"I'll not be threatened by that painted seagull of a devil. If you want to kill me, give me a weapon to defend myself and I will kill him first." Abel raised his voice. He wanted everyone to hear.

Transfixed like statues, the eyes and mouths of the audience widened at the sudden outburst. This moment of shock was short-lived by the raucous laugher that erupted from Lokai's round face.

"*Seagulli*? You think he look like a *seagulli*." Lokai turned to his people, gesticulating at the man described by the Venetian as a witch doctor, and spoke briefly in their native language. Soon after, the entire room of men and woman were laughing and cackling with their leader.

Masila became white eyed in rage and stormed away from the throne, pushing men and woman from his path. He was rough with some, but none sought to stop or rebuke him. He turned to Abel and Father Marcello before leaving the mouth of the meeting house. His teeth were clenched so strongly that a series of dark veins strained taut from his neck.

"Oua teke kata manuki he taimi 'e 'omai ai e kau papalangi honau 'otua ke talatuki'i 'aki ki tautolu," he said, spitting furiously at the ground again.

Father Marcello shook his head. There was a slight cringe across his face, as if something terrible was going to happen.

When the laughing had stopped, Chief Lokai let go of Mahina's hand and began a slow walk around Abel, examining him like a specimen horse he was purchasing.

"My daughter say you help her. She say you have friends who fight other palangis. My daughter is ready for marriage and must take root from Tapu Motu to give gift to husband. Husband is son of great Chief Doko so our family become one and make fighting against my ugly enemy to the North." He stopped in front of Abel again. "You understand my words in English?" he questioned proudly.

"Yes. I understand, lord," Abel answered. "It's very good."

"I speak English and three other language. Natui, Ha'amoa, Fisi. And play the palangi game, chess. I will play you. I am very good. Marcello is a smart teacher, but I am a smarter student. Yes, Marcello?"

Marcello stepped forward, and smiled nervously. "Oh yes Hou'eiki Lokai. Your skills have far outstripped my own in that particular game."

Lokai grunted in satisfaction before continuing. "My beautiful wife, Hiva, she not liking Chief Doko or Doko son but she loves our daughter, Mahina. If I lose Mahina, Hiva would be angry with me. She can be very angry woman so I am happy with you palangi boy."

The chief smirked slightly and looked over to where Hiva was resting, several feet from the foot of the throne. Her handmaiden Pua and one other young girl were leaning close by, waving palm fronds to keep her cool. She remained expressionless but kept her eyes fixed on Abel.

"Tell me palangi boy. Your friends on Tapu Motu. Do they have many spear for hunting and killing?" Lokai questioned slowly, wanting to ensure that his pronunciation was understood.

Abel considered the question and suddenly became wary of the chief's intention. "My friends are great warriors and have many pistols and rifles. I am also a great warrior, and I have received training in sword and musket." He needed to persuade his captors against believing his fellow castaways were an easy target.

The chief nodded slowly and pursed his lips. He appeared to be considering Abel's words before replying.

"We will see palangi, boy. We will see."

Lokai nodded to a servant who walked forward, and with a deep bow, handed him Abel's sabre. He turned it over with interest, examining its mirror blade.

"Beautiful."

Abel's eyes widened when the chief turned the hilt towards Abel and offered him the sabre. He took his weapon back and sheathed it.

With a motion of his hand, the chief dismissed the gathering while Father Marcello helped Abel to his feet and led him away. He looked back at Mahina whilst he was being escorted away from Lokai's meeting house. She watched him with sympathetic eyes but was interrupted by her mother, who grabbed her by the chin and turned her head away. A salty stare from Hiva was enough to break Abel's gaze, and he followed Father Marcello who was busy scattering away a group of piglets which had wandered into their path.

"Why are they letting me go?"

The thin-faced priest grinned. "They're not letting you go, young man. You can walk freely amongst the chief's people, but you are a prisoner. I've been informed by one of Lokai's more reasonable 'eiki, Lord Aunofo, that I am responsible for you. If you try to leave, I'll be punished. So I beg of you to behave yourself."

Marcello walked swiftly, pulling up his rough, tattered robes to avoid the muddy puddles. He was thin and tall and his long strides meant Abel had to hasten his steps in order to keep up. The young warrior brandishing the ornately blackened club watched them as they walked, and Abel caught his angry expression briefly before they passed back by the trilithon to the outskirts of the village.

"Who is he?" Abel said.

"That is Chief Lokai's first warrior, Kalafa, and he would kill you without a moment's thought. Stay away from him. Completely loyal to Lokai and one of the most brutal fighters I have ever seen with a war pakipaki. Tremendously brutal weapon. It's a long club with a wide head. He leads the chief's men into battle and has never been defeated in combat."

"Lokai called the white-haired man the chief's eye …"

"Yes, that's his role amongst the Natui. He is a matapule. A holy man and speaker for Lokai. He's also a miserable wretch who claims to know the will of their gods. Hates me dearly. The people call him by his inherited name, Masila." Marcello raised his eyebrows.

"That's what their people are called? Natui?" Abel ventured.

"Lots of questions. Yes. They call themselves the Natui and this island is called Natuini Lahi. In fact, the whole island

86

chain in the kingdom is all called Natuini. This land is the largest of them all. If you can call it a kingdom. In truth, it's actually a collection of chiefdoms throughout the island chain. The chiefs traditionally also call the lands they control after themselves. So you can consider yourself a captive of Chief Lokai in the lands of Lokai. Easy to remember, si?" Marcello grinned.

"This village is the seat of his power and is called Kahoua. Its meaning is gate or entrance way. Quite fitting, since it's the natural harbour for Natuini Lahi and the gateway to the rest of the island."

"Is he a king or chief?" asked Abel.

"Yes, that is complicated. He is Hou'eiki. Noble. A lord or chief. He is probably the strongest of all the rulers here. There are dozens of chiefs spread throughout Natuini and the outer islands, but only three of them are powerful enough to assert any proper control over the others. Each of them has proclaimed themselves 'Great Chief' over all others and call each other subservient chiefs. There is Lokai, whom you have just had the pleasure of meeting. There is Chief Doko, his distant cousin. He rules over a handful of villages here on Natuini Lahi but lives in a small collection of islands called Mo'unga Vela to the east. Finally, there is his great rival, Chief Maka of the northern isles. He controls a large tract of sea, a thousand seasoned warriors and rules from a near impenetrable fortress on an island called Natuini Si'i. Ono Hiva – his first wife – her family used to rule there until Maka overthrew them. Very bloody business."

"A fortress? I've not seen anything like a fortress here." Abel couldn't help but sound incredulous.

His companion looked unimpressed.

"Not in the traditional sense that you may have seen at home. But just as formidable. Maka has built his most populous village on a cliff surrounded by a rocky sea on three sides and has fashioned basalt blocks into an impressive wall on the landward slope. I've seen it in person. Very impressive."

Marcello led him towards a small hut made of sturdy branches and a woven dry flax roof.

"The one you call Seagulli convinced the elders that I was a bad omen, and they have made me live outside of the village's confines. Gives me a measure of privacy so I'm not complaining. Come in, young man."

He pulled open a mat which hung from the entrance to his abode, and the two ducked under the low doorway before moving inside. It was compact, but dry and comfortable looking. A series of mats covered the earthen ground, and Marcello gestured for Abel to sit down while he poured the contents of a clay jug into a coconut half shell.

"Drink. It will make you feel better. A recipe of crushed mango for sweetness." The priest watched excitedly as Abel drank the liquid gratefully. "You must forgive my obvious curiosity; I have few visitors and certainly none from our part of the world."

Out of a small wooden box, the priest pulled out a white strip of cloth and wrapped it tightly around Abel's bloodied leg. The pain had numbed, and he had almost forgotten about the wound sustained on the sharp coral as he jumped from the vaka. Now that he had been reminded, it throbbed painfully again.

"It's not so deep, so don't worry about getting an infection. The salt water would have taken care of that. I'm not a doctor, but that will have to do."

"There's a doctor back on the island I came from. Doctor Wickman. He could help if it goes bad, I suppose."

"A doctor, you say." Marcello raised his brow in sudden interest.

Abel looked at his surroundings. Several personal items were neatly placed on simply made wooden shelves, which were clearly not from the island. Amongst them he could see a leather-bound bible, a hooded brass lantern and a large sextant. Other small objects one would expect to find on a ship were neatly stacked or hung from hooks roughly fashioned from fish bones. Some hardened leather scroll cases were arranged in a pyramid in the rear of Marcello's home. It surprised Abel to see a timber chess board with several pieces made of carved sandstone. A number were unfinished.

"Robert, our ship's doctor, taught me to play chess on *Viritus*," Abel said.

"Chief Lokai loves the damn game. I'm fashioning him a new set." Marcello smiled and picked up the base of one of the stone figurines and held it out for Abel to see.

"The knights are the most difficult to carve. The Natui have never seen a horse before, so they think I'm making effigies of a monster. He demands we play every second night. I regret teaching him. He's very good, as he says, but he's grown bored with playing with me so he made me teach all of his nobles how to play. It matters not. They're all terrible. So he's always calling me, often waking me from my sleep at night when he wishes for a game." Marcello rolled his eyes.

"What are you doing here, Father? I'm grateful for your help, but I didn't expect to find a priest from Venice at the end of my journey."

Marcello frowned but was quick to answer. "Si, si, I was set ashore by my ship's crew. I was chaplain on the *Tempesta*. The captain took a disliking to me, and when I spoke about his mistreatment of the crew, he removed me from the vessel. Pushed me off on a longboat to the far side of this island. I was promised they would retrieve me in six months' time after their trade mission to the New Zealand Isles was complete, and here I was to await their return. Lokai found me hungry and lost. He recognised my value as a scholar and priest, so decided not to throw me into the 'umu.

"'Umu?"

"Ah, yes, 'umu. It means cooking pit." Marcello raised his eyebrows, nodding at his own revelation. "If that witch doctor had his way, I would've been thrown in immediately, but Lokai is a wise man and has seen the light of God. He wants me to teach his people and bless the great chief to a life of salvation. So he has forbidden any more enemies to be sacrificed in the old ways." Marcello spoke earnestly.

"You seem to understand the language well for someone who's been here less than six months," Abel said.

"Yes, well. It's been a little longer than that. My ship did not return in the season I had expected. I am hopeful they will come back this year."

"How long have you been here?" Abel took another sip of the refreshing drink and waited for an answer as the priest leaned back and turned over his now empty half shell in his hand.

"Six years this summer. I think. I didn't keep count of the days in the first year I arrived as well as I should." Lines appeared on Marcello's brow as his eyes lost focus.

After a few moments of silence, Marcello gained concentration once again and smiled. "So, tell me, are there others alive somewhere, or is it just you? Do you have a ship?"

Abel relayed the full story of the encounter with the French and their subsequent arrival on Tapu Motu. Marcello listened intently. He became especially interested when Abel described the fire on *Viritus*.

"The entire ship and its contents are ruined?"

"Mostly, but much of the ship was submerged in water on the reef and rainfall controlled the rest of the blaze. When last I saw it, half the ship was black like coal, but enough of the ship survived that some of the cargo may still be intact. Lieutenant Luther managed to bring much of the dry goods and powder ashore. We were lucky the fire didn't reach the armoury or powder storage or else we all would've been blown to smithereens."

When the story was finished, Marcello leaned back into a comfortable stack of soft mats and tapped his finger on the side of his slender nose, mulling over what he had been told.

"A shame. If I could, I would assist. Much like Jesus was, I am somewhat of a carpenter myself, so I could help rebuild the vessel, perhaps? Fire and gunpowder are the great equalisers of humanity. Quando finisce la partita il re ed il pedone finiscono nella stessa scatola," Marcello said.

"Ah, I'm sorry, I don't speak Venetian."

"Do not be concerned. God has blessed you, boy. A harrowing tale of course, but the lord has seen fit to rescue you, and now I have a fellow European to talk to. You can stay in my hut for now until you build your own fale. That's what they call them here. For now, you should rest, as I imagine you must be exhausted from the journey. Now, I have duties to perform and will take my leave. I can trust you to stay out of mischief, yes?"

"I want to live, so yes, I won't cause any trouble," Abel said.

"Bien. Very smart. They are watching you after all, and won't hesitate to drag you back here, upside down by your feet, just like a hairy bat, if you try to escape."

"Yes, I promise. But I must persuade the chief to let me go once he understands I have no ill intentions. I don't even know if my cousin is still alive, and I need to help him if I can."

Marcello frowned and nodded before standing up and abruptly leaving the hut in an unusual rush.

Abel was exhausted and welcomed the chance to rest on a dry and clean surface. He lay back and looked over at the scroll cases and the sextant. Father Marcello had a great many objects, and Abel wondered why an unwanted castaway was set ashore with so many valuable items.

⚮

It was a strange exchange. Hiva could barely contain her anger when she learned of her daughter's mistreatment at the hands of the intruders. This young man who arrived so boldly may have helped her return to the safety of Kahoua, but what lies may he have told to ensnare Mahina's trust?

Why will Lokai not punish them? He has not been so forgiving in the past, she thought.

The treatment of the Masila, his very own matapule, was also an insult to Natui traditions. Her husband's irreverence had not gone unnoticed amongst his loyal 'eiki, though she knew it mattered little; his power and reach surpassed all the sub chiefs on Natuini and possibly even the might of Chief Doko and Maka. As she had watched the arrival of her daughter and the strangers, she longed to embrace Mahina with all of her love. The many days away from home and the time spent apart were a rare occurrence between them. However, as Lady of the Natui and first wife to Chief Lokai, she could not be seen to display weakness through excessive emotion. So she sat quietly. Her blood boiled. And yet she still sat quietly.

When Marcello had escorted the palangi out of the chamber, she beckoned Mahina to approach and leant in, her lips close to her daughter's ears.

"We will speak of your adventure later, my love. I missed you so much."

"Mother, I was never scared. Not once. Perhaps Afah. But not me."

Mahina held her chin high in the air. Her expression serious. She always wanted to prove herself, but Hiva knew her daughter's heart well.

"It's okay to be frightened. I am. Perhaps my greatest fear was that you were hurt. Are you sure those strangers did nothing more to you? If they did, I'll have them gutted like fish."

"No. Just some bruises. Epeli … the boy. He helped us leave on our vaka. There was a fight, and we escaped while the men were killing each other. Their spears made a sound like thunder."

"Do not trust the boy. Your father should send him back. We don't need more of those people here. Marcello is trouble enough."

Mahina remained silent. Hiva could see the exhaustion on her face. She hugged her and kissed her on both cheeks.

"Go get some sleep, my beautiful girl."

Mahina smiled and bowed graciously. Soon after, Chief Lokai dismissed all present, though Hiva remained behind with Ruaka. He stood behind her with resolute posture, as if to fight off an oncoming army. His duty as his lady's protector was to be on guard for any would-be assassin or kidnappers who might seek to strike at Lokai's position. In truth, there were few who would dare attempt to harm Ono Hiva.

As she had told him, he kept his eyes averted from her slim frame to ensure that there was no suspicion of his feelings, but he was already familiar with her body. Intimately. Hiva knew their secret was the greatest threat to her life. Knowledge of their relationship would end with swift justice taken on both of them if their discreet meetings were discovered. Aside from their relationship, Hiva had little to fear. She was popular amongst her people and those of the many surrounding islands. She had taken the time to educate herself in the affairs of the commoners and ensured that she displayed a generous nature. Hiva was known to give back the gifts of koloa and crops she had received in tribute to those in need. This had made her many friends, and not just amongst the Natui. She had spent many hours as a young lady conversing with the elders about their history, oral traditions and the cultures of their allies and enemies across the seas. She knew she had become an important asset for the chief, so she was at least favoured for her ability to smooth relations with their rivals when war seemed close.

Now, standing before her husband, she would once again be called on to perform her duties as first wife.

As the last of the gathered villagers left the meeting house, Hou'eiki Lokai was being served a meal. His youngest and newest wife, named Becca, seated herself behind him. She massaged his wide shoulders with the oil of a pressed coconut whilst he stripped the flesh from a large roasted fish. It was surrounded by an array of yams, fruit and shellfish which sat on a plate fashioned from the hollowed-out stem of a banana tree, and would soon be devoured with some gusto by the portly Lokai. Becca was pressing herself lovingly against his back, smiling suggestively at Hiva as they waited for the chief to acknowledge them. Hiva ignored her.

After swallowing a chunk of fish, he looked up from his raised platform of stacked mats. "Malo e lelei. Ah, my lovely wife, Hiva. A strange day. Our pretty daughter came home safe but with a palangi boy by her side. I am thankful to the *one* mighty God that she was unharmed, and to our great relief it seems that she was not deflowered."

Lokai nodded to himself. He raised his hand up to stroke the hand of his masseuse, who was pushing her fingers deeper into his flesh with greater enthusiasm now that she had an audience. Hiva hated the idea of worshipping the palangi god, and her husband was hoping to provoke her to anger. He wasn't successful.

"Yes, husband, I am thankful. Great Maui calmed the ocean after the storm and pulled her vaka to shore and back to the love of our arms."

Hiva placed stress on the name of one of the old gods, which Lokai had encouraged his people to abandon. His expression changed to that of displeasure but soon turned to a smile once again as Becca leaned forward to kiss his neck, never breaking her stare away from the first and most important wife of the Natui chief. They had barely spoken since the marriage during the last storm season, although Hiva had tried to engage with her. Despite this, Lokai's new wife only saw her as a threat to the attentions of their shared husband.

"I could see that you do not like the boy," Lokai said. "But our daughter says that he saved her from shame and perhaps death from his own people. We should reward him. Not treat him with suspicion, my love."

Hiva shook her head. "Who knows what tricks the palangi boy has played on Mahina. He should be banished or sent back to his people. I tell you, husband, he will only bring us ill fortune." Hiva held the centre pearl of her necklace between her fingers. The touch of its cool shell calmed her.

Lokai laughed. "Ah, is this because of your dislike of the god-man? You worry that more of their kind will come and that our people will change forever? My love, Hiva. Change is all around us. Maybe it is time for changes, like the seasons, no?"

"You wish to replace our sacred matapule and holy faifekau with this foreign worshipper of just one god? That is what people say. And now you openly mock him in front of our noble families."

Lokai smiled, and for a moment his face changed to that of a cheeky young boy, as if caught spying on the girls as they bathed in the ocean.

"I do so, since I'm the only one who dares. He's grown powerful in his own right with great tracks of lands and servants who worship him like he is chief. Sometimes he needs to be reminded of his station." The chief nodded to himself.

He turned to stroke Becca's hair and touched her face, motioning for her to stop her massaging hands from digging into his back. She giggled and leaned back, taking a bite of ripe mango from the small feast laid out at their feet.

"Do not worry, my dearest wife. As chief matapule, Masila's place is assured amongst the Natui. The god-man serves another purpose."

"And that is?" Hiva asked softly, her brow raising with the question.

But her husband ignored her and reached around Becca's waist to caress her buttocks, whispering inaudible words into her ear. Turning back to face his first wife, he seemed in a pleasant mood.

"There is more good news. My young third wife, Becca, is pregnant with child and Masila assures me it will be a son. Maybe two!"

This was unexpected. He had tried for many years to have a son with all three of his wives. Hiva had decided his loins had been cursed for his arrogance. The matapule could be wrong, of course. He had been before.

Lokai stood up from his meal, wiping his face on a length of cloth already smudged with grime and stains.

"Nothing to say? Are you not happy that my family grows and so does my strength and influence?"

The chief grinned broadly as he walked towards Hiva. Standing before her, his foul fish breath enveloped her. He looked her over and with a quick motion, he darted his hand underneath her feather bodice and to her breast. Hiva breathed in deeply as he clenched her nipple firmly between his forefinger and thumb. She winced at the pain. This was his cruel game. He wanted a reaction. Some displeasure. Anything to show he was in control, and she was being worn down by his frequent humiliations. Even through the pain, she recovered her composure and gritted her teeth to harbour the sharp pressure. Ruaka moved towards them as if to intervene but stopped after a single step. She knew he wanted to strike the chief down. Her lover hated Lokai as much as she did, but Lokai's eyes flashed with anger towards him. The chief had noticed his concern.

The chief turned his gaze back to Hiva and squeezed a little tighter. The desired effect was reached when she breathed deeply in pain and a look of agony fell across her features.

"My lovely bird. If you had given me a son, I would have visited our marriage bed more often than I did. Perhaps then you would not be as bitter as an old taro leaf."

The slap to Lokai's right cheek was quick and loud, and the large man withdrew his hand in surprise.

"May I remind you, my husband, that I'm the eldest granddaughter of the great Lord Kavelu, and the Kavelu line outranks your own. Yours is of lesser blood. You have no right to treat me like this," Hiva said defiantly.

Lokai clenched his fists. She feared he would punish her for her outburst, but as swiftly as his anger flushed his face a deep red, it subsided in a smile and mirthless laugh.

"Yes, you may remind me of my lesser heritage, but I am still Hou'eiki. I will not punish you for striking me. I've always admired you for your strength and passion. You may have one strike upon me without retaliation, Ono Hiva. Just one." He hesitated for a moment, looking over her face for any hint of emotion. "Enough of these silly games we play so well. They're fun, but I'd hate to upset Ruaka. I think he almost slapped me too."

Lokai tightened the waist mat arranged around his belly as he strode back to his stone seat and rested heavily on several mats which draped across the breadth of the throne. In a gesture, he beckoned for Becca to massage his back once more, which she hastily obliged.

"Hiva, I must ask you to be the consummate lady of Natuini once more and represent me to Chief Doko in accepting the proposal of marriage to his son. It is time for our families to unite, and Mahina is now ripe of age to be gifted into union. Her children will ensure our strong bond with the 'Grey Hair' chiefdom." He spoke in a sombre tone, as if it was a great burden he was passing onto his wife.

Hiva could not hide her sadness at this request. She had known this time was coming near, but every day was a gift to help her prepare for the inevitable. Now that it had become a reality, her face showed the pain of loss for her daughter, even though the ceremony and marriage would be many months away.

"When must I leave?"

"You must take the kava root by hand and provide this to the son of Chief Doko as soon as two moons have become as round and shapely as a wasp's nest. You will need to whip the legs of your servants as they prepare gifts for the occasion. Then after taking the good news across our lands, your journey across the waters must be swift."

"And what of the palangi men? What if there are more upon my journey? You can only guess at their true intentions. You should consider sending the boy to another island from here. Or he may signal for more of them to come."

Lokai's laughter rolled like thunder. "He's of no threat. You can sometimes be as cold as I, lovely bird. No, much like the god-man Marcello, he will prove of value to me, and it seems that our little Mahina would not allow any harm to come to him. She says that he's the one who helped her and Afah to escape the others."

"She may have been tricked. He may be a spy ..."

"Enough, Hiva! The boy will remain amongst us. Anyway, I've heard rumour from ugly Chief Maka to the north that great Finau of Vava'u has captured a dozen palangi men and has taken one boy as a son, fighting beside him as if a favoured offspring."

"This intruder will never take the place of a son. It's a mistake to keep him amongst our people. More will come as they always have. He presents a danger, now you have given him back his weapon."

Lokai dismissed her with a careless wave. "One boy with a long knife is no threat. But a dishonoured boy, stripped of his only possession makes for a cornered beast. It is time for you to go, wife. Soon you must gather your servants and warriors. When you arrive, you will give my love and respect to Doko and invite his people to a betrothal feast in honour of our new union. Ruaka and his men will protect you on your journey."

Hiva lowered her head. She considered pressing her concerns on allowing the newcomer to remain in the village, though she decided this was futile, as her husband had already lost interest in her. His attentions were now focused on stroking the thighs of his third wife, beckoning her to sit on his lap. She turned to Ruaka and flashed her eyes in a signal for him to follow as she left the chief's presence. As they left and were out of earshot of anyone that may hear, she spoke in a low tone as Ruaka leaned in.

"If that boy and his people threaten my daughter again, I want you to kill them all."

❈

Inside the meeting house, Lokai grabbed lustily onto the thighs of his young wife while she mounted his sweaty lap and pulled up her waist mat. With a groan of pleasure, he thrust himself deeply into her willing body. She gasped and leaned into him, grinding her hips back and forward, her moist, pregnant belly heaving upon his.

"Not so fast now, Becca. I would be displeased if we hurt our baby boy."

He playfully slapped her behind and looked to his side, where a diminutive female figure lurked in the shadows of a flax curtain, hidden from the prying eyes of others.

"Come forward, young Pua. Don't be afraid of your liege." With one hand, Lokai reached out and pulled her close, his hand around her waist slipping to her taunt buttocks.

"Tell me about what you have witnessed between Ono Hiva and her handsome chaperone. The beast who looks upon me like a hunter viewing its prey?" He spoke with foreboding, but moments later his lips parted and a wry smile shone from his face.

SIX

If Abel was a prisoner, he had a large, expansive prison to roam freely around. Father Marcello explained Lokai had granted him freedom to go where he pleased as long as he did not venture further than the calm waters which surrounded the island. He was told not to go near an area of the island to the north, which the priest said were sacred cliffs to the Natui. They buried their ancestors on its rise, facing the sky towards where they believed their original descendants sailed from to reach this Pacific paradise. But Abel soon discovered that much of his time was not his own.

He kept to himself for the first few days, watching the goings on of village life from the outskirts. The people here treated him with caution, keeping their distance at first. Marcello was absent most days, and when he returned, he was exhausted and spoke to Abel only intermittently before drifting off to sleep. Some of the elder women of the village approached him during the day and would leave him with a parcel of food, which was mostly an assortment of shellfish and yams. This sustained him well enough. He was grateful, sparking more than a few grins when he attempted to speak Natui.

"Malo 'aupito." He would speak the words for "thank you", which was followed by a rain of giggles from the Natui villagers who heard him.

After four days in Kahoua, Marcello left the village on an errand for the great chief and said that he would not return for at least another week. Abel baulked at the idea of remaining alone, asking to accompany the priest. Marcello refused, explaining his mission would be made more complicated by Abel's presence. He didn't explain what this meant, but the outcome was the same, anyway.

The day after Marcello departed, Afah approached him as the sun was setting on a clear sky and beckoned him to come out of Marcello's fale; the word Abel had learned meant home or house in Natui.

Afah still sported the bruising he had sustained on Tapu Motu. Abel wasn't sure at first what Afah's intention was, and his anxiety heightened when he was led to the sandy beach as the sun faded in the west. When he reached the shore, a dozen young men and women, including Mahina, were gathering for an early evening swim. Afah smiled and pushed Abel forward towards the water before racing past him and jumping into the shallow waves with the others. The companions were playing, splashing around and pretending to fight in the surf's shallows. Abel watched them from afar. Mahina was examining a large shell she had found half buried in the sand, turning it over to feel the rough interior. Her hair was wet and dripping over her shoulders. Even in the dying light, her face shone with curiosity. Her eyes were focused, and yet to Abel they were also soft and intelligent. Uncertain how long he had been watching her, Abel's cheeks burned red when she looked up and noticed him staring. He smiled and she returned a brief nod in response

Some boys and girls pointed and giggled as they waved at him to join them, and though he was tempted to jump in, he felt too shy. Another boy, older and taller than Afah, shook his head and strode out of the water towards him.

"Maau." The boy touched his own chest lightly. "Maau," he said again.

"Hi, Maau. I'm Abel."

The young man nodded, then gestured out to the water, and raised his eyebrows expectedly. He had a confident face. Broad and serious.

"Fine, I'll come out for a swim."

He took off his shirt, boots and breeches down to his underwear. When he reached the cool water, his companions smiled.

Mahina swam up to him. "You … swim?" she asked.

"Yes, not too bad really."

With that, Mahina grabbed his hand and pulled him towards some of the other boys who were lining up, getting ready for a race. She pointed to a large rocky outcrop that stuck out of the ocean as a marker.

"Fast there. Fast here again. Understand, Epeli?"

"Okay, when do we begin—"

Before he could finish, five of the young men had dived into the waves, swimming towards the rock. He turned and dived after them whilst the spectators shouted and laughed at their attempts to best one another in the impromptu swim race. Abel was an adept swimmer but was clearly no match for any of the five boys ahead of him. They reached the rock and turned with Abel many lengths behind them, and when Abel reached the mark and finally made it back to shore, the others had already finished and were having a jolly laugh at his last place attempt. He was exhausted but laughed with them.

"Granted, I'm no match for the swimmers present, but I'll get better and best all of you next time."

Abel coughed up a spray of salt water he had gulped along the way. Mahina smiled at him, though it did not linger, and she turned to speak to the girls. Maau had won and had taken the victory in his stride, patting Abel on the back. They swam some more and talked, though he did not understand them well, Abel listened to their words as much as he could to recognise any patterns, or repeated phrases he might remember. When the sun had finally set, they returned to the village. Abel went to sleep in Marcello's fale, feeling refreshed and happy that he could have some fun amid this strange new place.

The following day, Afah, Maau and a few older boys gathered some materials to construct a simple shelter for Abel near Father Marcello's. It was built around four timber poles. The roof was a thick weave of flax and dry grass, clasped together by many lengths of coir rope. The lengths of rope were strong. Natui women laboured through the day to make dozens of feet, using the sinewy outer husk of coconut for its fibrous material. He had watched them pull out the thousands of fibres with stone scraping tools. When they were satisfied that enough material had been harvested, they soaked the remains in fresh water and beat it with large pestles to separate out the strands. He sat down with the group for a few moments and the younger girls giggled at his attempts to twist the weaves, using his feet to hold the bottom lengths taunt. Before his hands became chaffed, he was pulled away by Afah, who waggled his finger in horror at the young man's eager foray into Natui arts.

Taken to the foundations of his new sleeping hut, Abel did what he could to assist in its construction. However, the boys seemed content with him helping with lifting materials and gathering drinking water from a freshwater estuary which ran from the east bank of the village and out to sea. They didn't speak to him much, except for Afah, who would occasionally converse in sign language about how it was going to be built. The priest had told Abel that Afah was an adopted son of Chief Lokai. Afah had been taken in after his noble father and mother had gifted him as a child. He was the youngest of five sons and although as Lokai's adopted boy he was afforded some respect, he would never receive titles or lands. Afah didn't seem to mind. He smiled a lot and was a jovial boy who wasn't afraid to pick on the older lads. Abel decided that he liked his spirit.

They promptly erected the fale after only two days, and Abel thanked them for their work with an awkward handshake, which made the group laugh. They shook each other's hands repeatedly for hours afterwards, turning it into a friendly if not bruising wrestling game between them. Reluctant at first to be involved, the group soon turned their physical prowess upon Abel, and he happily joined in with the rough and tumble, arm wrestling and brawling. By the evening, when the night filled with smoke and mosquitos, the boys were covered in scratches and bruises, but they were in good spirits and they all took turns shaking Abel's hand as they drifted off towards campfires and their sleeping abodes. That night, Afah brought a small parcel of pork for his supper, and the two of them shared a few tasty pieces the villagers had cooked on a long spit. There were a number of healthy-looking pigs which freely roamed the village, eating the scraps of coconut husks and lapping up water from crudely fashioned troughs. Abel was tired from the exhausting day, and now that he was fed, he felt drowsy, longing for some sleep. Holding his hands to his head in the sign of a pillow, Abel mimed his intention to Afah, who signalled that he understood his meaning with a brief nod. He shook Abel's hand again with a laugh and raised his palm in the sign of farewell.

"Po'uli a," he said before walking back to his own sleeping hut.

Barely a few minutes after lying on the cool, soft floor of his abode, Abel drifted off to sleep.

Over the coming days Abel was heaped with attention from the local men, women and children from the village and guessed that now Lokai had granted him safety, they were now free to cautiously approach with curiosity. After waking early to wash himself in the morning seas and returning to his new shelter, the young girls of the village formed a great mob around him, feeling his blonde curls and suntanned skin. They were not unused to seeing a palangi since Father Marcello had been here for some years before the newcomer's arrival, but Abel was a much younger man, and he found himself the centre of some attention from more than a few of the braver unattached women in the village.

"Please don't pull my hair, ouch!" Abel yelped in pain as a pretty girl about his age tugged on one of his golden locks.

Mahina was quick to appear and scolded the other girls, shooing them away with an angry gnash of her teeth. With a rough yank, she pulled him towards Father Marcello, who had returned the day before from his journeys to the inner island and had heard the commotion from his low-roofed hut. When he came outside to see the spectacle, Mahina hurriedly spoke in Natui to Marcello, who was still rubbing his eyes from interrupted sleep.

"What's that you say Mahina?" He paid attention to her serious expression and looked over at Abel, who shrugged his shoulders.

"What's going on?" Abel said.

The older man raised his eyebrows and straightened his robes while peering towards the centre of the village. Abel saw him sway on his feet and noticed the smell of liquor on his breath.

"Well, it appears that the great chief has ordered that you replace me as English instructor for Mahina and that she is tasked with your learning of the Natui language. It makes little sense that *you* would be trusted to do this so quickly." He looked at Abel and hung his head low a moment later, as if in deep thought.

"I … teach you … Natui," Mahina said to Abel. "And you, my teacher. Father say because you need learn. You live here now."

Her English was broken, but Abel understood well enough. It surprised him to hear her speak English, and he now understood why she knew some of his words when he first helped her and Afah escape from Tapu Motu.

He smiled widely, and she blushed, hiding her mouth with her hand for a moment.

"I'm sorry, you speak really well." He gently took her hand away from her mouth and grasped it in his own. "It just surprised me, Mahina. I can't stay here. I don't belong here, so I don't know why your father is saying I'm going to live amongst the Natui. Before long I'll need to return to the island where I came from and help Lieutenant Luther."

Mahina's face scrunched up as she thought over his words and relayed the translation back to Father Marcello to confirm what Abel had said. He did simply with raised eyebrows and a series of nods.

"No. Stay here now. No going back." Her voice turned sharp.

"But Mahina, this is not my home …"

"You teacher. Me teacher. Marcello, you tell him now." Her eyes blazed at Abel, and she stormed away from the two of them.

"What just happened, Father?"

They both stared after her as she left, bellowing at some of the young girls who were still waiting on the edges of the conversation, pretending not to listen.

"It seems I've been replaced as her instructor by a younger stallion. Not sure what that wily Lokai is up to, but this is very strange indeed. He expects me to chaperone you like some glorified nursemaid!"

Abel noticed Marcello slurred his words, and his breath reeked of some pungent liquor.

Narrowing his eyes with a sudden fury, Marcello grabbed Abel by the shoulders, holding him at arm's length, his voice trumpeting loudly. "Don't think anything of it boy, I'm the only palangi of value here. You're just a ship rat. A newcomer. One misstep and they'll have your head for harvest feast!" Marcello's face had gone bright red, and he was shaking. Abel tried to pull away, but Marcello's hands held him with some strength and dug into his flesh. With a push to the older man's chest, Abel forced him away and kept his hands up to guard himself.

"Father, what's wrong with you?" Abel was shocked by the sudden change in personality and looked upon his aggressor's face, which was twisted into a wretched canvas of fear and horror.

Marcello was breathing deeply, as if having finished a lengthy run, but as quickly as the rage had appeared, it relented, and he looked about himself confused by his surroundings. His face sank, and he fell to his knees, sobbing uncontrollably.

Abel was unsure what to do next. Several villagers looked on with concern. He reached down and tried to bring Marcello back to his feet, which proved difficult since he was unable or unwilling to stand.

"Come now, Father. Return to your shelter. I beg of you, please."

Abel grabbed him by the arms to hoist him up. He pulled Marcello inside and assisted him onto the sleeping mat. The sobbing had turned into a quiet whimper, and he rolled into a ball, closing his eyes. Abel stayed with him for a few minutes until sleep had taken the priest. He looked around the room and viewed an open bottle he had not seen before which was branded with the mark "Rhum Anglais". Picking it up, he smelled the bottle's mouth. Rum. The priest had drunk more than half the bottle since Abel had woken up for his morning walk.

When he was sure that Marcello was sleeping and unlikely to wake for some time, he left the hut to allow Marcello to recover. At the entrance he stopped and looked back at the bottle of Rhum Anglais, considered Marcello and briefly re-entered to tuck the bottle under his shirt. Ensuring that no one was watching, he took a small satchel of food wrapped in banana leaves, which Afah had given him for supper the night before, and slipped his sabre into a leather scabbard around his waist. Walking down to the beach, he found an isolated rocky cove where he could be alone. Abel spied a dry rock to perch upon and looked out across the ocean, squinting in the sunlight, trying to make out the shores of Tapu Motu. There was a distant shadow of the land, devoid of features at this distance. He soaked his feet in a pool of sea water and watched a small hermit crab scurry away as his toes ventured close, scrambling to sanctuary in another nearby pool.

Marcello's rum smelled medicinal and tasted warm as he took a swig of the powerful spirit. The taste was familiar but smooth down his throat. A much easier drink than the rations held aboard *Viritus*. He drank in the heat of the sun, whilst eyeing up the state of his sabre. The sheath was plied with oil, but this would soon wear away. Salty, humid air would prove to be an enemy of the steel, which required constant attention to prevent rust. He wondered where he would find the oil and thought about asking Father Marcello if he had been set ashore with any upon his banishment. It seemed he had access to many things that Abel considered would have been spoiled or unattainable after so much time had passed. This seemed strange, but his thoughts were slowly dulled by drunkenness. The pleasure of basking in the sun along with the welcome dizziness calmed his mood. It was as if his heart had beaten at twice the normal speed ever since their arrival, but now he took a moment to relax and forget about his worries. Marcello, the English lessons, Smith and the *Viritus* rebellion. For at least a few moments, he wanted to forget it all.

For the rest of the morning, he attempted his daily sword practice which the lieutenant had drummed into him as necessary for readiness in battle. Abel took an uncommon stance he had always favoured, holding the blade over his head and pointed towards the enemy. This gave the advantage of allowing either a thrust or cut to an opponent with a high guard. It was important to keep his knees slightly bent and nimble to lunge forward or retreat as required. With a quick motion he began the blade strikes he had memorised into patterns. A thrust to the head followed by a slash to the base of the neck and another low swing to the upper thigh. He retreated, guarded from three invisible blows, and launched another attack upon his enemy, driving them further back with every cycle of attack.

The sun beat down on his face, and the rum in his system put a swift end to the blade dance as he heaved up his meagre breakfast and purged himself of the liquor. With some forethought he had also brought a fresh coconut with him. With the tip of his blade he poked a hole in the top to drain the fresh tasting liquid within. He could still taste the sickly bile in his throat but was determined to continue his training, feeling that he was going to need to become harder and stronger in the coming days ahead if he was going to survive this ordeal. He discarded the coconut and began with another stance. The traditional fencing mid-guard was encouraged in his basic training. He started a new routine but halted when he noticed a figure perched on an outcrop of rocks next to the rising foredune. He didn't know how long Kalafa had been watching, but he momentarily stopped breathing at the sight of the burly tribesman. Kalafa was only a stone's throw distance away, crouching low with a monstrous club in his hand.

Abel tightened the grip on his sword and held his ground. "I'm not afraid of you," he shouted at the hulking warrior and brandished the sabre. "I'll strike you down, you'll see." The challenge was issued with a broken voice. He kicked the ground, and it sent a billow of white powdery sand into the shifting breeze.

It was drunken bravado, but when Kalafa's eyes flashed in anger and the man leaped from his vantage point towards him, he felt a numbness overcome his body. Kalafa pressed his fist over his heart, and then sharply pointed towards Tapu Motu. Then a bellowed tirade of angry words, completely unintelligible to Abel, brought him to a sudden sobriety. Kalafa swung his ashen coloured pakipaki at Abel's thighs, and he was caught with a glancing blow, causing him to stumble backwards in pain. Before he could recover, he felt a further sharp pain as he took a kick to the chest, which launched him off his feet and into the dense, wet sand. He was winded, and as he tried to draw breath, a small wave washed over him.

Choking up salty water, he crawled away from the incoming tide and stumbled back to his feet to draw a breath as soon as he had recovered. The merciless assault did not let up. Another low blow was aimed at his legs, but this time Abel jumped backwards and it connected lightly, only grazing his shin. He could feel his skin torn and bloodied. The warrior pressed forth, this time jabbing at Abel's belly with the edge of his pakipaki. Abel swept his blade sideways to parry the elaborate club, deflecting the angle of the strike. In repost, he wildly punched his blade across his opponent's right arm and connected. It was a soft blow and delivered with little thought, but his blade was sharp and Kalafa's skin was unarmoured. The flesh on Kalafa's forearm parted, and a wet stain of blood flowed from the wound. As if completely unexpected, the much larger combatant became wide eyed, stopping for a moment to view the clean and skin-deep strike. But instead of a look of pain, his face turned to an expression of indignity. Kalafa brought the pakipaki high above his head, and Abel prepared himself for a strike to his temple. A blow he knew he was unlikely to defend from or survive. The larger man had clearly been holding back until this moment.

The blow never came. Instead, a scream from atop the outcrop of rocks stopped Kalafa from advancing, and they both looked back at the source of the cry. It was Mahina, and striding across the dune towards the two was another man he had seen before. Ono Hiva's guardsman. The other boys had called him Ruaka. He was holding an enormous multi-pronged spear over his right shoulder and although slightly smaller in girth, Ruaka was equally fit and looked a fierce challenge to Lokai's champion. They confronted each other and began to argue. Ruaka stepped in close, and his face was only a few inches away from his opponent's. They shouted over each other, all the while gesturing towards Abel, Mahina and towards the village. The confrontation escalated with Ruaka placing his free hand against Kalafa, shoving him backwards. He looked down at the wound Abel had inflicted and laughed at the blood which was still seeping from the cut. This enraged Kalafa further, but when he looked up at the girl, his expression changed from fury to embarrassment. With a sudden change of heart, he kicked at the ground in front of his foe and scrambled up the beach and away from the fracas until he disappeared amongst the island's thick foliage.

The danger was gone for now, but the pain inflicted during the one-sided fight became very real. Mahina and Ruaka helped Abel back to the village and into his own shelter, which was surrounded in shade and cool compared to the baking sun of the beach. Mahina motioned Ruaka away and looked over his wounds; mostly bruises to his legs and chest, but also several cuts on his arms from shells and coral fragments he had fallen upon. Lying down on a thick bed of reeds, Abel took a few laboured breaths as the room began to spin in relentless, nauseating waves.

"You live, boy?" Mahina asked.

"I'll be fine. I don't know why he wants to kill me. I haven't done anything to him."

She shook her head and examined his grazed knee. "He want give pain. No want to kill. If want kill Abel, you be kill."

Mahina's broken English confirmed what Abel suspected. The warrior was holding back. He was being tested. Toyed with. It just made him feel weaker hearing it said aloud.

The combination of pain, heat and rum was making him feel ill again, but as he looked up at Mahina's concerned eyes he saw again how beautiful she was as she looked upon him with obvious worry. He felt his senses being overwhelmed. The spirit and adrenaline through the battle brought about a mixture of emotions. Without thinking, he sat up and kissed Mahina on the mouth. It lasted only a few seconds. She didn't respond, but when she sat back, her face turned pale. For a moment they stared at each other, and then she touched her lips as if to feel that they were still there. There was silence between them, and Abel could feel he had made a mistake. Cautiously, Mahina stood and left the abode without speaking.

Abel was sure Mahina would tell her father. He looked from side to side, considering how he might escape if the Natui came for him. The reality became clear that there was nowhere to go, and certainly not in his current state of drunkenness and pain. But when Mahina returned alone, he knew she had probably not spoken of his indiscretion. Carrying a small green bundle, Mahina kneeled beside him while she unfurled the layers of banana tree leaves. Inside there were a few objects, but it was the sharp knife that Abel noticed first as Mahina snatched it up and held it firmly to Abel's throat. He held his breath while Mahina leaned in, pointing to her lips.

"If do again," she said, and then motioned the knife sideways across his throat without touching the skin.

He nodded hurriedly in agreement. "I'm sorry, I didn't mean to do that."

The girl relented and withdrew the knife, placing it back inside the parcel. However, she drew out a small clay pot and a tiny jug. Gesturing towards his face, she offered the jug with both hands.

"Drink. We call this noni."

Accepting the small container, he drank the liquid down. It tasted both tart and sweet, almost like a rich ale. When he finished, she placed her soft hands on his chest and pushed him down onto the leafy bed. Then, opening the clay pot, she scooped out a rough yellow paste with her fingers and rubbed it gently on his bruises, first his chest and then his sore thighs, causing him to wince more than a few times. It was cool to the touch. He soon felt numb as the pain subsided.

"This is bark of the hehea tree. You be better now," she said as she carefully wrapped the medicines back into the green leaves.

"Mahina, I am sorry."

With a sudden motion, she swept up the small package and left the hut. Abel was alone to ponder his predicament. He felt guilty, but was too tired to consider going after her to apologise.

The wounds were painful at first. They dulled over the following weeks, but the black and blue colours of welts and bruises became prominent for all to see and had taken some time to fade. However, if any of his Natui captors were concerned by his one-sided battle with Kalafa, they were more distracted by preparations for Ono Hiva to leave on her journey to the lands of Chief Doko. Men, women and children from many of the surrounding villages had arrived and were put to work, labouring tirelessly day and night in the crafting of dowry gifts. Prior to her departure, mats were weaved, mango wood bowls were carved and huge baskets of fruit and sweet potato were gathered aboard two large vessels Mahina had called "kalia". Lokai was sending his wife with two dozen warriors and almost an equal number of maidens and servants for the noble lady.

Two months after Abel's painful defeat on the same shore, a party of enormously muscular men stood side by side. They wore light cloaks made of a variety of woven feathers and each held a pakipaki and short spear as they lined up on the beach for an inspection by Lokai. At the centre of the group, Ono Hiva stood proudly, wearing an elaborate necklace of cone shells and her hair wrapped tightly with many strips of red-dyed bark cloth binding her long braids. Above her waist, apart from pearl bracelets on both wrists, she was bare-breasted. On her lower half she wore a layered tapa-cloth skirt to protect her modesty. Standing at a distance next to Afah on the beach head, Abel thought all at once that she looked as regal and dignified as any noble lady of England he had seen. There was an air of grace that surrounded her. Something almost otherworldly.

He didn't know how long Marcello had been standing beside them. Shadows dancing off his robes alerted him to the priest's presence, and he turned briefly to nod in his direction. Marcello nodded back, and they continued to watch the chief make his way down onto the sand and towards the departing travellers. The two had avoided each other for some days after Marcello had flown into a rage but had since spoken, and the awkwardness had now passed. In the months since Abel's arrival, Marcello had mostly left him alone, aside from being present during his mandated language lessons with Mahina. Before long, Marcello had grown bored with having to chaperone and would often saunter off mid lessen or fail to show up at all. Then eventually he stopped attending completely. At first, Abel thought this would have been seen as inappropriate, and he would not be able to meet with Mahina without someone watching over them. But the lessens continued, and he guessed he had come to be seen as a strange but harmless foreigner.

Abel wasn't entirely lonely. Occasionally Afah, Maau and some of the other boys would take him swimming or spear fishing in one of the nearby lagoons. His swimming skills had greatly improved, though his fishing skills remained amateurish, especially with a spear. The encounters had allowed him to form friendships with the younger Natui, who he knew were probably also watching to ensure he did not escape.

He watched the shore, peering across to Tapu Motu, and wondered what had become of his friends. As time went by, he felt a pang of melancholy thinking about Luther and what fate had befallen his crew. Occasionally he would plan to steal a vaka, but every time he stepped out of the village, he felt that someone was always there to watch. So he stopped thinking about it, hoping that, instead, Luther may eventually rescue him, and tried to concentrate on his regular lessens with Mahina and learning as much of the Natui language and culture as possible.

As they stood on the rise, it was the older man who broke the silence.

"I've heard that your mastery of the local language is becoming impressive."

"I don't think it's impressive. But I've learned a lot over the past months. Doctor Wickman always told me I have a good ear for languages."

"Good to see that you've made some friends, play fighting and socialising with some of the Natui boys." He nodded towards the hulking champion, Kalafa, who was accompanying Hou'eiki Lokai onto the beach below.

"Not sure you could call it play, with that one. I've been nursing a fractured rib which has only just healed, I reckon." Abel winced as if he was experiencing the pain all over again and rubbed his chest. "But that poultice Mahina gave me helped."

The priest stepped forward and fingered his crucifix, grimacing. It was likely the regular lessons between Abel and Mahina was irking him still.

"You would be with the saints now if Kalafa truly wanted to hurt you. There are few, except maybe Ruaka, who could face him in one-on-one combat with any hope of survival."

Abel nodded but kept his eyes on the procession, which had now reached its conclusion in front of the Lady of Natuini and her consort of travellers. Ruaka stood proudly next to her and bowed deeply along with all the others who had lined up to receive their liege.

"Ruaka was the one who stopped it. I feel that I should thank him, but I don't know yet how to express it properly in words. I want to say more than just 'thanks for saving my life'. I feel I need to talk to him. Really talk to him."

His companion laughed and shook his head. "It was not Ruaka who you should thank, young man. The young princess knew he would cause trouble. So she asked Hiva's champion to intervene. You would've walked away with real injury otherwise."

They both stood in silence again and watched the Hou'eiki place his arms around his first wife, kissing her deeply on the forehead. Lokai seemed jovial this morning, and he smiled broadly despite standing in the blistering sun of a cloudless day with a torrent of sweat pouring from his brow. Even from thirty yards away, the two could see a gush of perspiration leap from his hand as Lokai wiped his fat palm over his forehead. Beside him stood his trusted matapule Abel had called a Seagull. This seemed to have stuck. Younger villagers had adopted the less than endearing title, Seagulli. He was often at his master's side, whispering in low tones to the chief. The influence and trust afforded to Masila made him a powerful force amongst the Natui. But outside of his dealings with Lokai, he spent little time speaking directly to commoners. When he did, it was with only grudging tolerance. His demeanour was salty at the best of times, terrifying at the worst. His duties were mixed. Sometimes he was called upon to bless a marriage or adjudicate over a dispute. People would travel from faraway villages to ask Masila's consent to a child's name or even judge the ownership of ancestral lands.

Marcello sneered at the sight of the matapule. "Look at him, snivelling like a lapdog sniffing for a bone. You know his own people fear and hate him."

"So why do they put up with him?" Abel had seen others look down when Masila passed by, whilst some of the braver villagers spat in his wake.

"The title of matapule is his birthright. Handed to him by his father as the eldest son. It is his ancestors who have been the *eyes of the lord* for generations. They speak the chief's will and act as the spoken word of Lokai to his friends and enemies. It is folly to cross him and he wields much power. He is also a holy man, and they say he casts spells upon his enemies …" Marcello made the sign of the cross upon his chest and shook his head. "Heathen god this Maui. But I'm teaching his lordship the way of light. I feel soon he may repent his sins and cast aside these false idols."

Abel was indifferent to the religious leanings of Father Marcello. He was of Christian upbringing, but never understood why the churches of Europe had decided that it was their mission to convert the far-flung heathen peoples of the world. Particularly when they had worshipped their gods as long as most Europeans had worshipped theirs.

Ono Hiva's champion was standing at attention behind her. Abel wanted to approach, to thank him. But now that the party was ready to leave on their mission to formalise the betrothal, he couldn't see an opportunity. His lessons in the native language had begun some time ago with an exchange of knowledge between him and Mahina, and he hoped that by the time they returned he could speak enough Natui to express himself. For now, he was content to take in his surroundings whilst making himself as useful as possible in case his captors changed their mind about his relative freedom. Afah had also agreed to teach Abel about the ancient art of kava making. Ruaka was known to enjoy his kava circles, surrounded by his fellow Natui menfolk, and that may present an opportunity to speak with him.

From this vantage point he couldn't hear the proceedings but could see Masila holding a small green bundle bound in palm leaves. He gave it to Ono Hiva. When he pressed the package into her outstretched hands, she slowly lowered her head, bowing deeply. Beside Lokai, Mahina stood tall and proud. She glanced up the slopes of the dune and met Abel's gaze, smiling briefly before turning to face her mother.

"Let's get closer," Abel said.

"Don't think you can be so familiar. Keep your distance."

Abel walked down to the beach, pretending to ignore Marcello's protestations as Chief Lokai spoke. Marcello followed him anyway.

"My beautiful and gracious wife. Take this gift of union to Malohi, son of my second cousin, Doko of the Grey Hair. If Maui grants us favour, you will return with Malohi, and we shall hold a glorious wedding celebration for our precious daughter."

Ono Hiva straightened her back and beckoned to her daughter to come forth. They embraced, kissing one another on both cheeks.

"Husband, I gladly accept this honour and will return with a newly betrothed husband for our only daughter. Then we will be a stronger people and the Natui will praise your glorious name."

They kissed each other's cheeks before Ono Hiva and her people boarded one of the boats, laden with goods and gifts so that the hulls sat low in the water. It did not take long before they were settled and a dozen men jumped into the surf to push the vessel into the water. Those on board paddled with incredible strength and speed to ensure both kalia could clear the waves of the reef and move through the open ocean.

"How long is their journey?" Abel asked.

"It could take up to three days of island hopping if the winds are favourable. Longer, if not. But the lady will stop at many of Lokai's villages along the way to display the kava root and announce the marriage. And to remind their people of their duties to her husband's rule. This will extend the journey by some weeks, as she will be expected to receive gifts and show gratitude to the more important hou'eiki by staying with their families for a night or two. There are many islands east of here. Hou'eiki Doko and his people live on a large island called Mo'unga Vela, around an extinct volcano. All going well, you will meet him. Or at least see him upon their return."

Many had gathered on the beach to see the kalia moving swiftly out to sea. As they cleared the reef, the crews unfurled large triangular sails which bore them further out along the coast, moving away until they were just tiny specks in the distance. Servants stood with large palm fronds which were held high over the heads of the hou'eiki and his courtiers who had sat on the beach, being fed fresh coconut and raw fish while they waited. When Ono Hiva's voyage was entirely out of sight, Masila stood and raised a conch in both hands before blowing into its mouth. The trumpeting was heard across all of Kahoua and a raucous cheer spontaneously erupted, with shouts of men and women wishing their lady fortune and favour in her long journey ahead.

SEVEN

The truce had been hard fought. Luther considered the men on both sides of the grassy clearing and silently counted out the survivors. Exactly thirty-eight men were on the field, with eighteen beside him and the remaining standing at a distance in the shade of the forest canopy towards the clearing's opposite edge. The enemy had the numbers, but with his snipers, Private Cambridge and Rowe, hidden from sight, the imbalance seemed more pronounced today. He figured that six men had died since their arrival. Four were slaughtered on the first day of conflict, and a further two souls from the opposing camp had been killed during the constant skirmishing since. Some men were absent from the field on both sides. They may have been injured, or perhaps like Cambridge and Rowe, they were watching from a place of secrecy on the forest edge. Many of his own compatriots had sustained a variety of injuries. The blood on his white shirt was a reminder of the danger they faced even now, though the violence had abated somewhat.

It was important to display strength, so he ordered his men to stand at attention at the meet. Taking off his cap briefly, Luther swept back his light brown hair and wiped the sweat away from his face and onto his sleeve. The other marines had abandoned their crimson marine jackets for lighter shirts in the heat, but he had kept his on, enjoying the familiarity of the feel and the additional layer of protection it held in combat. Another part of him felt that his marines still required a reminder of the leadership his uniform conveyed and the need for respect for rank in a situation that could easily spiral into chaotic disorder.

Beside him, the other sailors and marines who had thrown in with his cause were perched in the long grass and waiting on orders. For an hour, the two sides had been watching each other for a clue of betrayal or deceit, with Master Larkin standing ahead of his faction to survey the field, as if to express his confidence and lack of fear, despite having no absolute advantage over his opponent.

"We have the guns, but they have the numbers," Luther said.

He kept his eyes firmly fixed ahead. A few paces away from him, Doctor Wickman and Petty Officer Worthstead heard and understood what he meant.

"And most of the fucking grub," Worthstead muttered, only just audible to Luther and the doctor.

Wickman gave Worthstead a disapproving glance. Luther shook his head, but his stomach was grumbling, and he worried about what the men would do if the stand-off lasted much longer. Worthstead had only voiced what his compatriots were thinking. He didn't doubt their loyalty to his leadership, but he feared they would become increasingly desperate if this went on any longer. In the days after the conflict began, he had secured the northern beachhead, looking out to the wreck of *Viritus*, and much of the equipment saved from the ship. This included most of the dry powder and rifles. However, Master Larkin's crew had made off with an ample supply of powder muskets and ammunition before they retreated further inland and were still in a position to bring arms to the fight. Since then, they had engaged in several fire fights, but neither side had gained any great advantage.

Wickman had astutely pointed out that in some ways their geography had been such that they were in a safer place than was previously understood. The beach and shallow caves close to their camp were located on a wide finger of land. It stretched out from the small island and created a defendable position from any inland attack. Cambridge and Rowe had reported Larkin's encampment was much more spread out, difficult to defend and easy to spy upon. Near the centre of the island was an abundant supply of water from a stream spouting from a large aquifer. Many violent encounters eventuated as they ferried water back and forth to their respective camps.

Despite the terrain advantage, one significant difference was the two groups' source of food. The other side had an abundance of it, and they had been well nourished since arrival. Somehow, they had located a large crop of yams and tubers. The hungry sailors were well fed and had protected it with deadly determination. Their own well defended area of land had some food sources, many identified by Timothy Millstone who had also spent his time building fishing poles and nets for the fish that swum close to the reef. The rough weather and storms had churned the waters, making fishing difficult, and collecting food from the island was a dangerous task. Larkin had taken advantage of the situation, engaging in guerrilla warfare each time Millstone had ventured out with marines on a search for food. On these occasions they would be forced to retreat to camp and could only comfortably forage in the area immediately surrounding the beach and caves.

The men were hungry and growing in frustration at being marooned on an island with no means of escape. Both sides were in a constant state of fear of being murdered in the middle of the night, so when a sailor approached their camp with a white shirt atop a branch, announcing Larkin's request for a truce, Luther had agreed to the proposition.

He had determined that their opponents were running low on ammunition or powder and had voiced this to the doctor privately.

"Before our people starved, Titus knows we would have needed to take their camp by force. Perhaps they don't have the powder to sustain the fight and know that we would have little choice but to make a last stand?"

Regardless, both sides were now facing one another with the prospect of lowering their weapons, and even their most blood thirsty militant welcomed this. Of course, there was always the potential for betrayal. Larkin had named this clearing for the truce and requested that whilst all men were present, only two could meet at centre field for the negotiations. Luther had selected Wickman as his second. From seventy paces away, Larkin was preparing to approach alongside Andrew Smith.

"Worthstead. Do you see anything unusual? Anything we should be worried about?" the doctor said.

The petty officer surveyed the edge of the clearing with a spyglass. They stood in a large clearing devoid of much vegetation except for an occasional low bush and long, sinewy grass. It was at least one hundred and twenty paces from north to south where the two sides had made their stand off and at least twice that east to west. To the west a shallow line of trees blocked a view of the ocean. They could hear distant waves breaking over a reef. To the east a thick layer of foliage with many miles of forest beyond. The clearing itself was unusually bare and seemed out of place on an island which was almost entirely covered in trees and thick bush. However, one object caught the eye of all present in its extraordinary nature. A towering pillar of rock covered with browning vegetation, motley grass and draping vines sat almost perfectly at the centre. It was at least three times the height of a man and Worthstead guessed that twenty men could link arms encircling the hulking monolith. Nothing surrounded it except an enormous expanse of grass which moved ever so lightly on the sea breeze. Carved into one of its sides was the face of a man, glaring angrily towards the east.

"Where in God's hairy armpit did that bloody thing come from?"

Wickman raised his eyebrows at his companion's blasphemy. But he was also dumbfounded with curiosity.

"Just focus on the task at hand. Do you observe anything of interest or concern that I need to know before we approach?" This time his voice was nervous and shrill.

Worthstead nodded solemnly, and his eyes widened.

"What is it, man? Do you see the makings of a trap? Is there something we should take as an ill omen? Is there a worry here?"

"Yes." The private nodded earnestly again. "For one, there's a fucking great big boulder, slap bang in the middle of an empty field."

"What …?"

Worthstead sighed and grinned, picking his teeth with a sliver of wood, and tapped his pistol, which hung loosely on his belt. "I don't see nothin' doc. If they got someone in those woods, then they're well hidden. Just like our two. If they're any good, I shouldn't be able to see them. But no, I don't see any blimmin' hordes of snakes waiting in that long grass to pounce upon yer." He peered around and squinted in the hot sun which had risen at its zenith. "If I was planning some ol' skulduggery, I wouldn't do it 'ere, mi'lord. Too much open air. Not enough hiding places to sneak around in for a bit of back stabby and sneaky wet work."

His appraisal of the day did little to calm their nerves, and when Luther turned to signal for the doctor to begin the approach, his heart beat in anticipation of the unknown.

If Wickman was nervous, he hid his emotions well. He bit his lip and straightened his back before marching forward, with the young lieutenant a few paces ahead.

Striding confidently in their direction, Larkin and Andrew Smith had also begun their short trek to the meeting point. They stopped just short of five paces from each other and stood directly next to the outcrop of rock that provided some welcome shade. It cast a slight shadow with the sun directly above, enough for the group to gain some relief. Luther keenly welcomed the respite from the striking sun. In this open field without shelter, the heat was palpable.

The four men eyed each other up for a short time. Master Larkin had arrived in full dress uniform but up close he could not mask his discomfort in the baking humidity. However, the message signalled was clear to all, and from a distance his rebellious marines and sailors were reminded of his seniority whilst the treasonous lesser officer's attire had been scuffed and torn from weeks of rough living.

At first, neither side moved nor spoke. Instead, Larkin pulled a water flask from his side and drank deeply from the vessel. The doctor could see that Smith was glaring at both of them with a look of both hatred and disgust which became even more pronounced when his superior lifted the flask and offered it to Luther who accepted it without hesitation and also drank, taking much of it down before lifting it away from his lips. When he was finished, he wiped away a few precious drops that had come free on his chin and expressed thanks with a quick nod. The water was still cool to his throat and had likely been taken from the fresh stream within the hour. The flask was given back to its owner, who carelessly shuffled it back into a leather pouch under his jacket, before taking a deep breath and breaking the strange silence.

"Gentlemen, glad to see you in good health. Doctor, I have some men who could benefit from your expertise. You are still bound by your oath, I take it? Three months on this island hasn't caused you to discard your ethical reasoning?" His eyes fixed squarely on Luther as he spoke, even though he was expecting an obvious reply from Wickman.

"Why yes, of course. I would be keen to check on the health of your – our – men." His voice trembled in response to the strict contrast of confidence displayed in being addressed by a superior.

"There will be time for all poor of health to receive treatment, though I'm also sure that you could forgive Robert for worrying about his personal safety." Luther also kept his eyes firmly fixed on his rival.

"Using first names so disrespectfully, Lieutenant? Have your people fallen to ill-discipline and savageness so quickly? The good doctor is your peer, not your subservient. But perhaps you have both forgotten your place."

"No, Master Larkin. We are all still British and understand the need to maintain steadfast. Even in this unfortunate environment."

Larkin baulked at Luther. His face turned red as his voice rose. "You talk of steadfastness in the midst of mutiny. How dare you, insubordinate wretch?" As quickly as he lost his temper, he closed his eyes, and with a deep breath he held his hand to his head where a deep scar had formed from the blow he had taken during the evacuation of *Viritus*.

"I apologise." A mirthless smile flashed upon his face. "It's a difficult prospect that we face here, and I didn't call you here to argue. I want to be blunt. This bloodshed cannot continue given the dangers we face, and it's time to stop this foolishness and fall to order once more."

Luther agreed with a nod. "Yes, sir, this is a truth. This has been a great dishonour for us all, and a truce should be reached," he said.

"Excellent," Larkin's voice rose once more. "Then we are in agreement. The fighting must stop, and we should bring back order where there has been none." He straightened his back as he placed his hand on Smith's shoulder, looking at him for agreement.

Smith gave a slight nod.

"Of course, Luther, we must move forward and pool our resources if we're to survive here. I will pardon you for the mutiny and you will admit your error."

"My error?"

"Yes, you can claim that you were sick or brain addled from the long journey. Either way, we'll fall back to the natural order of things. I'll assume command and we'll move to our next steps in securing our position here."

Larkin scratched his beard as he stepped back and surveyed the marines and sailors at opposite ends of the field. "One or two of your marines will need to be punished, however. A severe lashing will do. For their sins against God and king. If I'm going to command respect again, I'll need to set an example. It's completely up to you who, but this is something I insist upon."

Smith smirked. "Yes, we insist upon it. Also, the boy, if we ever catch him, I promise you I'll be flogging him to death, the little cunt."

Larkin gave Smith a rebukeful stare. "That's quite enough. We do not take pleasure in this undertaking. But it will be a necessary condition of the truce. Let's put an end to this. What do you say, Lieutenant?"

Luther scratched his chin and turned away from the group, pacing slowly in thought as the others watched on.

"Luther, what say you?"

The question was met with silence. Instead, he walked some steps away until he was close to the large outcrop of rock jutting proudly from the ground. Looking up to the top, Luther could see a red and brown bird perched above them. He hadn't noticed it until now, and it squawked a challenge as he caught its eye. The bird spread its wings to ward off the unwanted intruder and strutted around the edge of the mound. Luther guessed it was likely protecting a nest. Spying a long gangly vine which draped above his head and into the thick grass below, he grasped it between his fingers and felt its texture, rough and brittle. Leaning forward, he pressed his hand into the thick foliage on the surface of the rock. It was cool to the touch. A large centipede was disturbed and it weaved away from the rude intrusion, rearing its head for a moment before scampering back deep within the tangle of foliage.

Without looking back, Luther gave his answer. "So once the men are in order, and two of our own are punished, what of our plans then, Master Larkin? We have no ship and the French may still be out there searching for us. Abel is missing. What will be your orders?"

"I'm sorry about your cousin." Larkin approached. "You should understand those savages probably slaughtered him for meat. You know how these island natives are."

"What will be your orders?" Luther pressed again.

"It's simple. We must find where these savages are hiding. I suspect it's upon that larger island to the north of the beachhead. They'll have food and good shelter. We have the firepower to subdue a large village, and after a few of their men fall to our superiority, they'll see us as gods bringing a holy vengeance upon their heathen souls. Or something like that to their primitive minds. We can take some women to keep our sailors in good spirits and use the men as a workforce until we spy a friendly vessel to take us home, or perhaps even to one of the New South Wales colonies, where we can find a friendly captain to throw in with."

"A brilliant plan, aye Luther?" Smith laughed. "Maybe I'll find that little lass who your boy took a shine to and make her my belly warmer on the journey."

"Smith, enough." Larkin turned and raised his voice again in irritation. "Now what say you, Luther, do we have a truce?" He offered his hand and raised his chin in a proud pose, waiting for the other to turn and acknowledge the agreement.

Luther stayed in position, leaning against the surface of the great boulder, and gave nothing away to his thoughts on the proposal. Both sides of the crew watched from their positions in the clearing in anticipation of the outcome. They were all tired of the constant conflict. He looked back at his men for a few moments and considered the loyalty they had shown him. There was an expectation on their faces. But what did they really expect?

"They're relying on me to bring us to a peaceful understanding, Larkin."

"Absolutely. They need your leadership, and it's that leadership and your skill as a marine, which I value. That's why I'm willing to forgive this lack of judgement in the face of desperation and fear."

Luther grunted at the response. "You know that many people of the Pacific, from Hawaii to New Zealand, all seem to tell the tale of their god Maui. There is one story that I've heard. About

a large rock such as this not far from here on the Tongan Islands
…"

Larkin raised his eyebrows. "Yes? What of their heathen gods? Why do you bring this up? It's just a rock."

"Well, with respect sir, they don't see it that way. The peoples of these islands. Legend has it that Maui was so angrily awoken by a rooster that he threw great boulders and rocks to destroy the bird. It escaped to that island. The largest of the rocks thrown was the great boulder they believe to be a remnant of a god …"

"I'm still not following you, son." His voice grew impatient. "What is this madness?"

"You see, Master Larkin, you remind me of that demented bird. And you risk awakening the gods of these islands. To be clear, that's not you and me. It's the people who live here. Remember, we have nowhere to go. There is no place to escape to and you insist on wanting to kill your own men whilst feverishly plotting to enslave a people you know nothing about." Luther withdrew his hand from the undergrowth of the rock's surface. With some speed he reached under his shirt, drawing a pistol and turned towards Larkin and Smith.

"Vincent, wait!" Wickman shouted in horror.

Seeing his commander held at the point of a cocked pistol, Smith took two hurried steps back, grinning no longer.

The first mate held still, but his eyes were wide. "So, treachery, is it? I always thought you an honourable man. And what of us now? You kill me in front of all these men and show them what kind of loyal son of Britain you truly are."

There was a commotion across the clearing with men shouting in panic and anger, but no shots were fired. Instead, both sides looked at each other in confusion, and without their leader's orders took no actions. A few of the men with rifles took aim, but the distances were too great for an effective fire fight. Smith waved to his men, holding them off from pulling their triggers. He and his superior were in the middle of the crossfire. Luther could see him looking for a place to run.

"This is not gentlemanly conduct and absolutely not befitting of your oath to serve and obey," Larkin said.

Being berated by his former superior, Luther's face betrayed a look of shame for the reminder of his rank and station. This was not what he wanted. Not at all. Bringing a weapon to a parlay was an act of dishonour, but what more could he do? He had watched his men slowly dying, slowly losing hope, and the desperation of those who put their faith in him was increasing every day. He had hoped for a better outcome. For a more reasonable approach. It was clear now to him that this was impossible. So, deciding that the lives of his people were more precious than his personal sense of honour, Luther decided upon a contingency.

"Forgive me, Master Larkin. You have taken ill. Just like Captain. I think you and I both know that there has been little about this butchering of one another that could be considered gentlemanly. It pains me to do this, but you need to surrender yourself. Tell your followers to lay down their weapons and fall to my command. Let's avoid any further killing. You will be treated with respect, but you will not be in command any longer."

Larkin laughed loudly. There was little humour in his voice but much scorn as he turned to look at his men, who were currently dumbstruck. They looked at each other. Paralysed with indecision.

"This is pathetic. You won't fire that weapon at me. I know you well and I know the kind of man you portray yourself. Legend of St. Vincent. Nelson's favoured officer. Bollocks. You'll just prove yourself to be low born scum like the rest of those oath breakers. Now you are so ordered, put down that weapon." He finished his insult with a guttural roar, a line of spittle erupting from his lips and onto his bearded chin.

Luther hesitated. He lowered his weapon. At heart he believed strongly in the chain of command and strict regimented order of the military way. There was little doubt he had brought shame to his shipmates for his actions. For a moment he took his eyes off of his surroundings to look at the pistol.

The sudden turn in focus was all that Larkin needed to attack. He swiftly reached under his shirt, drawing out a razor-sharp dagger. Lunging forward towards his prey, he aimed high for the throat. He let out a mighty scream with the effort. All in vain.

Luther had seen the quick movement and his well-trained reflexes reacted at speed. Before Larkin could take a second step, the pistol was again lofted upwards and forward towards the face of the oncoming officer, a face which was twisted with a terrible rage. Pulling up the pistol and squeezing the trigger with one disciplined movement, a gunshot echoed through the clearing. Blood spattered in a torrent of brain and bone out the back of Larkin's head. A mist of droplets rained down on Wickman's horrified face and white shirt, soaking through with a damp warmness into his flesh. The body dropped, disappearing into the long grass, out of sight of all except the three men who looked on at the bloody spectacle.

"Damn you," said Luther. "Damn you and this madness."

Smith turned and ran towards the safety of his firing line. At first he stumbled, falling onto his face but picked himself up and kept going. Luther, seeing the man flee, knew at once that he had to stop him from reaching his men, otherwise this would have all been in vain and the cycle of violence would continue. He reached down and plucked the dagger from the chief officer's lifeless hands and spun towards the moving figure of Andrew Smith, flinging the blade towards his back. Smith had barely sprinted six paces before the blade struck his shoulder, causing him to trip on the uneven surface. He landed heavily and yelped in pain, clutching his back, trying to withdraw the knife that was deeply embedded. With a jerk, he wretched the knife free. Hearing footsteps behind him, he spun around on the ground and blindly thrust the knife up towards whoever was approaching. Luther kicked the knife from his hand, jarring Smith's wrist with crushing impact. The marine picked him up by his shirt collar and thrust him towards the line of his own men. They watched on, motionless. Stunned at the drama unfolding. Luther pushed Smith forward with a heavy hand.

"You cut me. Let me be. Fucking let me go!"

His protests were futile. Driven with an intensity of purpose, a fearlessness had overcome the lieutenant.

When they both reached the line of sailors, some of them angrily aimed their weapons at Luther, while others stepped back in nervous fright. None approached him.

He gripped his quarry's shirt collar tighter and hauled him downwards until he was on his knees just feet from the awe-stricken men.

"It's over, Smith. Tell them it's over," he shouted at the officer.

"Go to hell, you little—" Before he could finish, he received a firm blow to the back of the head.

"Tell them to lay down their weapons, or else the next one will send you to your master's side. Do it."

"By God ... please stop."

He was carelessly thrown forward again and landed heavily on his damaged hand, bruised from being kicked.

A few murmurs of anger emanated from the sailors but none of them moved.

"Put down those rifles. I said put them down. Tell them it's over. I'll let you live, Smith. Just tell them to yield. The fight's over, there will be no more killing of our brethren."

"Fine, fine ..." Smith's breathing was laboured, and the pain of the wound throbbed with excruciating agony. "It's finished boys. Master Larkin has perished. It's finished," Smith said.

Luther addressed the confused crew. "Brothers. I bear you no malice. Nor do your shipmates you took up arms against. My proposal is this. I will forgive all trespasses against me if you fall under my command. Your officer is dead by my hand, but you have nothing to fear from me unless you continue to take up arms."

Smith was struggling to his feet, grimacing at the effort. Buxley ran forward to help him up.

"You must choose your fate. Join me and we will prosper here and, with God's grace, find our way home. Choose a different path and we all might die, endlessly fighting, brother upon brother until our blood has run free. Decide, but decide this very moment."

With a few moments to look upon the weary faces of the men, he turned and strode back to Wickman. The two shared a sorrowful glance.

"Robert, we'll give him a proper burial."

"You think you haven't sent us all to our grave with this bloodshed?"

"It depends on what they decide. Tell me, Doctor, are they raising their weapons, ready to strike me down?"

Robert raised his eyebrows. "Why don't you take a look?"

Luther took a deep breath and closed his eyes, uttering a brief prayer. Then he turned and could see that he was being followed by every sailor he had addressed, their arms raised in surrender.

EIGHT

The Chiefdom of the Grey Hair was renowned for its lush beauty and abundance of heilala and frangipani trees. They grew voraciously on the several narrow islands of Mo'unga Vela, an archipelago of crystal-clear lagoons protected by coral reefs. As her procession of boats drifted slowly towards the largest of the islands in this chain, Ono Hiva could smell the subtle but lovely scent of the frangipani flowers. The tree line beyond the sandy shores was awash with brilliant shades of white, red, and yellow blossoms as they approached. A myriad of brilliant colours created such a vision of beauty that even the hardiest of her sailors paused and were awestruck by the landscape. The people of this land used the frangipani flowers to make a delicious tea. When mixed with honey, it was a refreshing drink and considered a cure for all manner of ailments. This, if nothing else about this paradise, Hiva looked forward to indulging in. She loved the tea. But she held no love for these islands. Of all the lands, she despised this place like no other.

Hiva's late grandfather, Lord Kavelu, conquered Mo'unga Vela as a young man with the aid of his ally Chief Maka. Much blood was spilt in its taking. For many years, Lord Kavelu had ruled over these isles and brought a long period of peace and prosperity. As a young girl, she could remember staying with her grandfather. She lived in these lush lands during the summer months and could remember how much he loved her, showing her off to all who could see by hoisting her atop his shoulders and walking her through the villages. It was a happier time, brought to an end by treachery. As Lord Kavelu grew older and increasingly frail, the family of its current ruler led an uprising. They massacred her grandfather in his sleep and killed all who were loyal to him. Hiva, because of her betrothal at a young age to Lokai, was spared. This avoided another war and allowed her to return to her home in the north, but not before she was forced to watch as Lord Kavelu's butchered body and those of his wife and servants were burned. The remaining ashes were rubbed into the hair of the victors to symbolise the taking of power from Kavelu. This morbid act became a fashion: men, women and children used ashes from their campfires to rub into their hair, making them distinguishable from outsiders. Since that time, they became known as the "Grey Hair" wearing the powdery ash like a mark of pride and honour. For Hiva, it was a reminder of horrific memories.

She grimaced at the thought of returning, despite the importance of the occasion. Yes, she hated the people of this land and its ruler. But she loved her daughter more than her bitterness towards the Grey Hair. With her daughter's marriage, a lasting peace would be secured, and Mahina would eventually rule over this land as the wife of its future chief. For this prize, Hiva could bear to walk upon these shores again but welcomed the prospect of a brief stay. Her duty was a necessary one; to present the kava root, which signalled the formal acceptance of marriage between the two chiefly families.

When they saw the first of the Grey Hair come to shore to view the approaching kalia, Hiva's sailors hauled in their sails and paddled with renewed strength towards a short wooden dock. It was tradition and a matter of respect to arrive upon the land of another chief at paddle, and not with the ease of a swift breeze that would bring them to shore. This symbolised a visitor had made an arduous journey and a tremendous effort had been undertaken in honour of the host.

Ruaka remained by her side. She had tried to hide her feelings, but he always seemed to know her heart. He turned to look at her, but said nothing.

"What's the point of just staring at me? Speak if you have something to say."

"Even if you were to lower your head to the level of the low tide, you would still be a mountain to any you see before you, Hiva. Remember that."

"You're a poet now? Enough. You don't need to tell me of my nobility."

"I see the lines on your forehead. It's a message as clear as a signal fire. You need cheering up."

"Must everything be in jest? Sometimes I'd like to be free to worry without your mocking."

"No mockery intended, my lady. Just the concern of a loyal servant. I wanted you to know that you're loved. Your people will die for you, as would I."

He grinned when she stood a little taller. Ruaka could be as annoying as an incessant kotare bird. But she loved him for it.

His irreverence somehow comforted her. She was not alone. He did not see her as a noble, only as a woman he cherished.

As soon as the kalia landed, Hiva touched the black pearl necklace to steady her nerves. Although it held many pearls, gifted to her by her grandfather so long ago, it also held a singular pearl which was a gift from Ruaka. He had found the oyster by chance in one of the pristine freshwater streams that ran across Natuini Lahi. When he was sure that no one was spying on them, he gave it to her to add to the necklace. Now it sat in the centre of the piece. Touching it calmed her mind. It also showed Ruaka he did not truly upset her.

"There are many here who wish me harm. Are your men aware of the danger in Mo'unga Vela?"

"They know. When I'm not near, I have assigned Seletute to remain close. You can trust him as you trust me."

Ruaka and his friend Seletute had fought many battles side by side. They had saved each other's lives more than once and had formed a strong bond between them over many years. Ruaka was born in the Tonga islands, and he had been brought to Natuini as a boy. He still remembered his older siblings and had a brother and sister he had not seen since his arrival. Seletute and Hiva's personal warrior guard were his family now. He often called them brothers, though they shared no blood bond.

On the shore Hiva was met by Chief Doko's very own matapule and several of the Grey Hair elders who escorted her into the heart of the island and towards the chief's bustling village, Kolo Mo'unga. Surrounded on three sides by thick vegetation and atop a small hill, the village was wrapped by a series of moats and palisades, protecting its inhabitants from intruders who would seek to raid their abundant storehouses, or worse, from slavers. The village within was built amidst hundreds of the hibiscus trees and now that they were in full bloom, the entrance to the village was a remarkable spectacle of colour. This brought back memories for Hiva, and with those memories, pain.

"You didn't tell me this place was so breathtaking. It's as if the gods have blessed this land with the beauty of a thousand sunsets. I've never seen such a place."

Ruaka studied the surroundings and protective palisades with curiosity. "And those walls are thick and at least twice the height of a Natui warrior. Indeed, this would be a difficult village to conquer."

"Difficult, but not impossible," Hiva said.

Her thoughts turned to her grandfather and the legendary warrior he had become when he had taken this land by force of arms. Ruaka stepped into pace beside her and kept a wary eye out for anyone who might get too close to his lady.

When they arrived, the large gates were already swung wide, revealing the village and the many structures within. The Grey Hair had built their village houses and meeting places closer together than those of Kahoua, and the crowded construction gave the appearance of a busy village. As Hiva entered at the head of her sizable entourage, a crowd of men and women was waiting for her and flanked her pathway as they shouted a welcome cheer for the visitors. Several young girls approached. They held wreaths of flowers, which they placed around her slender neck. Once she accepted this gift, her followers were treated the same way, with many of the inhabitants bidding them welcome with kisses upon their cheeks, and more wreaths of flowers placed around their neck and shoulders. Some of the Grey Hair were related to her people, and there were a few tearful reunions between her servants with relatives in the village. This made Hiva genuinely happy, and she could not hold back her smile. This small display of happiness pleased her welcomers. They let out hoots of joy at her arrival, which they had prepared for since receiving word of her daughter's coming of age and Chief Lokai's willingness to create a union amongst their people. It was a joyous occasion, especially since a noble marriage would be celebrated with a week of kava drinking, feasting and games to mark the marriage.

When the villagers saw her followers carry through the many baskets of yams, fruit, mats and ornamental goods brought as a gift for Chief Doko, a great cheer erupted from the hundreds of men and women. Some danced and sung, expressing gratitude for the offerings which they hoped would please their chief. If in a generous mood, he may share some of this bounty with his people.

A great open pavilion held aloft by ornately carved poles was the only building that was not in proximity to others, and outside of its raised timber floors a great number of people had gathered. Hiva could hear villagers talk openly about her beauty and, for those who had not seen her daughter, assumed Mahina was also pleasing to the eye and would produce handsome children. The compliment was welcome, though she remained regal and pretended not to hear.

Upon entering the clearing before the pavilion, Ruaka glanced at his ward, and she gave a brief nod, providing him a signal to step back and allow her a few paces ahead of the remaining entourage. Hou'eiki Doko was waiting for Hiva's arrival at the entrance. Behind him stood his family of six wives and twenty-three children, the eldest of which was his son Malohi, who would marry Hiva's beloved daughter. She had not seen Chief Doko for two years and was surprised at his changed appearance. His face was pale and gaunt. The healthy weight of the proud chief had been replaced by a thin frame covered by scaly skin from years of excessive kava drinking. He had the look of a sick man. Even the white bushy beard upon his face could not hide the hollow cheeks of the frail leader. The once striking man, who had wooed many a noble lady with his rugged looks, was now a ghost of his youth. Still, as soon as Hiva was within reach, he opened his arms and his mouth spread to a wide smile. Kissing Hiva on both cheeks, he embraced her with as much strength as he could muster, pulling her close to him as he whispered into her ear.

"Malo e lelei. Welcome to Kolo Mo'unga, beautiful Ono Hiva. It is our honour to host you again. This union will tear down the mountains of sorrow from years past. This is your home too now, no matter what has transpired before."

He pulled away and smiled again, this time raising his voice so that all could hear. "Bid welcome to the Lady of Natuini, wife of my cousin, the great Chief Lokai and mother to the future bride of my first son, Malohi. Ono Hiva you are received with joy and gratitude."

At this announcement, the men and women who were gathered let out a mighty cheer, and some of the older women began to spontaneously sing and dance as if to an invisible drum, though with a wave of his hand, the crowded entrance to the pavilion was hushed to allow for Hiva's reply. In her hands she held out the small and precious package she had carried from the lands of Lokai, carefully unwrapping the soft palm leaves to reveal the twisted and dry root of the kava plant collected from Tapu Motu.

"Malo e lelei. I, Ono Hiva of the Natui, wife of Chief Lokai and Lineage of the Kavelu tribe accept your welcome and bring you this divine message of acceptance."

Hiva carefully took the root from the package, letting the leaves fall to her feet and held the kava tendrils aloft so that all who were present could bear witness to its message.

"Chief Lokai accepts the proposal of marriage to his daughter, the fair Mahina, light of the moon. With her own hands, she took this from Tapu Motu. It is symbolic of the kava they will share on their wedding night. My husband brings you many gifts from our people and invites you to his home for the betrothal feast so that he may share his love for his cousin with festivities and feasting."

With both hands she offered the root to Doko, who took it from her gently. Also holding it aloft for his people to witness.

"We accept, Lady of Natuini. We accept with all of our hearts."

The aging chief almost shouted with joy, and his people were roused again to cries of happiness. Whilst her expression did not change, and she showed little open emotion, for a moment, Hiva let herself feel some measure of elation at the enormous expression of joy from Doko's people. She caught herself quickly, dismissing those feelings, and felt suddenly hot, standing in the open with the sun beating down upon them. She could feel the conflict in her heart sweep through her body as it had for all of her journey to Mo'unga Vela.

"Come Ono Hiva, join me and my son for food and drink. I know you're fond of the tea we make from the frangipani flowers and my wives have prepared a fresh tea especially for you, mixed with sweet coconut sugar."

"I accept. Please lead the way."

Hiva joined the older man as he turned and walked.

"Your warriors and servants are welcome to stay here as guests for as long as you are with us. I hope you'll remain whilst we prepare for the journey and travel with us for the wedding celebration. We'll require at least ten days to make arrangements."

"That's most gracious of you, great chief. Yes, my husband's intention was for me to accompany you and your son. I hope we're not imposing too much upon you."

"No, no, of course not, my lady. You have been very generous with gifts of crops and kava, so there is much kai for our hungry mouths. This year our harvests have been strong and the seas have been especially bountiful with scores of mahimahi caught by our proud fishermen. You know our fishermen are some of the most skilled of all Natui." The chief beamed with pride at this boast.

Servants led them into the heart of the pavilion, where finely woven mats adorned the clean, wide floors. A number of female servants ushered the small party to be seated around a dozen woven flax baskets filled with fruit, freshly cooked quail and other delicious delights in abundance for just the three of them. On one side, Chief Doko and his son Malohi sat together, whilst opposite Hiva was provided a seating place cushioned by soft reads. Coconuts were cut open in front of them, and they each drank the cool water within before engaging in further conversation.

"My son has grown, has he not? Eighteen years of age and he's just as big as I was in prideful youth." Doko gave his son a playful pat on his back and was rewarded with a fleeting smile.

Hiva looked him over. She was unimpressed by what she saw. Malohi was handsome. That was certain. He was well known for his good looks and had been the talk of many young noble girls from all over the Natuini. However, as a young boy with such rare beauty and noble birth, he had been pampered and groomed for much of his life. His servants had clearly applied warm hued colours on his lips and eyes. His hair was longer than that of a young girl and combed through with coconut oil until it was glistening. His body was also shiny, massaged with a layer of fresh oils to maintain suppleness and a healthy complexion. Coloured ribbons, which may have seemed better suited to tie the hair of a young virgin girl, were wrapped around his well-defined muscles and thighs in a decorative fashion, which Hiva despised. Much more so since she knew him to have an entitled attitude. She had hoped that he had matured so her daughter would not have trouble in her marriage. Hiva would gauge him properly in the days ahead.

"Tell me, my lady. Your husband. Is he well? The last I heard, he had taken up worship of foreign gods. Is this true?"

"Just one god. Lokai keeps a palangi holy man by his side and has accepted the fables he tells about one powerful god the palangi men believe in." Hiva tried not to show her bitterness and was embarrassed by the question.

"What is this god's name?" Doko asked, curiously.

Hiva laughed. "That is something of a strangeness. The holy man says that his god has no name. Only that he is called 'God'. He tells many stories about him just by looking upon layers of white tapa which are covered in strange pictures. When Lokai speaks to him, the holy man captures the words and can draw them inside the tapa. Many months later, he can speak the same words as if Lokai had just spoken them."

"This must be some kind of strange spirit magic. Indeed, the palangi god must have some power. Perhaps he's a descendant of Maui."

Doko nodded to himself and looked at his son, who shrugged with disinterest as he bit into a thick slice of melon. Hiva and her entourage had been told by Lokai not to reveal that more foreigners had arrived and were living on Tapu Motu. She was unsure why this needed to be hidden but did not question it and avoided talking further on the subject of the intruders any further.

The three ate quietly. The fresh fruit and yams were delicious, and Hiva was hungry from the long journey. She had been worried about coming here so much that she had barely eaten. Now that she was comfortable on solid ground, she could feel her stomach rumbling and her stomach pains subsided in taking in some refreshments. After an uncomfortable silence, it was Malohi who finally spoke.

"Ono Hiva. I truly look forward to meeting Mahina again. It's been many years, but I'm told she blossoms like a flower and that she is strong of spirit."

Malohi's voice was deep and confident for a boy who appeared more like the favoured daughter of a noble and not a son. His gaze was intense and fixed upon Hiva, awaiting a response.

"Yes, and I know she'll make you a proud husband, and she a dutiful wife. My daughter is also skilled. She can weave as well as any of our elder women. Also, she is not afraid to adventure far from our village and is a fine hunter of birds and fish."

"Ha!. No girl should spend her day's fishing and hunting. This is for men. When I'm her husband, these things will stop," Malohi said.

Hiva drew her breath slowly and carefully. As a strong, independent woman of the Natui, she did not appreciate his words.

"Were you so free and boyish when you were a young girl here amongst the Grey Hair?" he asked.

Chief Doko, who was eating veraciously, scooping the innards from a coconut shell, stopped mid-bite and put down his fruit, looking sideways at his son.

Hiva folded her arms and leaned back.

"I have fine memories of this village and your people. I remember playing here in this very meeting house, many years ago, well before you were born."

"You mean fine memories of your wicked grandfather thieving land from my subjects?"

Doko stopped eating. His face turned a blazing red hue. "Son, how dare you? This is our honoured guest and your future mother-in-law. You would dare accuse her family of thievery? I won't stand for it."

"But that's what the elders say, Father. I've simply reminded Ono Hiva of our history so that the lady may understand that when I'm high chief of the Grey Hair, I'll never let our lands befall an enemy's spear."

He was passionate, but again earned a look of fiery rage from Doko.

"That is enough, Malohi. Apologise to Ono Hiva. Now."

"But Father …"

"Apologise now, son. Or I'll tear that tongue from your mouth."

The boy looked away, but moments later, he turned back to Hiva and furrowed his brow. "I am sorry, honoured guest. Please forgive my words. I speak for my people's ancestors." The young man took another bite of flesh from the quail breast and tossed away the bone abruptly.

Hiva had not taken her eyes off Malohi but had also shown no expression. Instead, she picked up a small piece of honeyed yam and took a bite. When she had finished eating, she sighed and turned to the chief.

"I accept your son's apology. I cannot hold anger towards a host who has treated me so well. We will join as a family. His children will be blood of my blood. We all know families have the best arguments."

Doko looked relieved.

"I am sorry, my lady. Malohi will take his leave. He has to prepare the festivities for tomorrow night in your honour, and that of your daughter."

He shot Malohi a baleful glance and gestured outside with his chin, signalling his son to leave. Malohi stomped away from the pavilion, sweeping up a basket of fruit. He continued to eat while throwing pieces of food to the servants who had gathered nearby.

"He is young and he will learn." The chief shook his head.

"It seems he has already learned much."

"Please, Hiva … It's my fault. Over the years I instructed our holy men and story keepers to prepare him to take my place. I should've kept a closer ear on how he was being taught. There are many here who still remember the time of the rule of Kavelu, and they've told their children and grandchildren the worst of the tales. It wasn't a peaceful time, and Hiva, you were a young, innocent child so don't have the memories many of us elders do."

"Yes, I was young. That is true. But I remember some things." She spoke softly so the chief had to lean forward to hear.

"Yes, Hiva, what do you remember? The flowers of the frangipani tree? The games you used to play with my granddaughters?"

She reached out and touched the top of his cracked and rough hand, gripping it lightly in her own slender fingers, and pulled him closer. "My lord, I remember the smell of the burning bodies. I remember the screams of my aunties and uncles. I remember my beloved chaperones being violated and put to death by your people."

Duku's faced darkened, and he looked away, but she did not stop.

"Then, when the screams stopped, and the fires burned, I remember your people as they covered themselves with the ash of *my* people whilst they ate my grandfather's heart and liver, to take his mana, in honour of their bloody victory."

She let go of his hand, and he leaned backwards, keeping an expression of sorrow.

Another silence befell them, and it seemed it would last forever, until the chief's eyes softened and he looked upon Hiva once more.

"Those days have long since passed and most people have moved on. No longer do we pine for vengeance. Peace is upon us with this union and we shall make it so, the gods be our judge."

He sounded sincere. Hiva felt she should reply, but was interrupted by a pretty servant girl whose smiling eyes reminded her of her own daughter. She offered a freshly scented tea, and Hiva happily took the bowl, taking in the brew's warm aroma.

"Tomorrow we have our finest dancers provide you with joy. Whilst we feast on the fruits of our luscious bounty this season, we'll laugh and talk of family and our future tidings, whilst being entertained by my most talented people."

Hiva nodded, still enjoying the delicious tea. "I look forward to it, Chief Doko. I thank you for your hospitality."

She sipped the tea, enjoying its taste. The rest of the conversation was limited to exchanging pleasantries. When she was finished, Hiva excused herself.

"I wish to stroll the surrounding woods. There are many places I haven't seen with my own eyes since long ago, and I want to remind myself of the beauty of the land of Doko."

The chief stood and bowed. "Of course, Lady of Natui. It will be dark soon; I wouldn't like to see you in danger. I'll send some of my warriors with you ..."

"No need, generous host. I have my own servants."

Doko nodded. "What makes you comfortable and content pleases me. The grounds of my islands are yours. Be free to explore the places you once roamed and you'll have no interference from my people."

Before evening fell and as the light of the cooking fires glowed, Hiva walked out through the gates of the walled village. She had gathered a small basket, a blanket, and some ripe mangoes. Her hand maidens insisted they go with her, but she scolded them, telling them they would slow her down. After many days at sea with no privacy, she was glad to have some time alone to explore. Seletute had almost refused to let her go. His instructions from Ruaka were clear; she must always be protected. His eyes filled with panic as she raised her voice, reminding Seletute who his true master was. He eventually relented, but only after she had assured him that Ruaka was already aware of her plans to seek solitude. The poor man ran away to find Ruaka, hoping to confirm the orders. She felt sorry for her feigned anger. He was only doing his duty as one of her protectors. A less dedicated servant may not have cared.

Many noticed her leaving as she was now well recognised. The gates watchmen bowed to her as she left, but none enquired on her journey. Leaving the safety of the village behind, Hiva's heart raced to a swift beat, but once she was far enough away and could hear the sounds of birds as her only company, she calmed herself. Still, her heart continued its steady pace, and she quickened her walk to reach her destination.

As a child, when she wanted to hide, she would venture through the undergrowth to a place she had discovered on her adventures. She was relieved when she found the old path and her pace sped up. It was not an easy journey; Hiva pushed away tangled branches, clambered over bushes and stopped often to catch her breath. The heat was palpable. She took sips of precious water from a water vessel made from a polished coconut shell as the humid evening formed beads of sweat on her brow. Though darkness was falling, she continued on without considering a return to the safety of the village, and just before the last rays of light disappeared from the forest canopy, she came near to the end of her journey; a juncture where the path split into two directions. To her left she remembered the slope led downwards towards a brilliant white sand beach where she had swam in a pristine blue lagoon many years ago. However, it was the right-hand path she took. It dipped very steeply, so much so that Hiva had to hold on to sturdy vines to help herself down into a trench filled with thick foliage. At the very lowest point of the trench, she could see her destination. A large cave mouth sat under many layers of bush that had recently been disturbed. Inside, a soft light flickered. This was a welcome sight, given the encroaching darkness.

Bending down to ensure her head didn't strike the low hanging stone of the cave mouth, Hiva pulled away some vines which obstructed her and entered the rocky chamber. When she stepped inside, she could stand upright, as the cave was wide and its roof reached high towards the very top of the embankment. It was as she remembered it to be; the coolness of a chamber, hidden from the sun but also with the distinct sound of rushing water.

The chamber hosted a fast-running underground stream that ran through several passages springing off from the main cavern. She had explored many of them. Some were too narrow to enter, but she imagined they ran deep into the island's depths, and some waterways were powerful, their veins running swiftly into deep underground rivers. In some places, Hiva had avoided swimming for fear of being sucked into a deep, narrow hole, never to be seen again. Despite that horrifying thought, she had come here often and found this to be one of her favourite places to be away from the world, and it always cheered her to swim here on the hottest of summer days. She was rarely disturbed, as the people of this island believed it to be a place where dark spirits dwelled, and so only the holy men would sometimes venture into the shallowest of chambers to offer a sacrifice of the first crop or even the first large fishermen's catch after the stormy season ended.

Feeling her way forward, the flickering light became a small fire. It had been lit under a vent in the cave's ceiling so that the smoke could rise and escape without filling the chamber. As she came closer, she froze when a silhouetted figure crossed her path from the shadows of a rocky crevice and blocked her. For a moment her breathing stopped, and then, moving forward, she embraced the darkened figure who reached around her and felt the familiar warmth of her lover. She kissed him. Pulling away for a moment, their faces remained close.

"It has been so long, my Boko." Her tone was teasing, and she used his famous nickname.

He swept her up easily into his muscular arms, and then carrying her to the edge of a fast-running stream, he placed her down on the cold stone floor, pulling up her waist mat and slowly moving into her with a long awaited desire. The ground was hard, and she winced as she held on tight to Ruaka's shoulders.

"Wait, Boko, I have a soft blanket ..." Hiva breathed the words heavily into his ear, motioning to the basket she had dropped as he held onto her even tighter.

She could see only shadows cast across his face in the fire's light, but she was sure he was smiling as he again kissed her deeply. As they made love, their moans and heavy breathing were barely audible over the sound of cool, rushing water.

With each of them holding a flaming torch, the journey back to the village was well lit. Beyond the expanse of their light, the surrounding woods showed quiet sounds of life, with insects and the occasional gecko ducking behind a branch or tree when the intruders approached. Hiva was distracted and walked at a slow pace. It seemed forever since she and Ruaka had last been intimate, and she was grateful for the few moments they could share, but her mood was dark this night. She had barely spoken to him, either at the cave or on their journey back. He had not bothered her with questions. But he knew her well, and his worried stare showed he had already noticed.

A few flashes of lightning brightened the sky to the north, signalling heavy rain would soon be upon them. She wasn't looking forward to arriving back at the village, soaked.

"It's best we quicken our pace. If you wish, I could swing you over my shoulders and carry you back to your fale?" Ruaka said.

She didn't respond to his attempt to make her smile. Her mind was elsewhere.

"I am, after all, as strong as Maui in his prime and capable of carrying many fine women upon my muscular back. In fact, in the village of my father, I was well known for carting away dozens of young girls at once from their families. I even let some of them return home afterwards."

Hiva shook her head. "Must everything be in jest with you?"

Another flash of lightning appeared with a moment of brilliance before disappearing. Seconds later the distant sound of thunder rolled across the clouds, which had obscured the already thin crescent moon.

"I am a simple warrior, my lady, but even with my simple thinking, I can see that you're unhappy. Do I not please you tonight?"

Her face showed a slight look of annoyance, but with a sigh she stopped and faced him, placing her hands upon his bare chest.

"I walked through a swarm of mosquitos and prickly bushes to meet with you alone, risking my very life if I was found with you. You know you please me very much. In fact, these days gone, there's little aside from the love of my daughter and our time alone together which brings me much joy."

She took his arm briefly and pulled him onwards, letting him go when he relented and walked alongside her once more.

He smiled. "So what worries you? Whatever it is, my fist and spear will remove it from your mind."

"It's not a matter of strength that will unburden me. I'm worried about many things. My daughter. My people. Lokai."

"Your unworthy husband is a fat and greedy slave to his loins. He worries about nothing more than the tails of his fresh young birds and where his next meal comes from."

He pushed away the branches of a dense bush. Another bolt shook the sky and the shape of bat wings silhouetted above. They shrieked as they flew from sight.

"Lover, those bats look cute and harmless to the eye in the day time, but at night they are the terror of children's dreams. You should know that my husband is much the same. He's no fool and you should be wary not to think of him as anything except the most cunning of sea snakes."

The young warrior scratched his arm as he felt a hungry mosquito drawing warm blood from his exposed skin. "Tell me what's going on in that worried mind of yours."

Hiva thought carefully and turned to him as she spoke. "He plots. He schemes. These days he goes on long journeys but tells no one of his destination. There are so many secrets. I have often seen him and Masila walk northwards with his trusted men towards the sacred cliffs of our dead."

"And what of this? He's not permitted to visit the graves of his ancestors? Anyway, Seagulli is always with him. They're inseparable. He treats that holy man like he really is in touch with the gods."

"Is he not? The gods speak through our holy men and women and give them power. I don't doubt this and nor should you. They're listening. I don't like you calling him Seagulli. It's the name used by the palangi boy."

"As I said, I'm simple. You know I was once a slave to your people. I prayed but the gods helped me not at all. I fought for everything I have, and I only believe in what I see in front of me. I believe in my spear, my loyal warriors and these tatau upon my body that tell the tale of my ancestors and my warrior's journey. I believe in you. I can touch you. I can feel your warmth. But the gods ... who knows if they're truly watching us?"

"Please listen, Ruaka, there's more," she said, stopping again and placing her hands on his broad shoulders. "Think, my love. How long since our dead have been allowed to be buried on the northern beaches since the arrival of the first palangi. No one has been permitted to return to pay respects or talk to our people gone to the spirit world."

The warrior pursed his lips and nodded. "Yes, that is strange. But many places are forbidden on Natuini as have always been." He placed his arms around her and pulled her close. "You were forbidden to me once ..."

She pulled his arms away. "Ruaka, I'm serious. There's a danger growing. I feel it. He's more secretive now than ever before. He's taken to this strange foreign religion and spreads its teaching to each village. And now he takes no movement towards the new palangis. We don't know their minds or their strange ways, and he allows them to desecrate Tapu Motu. Have you considered why they're here?"

Ruaka pulled away the low-hanging branches of a tree to let them pass. He considered the question for some time before answering. "I have seen them from afar. They're strange people, but there are only a handful of them. They're hungry. The men loyal to me tell me they're fighting each other."

"Lokai allows the boy to spend so much time with Mahina. It's such a scandal. The people's lips flutter like the wings of a crazed butterfly."

"But the boy saved Mahina, and he's no threat. He behaves like a friend. It's clear he likes her, so I don't know why you wish him harm. I've grown to like him."

"I don't know why you don't see as I do! He's almost a man. You know that there are rumours that Marcello wasn't alone when he was found. That there were other palangis."

Ruaka looked away but nodded knowingly. "I've heard this rumour. My sister in the village of Koloa told me she had heard this. But you know the people of Natuini love to tell stories. Many are not true."

"Yes. You're right," Hiva said before her eyes widened. "But I have heard many hushed stories from my spies amongst the nobles, and this one I've heard more than once to simply be the tales of old women."

Ruaka's face became visibly uncomfortable as she continued. He was a great warrior and a man of great virtue, known amongst the Natui as being prideful but generous. However, his strength was in his skills with weaponry, not in subterfuge, and he was not well versed in hiding his thoughts from her.

She noticed his change in mood, even in the dimmed light. "What do you know, lover?" Her voice was now gentle, and she placed her arm around his waist as they walked. She knew how to bring his words out when he would otherwise remain silent.

"There is … I saw something when your husband first returned with Marcello. But it was long ago and my memory has faded."

"Your memory is sharp and you're holding something from me. You forget I know you well, Ruaka."

There was worry in his eyes. He winced, and it formed a furrow on his forehead in tight, pronounced lines.

"I am your lady and you have a duty to tell me what you saw." Hiva's voice remained calm. She also knew that his sense of duty to her was a powerful weapon.

The warrior motioned with his hand, pointing the way ahead. They were entering a more sparsely wooded area of gardens where thousands of frangipani flowers grew upon the groomed trees around the village of Doko. They were near the end of their journey and light could be seen at a distance from the campfires which still burned, marking the edges of the village. They doused their torches in a damp patch of earth.

"From here we must separate, but I'll watch you and ensure you reach the gates safely," said Ruaka.

He leaned in and kissed her passionately, holding her close to him. She responded by wrapping her arms around him, and after a few moments she pushed him gently away but held onto his arms and looked into his eyes with a determined stare. There would be no peace for him until an answer was given.

He looked down, avoiding eye contact, and spoke with a deliberate but low voice. "Lokai. Chief Lokai, arrived late when most were asleep. I was on duty at the edge of Kahoua. He was with Kalafa and some warriors from Koloa village where they had been hunting for many days."

"Go on."

"Marcello was bound by kafa rope. His face had the marks of being severely beaten. The men of Koloa were unclean. So, before they reached the light of our boundary fires, they washed themselves in the sea, so that no one could speak of it."

"Unclean?"

"Their bodies were filthy. Dirty with the blood of slaughter."

Ruaka leaned in again, and this time kissed her forehead. He pulled away and disappeared into the darkness. Hiva remained quiet and asked no more questions. It took her a few moments to move but when she did, she walked briskly away and towards the gates of Doko's village where she was welcomed by a pair of tired looking guardsmen. They stood at attention when she approached and let her through to the safety of their high palisades.

Hiva's servants had stayed awake for her return, and when they saw her, they showed Hiva to her personal sleeping abode, a newly constructed hut near the village's centre pavilion. A smaller hut next to Hiva's had been reserved for some of her servants. Pua had prepared her lady's chambers with mats woven from the finest lo'akau leaves to make a soft bed. Hiva could still smell the freshly cut timber which made up the floor of the spacious one-room hut. They asked no questions of her late-night disappearance and seemed relieved that they could also take some rest, especially when the heavens opened and the rain fell, followed by many flashes of lightning and the loud boom from the sky that followed at ever quickening frequency.

By morning, the rain had stopped, and Hiva awoke to the light of the sun streaking through the narrow gap between the roof and the walls of her sleeping chamber. The heavy rain during the darkness seemed only a memory with the heat of the day already drying away the evidence of the downpour. She was hungry and calling to her servants. Pua brought a breakfast of sliced bananas and pawpaw on a plate of freshly cut banana leaves. When she was finished, Pua returned.

"They made this fale especially for your arrival, my lady."

Pua motioned to the hut and smoothed out her sleeping mats before moving into a kneeling position behind Hiva's back. A dress of tight bark cloth was wrapped around the noble lady's chest, and Pua reached around to pull the garment down, exposing her upper half to make for an easier massage. She pressed her fingers gently into Hiva's back and caressed her flesh, smoothing and massaging muscle to relieve the stressful exertions of their sea journey. For a moment Hiva felt relaxed and took a deep breath, letting her servant rub her hands deeper and deeper into her skin.

"Malohi is a handsome one, isn't he Ono Hiva?" Pua asked in a delicate voice.

"Yes. Perhaps more pretty than handsome, though. He seems to have been raised as a daughter rather than a son. It's the curse of a boy who's pleasing to the eye that he would be treated like a polished pearl and not a future hou'eiki."

"I don't know about that. I've been told he's a man of many skills. And I heard that not just from the girls."

"His prowess as a man is the least of my worries. Stop encouraging the gossip."

"I don't think you should worry. He'll treat your daughter well, and many young ladies will be jealous of her fortunes."

Pua took a small bowl prepared with coconut oil and rubbed the precious liquid into the palms of her hands and began the massage again. Her hands slowly moved their way around her liege's back and arms and onto her chest. She gently caressed Hiva's breasts, cupping them and moving across her nipples with her slender fingers in a method she knew pleased the lady. After some time, she oiled her hands once more and moved from Hiva's chest to her belly. Her soothing arts plied more gently than before, rubbing across the faded lines of Hiva's child bearing marks.

"You're still young and beautiful Ono Hiva."

Hiva didn't respond to her servant, who was now, with knees apart, straddling close to her back to reach around her soft torso.

"There are many who look upon you with lustful eyes."

Pua pulled herself closer, letting her hands drop to Hiva's thighs, and then sweeping up close to her groin, she leaned closer to her ear.

"I have seen young Ruaka look upon you with such eyes. Do you sometimes cast your thoughts on your manservant? He could provide you with such pleasures."

The pleasure of the massage was replaced by a sudden burst of rage. Hiva turned and grabbed Pua by the throat. Pua's face went instantly white. The tight grip caused her to choke and gasp for air. Then, holding her down, Hiva straddled the younger lady and kept her legs pressed between her thighs so she couldn't escape. She pressed both hands into her neck even tighter, and Pua's eyes bulged from their sockets. Between the spluttering and convulsing, Hiva leaned close and spoke with her teeth clenched.

"You are my servant. I am the lady of Natuini and your words bring you close to your last breath."

"Please … please let me go." Pua could hardly spit the words out and tried to roll away, without success.

"You want to know my thoughts? I am the loyal wife of Chief Lokai and any who would dare suggest otherwise, I will have you skinned alive with a blunt knife. Am I understood, servant?"

Pua gave a hurried nod, tears filling her eyes. Hiva released the girl before she lost consciousness, pushing her back to the floor, watching as she coughed and fought to draw breath again.

"We're not all like you, a wanton sow, opening your fat legs to any man who wills it. Begone from my sight, hideous worm. Do not let me see you again this day."

The girl took no time at all to scramble away on her hands and knees. She sobbed loudly as she escaped the entrance.

Hiva lay back and looked up to the roof's tightly woven timber framing, kept secure by layers of skilfully spun coir fibre. Her heart beat loudly at thoughts of her secret being discovered. Perhaps her affair with Ruaka was now a rumour, and if Pua was brazen enough to speak such things, her husband would also have heard the gossip.

No, do not cast your mind to this, she told herself.

They had been careful. It wasn't possible that anyone could have seen them. They had always been discreet and kept their passion hidden from the prying eyes of others. They had not been careless. And yet, she felt their guarded union had been betrayed.

Stop it. There was no accusation. She could not possibly know of us. No, she's simply a naïve little girl who can't keep her mouth shut.

Hiva calmed herself and closed her eyes. She tried to concentrate on other thoughts. Anything to run from her doubts.

But her mind raced with the terrible possibilities of her exposure, and she didn't rest easy at all before night fell and the village festivities began.

News had quickly spread of the lady's arrival. Hundreds of families from the surrounding villages had travelled day and night to attend. Many of the well-wishers had brought a tribute of food for Chief Doko, and these would be used to ensure that all who attended were well fed after a long journey. It was seen as a significant mark of honour to offer a splendid feast for an important guest, and many of the Natui traditions were centred around festivals of feasting whilst guests were entertained with song, dance and great tales of their ancestors.

Under the shelter of the central pavilion, Chief Doko, Malohi and Hiva sat beside each other on many layers of tapa cloth, creating a soft flooring from which to rest and look out upon the village centre where the evening's performance had already begun. Seated beside them were a number of Doko's noble allies and his extended family, including two of his brothers and his very own matapule. The right hand of Doko was an elderly but energetic speaker who was well known for his sharp wit. In the land of the Grey Hair he was known as Vai Nonga or "Calm Water", a title given to him as the eldest son of his father, who also held the same title and served Doko's father as matapule prior to his passing. This was a common occurrence for the eldest sons of these important figures who spoke for their nobles and were the history and knowledge keepers of the Natui noble families. As a holder of ancient knowledge, he was respected and wielded much power as the voice of Doko, whilst also interpreting the will of the gods.

"A gift for you, from my Lord Doko." Vai Nonga stood and knelt before Hiva, presenting to her a bowl of ivory pearls, perfectly polished and round.

She accepted the gift, smiling warmly at the chief's trusted adviser. He had been a great warrior and leader of men in his younger days. Hiva remembered him being kind to her. Age had removed his muscle mass, and she could see that he struggled now to keep his knees bent. He was grimacing with the effort, so she gestured for him to be seated and he gratefully accepted.

"I've heard that my dear friend Masila has been named after a loud sea bird?" Vai Nonga chuckled with a light wheeze of laughter.

It was a deliberate insult to Lokai's matapule with whom he had a fierce rivalry. That was not uncommon amongst the matapule of Natui noble families. Doko overheard the taunt and widened his eyes but Hiva took it as light-hearted banter and responded with a wry smile to herself, knowing that the two men could spend whole evenings baiting each other with jibe and innuendo at the sides of their masters.

"Also, tell me, does he still bring fish to his marriage bed during the festival of Kele? As I understand it, his wife keeps her eyes open all night, in case he tries to slip a fish under her skirts." He gave Hiva a cheeky smile.

Doko's mouth dropped open at the crude joke, but his face relaxed when his guest laughed. Hiva would normally baulk at the disrespect, but she was surprised when the jest provided her with a sense of relief. She knew that the old man was only attempting to lighten the mood.

"Vai Nonga, you should lower your voice. You know Masila has spies all around and that they'll report back on your challenge to his honour."

"Bah!" he grunted. "I don't care if his people overhear me. Let them speak my words from many oceans away. I'll send a mahimahi back on your boats. He can learn of my insult while he provides pleasure to his fat mistresses through the lips of a sea creature."

Even Doko chuckled at this, and the three smiled at one another.

"I will tolerate your insults because I have heard more terrible barbs in your direction from Masila's lips. I admit also I missed you dearly, old man," she said.

"And I also missed you! We have not laid eyes upon each other since our visit to the lands of Doko when we first discussed this betrothal. So wonderful we can now plan for the day when finally, our people can be strengthened and form this alliance. I have advised my lord for many years to seek this outcome and your arrival brings us many favoured tidings."

"Yes, good news." Doko leaned in and poked his finger at the matapule as he spoke. "But I had to endure this old man's constant jabbering about it for years on end. I'm glad for the union; I'll be just as glad for Vai Nonga to shut up and hopefully retire so my ears can get some peace."

Doko laughed at his own mirth, but this was quickly followed by a fit of coughing. Vai Nonga quickly handed him a cup of fresh spring water and he drank it whole to stifle his rasp.

When he wiped away the water from his lips, Hiva was sure that she saw specks of blood.

"My longevity is a gift from the gods. I'm just doing my duty as your most trusted adviser." Vai Nonga lowered his head in mock supplication. "You know, my lord, as your matapule, my duties die with me. Therefore, I will be speaking on your behalf for many years to come. I come from long-lived stock, as you are aware."

"I've heard that some chiefs solve the problem of a long-lived matapule by having them accidentally fall into the 'umu fire pits. You might yet make a useful stew for a starving child."

Vai Nonga straightened up his back and ripped a chunk of suckling pig from a passing servant holding a platter of food.

"How is your health?" Hiva said. The elder chief was unwell and was clearly trying to hide his pain.

Instead of a reply, she received a dismissive wave of his hand, and she decided not to raise the subject again.

The evening continued with a great many delicious dishes. Hiva's hosts were generous and before long her hunger was satisfied many times over. She felt like she would burst if she ate just one more mouthful of food. Whilst they ate freshly prepared fruit and sipped on frangipani tea, they watched as a troupe of men and women began a traditional dance, depicting a fierce battle, followed by the celebration between men and women upon a warrior's return. Two dozen men lined up with pakipaki and when the loud, fast beating of a boar skin drum sounded, the warriors whooped and cried as they swept their battle oars in unison, at first as if they were paddling their vaka upon the water and then as a weapon in battle between each other. Sweeping the pakipaki toward each other's feet, they leapt high, hitting the ground hard before dancing around each other like circling hunters. At the end of the feigned battle, the men made a space for an equal number of women to move forward and begin their own dance, which was more subdued than their male counterparts. Bending their knees and staying firmly in place, young ladies moved their hands gracefully in perfect unison, making shapes in a choreographed display to tell an ancient story. Hiva was skilled at this style of dance and understood the tale being told as they swayed their hands with care and restraint. As they moved, the dancers were signalling to their men returning for battle, with gestures of love, and also of painful heartbreak of those who did not. The men thrust their pakipaki with great speed and strength towards the females in response as the girls gently touched their waists and welcomed the men towards them. However, the thrusting of their weapons was not a symbol of violence or aggression. Instead, it was a sensual message. The movements signalled the return of the warriors to their marriage beds and the children that would soon swell the women's bellies.

Surrounding the pavilion, a throng of people watched the revelry and were cheering on the dancers. A few of the older married women, who had long since given up the art, joined in with exaggerated movements to the joy and laughter of their families. This was not mockery of the young girls or boys who took part; it was viewed as light-hearted and to support the younger, shyer girls.

At its conclusion, the crowd cheered loudly, clapping and leaping up to embrace each other in lively spirits. The Natui were a hardworking people, but equally they loved the celebrations and dancing marking their many feast days. Tonight, Hou'eiki Doko had been generous and had slaughtered twenty fat sows to share with the revellers. This had brought even more people to his village, and with so many Natui families together, a great feeling of collective happiness had overcome them, bringing about much generosity from their lord and nobles whose homes were well stocked from a bountiful year of good crops. Lokai had often complained bitterly that the soil of Mo'unga Vela was more fertile than his own lands and wondered if Doko had made some pact with Touia Fatuna to provide good fortune to their plantations. The rumbling of the earth beneath the feet of the Grey Hair was a constant reminder of their angry mountain, kept at bay by the goddess of the deepest rocks within the earth. From her fruitful womb, this land and many others had sprung to life, birthed from the fiery recesses of her immortal body.

The crowds were unrelenting in their elation, but it was Malohi who finally stood to quiet the people. When they saw their future chief motioning with his hands for their silence they settled quickly, taking their positions on the outer circle of the pavilion clearing. Hiva noticed that the young man was equipped for battle. Across his chest and abdomen, he wore a thick breast guard made of woven coir rope. On his shoulders he wore several layers of stitched coconut shells and hanging from a coir belt, a series of packed bamboo thigh guards were held firmly together to protect his upper legs. When the people before him were completely silent, he stood before Hiva and his father, bowed and stood again upright, holding his head high.

"Future mother. Your daughter, the lovely Mahina, deserves to feel safe by my side. Tonight, I will show you my prowess with weapons of war, so that you may know my strength and skill to protect your daughter."

Malohi spoke with a regal confidence from a lifetime of preparation. A necessary skill for a further lifetime of rule over his people.

Arrogant little pig, Hiva thought.

Doko leaned in closer to Hiva at the display of bravado shown by his eldest son. "He likes to show off his talents with the spear and pakipaki. He's very skilled. Self-taught in a unique style of fighting. He's a natural with all manner of weaponry, but I dare not tell him in case his head expands to the size of a puffer fish."

Hiva allowed herself a smile at the description.

Malohi signalled to several servants who were waiting nearby. They pushed back the crowd, which formed a large empty space at the forefront of the pavilion. He tied his long hair back before again signalling for a servant to apply oil to his limbs, making them slippery, with a bright sheen in the light of the campfires. Hiva noticed his makeup was especially thick tonight, and his reddened cheeks made him look like he had returned from a tiring run. The thin line of charcoal applied under his eyes made them appear large in the firelight. There was no doubt he was unusually handsome.

Such a shame about his personality. Mahina will need to watch out for this one.

Ashes had been thickly applied to his black hair and as he moved, it left a powdery trail of white smoke-like vapor in his wake. Stepping off the pavilion platform, he walked with more grace than some of the young female dancers whom had moved across the same ground just moments before. She wondered how a boy with such a pampered upbringing had also found skill in battle.

A warrior from Malohi's personal guard came forward and unwrapped a tapa cloth, exposing two strangely shaped weapons in the shape of crescent moons, offering them to the muscular nobleman. He took both, one in each hand, and stretched out his arms to show the crowd. The weapons were a set of curved pakipaki lined on the inner side with razor sharp sharks' teeth, each tooth descending from large to small along its surface, forming a fierce tool of war.

Several of Hiva's own personal guards and servants were bunched together along the outside of the throng of villagers who were edging forward to get a better vantage point. Amongst them, Ruaka and Seletute pressed forward to the front, moving others forcibly aside to let them through. She could see that Ruaka's face was etched with curiosity and that he was spying the hooked weapons with interest.

The crowd on the opposite side of the clearing made a corridor. They clambered to make a passageway in a deafening commotion of shouts and excitement. From the crowd, an armed cohort of warriors thrust four men forward; each man bearing a branded mark of a circle on their right shoulders. None of them had their hair doused with ash, as was common with the Grey Hair, and it was clear from their protestations at the rough treatment they were not here voluntarily.

"The Ha'amoa slaves, Hou'eiki Doko? I thought you had forbidden him to use these men for this bloody sport?" Vai Nonga said, his face a mix of exasperation and confusion.

No answer came. Instead, Hiva saw that the old chief simply looked away and, in that moment, seemed more exhausted than ever. He coughed loudly several times before wiping away the spittle on his lips. His face scrunched painfully from the exertion.

Vai Nonga was furious. He smacked the floor with the palm of his hand while he spoke but kept his voice low so only Hiva and his chief could hear. "Whale raiders from far off Ha'amoa. Malohi and his men caught them three or four full moons ago and have kept them at work on his beloved 'uta plantation ever since. He caught thirteen in total. A couple escaped. These are the last ones left alive …"

Hiva was surprised by the lapse in decorum but kept her attention on what the young warrior was planning to do with his slaves.

As Malohi bowed to his elders in the pavilion with a quick nod of his head, he strode onto the field, coming to a stop at its centre. The four men were all older than the armoured nobleman and each of them unclothed except for a small loincloth. They had bruises and cuts from recent injuries. One of the men walked with a pronounced limp and patches of his raw skin were infected. Hiva winced at the sight, imagining the pain he must have felt. His arms and thighs had suffered terrible burns where tatau had once been inked, but now were reduced to an unrecognisable mass of horrific scarring. The men were pushed beyond the reach of the crowd as the masses hollered and jeered. Their excitement grew when two servants carried out an array of boar skin shields, spears and pakipaki, throwing them unceremoniously at the feet of the dishevelled four. They peered with mouths wide open at the motley pile of weapons, and after a moment of hesitation, they scrambled towards the paltry collection and picked up whatever they could get their hands on. Eventually each man took hold of at least one weapon after a brief struggle over the choicest equipment. Two of the reluctant warriors took hold of a shield, including the one with the injured leg. He struggled to stand upright, but lifted the shield with whatever strength he had left. It was a piteous sight. Hiva saw a mass of cuts and bruises on his right thigh. Even at a distance from the safety of her position, the unhealthy state of these men was obvious.

"Noblemen. Revered Lady of Natuini. My people. Men and women of the Grey Hair. Witness now, your future chief. Betrothed of Mahina. I am the great protector and I will show you how a true warrior of the Natui defeats his enemies and shelters his people from the darkness of foreign invaders."

Malohi thrust his weapons towards the dishevelled unfortunates. Vai Nonga did not hide his obvious disdain, rolling his eyes at the grandiose announcement, but kept quiet whilst shifting his folded legs uncomfortably.

"Cha-hoo!" Malohi shouted in a high-pitched shriek.

Other men in the crowd also shouted with the same scream, supporting him in his battle cry. Then with gritted teeth he stretched out his arms with each pakipaki held aloft and motioned the four slaves towards him in an invitation to do battle.

Wearily, they each glanced at each other with a look of resignation to their fate, but with the throng of people hurling abuse and screaming for blood, they raised their weapons and shields, moving forward towards the young warrior with steady caution.

Someone in the crowd threw a stone towards the lame man, but despite his slow movement he was able to dodge the attack. In the effort, he stumbled and fell onto his knee. His cry made the hair on the back of Hiva's neck stand taut.

One of the slaves leaped and sprinted forward. Malohi steadied himself for the attack. When he came within reach of the future chief, he thrust his spear towards his belly, grunting with the attempt. However, with a subtle movement the younger warrior easily parried the blow with his left pakipaki, jolting the spear to the side. He swept the weapon in his left hand down upon his opponent's shoulder as he attempted to pass by, striking it with the tip of his hooked club and pulling it downwards in a swift stroke. The blow easily tore open a swathe of flesh. It was a deep wound, with a flash of blood bursting and gushing down the man's body.

Malohi turned gracefully and swept his leg up into a high kick to the back of the bloodied man's head, causing him to fall forward onto his face. The slave gasped in pain, rolling away to avoid any further attacks. None came. Instead, Malohi pivoted back to face the three others and raised his weapons above his head in a peculiar stance which made him appear like a wicked bird of prey.

His agility and speed came as a surprise to Hiva.

When the two slaves holding a simple pakipaki both attacked him at once, he easily defended himself with a series of blocks and parries. He dodged one clumsy blow then swiftly reversed his own crescent-shaped weapon and struck the man on his thigh with the blunt side. It was a deliberately light strike, as if Malohi was playing a game with his attackers. He moved with the rhythm of a dancer and not the wild fury of a Natui warrior in the heat of battle.

Following up the leg strike, Malohi pressed his attack, relentlessly raining blow upon blow on each of the two standing attackers who could barely raise their weapons aloft to fend off each strike.

As if to impress the baying crowd, he broke off his attack for a brief moment and daintily jumped backwards and onto the back of the injured slave he had struck to the ground. Using the man's back as a platform, he launched at the closest of his opponents with both curved pakipaki raised high and swung them downwards, striking deeply into each shoulder. Then with the butt of his right club, he smashed the face of the injured man. Even with the noise of screaming villagers, Hiva could hear his nose break in a sickening crunch which followed with a spray of glistening blood. His victim dropped his weapon and crumpled to the ground lifeless.

A third man attacked from his right, this one charging directly at Malohi with a shield barge. It knocked the nobleman backwards. When he tried another shield barge, Malohi simply hooked the shield with his left pakipaki and pulled it away. The move exposed his aggressor's torso to a devasting front kick. Malohi followed by slashing at the slave's exposed torso with his tree hand. It drew a deep wound across his abdomen. Injured and partially winded, he withdrew in a gasp of pain.

This was all the opportunity Malohi needed, and taking advantage of the retreat, he swept forward and hacked again at the side of the shield, pulling it fully out of the slave's hands. When it dropped to the ground, the slave knew he could not defeat the more skilled combatant and dropped his weapon, throwing his hands into the air in supplication. Malohi scoffed in anger at the surrender. He made his displeasure known by kicking the slave in his lower abdomen, forcing him to double over in pain.

A cry of excitement leapt from the crowd, ever shouting on their future chief whom would one day be solely responsible for the future of his people. He would lead them to victory in battle against their enemies and the people understood that a ruthless and capable leader would provide their children's safety for a generation. He revelled in the attention. Smiling broadly with pride, he looked back to his father who returned a half-hearted grin in support of his son.

In the excitement, he was completely unaware the slave had recovered from the painful fall and was now upon one knee holding a spear aloft. Malohi had forgotten about the slave who had slipped in the first moments of battle. With a well-aimed throw, the injured man pulled back the spear behind his shoulder and with a scream of defiance, threw it with remarkable strength at the young warrior's head. The distance was no greater than twenty paces but the slave was worn from his injury and with Malohi turned to his side, he was a harder target to hit. Nonetheless, the spear tip sped silently towards its victim and sliced across his left cheek. Malohi stepped back in shock, watching the spear continue on, only to fall limply to the ground at the edge of the crowd, making the surprised villagers run sideways to avoid being struck. From his cheek a slice opened up and blood poured from the lengthy wound. Whilst still holding onto his pakipaki, he touched his cheek and felt the blood. It smeared thickly over his wrist, dripping onto his fingers with a bright red sheen that glistened in the fires of the surrounding torch light.

Malohi's face was filled with shock at the sight of blood. But then shock turned to rage as he faced his attacker. The slave balked at the sight, looking side to side for an avenue to escape. Malohi clenched his weapons tight and marched towards him with alarming determination. The injured man tried to flee but it was a useless endeavour, and as soon as he rose to stand, his legs gave way, his thin and starved frame crashing forward into the dry soil of the arena. Knowing he could not run, he crawled away instead, pleading for his life as he made a futile attempt to outpace his stronger and faster opponent.

Malohi's fury was unabated. He raised his weapons to finish the bloody task, but Doko awoke from his disinterest and shouted over the screams of the crowd.

"Son, you have defeated the enemy. Take your victory and let the slaves be. The battle is over."

Malohi did not stop. Instead, as he reached the struggling man, he brought his weapons up and over his head. The slave looked up with terror, raising his hands to protect himself, but this was in vain as the first of the angry blows struck.

Feverishly, Malohi rained down a series of strikes. The first sliced through the slave's outstretched hand and tore a jagged chunk from his palm. The second blow carved a sickening blow through the man's left shoulder, leaving flesh and bone exposed. With no hesitation between strikes, each brutal hit cleaved bone and tore muscle in a gruesome display of unbridled aggression. The battle was no longer a display of skill and heroism but had given way to the young noble's senseless brutality. The people of the village, only moments before screaming the name of their champion, fell silent at the sight of an unarmed man being unceremoniously hacked to pieces. They gazed in terrible fascination as he turned a captured slave into a mangled mess.

Hiva looked on in horror. Her stomach wrenched at the sight. Chief Doko had given up trying to stop his son from this vicious display and was looking downwards.

The slave was now lying in a bloody pool on his back and had stopped struggling. Malohi had turned his pakipaki around to show the rounded blunt side before bringing down another series of crushing blows to the man's broken body. The slave jolted involuntarily under the heavy weight of each strike, and the sound of his back breaking was audible to the hundreds of surrounding men and women.

He would have continued if not for an angry bellow interrupting the massacre when Ruaka burst from the ranks of the crowd and shouted a challenge. The younger warrior stopped and turned to face him. At his feet, the blood soaked and butchered frame no longer moved. Everyone seated in the pavilion, including Hiva, rose to their feet when they saw the oncoming danger.

"Malohi. You are nothing. You are the whore of a wild pig. Bring your coward's weapons to me, and I will show you the honour of a warrior's death," Ruaka said.

Ruaka held no weapon but marched forward towards Malohi and beat his chest loudly with a clenched fist, his teeth bared in rage. Ruaka had a reputation as a powerful warrior. Hiva had seen him battle in weapons practice with his men, but she had never seen him as fiery as this very moment. His darkened features were that of a fierce god bringing great punishment upon his enemies, and she feared what he might do while his blood boiled at this outrage.

"Ruaka, you must stop," Hiva said. She shouted but knew he couldn't hear her. Not in his maddened state. She hoped she could prevent him from making a terrible mistake. The chief's son was an 'eiki, and although Ruaka held respect amongst the Natui, he was a man of common blood and whose lineage could never match that of Malohi. Everybody knew that even the act of raising a weapon in threat towards a Natui of noble blood could see him punished with death.

Emboldened by his victory and with the confidence of weapons in hand, Malohi sneered at the challenge and took to the battlefield to face the approaching warrior. Taking a few slow steps at first, he quickened his pace, and then ran at Ruaka, sweeping back his right-handed pakipaki over his shoulder and then, just only a few feet from meeting his opponent, sprung into the air with a high strike towards Ruaka's head.

The young man moved with incredible speed. His fighting style was unfamiliar to the seasoned warrior, but as quickly as the attack came, Ruaka manoeuvred his body away from the high angled blow and barged forward his chest. Ruaka was a much larger man, and the weight of the impact drove Malohi off his feet and onto his back. He was quick to recover, however, and as swiftly as he fell, he arched his back and, thrusting his legs forward, he leapt back to a standing position. Ruaka had not stopped his assault. As soon as Malohi was on his feet, Ruaka grabbed his right wrist, twisting it violently. The young warrior screamed as his wrist bent sharply and he dropped one of his weapons. However, he surprised his opponent with a well-aimed knee to Ruaka's groin. The effect of the impact was instant. He groaned in pain, releasing Malohi's wrist, and took a few steps back. With the remaining pakipaki, Malohi slashed it inwards at Ruaka's torso and connected, tearing a light gash into his chest.

Ruaka recovered with haste, again leaping forward, he grappled Malohi's left arm and with his free hand grabbed him around the throat. Moving forward with all his weight, he lifted Malohi into the air and threw him downwards, dislodging the club from his hand as he hit the ground again. Malohi was clearly in pain from the fall but again recovered quickly, successfully wrapping his legs around his attacker's to unbalance him with a follow-up punch to his lower stomach.

The manoeuvre was successful. Ruaka doubled over and was pulled forward onto the ground by the grapple and strike. The melee had turned into a chaotic mess of fists and wrestling. Warriors from both sides ran into the clearing and tried to pull the two apart. The men were rolling back and forth in the blood and dirt with no intention of separating. A Grey Hair who tried to pull Malohi away was caught in the struggle with an elbow to the lip. It split painfully upon impact. He spat blood, stumbling backwards at the blow. The rest of the men pried them apart, dragging them away from each other.

When they were pulled to their feet they shouted curses, with each threatening to kill as soon as they were free.

Hiva's heart was beating quickly, and she was fearful of what may happen next. For a moment she thought that her beloved Ruaka might have killed the younger man and her mind raced with the consequences. It was with some relief the battle had been stopped and both men were still of sound body, but she could not show her fear. She could not betray her feelings for a man who was only a servant. Now she had to face the possibility that her champion may be punished for his intervention and felt helpless in her place. It was Vai Nonga who stepped towards the throng of men.

"Silence, brave men." He issued the commandment in an intimidating voice.

His skill in oratory was a powerful tool and as he spoke, he was considered the voice of the chief. His sudden authority made both men pause their assault. Vai Nonga hesitated before speaking and looked back at Hiva and his chief before continuing. Thoughtfully, he nodded at the two warriors who were caked in flowing blood and dirt, their hair and garments soiled after their brief struggle.

"A powerful performance of the noble's skill with the pakipaki. A well-rehearsed display, my lord Malohi. Honour to you also Ruaka. We offer thanks to your noble lady in showing that the passion of our brethren from the land of Lokai matches that of our own warriors. Imagine what we could do as one mighty force against our enemies? Maui, give these warriors your blessing."

He thrust his staff into the air, and at the gesture the crowd shouted in a cacophony of joyous voices, strengthened by their relief at the praise for both warriors. This took Malohi by surprise, and he again showed a look of indignity upon his face.

Vai Nonga could see this and motioned the crowd to be silent once more.

"Great lord of our people. These slaves were no match for your Natui prowess. Your enemies will tremble at the thoughts of battle with you. And now that you fight alongside the greatest warriors of your new people, in your marriage with the lady Mahina, you are now battle brothers with Ruaka." He smiled and widened his eyes at the young man.

There was some hesitation from Malohi but with the eyes of his people upon him he relaxed and faced his opponent. They looked at each other with disgust, but stretching out his arm, Malohi made a gesture of peace, which Ruaka reciprocated, clasping Malohi's hand with a strong grip before they both released and were led away by their own warriors.

Vai Nonga motioned for the injured to be taken away and for the body of Malohi's victim to be dragged from the field. The grounds were opened up to the people once more and a rush of servants brought forth roasted pigs and yams. They also carried in several large kumete; four-foot-wide kava bowls carved from timber. The bowls were brimming high with kava for the masses to continue their feasts and celebrations. The fight between Malohi and Ruaka was the subject of animated discussion for the rest of the evening, with young men picking up pieces of firewood and pretending to battle, mimicking the best parts of the fight. Vai Nonga returned to his place, sighing as he sat. As the night returned to normal, an awkward silence persisted between the three until Doko addressed his guest.

"If my son had been killed ..."

"I apologise for my servant, Chief Doko. He will be punished," Hiva said.

Doko nodded. "As you see fit my lady, but I would not do so with a heavy hand."

Vai Nonga slapped the floor. "Lord, he disrespects you with his disobedience. He was told to release the Ha'amoa captives directly and surely. Instead, he parades them in front of you and his uncles. As if you were already passed. As if he were already chief," he said.

"Yes, I know it. But what can I do? I'm not as strong as I used to be. He's my successor. He must learn the right way and I have little time left to guide him. In many ways, this is why I wish so dearly for the match between our peoples."

Doko's face was solemn as he addressed Hiva. "His own mother, Ono Huelo, she means well, but she has turned him into this. Gives in to all of his whims and treats him like the rarest of pearls. So he acts like one. Hiva, he is sometimes misguided, but he is also passionate and with grand ambitions. I know with your influence that you can help him become a great leader."

"I understand, old chief. The union between Mahina and Malohi is so important to our people. Boys can be changed with the right influence. A good wife can temper a young man's avarice for rebellion."

"And I know your daughter will be such an influence. But it is you who can watch over the couple and help them. Perhaps after the marriage you could live in Mo'unga Vela for a time?"

Hiva was surprised by the suggestion. Once a marriage had been concluded, it was a tradition for a young bride to move to her husband's village. She became part of his family and unwanted influence from her own family was frowned upon. Amongst nobles, the influence was still expected, but to be asked to accompany her daughter to Mo'unga Vela was an unexpected request.

"That would be highly unusual, Hou'eiki Doko. What would Ono Huelo think of such a suggestion? What of your people?"

"Yes, unusual. But you were once an heir of these lands and in such an important union we would make a display of the coming together of our two people. I would invite you openly, in front of the people after the wedding, so they knew that the honour was ours to have you remain with us. It would be just for a season, no longer. Please think on this great lady."

Hiva kept silent, picking up a cup of coconut water. Inside she noticed a tiny mosquito had found its way into the bowl and was drowning in the cool liquid, unable to escape. She carefully picked it up with her little finger and examined it for a moment before wiping it away.

The opportunity to leave Kahoua and the watchful eye of her husband was a possibility she had never considered. At least for a time she would be free to be with her daughter and guide her in the first year of her marriage. Most Natui mothers would beg for such a privilege. Ruaka would be by her side. Also free from Lokai's spies. They may have some time to spend with each other. The thought of staying so long in the land of the Grey Hair sickened her, but being able to remain with her daughter would far outweigh her hatred of this island and the memories it held.

The old chief did not press for an answer. Instead, he sat under a dark cloud for the rest of the evening, speaking only occasionally and without mirth. When the evening was complete, Hiva excused herself and returned to her sleeping hut. During the short walk back with her servants beside her, she could see the lifeless body of a slave being dragged beyond the gates of the village, where his body would be thrown from high beach cliffs and into the ocean. There his soul would remain and swim aimlessly and lost for all of eternity. He deserved a warrior's pyre, she thought, to be burned along with his weapons and to be made whole with the land again. But he was a slave and as a slave he was to receive no such honour. Ruaka watched from a distance, his torso still covered in blood from his wound, and as she lay down her tired head to sleep, she released her tears with thoughts of her guardsman perishing, and it was then she knew the depth of her love. Her world had become ever more dangerous. They were both doomed for their betrayal.

NINE

Abel's best skimming attempt landed just four bounces off the still water of the inland lagoon before the pebble was lost to its depths. It was a deep pool fed by a low and lazy waterfall that barely churned into a white froth below. The smooth rocky face it fell from was covered in a green moss, but beyond its descent the pool was clear. Mahina chuckled at his throw and picked up a stone she had found after briefly scanning the surrounding ground. She placed it in her palm, examining its width and surface. Then, without looking at him, she brought it close to her lips and spoke in a whisper to the stone.

"The shape is soft and smooth. Watch me fly."

She carefully aimed and threw the stone with speed parallel to the water. As it touched the surface, it skipped merrily at least fifteen bounces before disappearing into the light waterfall spray.

She turned with her arms on her hips and smiled wryly at Abel while he shook his head.

"Damn, show off," he said. He raised his voice with feigned anger.

Mahina cocked her head to one side and repeated the phrase. "Show … off?"

He bit his lip and tried to think of a way to express its meaning. Abel was no English teacher, but he had become used to explaining the meaning of more complex words with pantomime. His wild gestures were met with raucous laughter, but he took it in good humour and enjoyed the time he was spending with Mahina. He was also learning as much from her as she was from him, which was making his stay with the Natui a much easier prospect. His understanding of the Natui had tremendously improved with his immersion in the language, forcing him to listen and learn. The experience was improving his relations with the residents of Kahoua, who were now used to his simple greetings, trying them out on the locals. They merrily responded with a smile and few words of encouragement. The small notebook he kept was now full of useful phrases. Sometimes, Mahina would look on with curiosity as he wrote the phrases he learned, until one day he decided to teach her how to form letters and words from the English alphabet. There was some reluctance at first; Hou'eiki Lokai had forbidden Father Marcello from teaching anyone but his loyal nobles how to read and write, a skill they had begun to use with an occasional written message delivered by a servant courier from the outer villages. Marcello hadn't explained why this wasn't allowed. In any event, after consulting with Lokai in private, he invited Abel to play a round of chess. It was an awkward game; Lokai said very little and concentrated on moving his pieces around one of Marcello's handmade boards. The wily chief won and grinned in satisfaction before giving permission to teach Mahina the art of reading. Both Abel and Mahina were happy about the decision. Before long, her handwriting had become neater than his own. She treated every stroke of the quill like she was creating a work of art in every letter she scribed.

"How can I explain 'show off'? Right, how about this?" Abel mimicked her pose and then strutted about, exaggerating his walk with an air of confidence. "I am so great. I'm wonderful. I'm pretty. I'm good at everything. Me, me, me, me, me. Look at me," he said.

Mahina evidently thought this was hilarious, and she burst out laughing, pointing at his strange movements. He couldn't help but join her in the mirth as he realised how silly he must have looked. When she finally recovered enough to stop and consider his actions, he saw the look of understanding in her eyes.

"Fie lelei. Fie lelei. I think this is Natui word," she said.

They smiled at each other warmly.

"Come with me. Another place now." Mahina motioned for him to follow as she took their classroom of two close to the beach where they could watch the anglers bring in their morning's catch.

When they reached the shore, they settled themselves under the cool shade of a broad-leaved palm tree and relaxed in the soft sand. For a while they watched the procession of small boats come onto shore and the delicious bounty being hauled into the village for what would be that evening's fare. Two fishermen cut open the flesh of a mahimahi and dug the meat out with their bare hands, scoffing it with a hunger driven by their tiring work at sea.

"Koe kakai tangata 'oku nau toutai ika. The men are catching fish," Mahina said.

She spoke slowly, and as Abel repeated the phrase, she corrected his pronunciation. They continued to describe what they saw. The hermit crabs burrowing deep into the sand; the waves crashing upon the shore and the white clouds drifting above. For Abel, these lessons had become a daily event that he looked forward to.

It had been some weeks since the Lady of Natui had departed on her mission, and the two had spent part of the morning each day engaging in conversation. At first it had seemed like a chore required of them by Chief Lokai and had been limited to the confines of the village. Mahina's annoyance was obvious in her initial reluctance to take part, and most days the lessons had started with a scowl. However, as time went on, they were enjoying the company and their time together grew longer each day. Eventually they wandered from the village to different spots on the beach or on the low hanging cliffs overlooking the deep blue waters between Natuini and the other smaller islands nearby.

A warm breeze picked up the light grains of sand. Abel squinted and rubbed his eyes. For a moment his vision was blurry with a mixture of grit and tears, but when his vision cleared, he looked out beyond the blue waters, towards the distant silhouette of Tapu Motu. His mind drifted as he wondered what had become of Luther and Doctor Wickman. Mostly he was fearful he would not see them again and had considered returning by stealing one of the smaller vaka and attempting the journey back. Each time he was stopped by the thought of Lokai's wrath if he were caught and also what might happen if he were to return only to find his cousin captured or perished.

"Tell me of England. Your people. Your island. Marcello speaks sometimes, but he only talks about his God. I want to know how you make such big kalia."

Abel thought of London, and it made him homesick.

"I was born in a place called Dartford. But soon after I was born, my mother and father moved to London for work. It's hard to describe. It's not just the ships – kalia – that are big. My people build out of timber, stone and brick and the largest of the castles tower into the sky. The cathedrals are especially tall. They really are a marvel. London is such a big place with so many people. I don't know if you would like it or not. It can excite, especially the street theatres with their dancing and singing. I once saw a man eat a stick of fire whilst balancing on a tightrope! We like a good joke as much as a good cup of tea, I guess. And we grow up on stories of the old kings like King Arthur. I don't think he was real, though. Richard the Lionheart off on his crusades. My favourite stories are of the creatures and monsters like ogres and will-o'-the-wisp."

"You have monsters?" Mahina asked.

"Not real ones. You might think a horse is a monster. Beautiful creatures with large brown eyes that we tame and ride. We are expert horse riders, I'd say."

Mahina thought about the answer and nodded. "We are not different. We like stories, and laughing. We sing and tell stories of long ago. Many stories we have of war and fighting. Many stories of the gods like Maui-Kisikisi who learned the secrets of fire and gave this great knowledge to all peoples. I think your god is also Maui. Maybe your god is all the gods together."

"Maybe. I don't know much about that. Marcello could explain it. The palangi god is said to have created all things but his holy men seem more intent on keeping God's secrets rather than teaching them."

"I think my father has many secrets. He says there is much power with a secret. That is why Marcello cannot teach your English writing to all the people. My father believes that this power will be taken away from him."

The two fell silent again for some time until Mahina spoke.

"You want to go home?" Mahina said.

"Yes, but I can't. Lokai won't let me go." His eyes remained fixed on the horizon. "I have family out there. He saved us and I abandoned him. Luther, and Doctor Wickman. They are my people and they could be dead. It's difficult not knowing."

Some moments passed before Mahina spoke again. Lines formed on her brow as she tried to remember the right words. "You help me and Afah. Maybe you die if bad palangi catch you. But you help me. So … I help you go back to Tapu Motu if you like. We take vaka. Me and you."

Abel turned to her and smiled. "Your English is getting extraordinarily better."

"Yes. And you understand me. I will help you, Abel. You are my friend."

"I believe that you would. But you would face danger. You could be hurt. I don't want that to happen. You're certainly braver than me," he said.

He meant it. Abel had tried to be courageous and had stood up to the adversity of being a prisoner in a foreign land, but in his heart, he was terrified of returning to Tapu Motu. For the truth he may learn if he were to return.

"I like you too much, and I couldn't risk your safety. Anyway, as much as I hate to admit the truth of it, I'm scared."

"You like me?" she repeated.

Abel's knees weakened. His heart raced as his words quickened. "Yes, of course I do. I mean. You have been kind to me … And we have spent time together. I really … Is it acceptable? To say this? You are betrothed … to be married …" He was lost in his words now, and Mahina's expression gave nothing away as she stared at him in silence.

"I like you too," she said.

His face went red as she stared at him. Neither of them could pull their gaze away. Before anything further was said, they were interrupted by the arrival of Masila who poked Abel in the back with a blunt stick. He had appeared silently so they were startled.

"Tuku ho'o hange ha ki'i tamasi'i vale. 'Oku fie ma'u mai koe," Masila said. His voice bellowed impatiently.

"How in the hell do you manage to walk so quietly? You're like some bloody ancient ghost." Abel stood and wiped the sand from his shirt. He knew Masila couldn't understand him, but clearly understood the disrespectful intent.

Masila leaned forward waved his stick towards Abel like a wizard from an old fairy tale casting a spell.

"'Oku ou siofi peau ilo'i koe faha'i kehe koe."

Abel heard the words for "evil spirit", but not much else. He didn't need to, since he understood the matapule's sinister tone. Masila turned to Mahina and after a short conversation,

Masila spat disdainfully on the ground in front of Abel and walked away in anger.

"It is the voice of my father he brings to you." Mahina stood and touched his shoulder gently. "You must go to him now."

Soon after Ono Hiva had left Natuini, Abel watched Hou'eiki Lokai leave Kahoua with a large group of male villagers, including several warriors, and had only returned briefly on two occasions. Father Marcello had accompanied them on each journey. Before they left, he had enquired with Marcello on where they were headed, but instead of an answer, he simply received a curt reply to mind his own business. Although the priest had been pleased to have another European companion to speak to when he first arrived, the older man's attitude towards him had become estranged. These days, Marcello would often ignore him even though their fales were built so close together.

"Concentrate on your teaching duties. The chief has high expectations of you. And let me tell you, if you try and escape, all will be punished, including me, so you best be here when we return."

On each occasion, Marcello and the troupe of men would return exhausted and their hands rough with bleeding callouses and torn skin. Abel had received little attention from the chief until now, and he wondered if his captor had decided that he had outstayed his welcome. Walking through the village and between the mossy pillars of the standing stones which acted as the entrance to this bustling heart of Kahoua, Abel was once again unsure if this would be his final moment of breath.

As he entered and looked at the faces of the Natui, he saw no hint of danger. Now that he had been an inhabitant of Natuini for almost four months he was no longer glared at with curious eyes. He had made friends with Afah and the young men of the village who were eager to help him with language and customs, the favourite of which had quickly become the nightly kava drinking circles on the sandy moonlit beach. Afah and another tall friend named Maau were waiting for him beyond the trilithon and were laughing together as he approached. Their good humour was a stark contrast to his own sense of doom, but their mood gave him some relief. Maau was normally a serious boy with a brooding temperament but had shown a patience and interest in Abel from the first day they met. Today he was in unusually good spirits. The three had become friends, and this gave Abel a chance to practise his improving language skills.

"Come, come," Afah said in English when he reached them.

The three boys walked together towards the edge of the village and, with some surprise, led him towards the Red Grove, where Marcello had been building his chapel. Until now, Abel hadn't seen this sacred spot as no one was permitted to enter the grove without a faifekau present, with the exception of the Hou'eiki. Abel had once asked Marcello to take him, but Marcello had dismissed his request, saying that he could see it when his project was finished. Masila, who was also a faifekau, only performed sacred rituals there on special feast or holy days. The journey along a thin bush trail took almost half an hour and as they emerged into a large clearing, they saw a group of warriors gathering together with spear and bow in hand. Maau's father and uncle were amongst them.

The Red Grove was a large circular field covered by a green floor of lush grass. It was devoid of low shrubs but took its name from the many beautiful heilala trees which grew there, and the distinctive red flowers that covered the trees and moved gently in the warm breeze. A partially constructed building sat in the centre of the clearing. It had features of both Natui and European styles of architecture. This was Marcello's chapel. An A-frame roof which was covered in thatch and was raised from the earth by a platform of long timber to prevent flooding. It was by no means a large structure, but appeared sturdy with thick poles lining the sides and partially attached walls that reached only halfway up the building, providing for a well-ventilated building that would also keep out the weather. Outside, a saw horse and a pile of uncut timber were stacked to the side. The priest had been busy.

A few more men arrived in the clearing carrying spears.

"Where are we going?" he said slowly in Natui.

Maau and Afah turned to each other with a knowing look, which annoyed Abel.

"You are learning quickly," Maau replied in Natui.

"Thank you, but why are we here?" Abel's concern heightened.

"Don't worry, Abel. Today we become men. This is a great day. And we are happy to have our new palangi friend share in our happiness."

This time it was Afah who spoke and as he did so, Maau's father Aunofo, an aging but strong nobleman, approached the three young men with a bundle of spears, handing one of them to Maau. They spoke some quiet words between them before closing their eyes and pressing their foreheads together solemnly for a few moments. The two of them smiled broadly, and Maau received a hard slap on the back from a very proud-looking father.

Abel counted around a dozen warriors. These men were seasoned Natui fighters, judging by their equipment and the tattoos they sported on their limbs and torsos. Father Marcello had explained that although all men of Natui were expected to know how to fight to some extent when called to war, there were warriors of the tribe whose very existence was devoted to hunting and warfare. Intricately etched tattoos were common amongst the adults of the tribes, but a particular spear and turtle shell design was customary amongst these men. He had also seen those symbols on female warriors chosen to protect a young noble woman who didn't want to be shadowed by a man at all times. Each tattoo was unique in its own way. On one man, a large and ornately carved turtle shell had been drawn over his chest with dozens of black curving lines to depict the crashing waves of a stormy sea. On another, an angry face peered out from his shoulders and two spears crossing over a turtle shell were tipped with a prong of shark teeth. As well as their upper bodies, all of them had also undergone extensive etchings into their lower torso and upper legs with similar patterns of triangles and solid black bands stretching completely around their waists and thighs.

"Tatau?" Maau raised his eyes at his foreign companion, noticing his interest.

Abel nodded and noticed that neither of his friends had tattoos yet.

Maau pointed at the men and spoke in Natui. "Earth, wind, fire and water. Sometimes a spirit or a great beast. But always, earth, wind, fire and water."

"I understand." Abel nodded again.

His two friends had kept their language simple when they spoke to him, and he had learned a lot from both of them. Outside of the warrior caste, he had discovered that a villager's position or duty sometimes denoted the tatau they had adorned. The fishermen had many symbols of the sea. Warriors, like the ones in front of them, had drawings of arrowheads, spearheads and sharks' teeth denoting ferocity. Masila, a holy man and keeper of stories, was covered in angry faces, swooping birds and lizards, which Mahina had told him were symbols of their ancestors, gods and spirit creatures. Abel was no stranger to seeing these markings on the bodies of other Pacific peoples, and many of the sailors aboard *Viritus* also wore tattoos of their own. When he had spoken to Mahina about it, she was surprised to hear that the people of England, especially sailors, commonly decorated their bodies with depictions of life at sea, anchors, coats of arms and mythical creatures of the deep, such as mermaids. His cousin Luther has marked his chest with the Southern Cross constellation given his love of the Pacific Ocean and its skies.

"You want to feel this pain, Abel?" Afah said.

"I think so. I've always wanted one. Not so sure about the pain though."

"Me too. I'm ready now for a tatau. I'm old enough," said Maau.

Afah laughed. "Yes, Maau wants a big tatau of his mother's huge tits, right here." He bent over and pretended to draw two large circles on his own buttocks. Maau moved forward to kick him in the behind, but his mocking companion jumped away before he could strike.

By the time the laughter stopped, Maau was ignoring him and had stepped in closer to Abel, trying not to pay attention to his tormentor.

"I'd quite like a spear and sharks teeth pattern," Abel said.

"You? No, not for you."

"Why not?"

Maau regarded him thoughtfully. "You are palangi. The spear is not yours. This long silver knife is your tatau." He touched the scabbard by Abel's side where he wore his marine's sabre. "You need sky and blade. And great fire."

"Why the sky and fire?"

"You are palangi. You are … great fire from the sky."

"I don't understand. Do you mean the sun?" Abel asked.

"No, only *I* am the Sun." Another older voice approached from behind, taking them by surprise, and when all three of them turned, Chief Lokai was beside them. Kalafa stood closely behind.

"Palangi means something different. But I will explain this on our journey."

"With respect Hou'eiki Lokai, if I might ask, where are we going?"

No answer was given. Instead, the first warrior of Chief Lokai bowed his head and offered a finely carved short spear with a razor-sharp tip over to the chief, who took it in both hands and moved with a smile towards Afah. The young man, with hands outstretched, carefully accepted the weapon and fell to one knee with his head bowed low. Lokai motioned him to rise again and playfully ruffled the long hair on his head with a grin that spread from ear to ear.

"It is tradition that before the great hunt, that a father gives his son a well-made spear as a sign of his love and his family duty. Today you will, all three of you, walk into that forest as only boys, and when we return, you will be men."

The surrounding forest had become quiet. Birds which would normally squawk and rustle through lush green undergrowth had gone silent and the humid air seemed to drown everything in an oppressive moisture. In the unnerving silence, the beauty of the Natui islands was even more pronounced and all the senses seemed focused on the vibrant colours of the bush, wildflowers and a glimpse of deep blue sky beyond the canopy of trees. The hunting party lay low upon the relatively cool ground. Some warriors crouched, but most stayed hidden with such stillness that they seemed to disappear completely in the thick surrounding foliage. Afah was further forward than the others and stooped low. He held his back firmly upon the thick upstanding vines of an old banyan tree. Soft branches had been loosely draped over his shoulders, and his smaller stature and sinewy body seemed to blend into the twisting vegetation. He was careful to make no movements. The green camouflage was so skilfully applied that if a passer-by were to look in his direction, he may well remain completely hidden.

Beyond Afah the vegetation was unusual in that a thin pathway tracked through the forest, and the grassy surface had been quite firmly trampled. It wove its way around a large group of banyan trees for some distance before disappearing out of sight.

Most of the men had hidden themselves from view beyond the path which up ahead gently snaked from side to side and wound passed them. However, it was only Afah, Maau and Abel who remained on the very edge, just out of sight but within touching distance of the narrow space that had been crafted unnaturally.

Maau's body was pressed against the ground on the opposite side of the path from Abel. They could barely see each other through the grasses that separated them, and they did not speak or move for fear of disturbing the silence. Abel was becoming uncomfortable, having held this position for more than an hour, and his muscles ached. Bringing up his knees to his chest, he leaned forward to peer down the beaten vegetation but was rebuked with a glare from his companion, who flashed his eyes wide in such a way that Abel knew exactly what he was saying without any words spoken.

Lie down and stay quiet.

And so he did, but he quickly grew weary in the same position and the heat of the day was making him drift towards sleep. As his eyes grew heavier, he would pinch himself to keep alert. The shame of drifting off to sleep was not something he wanted to experience.

Abel thought about the high expectations his cousin and mentor Lieutenant Luther would have of him.

"You will meet many people of this world during our journey," he remembered being told by the lieutenant on his first day on *Viritus*. It was also the first day he had met his cousin. His father had sent him to Luther after consumption had taken his mother. He could still recall the terrible agony his mother endured from the disease, which made her cough so heavily that blood would

spatter on her bed sheets nightly as her breathing became desperately laboured.

"Remember that you take with you your pride and reputation wherever you may go. If you dishonour yourself amongst strangers, you will dishonour England and your countrymen. You must hold your head higher and stand straighter so that they may see you are a man of honour and worthy of respect."

It was one of many lessens he was taught, and he relished each opportunity to listen to his cousin's stories and words of wisdom. There was no truer hero in his mind than the lieutenant and no man or woman that he had ever met had displayed such courage. He would not disappoint him.

A distant shout woke him completely, and he could feel a rush of excitement enter his body. Around him, despite the calm of his surrounding companions, he could also hear murmurings and movement amongst them. Across the pathway, Maau nodded and pulled up a spear from his side so that the sharpened head was exposed and held ready. Abel unsheathed his own sabre, holding it firmly, for fear that the sweat on his hands would make the grip slippery. The hilt of the weapon in his hands felt familiar. He felt safer with the blade in his grasp, and now that he held it ready for action, his mind steeled, he felt strong, ready to take on the approaching danger.

The shouting ahead became louder. Now there were several voices. The sounds of snapping branches. They were chasing something. Something that grunted and squealed with an angry desperation. An anguished beast was moving with unbridled speed towards them, down the narrow path. He could feel his heart beating against the wall of his chest as each second passed, anticipating the moment he would need to leap from his hiding place. With an expectation that he would see a movement of bush or some other warning of its approach, it was with some surprise that the enormous beast appeared in a burst of flying dirt and broken shrubbery. It was a feral boar that charged with surprising speed and within a few moments had already reached the banyan tree where Afah was hiding. The pig's squeal erupted once again, and it showed its large, blunted teeth inside a red frothing mouth. It was covered in short grey-brown hair which was matted with freshly dried muck. A solid layer of muscle and long strides in its run demonstrated a full-grown adult that threatened to destroy all in its path who dared counter its escape; a mission the young men had been tasked with. The pig's head was enormous and long, featuring bulbous eyes, wide and feverish.

Afah pounced into action. When the pig rushed past, he flung a thick coir rope tied with a lasso at its head. He had tied the opposite length of the rope to the thick roots of the banyan tree. His throw hit its intended mark, looping the head around the creature's neck and in its stride the slack of the rope unravelled behind it. Afah and Maau held still but readied themselves to spring from the ground as soon as the rope had reached its full length and tightened around the boar's neck. They were both relieved that Afah's throw was true, otherwise they would have been forced to try to kill the creature with spear and sword whilst it remained at speed, a prospect they were told would be dangerous. It hurtled towards them, unaware of the trap, and as the rope was fully stretched, the noose tightened, knotting around its thick neck. The beast's heavy canter was cut short and its grotesque body flung upside down, leaving the ground for some moments before coming back to earth with an audible thud. However, as the rope reached its zenith and the weight of the animal strained the length of coir, the knot snapped free of the roots and the pig hurtled forward in a terrifying mess of flesh and dirt.

It lay on its back, momentarily stunned. But now the animal was in front of him, Abel hesitated in awe of the wild scene and its bestial chaos. It was Maau who reacted without fear and leaped from his hiding place towards the prone beast. With two hands he wielded the spear in a downward strike, piercing its belly with a well-aimed thrust. Blood ran from its underside and it shrieked in pain. A chorus of cheers rang out from the hunting party of seasoned hunters and warriors who now emerged from their hiding places and ran forward to witness the spectacle. The pig was not dead and rolled angrily away from the spear which was now dripping with red gore. Once on its feet, the beast ran back towards Afah momentarily and then, seeing its path was blocked from that direction, spun around again, lowered its head and charged with even greater speed towards its enemy. Maau braced for the attack. He lowered his spear, but the boar's rage and speed caught him off guard. The tip of the spear only scraped along its hide. With a look of abject terror, Maau was bowled over, his legs not having any time to brace for the charge. He hit the ground heavily and was instantly winded as the boar sped past. Abel saw the danger too late as Maau was swept onwards by the pig. Maau had stepped into the path of the rope which had looped around his leg and was being pulled along with the boar's escape. After a dozen feet, the boar slowed with the weight of its human anchor. It could not get away so turned to face the attached victim. This time, the boar positioned its head low and charged towards at an even more frantic pace than before, determined to smash itself into Maau to free itself. Afah was desperately attempting to reach the mayhem, spear in hand to help the felled boy, but he would not reach his friend in time. Abel launched from the grass and stepped in between his friend and the oncoming boar. Taking the blade in both hands he ran forward to meet the charge but with a well-timed step, leapt to its left flank and swept the sharp blade towards its lowered head. The sword connected with the top of its muddy brow and cut deeply through its flesh and bone.

The boar's squeal was deep and otherworldly. Blood erupted from its angry face whilst the beast lost its footing and tumbled forward. It rolled towards Maau, and it stopped only a few feet from where he was still struggling to stand. It was enough time for Afah to reach his friends, and now that the pig was prone, he took advantage of its vulnerable state and jabbed his spear into its neck, causing another grievous injury. With his breath returning, Maau retrieved his own spear and the three boys set upon the doomed creature, stabbing and thrusting its body with their weapons. In its last moments of life, the creature spun desperately to free itself from its attackers. The three boys seemed possessed, their attacks relentless, until they had to be pulled away by the elder members of the hunting party. It was Kalafa who grabbed Abel's sword hand and stopped him from any further violence. He jerked him backwards roughly. Kalafa gave him a look of amusement before letting him go and turning to the felled animal.

"Back off little men."

Abel understood the words that boomed over the ruckus. Even in the chaos of their feverish assault, his friends had enough sense to stop and move away quickly. Taking his own weapon, an impressive club adorned with ornate etchings and elemental symbols, Kalafa raised the pakipaki above his head and with a well-aimed blow, shattered the boar's skull, instantly killing it and stopping its desperate grunts.

"Che-hoo!" The hunting party shouted in victory, with many coming over to inspect the carcass, patting the boys on the back and admiring the large specimen of a kill. In stark contrast to the smiles of most warriors, Abel, Afah and Maau could barely speak or move, looking at one another covered in blood, shocked at their own savagery and still reeling with the terror of the event. Maau's father, Aunofo, leaned down and pressed his hand into one of the boar's bloody wounds. When he stood, he ran his fingers down the faces of Abel and his companions, making a streak of five bloody lines upon them. First his own son, who smiled proudly at his father's gesture, followed by Afah. When Aunofo reached Abel, he stopped first to dip his hand again in the blood of the perished boar before running his fingers down his face and then placing both hands firmly upon his shoulders. With some surprise, he could see tears welling up in the man's eyes, which were firmly locked upon his. Although he was lithe and fit, his face seemed at once very old, with a mixture of anguish and relief.

"My son … is your brother now," he whispered to Abel in Natui.

This made Abel smile, but he was without words and simply nodded in understanding towards the 'eiki. Aunofo wiped a tear from his eye and took a deep breath before turning away, letting out another joyous cry. "Che hoo!"

He was joined by a chorus of tribesmen who shouted in gleeful response.

Abel, like the others was surprised to feel exhilaration beyond the initial fear but this was interrupted when Kalafa swiped his pakipaki towards the brittle bark of a tree trunk and shattered its surface. The sound gained the attention of all three. He pointed the tip of the weapon towards them. This time Abel could not understand the words he used until later, when he asked Afah to explain.

"We Natui have an old saying. A worthy enemy deserves a quick death. But today all of you are lucky that you were not the meal. I do not believe the beast considered you children worthy of eating." He ended his insult with a self-satisfied grunt. Smirking to himself he walked away with Aunofo, leaving them behind to survey their handy work.

Abel and his friends were tasked with carrying the boar a short distance, where the hunting party set camp. The group took advantage of a short but powerful rain to fill their waterskins fashioned from dried bull-kelp. The Natui had used this natural resource for a great number of purposes, but one of the most important was the transportation of fresh water and food over long distances, especially across the sea. Abel had watched the kelp being hung to dry in the cool ocean breeze along the coast of the Natuini Lahi. It had strong inner pockets which could be filled or inflated like a balloon. Food, like pickled shellfish, salted fish and even seabirds, could be preserved in a good quality pouch for many months and years if stored properly, and the skins were completely airtight. When inflated they made useful buoys that signalled the location of submerged crab nets.

With the water skins filled and the fleeting rain giving way to the heat of the afternoon, a fire was prepared and the boar's skin and flesh quickly rendered. When the hunters were finished, they had stripped the animal of its edible meat and organs, prepared the thick skin for drying and scooped marrow from the remaining bones. The bones themselves were stacked and wrapped for transport. Later they would be used to make tools and knives. It was impressive to Abel that almost no part of the beast would go to waste, and the expertise of the huntsmen in their work was incredible to watch.

As the sun went down, the hunting party had made a circle around the large campfire, and spirits were high while they feasted on roasted boar and baked 'ufi wrapped in the leaves of the taro plant. It was delicious and a welcome feast for all after an arduous day. Everyone was hungry from the day's efforts and the chunks of meat were carved from the pig so quickly that the flesh had barely felt the heat of the campfire's flames before being devoured. Abel, Afah and Maau sat beside one another, and after Chief Lokai was served first, the three companions were given the juiciest of meats as their hard-fought prize and were heaped with praise and stories told and retold of the struggle to defeat their dinner. There was much laughter and revelry, and after the day's events had been relayed more than a dozen times, others began to relate their own stories of their boyhood rituals to become "men of Natui". There was much embellishment with each story being told in more grandiose details than the last until Chief Lokai announced to great laughter that as young men, every warrior present must have been as tall as a coconut tree and killed twelve boars with their bare hands to earn their place in the tribe. Abel's own stature amongst the hunters seemed to be suddenly elevated. His actions, although belated, were seen as courageous. He had risked his safety for Maau, a Natui, which was not lost on those present. More than a few of the warriors came to sit beside him and his friends to congratulate them on their victory. Abel could not understand all that was said to him but had gathered enough to understand that each was welcoming him, as if they were meeting him for the first time again. He noticed that both Afah and Maau nodded in earnest agreement as each elder warrior would approach to offer words of encouragement or wisdom. However, the seriousness of the talks took a humorous turn, when in a wild demonstration of the hunt, a few of the younger warriors stood up and acted out the battle. One man pretended to be the boar, diving headfirst towards the other whilst his opponent pretended to draw out Abel's sabre, using a stick as a prop, and as the man ran past he was struck in the belly, with the sabre being swept about in an exaggerated fashion. The warrior acting as Abel let out a loud and farcical battle scream as his companion fell into a heap. Then the other warriors swept in and proceeded to hit the "boar" with imaginary clubs. The man rolled from side to side, letting out a tiny but audible cry of pain with every hit. With a feigned high-pitched voice of a child, Chief Lokai stood up from his place of honour at the head of the circle and spoke.

"Is it dead yet?" His arms flung to the side as he asked the mocking question.

The rest of the hunting party could not contain themselves, rolling about and holding their bellies. Even Kalafa laughed so much that he excused himself to relieve his bladder. The boys joined in on the banter. When the laughter subsided, kava bowls were passed around the circle and the group became more subdued, with conversation quietening to a murmur. The drinking of kava had deep cultural and spiritual significance. Its ritual was well defined but could change depending on who was present and how important they were. Abel had witnessed the drinking of kava in both formal and informal situations. Commonly, a tou'a, a young virgin girl of marrying age, would be invited to serve the kava. The men would be free to talk to her and if one amongst them took a liking or was considered to be a good match for the girl's family, he would be allowed to flirt or even tell suggestive jokes for her amusement.

Without a tou'a here, Aunofo sat next to Chief Lokai on his left-hand side and would ensure the ceremony was observed correctly. The chief cupped his hands and clapped once loudly. Aunofo ladled a serving of the milky liquid made from a mixture of water and kava root.

"Koe la'a hopo," said Aunofo before passing him the cup.

Lokai drank quickly and finished the bowl made from a half coconut shell. When he put the cup down, several warriors cried, "uloula'avaɪ". Then, clapping once himself, Aunofo scooped the precious liquid up into a bowl and also drank.

During this ritual, Abel knew that each man had a second title, either a nickname they had held since childhood or a noble title bestowed upon them by the chief. Each warrior to his left would clap and his bowl would be filled by Aunofo, who would pass around the kava for them to drink. When it was Abel's turn, the others watched him as he nervously clapped.

"Palangi," a few of the hunters proclaimed.

With some disappointment he did not have a nickname and since they could not call him by his real name, he had only become known as "palangi" for the ritual. They had only given him a tiny portion. He drank without hesitation, but it was barely a mouthful. Aunofo looked at him with concern.

"You are new. Just a little," he said.

The second time around, he clapped louder and held his chin high in challenge to say he could drink more.

"Palangi!" his companions shouted again.

There was even less liquid inside this time.

Aunofo looked at him again. "You are young. Do not drink too much."

Several warriors near them nodded in agreement. Abel's face went red when the kava vessels were filled generously for Afah and Maau.

Another round of kava was being served. As his turn came, he brought his hands together to clap when Chief Lokai stopped him.

"Wait, palangi. Come and sit by my side."

Abel looked at Afah, whose eyes were wide in shock.

"Go, Abel. He has summoned you." Afah took his arm and pushed him forward.

Abel walked around the circle until he reached the chief. All eyes were upon him with looks ranging from curiosity to bemusement.

"Sit." The chief motioned to the ground to his right.

Abel obeyed quickly, but felt nervous at the invitation. He sat still and the kava ritual continued, with each warrior drinking deeply from the vessel. When it was again Abel's turn, Chief Lokai motioned for everyone to pay attention with the sweep of his enormous hand. When everyone was silent, he wiped a river of perspiration from his brow and smiled.

"It is hot tonight. I'm sweating like that pig we just devoured," he announced to another bout of laughter. It subsided when he motioned with his hands again. "Today, two youngsters of Natui have begun a journey of manhood. The hunt is not about the taking of life. It is about the giving of life."

Chief Lokai now rose to his feet to address the warriors and each of them rose with him until the whole party stood at attention, including Abel and his friends.

"When one beast is sacrificed, others may live. We eat from the gift of its flesh and we build our homes with tools made of its bones. We defend ourselves with the shields made from his skin. In this we pay respect to the beast. As we pay respect to the warriors who provide for our people." As he spoke, the circle of men nodded and spoke out in hardy agreement.

"There is some hardship ahead for these boys in the days ahead, but for tonight they eat and drink amongst the most seasoned of us." He looked at Abel, staring at him for several moments with no expression upon his face.

"However, there is one foreigner amongst us. A 'palangi'. Today, he showed honour and courage. His own father, who is not here to see him, would have wept with pride at his strength. And in showing the courage of his people, he stood side by side with our own and in that moment our people became one."

Lokai's voice grew louder with every word while the hunters nodded in agreement to each other.

"The palangi has shown once again he is willing to give his blood for strangers in need. It is my hope that we may become friends with the palangi peoples. It is my hope that the palangi Abel will become a man amongst us and that brings our people together so that the Natui can be strong with powerful allies from far away seas."

"Koe tamasi'i falala'anga 'e hoko ia ko ha to'a. Io!" Aunofo shouted loudly to support his chief, and this was followed by a barrage of agreement from all the warriors present.

"It is my decision that he be considered to have begun the rituals of manhood today. But if he is to become one of us, he must have a worthy Natui name, born of his actions." The chief looked again at Abel, who was struggling to comprehend all that had been spoken.

"Kafa e faifolau," he said. "Your name to be spoken in the great ritual, and the name to be spoken by your warriors' side by side when in battle will be Kafa e faifolau. This means 'he binds us', who brings us together as one. He who makes stronger. KAFA E FAIFOLAU!"

As this was shouted by Lokai, it was loudly repeated by the men several times until it was well known amongst them.

Abel had a special name now, and he beamed in pride at the gesture. "Thank you, great Chief Lokai," he said.

"My lord, Great Sun of the Natuini lands. There is another task tonight that must be accomplished before the title becomes official," Aunofo said.

Everyone quietened down and listened in interest. With a grave and serious expression, he held a kava bowl in his hands.

"The boy must drink one more serving of kava before he takes his new name and can be considered a man of Natui, like Afah and my son Maau."

"Really, is that so?" Lokai raised his eyebrows. "Well, give him another drink. Let it be done."

He turned to Abel again, addressing him in English. "You are ready for the kava. One more and you become a man of Natui."

Abel smiled. "Not a problem at all 'Great Sun'. That may be the easiest of today's challenges."

Aunofo picked up the communal kava cup with his right hand and reached out to scoop up some liquid from the large kumete bowl. However, just before he touched the kava, he hesitated and looked at the gathered hunters. His serious expression turned to a mischievous smile. Then he raised his left hand from behind his back to expose a gigantic half coconut shell. It was enormous and perhaps the largest shell Abel had ever seen. As if it had been planned from the start, the gathered warriors again burst into joy and laughter as Maau's father scooped kava into the bowl to the brim and then handed it to Abel.

"All must be finished at once." Aunofo winked at him.

Not wanting to embarrass himself or seem weak, Abel took the challenge to heart and, taking a deep breath, began to drink. The dusty tasting liquid swept down his throat like a waterfall, and although he almost gagged at the effort, he managed to finish the bowl, passing it back to Aunofo when he was finished. Kava dripped from his chin onto his bloodied shirt, and he was relieved when the chief motioned everyone to sit down with him so that he could rest and look at his new friends with a sense of accomplishment.

As the night wore on, the effects of the kava set in, and the warriors' faces turned calm and subdued.

Abel felt very relaxed and very full. Some of the hunters began to sing songs amongst themselves whilst the kava was pressed into hands around the circle at more regular intervals. Abel had seen more than his fair share of drinking circles with his *Viritus* companions as they stopped from port to port, but a night of drinking rum and ale turned rowdier as the night progressed. Some ended up with a bloodied nose or loose tooth. In contrast, the mood of a kava night became ever more peaceful.

"Well done, young Kafa e faifolau. I am pleased that you have joined us," Lokai said.

"And you have treated me well. I'm thankful you have decided not to kill me."

"Aha! Yes, I think that is something to be thankful for. I don't think I would want to face the wrath of your cousin, the one they call Lu'fa."

Abel nodded. "Luther? Yes, he is a great warrior, as strong and brave as Kalafa. Except the lieutenant is a kind and generous man."

"Ahh, you do not think that Kalafa is kind? Kindness is not something I like much in a fighting man. His duty is to fight strong. And make me safe from the spear. I am chief and only I decide when my warriors are kind or unkind. It is Kalafa's duty to kill my enemies, before they kill the 'Great Sun'. Nothing more.

Maybe palangi chiefs are different, yes?" Chief Lokai sounded rhetorical as he took another drink out of his bowl.

"You told me you would explain what palangi means," Abel said.

The older man fell silent, and for a moment, Abel thought he may not have heard the question. Lokai took another bite out of a tasty roasted leg he had sheared from the boar's carcass earlier.

"When I was a young man, perhaps no older than you, I saw your great kalia for the very first time. There were two ships together. At first, when my people saw them coming near, we were frightened. We had not seen your people before, and the ships were much taller than ours. And beautiful ... so beautiful. As they came near to the shore, we thought that a giant enemy from distant lands had come to fight us and take our people as slaves. But my father, the 'Great Sun' before me, he led the warriors of Natuini out on as many kalia and vaka as we could sail and met them at sea. I stood proudly by his side while we shouted for the giants to come closer, calling for them to face our spear and shield. When we could see the men on the ships, they were not giants. But their skin was pale, and we thought they may be ghosts from the 'Lalo Fonua', the place of darkness, and they would take our lives."

Others near the chief were curious at the conversation and Aunofo began to translate the story to those who were listening.

"Still, we stood strong and shouted for the ghosts to come down from their kalia and fight us if that was their will. They did not. Instead, the pale ones raised their guns and cannon to the air and the sky shook with thunder that day. We returned to the beach and every man and woman who could hold a spear, bolo or pakipaki waited for the attack, but it never came. Before the sun left beneath the sea, the ships sailed on and we did not see them again. My father, he called them palangi. 'Pa' is the sound of the loudest thunder before the rains, the sound which shakes the land. Langi means from the sky and so that is the meaning of palangi." He chuckled and shook his head.

"When Marcello arrived, we understood the palangi were not ghosts or giants. Just men. But when he could speak Natui, I also understood that the palangi people are many, and they have much strength. They build mighty spears that kill a warrior from many steps away and they travel far in their great ships. And they have only one god …" Lokai raised his hands as if in exasperation and turned to Abel.

"How can there be only one god? I asked Marcello. This god must be powerful. Maybe the most powerful. His stories are found in pictures for all palangi to know, so I ask many questions of the book he looks at every day. I thought, 'A great god he must be if his people are so strong with many sons and many ships.' I wanted to know more, so I told Marcello to teach me the stories."

With a grunt, Chief Lokai lifted himself from the dry ground and stood before his people to address them. Aunofo hissed at the circle of hunters and each woke from their mellow rest and stood upright and silent in the presence of their chief. Lokai puffed out his chest and pointed his finger at all who stood before him before speaking in perfect English.

"The holy book says, 'Let every man and woman be subject unto the higher powers. For there is no power but of God and the powers that be are ordained of God.' The holy book also says, 'And I will make them one nation in the land, on the mountains of Israel. And one king shall be king over them all, and they shall be no longer two nations, and no longer divided into two kingdoms.'"

In unison, his warriors stomped their feet and shouted, "Amen."

Lokai looked proud, and as soon as he had completed relating the scripture, he motioned for everyone to sit down again, something that they were all grateful for given that many were half asleep from the excessive consumption of kava.

"I thought that you also believed in Maui and the other Natui gods," Abel said.

"Of course." The chief smiled, with one eyebrow raised. "I have taken the palangi god as one of my most favoured, but now he is one of many others worshipped by my people. We must pay respect to all. One day, I think he will become our only god. I cannot change the people's mind in one night."

The answer seemed strange to Abel. He picked at his back teeth with a small stick to dislodge a sliver of boar meat, thinking about what Lokai had said. He knew the Christian Bible also taught that there was no other God except the one taught by the church and wondered if Marcello had explained that to the chief, but thought better of contradicting him, especially while he appeared to be in an unusually good mood. Instead, he queried something he had been pondering since his arrival in Natuini.

"Great Sun, I do have another question. Why did you ask Marcello to teach you English? He is Venetian and his language is Italian ..."

With a slow and steady nod, the chief's bottom lip poked out. "No one has asked me that before, but it is a very good question."

He took another large sip of his bowl and threw it to the ground. Aunofo promptly picked it up and filled again.

"Easy to answer. Marcello told me that Venice was once a great nation upon the waters. Now it is not. The English are kings of the oceans now, so I want to learn the language of your people. I also want to be a great king of the ocean, and I want to make friends with King Siaosi.

"Siaosi?" Abel asked

The chief sighed before speaking slowly and deliberately. "Gee-or-gee. Your king's name is a difficult one for my tongue and so we call him Siaosi. Maybe one day I will take my kalia and visit your king so that we may share stories of battle and I can drink kava with him."

"The king most likely drinks wine, or ale," Abel ventured.

"The palangi drink makes men stupid. Look at Marcello. A man who speaks to spirits but fills his body with poison and makes him angry for all the world. I will one day send all his rum into the sea and watch fish fall about themselves and swim into the rocks. Kava makes men think. Enemies who would kill each other in the daytime will tell stories of our ancestors and embrace each other as brothers after a kava. This tradition makes our people strong and with our tradition, my people have time to remember they are my subjects, and I am their ruler."

Abel started to feel sleepy and stifled a yawn, but Lokai was still interested in conversation.

"Lu'fa is a good ruler of men, yes?"

"Luther is a good and fair leader. He treats his marines with respect and they respect him. I think that each man would die for him if his life were in danger."

"Ah, that is the warrior every chief needs. One that makes much loyalty. I would very much like to speak to your cousin. When we return to Kahoua, it is my decision that you will return to Tapu Motu and request that Lu'fa be a guest at my daughter's wedding feast."

Abel's eyes widened. "You will let me return to my people?"

"Yes, but only for a short time. I send men with you to make you come back safely. You are guest in Natuini and for now you must remain by my side. But your cousin would bring great honour to me if he were to be my guest. He may bring along with him the healer or one of his loyal men if that is his wish. We will treat them well, and then I will send them back to Tapu Motu with gifts. Will you do this?"

"Of course. I will go as soon as you allow it. I much desire to see my cousin and my people again. Thank you, Chief. Thank you dearly."

Abel smiled and felt relieved he was being trusted with leaving the village, even if under escort. If Lokai felt some benevolence towards Luther and the remainder of the *Viritus* crew, then he would be more likely to tolerate their ongoing presence on their sacred island. He had heard Masila rail against Tapu Motu being desecrated by the palangi, sustaining themselves from the bountiful food that was grown on the island, and many people agreed with him. Marcello believed that it had only been Chief Lokai's insistence that they be allowed to remain peacefully that had kept them alive, and if the Natuini could make friendships with Luther and his fellow crewman, this may increase the likelihood of a sustained peace.

The kava overcame Abel, and he felt his eyelids grow heavy. This was no shame since Maau, Afah and many other warriors present had already slipped into a deep sleep with the lush green canopy above. He lay on his back, staring at the clear sky through an opening in the tree covering. The clear night provided a wondrous blanket of stars for the weary hunters.

The following day the three friends woke at the break of dawn and were led by Aunofo away from camp. They rarely spoke along the way, and all of Abel's questions about their destination were ignored. He suspected he was the only one that didn't know where they were headed. Afah looked worriedly at Maau who kept his own eyes forward, with a sense of determination on his face.

Another test perhaps? he thought.

They travelled towards Kahoua, but before they could sight the village, Aunofo turned west and closer to the shoreline. When they finally stopped, they were confronted by another campsite with a smouldering fire and a single hut built on the edge of a sandy clearing. Abel was surprised to encounter Masila waiting for them. He sat in front of the fire with his eyes closed, and he was rocking back and forth with a mortar and pestle in his hands, grinding a blackened paste within. They could hear him whispering to himself as he moved, though he stopped as they approached, then stood to meet them.

Masila's gaze immediately fixated on Abel before turning to Aunofo and raising his eyebrows in silent questioning.

"It is the will of Chief Lokai. It is my will also. All three boys will receive their mark." Aunofo looked at the friends and nodded solemnly. "When you return to your families, you will be men of Natui."

Abruptly, he turned back to the path and left.

Masila pointed to the structure behind him, which was perched on a ridge overlooking a break in the trees, and beyond they could spy the blue ocean. The timber structure was without walls but wooden poles held a high roof and, on the inside, a table with several pots, small clubs and strange comb shaped implements carefully laid out in neat rows atop.

"To be a man of Natui, we must wear the tatau of our people. Stand and wait until I call you."

Masila strode into the shelter, leaving Abel and his companions to sit on the cool ground.

A sound of thunder rocked the sky above them where thick cloud cover had been gathering since morning. Soon after it rained, thick and heavy. Abel moved towards the shelter, but Afah took his arm, preventing him from walking any further. He gave Abel a stern shake of his head, eyes wide open in warning.

"Don't interrupt Seagulli."

They soon became drenched as the rain grew stronger. Maau closed his eyes.

"Have you ever wondered where the rain comes from?" Maau said.

Abel had grown used to these questions from his friends, who often seemed preoccupied with the mechanics of nature.

"They are Tangaloa's tears. Masila says he cries for us humans that we cannot witness the beauty of all the world from where he sits in the clouds," Afah offered.

"That's silly. No, I don't think so," said Maau. "He seems to cry a lot for a god. Look at the clouds. I wonder if they are like the steam of the cooking fires."

"Maybe the gods of the underworld are cooking under the mountains of Mo'unga Vela where the rivers of fire flow? The steam from such fires would make clouds so thick that they might rain on us."

Maau scoffed. "Why is it always the gods with you, Afah? The sea and sky move in patterns. Each season is no different from the last. Every year it rains for many full moons, then stops and returns again for the same amount of time. This is not the work of gods, waking up to boil your mum's unripe yams."

"Shh!" Masila hissed, hearing the boys' chatter.

The matapule ushered them into the shelter and summoned them to sit whilst he prepared the tattooing combs and ink. At first the matapule examined each item, picking them up and placing them back down again in strict order. When he touched each piece he would utter words quietly, blessing his tools for the task ahead. When the tatau combs were taken from the table, Abel noticed how razor sharp they were and worried about the pain they would cause. As they waited for Masila to complete his ritual, Afah and Maau tried to relay as much as they could about what was about to occur, and Abel could feel a mild panic setting in. It was Masila's duty to perform this ritual which would bring the boys into what the Natui considered adulthood. Masila had been preparing ever since they left on their hunt and had blessed the implements and the site of the ceremony to ensure his hands were guided by the benevolent gods of the Natui. The location was important, as they could look out across the ocean where the spirits of their ancestors could watch them as witness to their coming of age. Whilst Natui men would receive many tattoos over a number of years, the three were to first receive arm bands to signify their strength and entry into the brotherhood of warriors. Importantly, they could not return to the village until this process was complete, or else they would bring shame and dishonour to their families.

Abel watched on in curiosity and then growing horror as Maau was taken to the centre of the abode and the tattooing began. Masila used a fine dark chalk to outline a pattern – a series of stylised triangles around the upper half of his arm in a wide band. Once the matapule was satisfied with the outline, he took one of the sharp combs and dipped it carefully into the prepared ink. With his other hand he held a thin but sturdy stick and, placing the comb against Maau's arm, he began a series of repeated strikes, embedding the sharp points of the comb into his arm and darkening the pierced skin. Maau's face scrunched, and before long he groaned unhappily as the pace of the strikes intensified, gritting his teeth to stop himself from moving. After just ten minutes, Maau asked Masila to stop and insisted he be given time to rest. However, the elder man grunted angrily and continued to apply his well-honed skill. The suffering did not stop for at least an hour when Masila finally relieved Maau with an order to rest. When his friend sat with them again, they could see that he had been crying silently from the pain and was sweating profusely, water dripping down his face and body. He placed his hands over his face to hide the tears, but before either companion could talk to him, it was Afah's turn to be seated in front of Masila, who started quickly and mercilessly with every strike of the tatau comb.

Afah seemed to suffer more than his companion and his fidgeting earned the ire of Masila, who stopped only to scold him for moving and reminded him that the tatau would be ruined if he moved too much. After Afah, it was Abel's turn to step up and receive his own tatau. Masila stared at Abel with stony grey eyes, and with a slight movement of his chin, summoned him to sit on a low tree stump that had been fashioned into a comfortable seat. He nervously stood and turned to his companions for support. It was Afah who looked up and gave him a smile, mixed with a grimace because of his aching arm, and spoke to him in the Natui tongue.

"You will receive the sky. It is the will of Chief Lokai," he said.

Although he suspected the matapule disliked him, he gave no indication of his disdain as he prepared the delicate comb and carefully began his tatau. He was a truly gifted artist, and the task was undertaken with a measure of profound solemnity. Masila cleaned his arm with a wet bark cloth drenched in seawater, and when it dried, he drew the careful design that was to be etched into his skin. Abel could make out a simple row of figures in the shape of people. They were holding each other's hands, encompassing his arm and forming the canopy of a cloudy sky. He then inked the teeth of the tatau comb, placed it carefully upon the first drawing and tapped with a rhythmic motion.

The pain was immediately intense, and Abel struggled to keep still. Clenching his fist, he could only think of the pride of this moment and the acceptance he would have from the people of Natui. When the thought of pulling away from the sharp tatau implement crossed his mind, another thought overcame him. That he deeply wanted to impress Mahina and the very notion of bringing shame to himself by rejecting the process kept him strong. He knew she was meant for another, but it mattered not. He felt light-headed and happy whenever he thought of Mahina, and it was clear to him how much he cared for her. In the agony of the incessant needle pricks, he kept his mind steeled, hard and focused on the task. He was unsure when but some way into the process he blacked out from the pain and had to be woken by Masila with a slap to the face. Sitting up in shock, the tatau continued until Masila was finished with the first session. All three boys were told to wash themselves in the ocean, and when they leapt into the cool waters their arms stung horribly. The seawater would cleanse the wound and prevent infection, but the salty water and carved flesh felt like a hundred bees had stung him all at once.

They were allowed to rest for the remainder of the day, but Masila did not speak a word to them. Instead, he slowly cleaned all of the implements, wrapped them carefully in thick green banana leaves and then sat before them, crossed legged, chanting in the ancient Natui tongue for the gods to bless and sanctify these holy instruments. Their tataus were incomplete, and the process continued the following morning and for five more harrowing days, each session becoming painfully longer. Every day they woke, and the ritual began again. Masila would complete a segment of each tatau, they would wash their wounds, gather food, water and firewood for the night, then settle into a restless sleep. They dreaded awakening each morning, but on the fifth day, to their great relief, the matapule had completed his work. Abel's arm was finished just prior to sundown. The three boys rushed to the sea together and winced in pain at the salty sting which they both abhorred and loved. After the initial agony, the cool water mercifully dulled the pain.

Abel learned that the tatau would not heal properly for many weeks and that he would need to keep the wound cleaned in the sea every day, but he was eager to see the final result as the redness and swelling subsided. When they had rested and awoken the morning after the last tatau ritual, Masila was clearly exhausted and slept much longer that morning than usual. With the twisted vines strewn through his hair turning brown, and his white painted features faded from many days of sweat and focus, he looked frail, with lines of age clearly etched deeply in his face. At one point he caught Abel looking upon him, but instead of berating him for being disrespectful, he simply locked eyes and considered the boy with curiosity, only looking away when Abel became embarrassed and turned his own face downwards.

They were greeted warmly when they returned to Kahoua. As soon as they entered from the northern forest pathways, word spread of their success, and they were soon surrounded by well-wishers who congratulated them for completing their trials. Even Abel was welcomed with enthusiasm, and some of the older warriors took an opportunity to press their cheeks against his, nodding in an unspoken understanding of what he had endured.

His spirits were lifted, and he was warmed by this sudden turn of acceptance amongst the Natui. For a moment, he forgot that he was anything more than just a privileged captive. Whilst Afah was hoisted skyward atop the shoulders of several men, Abel looked out into the crowd to see if he could spot Mahina. He pushed through the crowds to see if he could locate her. When he did, she was standing far away and alone, watching from the edge of the village and beside the trilithon that marked the entranceway to Kahoua and the pathway to the beach beyond. Although she was far, he could see that Mahina's face was dark. Her frown deepened as he approached, and she looked away from him with disinterest.

"Mahina, are you not happy with my return? I missed you dearly. It was an amazing hunt. I have so much to tell you."

Abel moved closer to her, but she stepped back and kept her distance. A look of suspicion cast across her face.

"I did not miss you," she said.

Abel's mirth took a turn, but he persisted further. "If I've done anything wrong, I'm sorry. I just don't know what I've done. We have spent many days travelling, and I can't possibly understand why you would be angry with me. When I was away, I wondered how you—"

"Do you think you are a man now?" Mahina interrupted him while she peered at his new sleeve tatau. "And that you are a great and powerful warrior?"

"No."

"So you are not a man of Natui? You finished the rituals, did you not?" Mahina was quick to ask.

"I did. It's just that I don't think I'm a great or powerful warrior. I'm a man … I have a tatau. Its means 'I am of the sky'."

He leaned forward to show her the intricate patterns. She looked down her nose, showing no additional interest.

"I have more skill with the spear than you. I think I could beat you in a fight. You know I am well trained as a strong woman of Natui. Will you now go into a battle and be killed so you can show you are a man?"

Abel stood silently, unsure what to say. So he said nothing but continued to watch Mahina as she grew more agitated.

"You will go back to your people?

"You know about that? Yes, it's your father's wish that I bring Luther to Kahoua. I must return to Tapu Motu, but I won't go until Ono Hiva has returned."

"And you will return to us?"

Abel's heart was beating quickly. He didn't like being berated, and it wasn't clear what he was being berated for. He only knew Mahina was upset, and this made him uneasy.

She pressed him. "You will not run away and join your people. Maybe you forget about us and you will hide on that island."

"No. I will return," he said emphatically. "I want to return."

He sighed and stood straight, conjuring up some courage before continuing, but looked around to see if they were being watched.

"Mahina. I want to return to you. Of course, I've made friends here. And I don't care you're to be married. I just don't care, and I'll return here because I want to be near you. That's how I feel. Please don't be upset with me."

Abel wanted to embrace her but knew that would provide for dangerous gossip.

Instead, it was Mahina who stepped closer. Her face had softened. She dropped her eyes again to his tatau and for a moment a slight smile appeared on her face. Then suddenly she slapped his shoulder.

"Ow! Why did you do that?" The tatau was still very raw and he winced in pain from the blow.

"Good," she shouted. "You still cry like a little boy. If you return from Tapu Motu maybe I will hit you again."

She walked past him to join her fellow villagers to welcome back her adopted brother. The villagers put Afah back on his feet and Mahina gave him a tight hug and kiss on the cheek.

"What in Jesus's name just happened?" Abel said to himself, nursing his arm, sore from Mahina's swift attack.

TEN

Abel bathed himself in the cool sea and gently washed his slowly healing arm. He was proud of his decorative sky which was now a mark of interest and broken conversation for everyone he met and spoke to, and a great deal of the Natui seem to be friendlier with him since his return five days earlier.

Chief Lokai had arrived with his party of warriors the previous afternoon, and as Abel was walking back from the shore after cleaning his wound, Masila also returned. Unlike the three friends, Masila received no such favourable reception. Instead, most people looked down or pretended not to see him, and even those whom he encountered on his way through the village only briefly exchanged pleasantries with him. He was a lonely figure. Apart from a few of the older men he sometimes drank kava with at night, he was largely disliked because of his unsociability and his habit of berating anyone who found themselves on his path. Few dared to speak against him openly. His influence and his power to converse with the ancestor spirits provided for a fearful reputation. He was chief amongst the faifekau who communed with their beloved gods. As matapule and a faifekau himself, he was key to providing people with the precise knowledge and traditional rites that appeased the gods to grow healthy crops, to bless the new-borns of Natuini who would come from all over the island to receive a ritual of purity which would determine the health and future fortunes of the children.

The matapule was also a master of spies and seemed to have knowledge of many events days before anyone else. Abel noticed the occasional stranger enter the village, sometimes as if having arrived from a long journey only to slip into the chief's meeting hall to provide a message to Masila. Kalafa himself along with a handful of the chief's most trusted men would stand guard. Sometimes the meetings would take hours, while others finished just minutes later.

Although Mahina was still shooting cold stares at Abel, their language lessons commenced again much to the insistence of the frequently inebriated Marcello. It was during one of those lessons some days after his return, Abel saw an unfamiliar warrior entering Kahoua and being taken to a private meeting with Masila and Chief Lokai. A short time later, that same messenger exited the meeting hall, but prior to leaving stopped by Father Marcello's sleeping hut holding a shiny object. The priest walked out to meet the stranger, exchanged a few words, and was given the object, partially obscured by a wrap of banana leaves. However, when Marcello unfurled the leaves, to Abel's astonishment the object was a large bottle of rum, which Marcello took no time in opening. He drank deeply from the bottle, nodding happily at the stranger before disappearing back into his hut.

Mahina had been in the midst of teaching Abel the names of the brightest stars the Natui used for navigation across the seas. Abel stopped and stood to watch the stranger leave through the edge of the village and into the northern tree line

"Is my lesson making you bored?" Mahina raised her eyebrows.

"Did you see that?" Abel said, still looking towards where the visitor had disappeared. Where did that man go? The one who gave the bottle to Marcello."

Mahina shrugged her shoulders. "I don't know." She stood up and playfully yanked on his ear.

"Oi! You enjoy causing me little injuries, don't you?" Abel rubbed his ear.

Mahina giggled with a mischievous look on her face. "It wakes you from your daydreams." Mahina paused with her hands on her hips. Her lips pursed together. "I don't think he is from our village. Let us find out. I am also bored."

"Really? You want to go?" Abel said.

"Yes, it will be like we are hunting. I know the path he is taking and it leads to many others. If we are quick, we can catch him before he takes another. But I warn you, it could take us all day."

"I need to know."

They hastily snatched up water-skins with some provisions for their journey. Abel took his sabre, and Mahina picked up a short spear. Then they quietly left through the back of the village and under the cover of the forest's edge in order to avoid the prying eyes of Masila's spies.

They moved quickly but stepped lightly to not make a noise as they moved through the well-trodden brush. This northern leading forest path was often used by hunting parties and traders from Kahoua and other villages controlled by Chief Lokai, as it connected much of the island to the village in a trade route. Abel had become familiar with its many turns and bulging roots in his adventures with Afah and Maau.

Even though they kept a good pace, Abel was worried that they had lost the man, and he had stepped off the trail at an earlier point. However, he was halted by his companion and told to crouch. Mahina put her finger to his lips to ensure he said nothing, and then pointed ahead of them towards a slight rise in the forest where the path turned upwards and over a small embankment. On top of the rise was the man they were looking for. He had stopped to relieve himself on a tree and was scratching his behind with vigour at the same time, and when he was finished, he turned northeast and left the trail into the deeper and denser woods.

"He should not be going in that direction," Mahina said.

"Why? What's in that direction?"

"That way leads to the resting place of our ancestors. Many years ago, we would go there to grieve and remember our lost ones, but Father and Seagulli have forbidden that for many seasons. No one, except my father or Seagulli may enter."

Mahina waited a few moments and then moved forward again.

"Well, are you coming?"

The young couple followed their quarry at a distance. Despite the man moving slowly through the bush, Abel and Mahina were becoming tired, being forced to scramble low through rough grass and overgrown roots in order to keep hidden. Mahina was significantly more sure-footed and fitter than Abel, having lived and traversed this kind of terrain since a child, and found herself having to guide her companion through some of the denser undergrowth. Abel had always found himself impressed by both her physical prowess and strength. Her body had become lithe and fit from her training with Ruaka. Ono Hiva had insisted the warrior teach her martial skills to protect herself, and she had become adept with the spear and bow with his guidance. Since his arrival, Abel had struggled to keep up with her on their hiking and swimming adventures, but he felt even more endeared to Mahina for thinking nothing of teaching and helping him to survive here. Without her, he was sure he would not have adapted to this environment so quickly.

They reached the top of a high ridge where the trees dissipated and open grass with only sparsely wooded shelter began. They stopped on the rise. Mahina scrunched up her face and faint lines appeared on her forehead.

"I am scared," she said.

"You, scared?" Abel scoffed loudly.

She shushed him, raised her fingers to her lips in alarm. When he realised his voice would carry, he shrugged an apology before stooping even lower amongst the green bushes which kept them hidden from prying eyes. From here they could feel a cool ocean breeze and knew they were close to the seashore when the distant sound of waves became audible. However, their attention was on the unusual sight beyond, where they could see the man they had followed had encountered a larger party of travellers. He appeared to be familiar with them, greeting them with a wave of his hand. Some men and women in the party were transporting live pigs, and some held bundles of supplies, such as baskets of coconut and bundles of rope. Two of the larger men held at least twenty throwing spears between them and once they had spoken to the messenger, all of them continued on their way down a slope towards the coast.

"These are the people of Hule, ruled by my stepmother, Ono Tihani. It is a large village loyal to Chief Lokai in the island's north. They are few in number but the lands there are rich and they produce much food through healthy crops. They are also very good fisherman and strong sailors. Perhaps they are preparing for a long journey. But we are close to the resting place of our ancestors and would not be allowed here unless given permission from my father."

The terrain was more open here so they hid in the long grass until they were certain they could not be seen and then followed the group once more, risking alerting them with every break of a twig or crush of the dry grass beneath them. The path down which the party had walked looked well-worn, sloping steeply towards low cliffs looking out to the ocean. Several smaller islands and patches of a coral reef were in the distance, creating a natural barrier from the rough seas. As they moved further west, they could now see where the island formed a deep, crescent-shaped inland lagoon. The calm water here was deep, pristine and held smooth colours of green and blue, giving the water an otherworldly appearance. On either side, two cliffs leaned out towards each other at a narrower point, as if with hands that longed to touch one another. The dozen men and women set foot on a white sandy beach, which edged around the outside of the lagoon. A pig came loose and there was some light laughter from below, and a younger man ran into the wet sand to retrieve it, falling in the attempt but tackling the pig. The pair soon lost interest in their movements, when their eyes simultaneously caught sight of a dozen other figures hundreds of paces beyond the shore and at least thirty Natui sailing vessels, all under different stages of construction. The grassy banks high upon the dunes had been turned into a makeshift camp where men and women had gathered a large amount of rope and timber material for the vessels. All of the kalia on the shore were in different stages of construction by a team of ship builders. However, it was the great floating object nestling peacefully between those cliffs and anchored in the gentle waters that shocked them the most.

No more than five hundred paces from their hiding spot was an intact and safely anchored three-masted palangi sailing ship and although at a distance, from where they knelt the two could clearly see the movement of several men on board the upper deck of the vessel. It was the nature of the men which provided additional shock to Abel. The figures aboard were both European and Natui.

"Are these your friends?" Mahina said.

"I can't see the faces of those men. They're too far away. I can't understand why Marcello didn't tell me about this."

"His palangi drink. The one you call rum. This is where he takes his rum?"

"It explains why he has so many things and a never-ending supply of ship's grog after so many years. He's been taking what he wants from the ship. This must be the ship he arrived on, but that kind of barque would require dozens of men to sail. So what happened to the rest? Can we get closer?"

Mahina surveyed the beach and cove, shaking her head. "No. The land has nowhere for us to hide, and it would be impossible to walk closer. The men would see us. We could walk back to the cliffs, but we would still be far and could not see any better than now."

Abel slumped into a sitting position in the tall grass and placed his head in his hands. Anger welled from his chest to his head. "All this time there has been a means of leaving and I wasn't told. How could your father keep this from me? What's he planning with all of those other kalia?"

"I do not always know my father's mind, Abel." Mahina sighed and sat beside him. She took his hands from his face and held them in hers. "Are you so much sad you cannot leave Natui?"

He thought about what he had said and realised that it must have sounded uncaring to someone he had grown so close to.

"Now that I'm here, I sincerely do not wish to leave your side at all. My heart belongs in two places. Mahina, please understand that I have a duty also to my people. I have family on Tapu Motu and there is the doctor. He was always good to me. They want to return home."

The two sat in silence, watching the beachscape for a further sign of what was afoot. Suddenly Mahina stood up, pulling Abel to his feet.

"Are we going home?" Abel said.

"No. We are finding the answers you seek, and I know someone we can ask."

❈

From an early age Tihani had always been told someone gifted her with unusual beauty. As she grew from child to comely young maiden, her name, which meant "fortunate girl", was often spoken of as mirroring her startling appearance and highborn bloodline. With her long dark hair resting on her shoulders, servants would say they heard the people call her the most beautiful woman in the world. At ten years old her mother told her that her eyes were as gentle as frangipani flowers and many a suitor would be so allured that she was destined to marry only the greatest of hou'eiki. She had also grown tall and lithe; as tall as the sturdiest men of Hule. She had known that her extraordinary looks could be both alluring and intimidating. So, as Tihani grew, she turned this to her advantage and coupled with a calm and whispering voice, she found she could easily persuade others to her will. Men and women alike.

In time, with her marriage, she found that power of her beauty had found its limits. For her bountiful womb, promised by her mother and father in exchange for a special relationship with far-off lands, had produced no boys. In fact, no offspring at all. When it was clear after some years that no children would come of her marriage, she was unable to keep favour with the chief, who cast her aside and, in a bitter rage, banished her to the furthest point on Natuini. More than that, so angry with her and believing her to be negligent in her duty to produce heirs, Lokai ordered her never to leave Hule – a village that had become her prison. Time had passed, and she had seen five harvests and as many seasons of merciless hurricanes batter the world since she last set foot outside her new home. In that time her husband had not travelled to see her even once.

Perhaps, as she now thought, it was a curse and not fortune that destined for the great chief of Natui to lay his eyes on her as she journeyed to Natuini many years ago with her mother and father. Both were nobles of Ha'amoa known as Matai amongst her own people. At barely sixteen years of age, she was brought to Natuini with her parents as part of a diplomatic approach to Chief Lokai to procure an agreement of trade between her Ha'amoa and Natuini. The islands of Lokai were now called home, or now during her darkest days, her luxurious prison. Though she didn't learn of her fate until her wedding day, Lokai had already arranged for the strengthening of ties to Ha'amoa to be consummated through their marriage. He desired a son or many sons to ensure his blood lineage would rule into distant generations to come. She could remember the day vividly when she became the second wife of her estranged husband and the nightmare that ensued. Fate would prove he was neither handsome nor kind and his appetite to conceive a child was voracious. Though ultimately futile. She still remembered the tears when she said her final goodbyes to her family and longed more than anything to one day see them again. Dreams of escaping and returning to her family invaded her sleep most nights. Perhaps she could run to a trusted uncle. This would be a breaking of custom even if marriage suffered greatly between husband and wife but was not entirely unheard of. However, Lokai had kept her captive, and without the ability to communicate or leave beyond more than two hundred paces in any direction, the dream to be reunited with her loved ones was starting to drift into fantasy. Not that she had lost hope in her loneliness. For she had bided her time, and in her captivity, had slowly regained a semblance of power, albeit slowly and discreetly.

In the light of a fire, she stood naked at the centre of her spacious fale which was adorned with the finest tapa mats, precious ornaments and many other gifts from her vast entourage of admirers. Two handmaidens, their hands working rhythmically, massaged her skin from shoulder to foot with cool coconut oil. She closed her eyes and breathed deeply, loving the sensual hands of the young ladies who she had handpicked for their own not insignificant beauty and had become her trusted companions and confidants. When she had signalled she was ready, they carefully pulled tight her bark skin ta'ovala, wrapping the knee-length skirt around her waist with the finest of black woven coir rope. Then a necklace of pearl and cowrie shell was draped around her neck, crossing over her bare breasts. Kneeling to her side, one of her maidens slipped a natural fresh water pearl bracelet onto her wrist whilst the other placed a light crown of dyed red feathers of the fruit dove upon her head.

"You're beautiful, as much today as you have ever been," said Lulu, the eldest of the two Ha'amoa servants who remained in service to Tihani after her marriage. They had remained by her side since arriving with her many years before. Her younger servant, Samena, was only sixteen years old but had been moulded into a loyal and well-educated young lady.

"Just lovely." Standing back and gazing over her lady, Lulu nodded approvingly. "Your guests await you outside."

"Refreshments," Tihani said.

Samena left the fale to prepare food and drink for Tihani's unexpected arrivals.

"You say Mahina is with the favoured palangi boy my husband has kept all to himself for so many months? Tell me. What does he look like?"

"Hmm. I don't know," Lulu said. "It was dark and we dressed them both in the tapa of mourners so they would be covered from head to toe. No one in Hule can see their faces. Though, if I am pressed for my opinion, he probably looks like the black clothed god-man, Marcello."

"Surely not? Marcello is an old man and, as I understand, this boy is not much older than Samena."

"They all look the same to me," Lulu said dismissively. "But I suppose this one has younger features and is less brain addled by that palangi juice you love so much."

Tihani smiled. "I've heard that he's more than a boy. I've heard from some that he's most pleasing on the eye."

"What does it matter, my lady? Take your mind off such things. You're not permitted to be alone with a man and its best that you turn such matters from your head."

Lulu was being sarcastic, of course. Tihani followed her own set of rules, though this took some level of discretion from those trusted favourites she kept close to her. Her servant gathered up the spent cups which had held the coconut oil used to rub upon her now glistening body.

Tihani still kept a slight smile. "That has never stopped me before. Anyway, I may look at any man or woman I choose. There is still freedom in my eyes and I will look at whom I please. Now, take me to my chair and when I am comfortable, I will have the visitors summoned. This night may yet end with a touch of excitement."

Her sleeping chambers were connected to her meeting fale by a covered corridor which branched off at its mid-point to a large garden, surrounded by a palisade of tall wooden stakes. She could not leave the village. But the chief had ordered the construction of an enormous living abode so that she would at least have space to wander within her own chambers, and when she wanted to spend time outside, she could do so in privacy. She maintained a garden area to bask in the warm sun during the day. Her large fale was also deliberately built in the centre of the village to ensure that she could not easily leave without being noticed by people of her village who were loyal to her husband. However, for many years she had bided by her orders and had given no reason for the Natui chief to be concerned that she would break away from his prison, and this had meant that the attention of spies had dulled to boredom.

Tihani, through her significant charm and wealth as the noble of Hule and wife to the chief, had turned most of those spies into her own loyal servants. Much of the information that flowed through Kahoua was first spoken to her own ears for approval prior to its dissemination across Natuini. She was not so naïve as to believe she was not being watched; however, these days, most of Lokai's people were distracted by the grand construction of a fleet of ships on the northern beaches. The village was also less populated for the time being, as a large camp had been set up by the coast so that the workers, sailors and shipbuilders of Hule would not have to travel back and forth as the work progressed. A great many visitors from around Natuini would come to pay tribute to her, and so it was not entirely uncommon for people to arrive at unusual hours. Whilst they would be rejected, if not convenient to Tihani, this unexpected announcement of visitors was decidedly special, given the secretive nature of the approach.

Her living and visitors fale were as equally spacious and ordained with all manner of decoration. Some of the tapa mats which lined the entire timber floor of the chamber had taken months to weave by the ladies of Hule, but she was also prudently generous and had given away as many fine Natui crafts as she received, often to influential nobles of Natuini, who in turn would ensure that they remembered her during a fair harvest or when they had themselves enough crafts to share with her. Some of them were young men or the mothers of young men, hopeful with the dream of one day being able to woo her in marriage if the chief were to pass, and some of the mothers attempted to gain her favour, hoping to offer their sons up for the same purpose.

Checking herself, she stood in front of a low seat draped with layers of soft and colourful bark cloth facing the entrance. She made herself comfortable and summoned Lulu.

"How do I look?"

"Beautiful, my lady. But you know that already." Lulu smiled sweetly.

"If that's true, then I am ready to receive these mysterious guests. Let them approach."

Lulu ushered the two travellers through the heavy covers of the fale. As they lowered their mats, Tihani welcomed the two and leaned forward to kiss their cheeks. She smiled as she sat down and then gestured with her long delicate fingers towards the seats that had been prepared opposite.

Mahina had found Samena and persuaded her to keep their visit secret. She had given them funeral mats for the couple to wear. The mats extended behind their heads, helping them hide their faces. They walked into the village unrecognised, and if they were seen by the dim fire light, they would be considered mourners, a weary couple travelling through the village on their way to pay respects to the family of the deceased. The mats were uncomfortable but suited their purposes, and now that they were settled, they squirmed in the itchy body length coverings.

"My love. Little Mahina. You're not so little now, are you? All grown up since last I saw you at least two seasons ago?"

The travellers were hot and weary from the day's travels and her faced turned piteous with concern as Samena entered with a wicker basket of fresh fruit, dried fish and ripe drinking coconuts.

"Thank you, Samena."

"My lady." The young lady stepped away.

"Please, be refreshed. The mangoes are perfect."

They were grateful for Tihani's offering and were famished, so didn't hesitate to drink deeply from the opened coconut and the lush water within. The young man picked up large slices of mango and bit a chunk, sighing with relief as his hunger abated. Tihani noticed his occasional gaze. When she made eye contact, he looked away with embarrassment. She was used to the stares from young men and smiled as he tried to hide his interest in her. He was handsome and exotic, and certainly nothing like the god-man Marcello. Even Samena was staring unashamedly.

"You look like you've travelled far and without comfort to be here. To be so far from home at such a time of night, the lovely daughter of the great Ono Hiva must have important news to share?"

"Important questions, Ono Tihani but please forgive us for intruding so late. I bring with me a friend. His name is Abel and I trust him to share our words."

"He is also very handsome. I think I'll take a closer look."

The lady leaned forward. With her face very close to his, she took his chin between her thumb and index finger, examining his features.

"You are a good-looking young man. And your eyes, so blue. Just like a calm sea during the light of mid-morning."

"Thank you, lady." He sounded nervous.

Much to Tihani's pleasure, Mahina's face tightened and her lips pursed together tightly.

Not the reaction of a mere friend, she thought. *This could be interesting.*

"He understands Natui?" Tihani leaned back again and took a sip of her drink. "I'll need to be careful with my compliments so you don't think I'm trying to steal you away from my beloved step-daughter."

"We're not together, as you insinuate." Mahina's voice raised an octave. "I'm to be married to the son of Chief Doko."

"I only intended to have some fun with you both. A little laugh? After all, it has been many years since I saw you last. In fact, your visits to my lovely cage could not be considered frequent."

Mahina took a breath and looked embarrassed at the rebuff.

"Never mind, daughter. Even in marriage, you may still look upon a handsome face and, if you like it, there are many hiding places for young lovers to keep themselves away from the prying eyes of others."

She looked over at Abel and winked. He blushed, his cheeks turning a distinctive red hue in the dull fire light. A blush she loved to see.

"If she's not interested in your beauty, I might welcome a visit from you another evening when you're without a companion. Perhaps I could help you remove that warm ta'ovala and free your body to the midnight air. I've not seen the body of a young palangi man without the trappings of cloth."

"Enough Tihani." Mahina raised her voice again and sprung to her feet.

"Ah, I see you *do* care for this one. Please take a seat once more. I did not want to offend."

She gestured for her to sit. Mahina did so reluctantly and only after providing a baleful glance at Abel. He was still red-faced from Tihani's flirtatious advances.

"I apologise. It's late, and I'm still within the lands of dreams. Such wonderful dreams. It's a place I like to be. You must understand, these days the walls of the village of Hule are my boundaries, and I'm unable to venture further than a hundred steps from this very fale.

"We are sorry to disturb you, Ono Tihani. Mahina said that you could help us understand something we have seen today." Abel spoke with some renewed confidence but she could see the worry in his tired face. What could be so important that they would risk capture and punishment if they were caught with each other so far from Kahoua?

"Your Natui is crude, but you have a smooth voice, which I like to hear. Tell me how I might enlighten you?"

Abel started to reply, but was interrupted by Mahina.

"I will relate what we have seen, so it is clear. And I will translate for Abel if he cannot explain himself in our language. He will speak English and I will tell you his words," Mahina said.

She told a story of how she met Abel and his acceptance into the village by Hou'eiki Lokai. It was an incredible story and left Tihani wondering why her husband had let a young man spend so much time with his daughter. A dangerous decision no doubt. She was also told about the messenger who met with Marcello. That when they reached his destination, they saw a foreign vessel and a boatbuilders village constructed on the northern beaches.

When she finished, Tihani gestured to Samena. The servant left the fale but returned shortly after with a wrapped parcel and three coconut shells which she arranged before them. Samena stepped back with another gesture from her lady. Tihani unwrapped the parcel and exposed a glass bottle.

"You drink rum? Where did you get it from?" said Abel.

Picking up the bottle in her hands, she uncorked the neck and offered to pour the dark liquid into their cups. Mahina leaned back with a look of disgust. Abel nodded and accepted.

"Good," she said, pouring a small amount into their vessels. She took a half shell of coconut water and diluted the alcohol before picking it up with both hands, sipping the concoction, eyes closed and with a pleased expression.

"I have grown a taste for this *palangi* drink. Most of all for the way it makes me feel."

Abel drank and winced at the harshness of the flavour.

Opening her eyes, Tihani stood and walked to the entrance of the fale, pulling open the draped curtain to catch a moment of evening breeze.

"Some time ago I was also curious as to why your Marcello wanted this rum of his. So I persuaded one of Masila's messengers to bring me a sample. Ever since, when Marcello receives his, I also receive mine. The shipbuilders tell me there are hundreds of such bottles, even after so many seasons passed, and that Chief Lokai rewards the palangi priest with some paltry gifts from the ship in exchange for his teachings. And his silence. At first, I didn't like the taste, but mixed with coconut water I have grown accustomed, and it makes my lonely nights in Hule bearable." She raised the cup and sipped again.

"What's happening down there?" Mahina said. "Please, Ono Tihani, tell us."

Returning to her comfortable seat and resting the bowl on her lap, she considered how much of her knowledge she should share. Not everything. That wouldn't serve her at all. Just enough of the parts she wanted them to hear. And there would most certainly be a price.

"I don't know what he's planning. I've tried to understand his mind, even from as far as Hule. His games are a mystery to me, that I promise you. However, I am willing to relate to you a story. I will tell you what I know and more, but I must ask a favour of you in return when this is done."

"And that favour is?" Mahina said, raising her eyebrows.

"Not something I ask of you. It's a favour from your friend, Abel."

The two friends looked at each other.

"Of me? I have little I can give."

"I don't ask of material things. Only that you will consider a favour in the future. I will not ask you to work against the direction of your heart, but that you consider what I might ask of you in a time of need. In return, I will continue to share the things I know, and given my knowledge, that is a generous gift."

Abel's faced turned to the side in confusion. "I'm sorry. Please say that again. It was difficult to understand. You want a favour of me?"

"Explain this carefully to your friend," Tihani said to Mahina. "I want him to understand what I have asked of him."

Mahina grimaced, but translated. Though Tihani could not understand the words spoken between them, she was certain her daughter-in-law would be warning him not to accept her terms. They spoke briefly, and from the look on Mahina's face, he had made a choice she did not approve of.

Abel turned back to Tihani. "I agree."

"Good. Now we may speak." She smiled and told them at least some of what she knew.

Ship's arriving from foreign lands were a rare but remarkable event. Many witnesses were reluctant to speak of it. But Tihani, through her patronage of the village and its inhabitants, had gained the trust of the people of Hule, and the wives of its warriors saw her as their finest treasure. Despite her own imprisonment, she had brought much wealth and favour to their farms and villages. Traders with plentiful stock would stop regularly through Hule to call upon the lady, and this meant that the village had a frequent flow of goods and materials for the people here to thrive. The women and some of the fakafefine had become her ears as they lay with their husbands and lovers, the warriors, defenders and fishermen of Natuini. The tales men would tell at night with the promise of earthly pleasures had garnered much information for Tihani. Of all the stories, the night of the palangi's arrival during the first year of her banishment was still the most intriguing.

The monstrous ship had arrived during peaceful weather and had anchored in the gentle but deep lagoon, close to the burial ground of the Natui ancestors. There had been tales of palangi vessels before and the people were wary of the pale-skinned people who had come from afar to trade or explore. When Chief Lokai learned of their arrival he travelled with Masila and his personal guardsmen, including the mighty Kalafa.

The palangi had been cautious to stay within the bay and did not venture far onto land. The people of Hule also stayed at a distance until Chief Lokai arrived, but when he did, he ordered every man of the village to attend with spear and shield.

He led a party of two hundred warriors to the lagoon, keeping the host of men hidden in the forest and just a small group of personal guard surrounding him. When he stepped on the beach, the palangi leader and Marcello came out to greet him. It became clear that the palangi travellers wanted to trade and not fight, and they had many questions about where they could find precious stones from the earth. They needed fresh food to replenish their ship and they had travelled through a number of friendly lands, having stopped in Fisi, Tonga and Ha'amoa before reaching their shores. She explained that even then, Father Marcello could speak some of the Natui language, which allowed for both sides to be understood. This proved to be a slow process and required many days of talks for the Palangi's to explain themselves and for the Natui to agree for an exchange of trade items.

After five days, goods were traded and relations between the two sides had been amicable, to the point where some of Chief Lokai's men could board the great palangi ship and feast with their men aboard.

Marcello and the leader of the palangis did not know the extent of Lokai's hidden warriors, and they did not understand the true danger that awaited them. They were completely unprepared for what happened next. Although there had been a peaceful exchange of words and goods, a few of Marcello's fellow journeymen and an equal number of Lokai's' warriors began to fight on the beach. No one could say how it began, or who was responsible, but men on both sides were bloody and hurt from the battle, including Marcello who had been eating an evening meal alongside his leader on the beach.

Chief Lokai ordered his men to attack the ship, and they swarmed from the forest in droves. Some of the foreigners had tried to come ashore to save their captain, but they were dragged off their vaka only to be beaten or killed. With the fighting on the beach, and the havoc caused by a dozen warriors already on the ship, the palangis were in disarray. When the bulk of the chief's men reached the beach, they dragged down dozens of small vaka which had been hidden just out of sight that very evening. Chief Lokai had some of the palangis captured. But before it was done, Kalafa took his pakipaki and struck the leader of the palangis dead with one blow to the head.

It didn't take long for the foreign ship to be taken and with it the palangis' surrender, seeing that their leader was lost and they were outnumbered by the sudden arrival of Lokai's hidden tribesmen.

Taken to the beach, most of the palangis were made to kneel in a long row, entirely surrounded. Tihani explained that in defending themselves, the palangis had killed more than a dozen Natui with their loud weapons which kill without touching, and showing the men of Hule the bodies of their fallen brothers and cousins, Kalafa sent the warriors of Hule into such a fury. He told them the palangis had planned to kill them all and take them as slaves and had now taken the lives of so many Natui. That's when the killing began. The palangis, surrounded and with nowhere to run, tried to fight back, but Lokai's men butchered them. Some drowned attempting to escape after swimming into the deep lagoon.

Only eight men were allowed to live. Marcello and seven others. When Lokai returned to Kahoua, he took Marcello, and kept the others as slaves; their only duty to be to maintain the ship. They would keep it harboured safely and repaired as needed.

Tihani had been told that some of those men had died since trying to escape or through sickness.

The ship had remained harboured beyond the northern beaches. No one had been allowed to return there under threat of death. For reasons unknown to Tihani, the men of Hule were ordered not to speak of what happened, their lands and women to be forfeit if any of Hule's people were to relate to others what happened that day. The Natui of Hule kept their word, and over the years the memories of that day began to fade. Only a small contingent of Hule's warriors watched over the ship and the remaining palangi. However, almost four full moons ago Lokai ordered his ship builders to construct dozens of kalia in the same lagoon. The northern beaches are peaceful and well hidden. It was some distance from any major village so served no purpose as an entry into the island for trade. Being sacred, many of the superstitious Natui would stay away from the lagoon and avoid fishing near its waters. Few would dare venture to its beaches; except of course for a few dozen inhabitants of Hule who had been entrusted with its secrecy and to be jailors to a couple of pitiful souls, captured many years ago. Now, a hundred men and women lived on its shores, building ships, growing crops and creating stocks of food and supplies. Its secret was becoming harder to hide.

Tihani had learned of travellers caught trying to venture close to the area, only to be turned back by Hule's scouts, and more than one trader from the outer islands had questioned Tihani about rumours they had heard of shipbuilding and the amassing of rope, livestock and weapons. Beyond what she knew of the sudden work and goings-on beyond Hule, the reason for the sudden build-up of vessels was unknown to her.

"Beasts. Kalafa is a beast. The people of this place are murderers. They butchered those men for nothing!" Abel said.

"Not so, my newest friend. You see, the men of this village, when the blood spilling was done, and they spoke to each other of the events of that evening, no one could remember how any of it began. Lokai told the men of Hule that he believed the foreigners had ill intent all along, but we are not foolish. Not one man can recall the palangi raising their weapons against us. There was some shame and regret. You must understand that we're all subject to the rule of the hou'eiki, and their orders must be obeyed without question. Soon after the events their sense of shame was replaced by the distraction of life that we must all live, the children we must birth, the crops that we must grow. When people leave this earth, we must sometimes let our emotions leave with them for we would cry forever otherwise."

"I can't understand any of this. Why would Marcello hide this from me? Surely if it was all some mistake, they would know I would not be afraid of the truth. And what of the fleet they're building? I want you to tell me more."

"There is nothing more to tell. Though it is something I am afraid of ..."

Tihani lingered on the last words and looked into the fire light which was slowly dying. She was being deliberately coy. Tihani always kept some information at hand for use at a later time. Her knowledge empowered her. The young man's friendship would be needed in the future, so she gave away just enough to secure a promise.

"Now I've relayed to you what I can. I'm tired and neither of you can go home tonight so you'll be my guests. Abel, you'll sleep here, and Mahina will stay with me in my chambers. Before first light, Lulu will awaken us and I will bid you farewell."

Next morning, Samena woke Abel and Mahina gently. A small package of fruit wrapped in banana leaves was provided to them, and they quenched their thirst with coconuts and prepared to journey back to Kahoua.

Standing in the entrance of the fale, Tihani awaited them, wide-eyed and awake, as if she had slept many more hours than they had. The couple were stifling yawns, still exhausted from the previous day's journey.

Mahina thanked the lady for her hospitality, though there was a coldness in her voice.

Tihani regarded her with a solemn gaze. "I know you despise me, child. That is because your mother scorns me and still blames me for taking our husband's gaze from her fading beauty. You should understand, daughter, that I didn't wish for any of this. If I could go back to that day, when your father chose me, I would've run to the cliffs and dashed my body upon the sharpest of rocks below."

She could see that Mahina's eyes were glistening, but she held back from releasing any tears.

"I'm sorry, Ono Tihani. I've treated you so poorly. You provided us with shelter and I've been so rude to you …"

"Do not apologise, young one. For nothing is given entirely freely." Tihani turned to Abel and took his hand with a firm grip. "There is something I wish to ask of you and your palangi friends, in exchange for the knowledge I gave in such detail. I have risked my life for your curiosity and now I seek something in return." She could see he understood.

"Fine then. I've already promised to help you. Tell me what you want," said Abel.

"No, not now," Mahina said. She tugged on his shirt, trying to pull him away.

Abel turned to her with surprise. However, Tihani took his face in her hand and swiftly pulled him back, ignoring her step-daughter.

"If you and your palangi friends take the ship and leave this island, I want you to promise to take me with you and return me to my family in Ha'amoa." She narrowed her gaze and pulled him closer.

"You want me to take you back to Ha'amoa? On that ship? Is that what you want?"

"Promise me. It is what must be given for my knowledge. Promise me, or I'll curse you and your people."

Abel looked at Mahina, his confusion clear, but when she translated Tihani's words, he steeled himself and turned back to her.

"Very well. I will do what I can. You must understand this may be beyond my control. I'm no chief. I'm captain of no one," he said.

"Your promise to try satisfies me enough."

She nodded to Lulu who ushered the two to leave. But as they did, they were confronted by a strange figure at the entrance and were startled by his abrupt appearance. A grizzled man of almost fifty years, with matted hair and sun scorched skin. He wore a ta'ovala, but was bare chested, his body from ankle to neck covered by tatau of snakes which in the glimmer of torchlight seemed to move as if alive on his leathery skin. He stared wide eyed, not at all happy with their presence.

"Are we to be alone?" His voice was as leathery as his face.

Tihani nodded at the entrant. She was expecting his arrival.

"The lady must see her guest. It is time for you to take your leave." Lulu bustled Abel and Mahina out of the fale and into the morning sun.

The sun was already above the horizon when they returned from their journey. Little was said between them along the way, and they had rushed home as soon as they could. They had considered sneaking closer to the ship but changed their mind at the thought of being discovered. Emotions ran high. Abel was overcome with confusion after hearing the story from Ono Tihani. He was equally fearful of being questioned about their whereabouts and when they finally could see the campfires of Kahoua their fears seemed realised as they saw a great commotion from the village. It seemed the entire inhabitants were crowded together, standing and shouting with excitement.

"Are they looking for us?" Abel stopped short before entering from the edge of the village. Kahoua's surrounding forest was sparse but provided some cover from view.

"I'll go alone, Abel. Stay here until it's safe. I think I know what's happened."

She glanced at Abel for a moment before turning and moving into the village, whilst Abel moved further around the edge. A copse of trees provided a vantage point where he would not be seen. Rising voices from the villagers became louder, but when the cheering began he knew the commotion was unrelated to their disappearance.

He emerged to see dozens of villagers gathered outside in a throng of excitement, bunched together with gleeful faces. A small huddle of faifekau hurried to Lokai's meeting fale, pushing through the crowds. Lokai's aunt Sieta marched with purpose amongst them. A powerful matriarch of the family, even Lokai spoke to her with the utmost respect for fear of a firm rebuke. She was flanked by a retinue of servants whose shoulders and arms were weighed down with heavy mats and decorative tapa. Abel knew that if koloa was being prepared, there was a celebration planned.

Abel was spotted by Maau and his father Aunofo.

Aunofo smiled when he saw Abel and strode towards him.

"Great palangi warrior, Kafa e faifolau. Where have you been? We've been looking for you."

"Nursing my tatau. It needed cleansing in the ocean, but I fell asleep on the beach."

He patted his arm to emphasise the pain and winced with the genuine agony. It was easy enough to show the effects of the grievous wound caused by Masila's art when it was strikingly real.

"You and my son have been brave. He and you have become like brothers. There is much to be joyful for, and my spirits have reached such a moment of mafana. Abel, I would like you to think upon a request. Something that my wife and I have given great thought to."

"Of course, 'Eiki Aunofo. I'd be happy to help with anything you need. Maau has become a good friend."

Aunofo looked pleased and nodded. "I hope that you will say *brother*, Kafa e faifolau. Your own father is far away. I know you have told us he is alive, but if I could speak to him, I would ask that you could also be my son. To live in my household and to have a family of Natui for yourself. Maau has no brother, and my wife and I have not been able to give him one, so I want to ask you this solemnly; will you become my son and allow me to adopt you as one of my own?"

Maau was smiling and nodding feverishly, pleading with Abel to agree. He was sure he had heard the Natui correctly. Aunofo, a noble and closest friend of Chief Lokai, had asked him to be his son. It was a shock. Especially with so many other events racing around his head. He was lost for words, simply staring in disbelief at the older man and his friend. He had formed such a powerful bond with Maau and Afah.

Aunofo's face softened from happiness to gentle understanding. "It is much that I ask of you, and I know you'll need to consider your own heart for the answer. Take your time, Kafa e faifolau." He placed both arms around Abel, giving him a powerful embrace before stepping back a pace. "There is more good news. The lady of Natuini is returning. Our people have seen her kalia, and she brings the Hou'eiki of Mo'unga Vela with her. The people are so very happy."

"They're arriving tonight?"

"Before marriage, it is a Natui tradition that a betrothed nobleman enters the home of his wife to show dignity and respect to her family. This must be on foot, with the offerings of the land

and sea before him. They must enter through the great gates. Masila's duty is to welcome them."

Aunofo looked down at Abel's appearance. His shirt and pants were covered in the muck of travel. He only had the one set of clothes and over the months they had become frayed and worn with noticeable rips.

"You must be ready and dress properly for the celebrations. Your palangi clothes are unclean. Maau will give you one of his finest ta'ovala to wear around your waist while your clothes are soaked."

The nobleman placed his hand on Abel's shoulder. "You are not of noble blood like my son, but you are noble in spirit. You are palangi but you are one of us now, so you must look like a man of Natuini."

ELEVEN

"You say they've been sitting out there just waiting and waving a white cloth?" Luther stood at the water's edge beside his most skilled scouts, Cambridge and Rowe.

"Yes, sir," Cambridge said. "We spotted the vessel travelling to about that point, two hundred yards out from shore. We guessed they wanted to be seen but didn't want to come too close. They just wave that same white cloth. Haven't stopped at all since they arrived."

Private Rowe handed his lieutenant the spyglass. "And then we looked closer. Take a gander at *who* we saw."

Luther rubbed the lens with his shirt sleeve before bringing the spyglass to rest on his right eye. A double hulled canoe floated lazily on the water.

The sail boat held just six men on the vessel's single deck. They stood calmly aboard and had perched themselves in the calmer waters of the reef with their sail furled. When he turned his attentions to each of the men, he was astonished to see Abel. He was dressed in the same fashion as many of the Pacific Island males he had encountered; bare chested but with a woven bark skin waistcloth around his lower half. His young cousin's blonde hair was much longer than when he last saw him, and he seemed taller and much more muscular.

"My God, it's Abel. He's alive. Doesn't look like he's a prisoner. I can't see any weapons on the others with him," Luther said.

"They're not here for a bout of fisticuffs." Rowe chuckled as he jabbed his fellow marksman on the arm. "Certainly not with just a handful of men, sir."

"Maybe. But I'm not taking any chances. So the both of you need to move with haste and fetch the good doctor. Also, send back three other reliable marines. Only a few with a bit of sense who can follow orders. I want our people armed and on the beach with me, but I want you and Cambridge out of sight. Rifles ready. If there's trouble, you know what to do."

Cambridge, the staider of the two men, considered their surroundings and gestured towards a steeply rising dune covered in dense shrub some forty yards away.

"Some ample cover on top of there, aye? Close enough for a couple of accurate shots." He tapped the stock of his Baker rifle.

Only the two privates had been issued with these special weapons. Baker rifles were a newer design. Lighter, slower to load and less powerful than the Brown Bess which were a mainstay of British marines. However, they were significantly more accurate at a longer range. This suited the keen-eyed duo, who were light on their feet and expert shots at tremendous distances. Each of them also enjoyed telling anyone who would listen about how they were much more accurate than the other, bragging about how many men they had killed between them becoming a running competition. If the two were to be believed, they had downed dozens of men each, though the figures changed frequently and altered depending on what was most recently reported by the other man.

Vincent agreed with the location for their sentry. "Fine. But listen. Don't let Smith know we have visitors. I don't want him out here causing trouble, and I'm determined not to shoot anyone today."

With a grin and a nod, Rowe and Cambridge saw to their duty, leaving Luther alone. He couldn't help but smile at the knowledge that the young man was alive. He had feared after such a lengthy time without returning, his courageous ward had perished. He had cursed that he did not try to find him. His guilt was deep. But he had his men to think about and he could not have sent his men to their deaths or abandoned them to search for Abel by himself. Now that Abel was returning, his mind became awash with questions of what the poor lad had endured and why it had been so long before he finally came back.

As soon as Luther could see Doctor Wickman and another three marines emerging from the inner island trail, he took off his white shirt and waved it high in the air, signalling to the crew they were safe to approach.

In response, there was a movement on the sailboat. It turned with speed, heading towards the beach. The wind was light but favourable as they unfurled their sail, and he could see the crew were also paddling at pace.

As he donned his white shirt again, the doctor and his company arrived. Wickman was rushing. He stumbled on the sandy beach more than once in his attempt to reach Luther's side.

"You're still the clumsiest man on the crew, Doctor," Luther jested at the physician as he arrived in a puff. "Are you aware that the next stage of human speed, after the walk, is considered the humble run, something you seem incapable of."

"Running is for younger men and soldiers. True gentlemen walk." His voice was indignant as he tried to catch his breath. "Enough of this mockery. Rowe tells me that we have company and Abel is amongst them. Is this true?"

Luther nodded towards the arriving party. "Look for yourself." He turned to the three marines and positioned them several yards away. They were armed with rifles, and each had a sheathed cutlass at their sides.

"Stand at a distance and keep your rifles at ready, but do not menace the natives with them. I don't want any unnecessary bloodshed. Abel is amongst them, which means they may not be hostile. If anything goes awry, I and *only* I will order a volley. Am I understood?"

The three men nodded.

He turned his attention to the party who had anchored their boat in shallow waters twenty-five yards from the water's edge. To his surprise, it was only Abel who disembarked, and while the others on the boat stood and watched Luther's crew on the shore with curiosity, they did not make any move to step into the surf.

Abel waded through the waters towards Luther and Doctor Wickman. His face appeared a mixture of elation and desperation, and as soon as his feet reached dry land, he ran towards his cousin and embraced him with a mighty hug. Luther wrapped his own arms around Abel. For a long time, the young man held tight. Then suddenly he began to weep uncontrollably, his head buried in Luther's shoulder.

"It's all good now, my friend. You've returned home." Luther held him close. More than once, he steeled himself to prevent his own eyes filling with tears.

Abel, Luther and Wickman had taken shade and sat underneath a crop of young palm trees where they could still see the open ocean. Three marines stood at a distance in between them, keeping watch on the Natui crew, who were keeping watch on them just as intently from their vessel. Wickman poured a cup of water for each, and Abel drank deeply. He shook his head and gave the two men a warm smile.

"I've missed you both ever so dearly. I had feared for what had happened. Sometimes I thought you had even left without me," Abel said.

Wickman was transfixed by his tatau and leaned forward to grasp his shoulder. "What on this God's earth have they done to you? They've marked you with their heathen symbols. The torturous beasts."

Abel winced at his touch and pulled away. His tatau was still red and healing. "No, it's not like that. It was all my choice. It was an honour to be marked, and I wear the sky as a warrior of the Natui. I'm one of them now. I mean … I've been accepted by these people as a Natui man, and I am well-disposed with Chief Lokai, one of their great rulers. I'm teaching his daughter how to speak English, and Lokai plays chess with me on occasion. He's amazingly skilled at the game and beats Marcello all the time."

"Slow down, son." Wickman raised his eyebrows. He was about to speak when Luther interrupted.

"Wickman, wait. I want to hear more".

The lieutenant leaned forward. "Tell me everything. Everything from the moment you left to now and the circumstances of your return. Who is Marcello?"

Abel nodded and took a smaller sip of the water before beginning. Wild stories of his exile grew more excited and at times Luther had to motion for him to stop and slow down. He told them about Kahoua village where he met with the Venetian priest, who acted as his translator. He was friendly at first until the relationship turned sour. Abel told them about Chief Lokai, Ono Hiva and his friends Mahina and Afah, whom Luther remembered from their first encounter many months before. They had become firm companions to Abel. Luther listened intently when he relayed the journey he had undertaken to become a "man of the Natui" and the pain he endured to receive the tatau.

"Bloody heathens," Wickman muttered, earning him a baleful glare from Luther.

The lieutenant encouraged Abel to continue his story despite the interruption. When tales of his travels to the northern shores and the discovery of an intact ship came up, Luther's interest was piqued.

"A sailing ship, with cannon? You're saying there's a vessel harboured and seaworthy? On the other side of the main island?"

"Yes, sir. Seaworthy. And as I said, I think that there were European sailors aboard. I counted as least two, but we dared not venture further. Otherwise, we would have been caught. There's more." Abel told them of Tihani's story, including the killing of Marcello's Venetian crewmen.

"The Natui are building dozens of large vessels, they call 'kalia'. They can transport a great deal of sailors and supplies and are much larger than the vaka I arrived on."

"We? You said we. Who else saw it? Was it the young lady who took you to see one of Lokai's wives?"

"Mahina took me. She was just as surprised as I was with the whole mystery. You can trust her. She's become a really true friend to me and she would never betray me. You can surely trust her."

"A special friend?" Doctor Wickman questioned with raised eyebrows.

"Not like that, Doctor. She is to be wed. But we've become close, and she's helped me learn their language. I've become quite adept and can understand much of their tongue now. It's really a beautiful language."

There were a few moments of silence between the three as Luther mulled over the new information.

"A fleet of ships, but for what?" Luther said. "Abel, I know you want to trust your new friends, but it sounds like they have a history of slaughtering European sailors, and I have to assume any possibility." Luther cast his gaze to the sailing boat and the five men aboard. "What about them? Do we need to be worried?"

"I'm well liked amongst the Natui, and I've told Chief Lokai you mean no harm. They could have attacked you already, but they haven't."

"Tell me, cousin. Have you been able to leave Natuini until today?"

"Not exactly. I have permission to go to all the places the Natui are able to walk themselves, but I wasn't able to leave."

"Then you're an honoured prisoner it seems," Wickman said.

"It's not like that, sir. Chief Lokai has been kind to me, and he says that he'll ensure your safety here. And you have nothing to fear from the Natui people. Those men on that kalia cannot even set foot upon this island since it's so sacred. It's okay for us though. Palangis are unknown to the spirits of the island, and we meant no harm by landing here. The chief has proclaimed this a sanctuary for you."

Luther looked at the doctor again with concern before standing and stretching his back. Turning away from the others, he looked out to the water, straining to see the shores of the opposing island to the north.

"Whatever they've told you, please consider that some of it may not be all true." He stood in place, only moving to swat away a sand-fly buzzing close to his cheek.

Abel stood and walked beside him.

"I believe that Chief Lokai has the best of intentions. Vincent, I have lived amongst them for almost half a year and they've allowed me to be part of their family," he said.

Luther noted the use of his first name as a display of familiarity. That would not be unusual if they were alone, but in the presence of others on the crew it had not occurred before. Luther decided not to react poorly. Regarding Abel, he was unsure what he had been through. It was clear to Luther that this

Abel was different. Despite the initial tears, his young ward had come back looking older and stronger. He stood straighter and carried himself with confidence, not the walk of a subdued captive. Abel had been taken in by the natives and had spent time with a people whose intentions were unclear. But they may have taken advantage of an innocent young man stranded and far from his own people. Luther suspected Abel had seen only what his new friends had chosen him to see.

"You say those men cannot step ashore?" Luther asked, still staring out to sea.

"It's forbidden. Only those of noble blood or a priest or a matapule can set foot on the island. Why?"

"Right now, our scouts are training their guns on your Natui from those far dunes. Cambridge and Rowe have been watching for movement from the mainland for quite some time. More than once, they've seen the arrival of small canoes manned by one or two natives at a time. Your friends are spying on our camp by the freshwater spring. The Natui are skilled traversing their own land but, probably because their spies don't know this island well enough, they struggled to keep themselves hidden. My scouts, who were already expert woodsman, have had almost half a year to map and explore the whole damn thing. And so that advantage has been ours."

There was silence from Abel, but he could see he was considering what this meant.

"I don't understand. No one's allowed here. Vincent, why haven't you repaired *Viritus* and attempted to leave?"

"Soon after you took that girl – Mahina – and her brother to safety. I took command of the remaining crew. Some men died, but we have order now. For the most part, anyway. After that we set about repairing the ship to take advantage of the fit weather. There was extensive damage. Jack Horton thought it possible to repair and refloat the ship at high tide and with the help of other smaller anchored vessels. So we started the repairs and set about stripping the ship to lessen its weight. Horton started to oversee the construction of smaller craft for the job. It was painstaking, but we were making progress until one night about two months ago we found *Viritus* burning once again."

Abel's eyes were open wide in surprise. "Was it one of the crew?"

"Don't be bloody foolish, Abel. We may have some ratbags amongst us but every last one of them is destined for home and would never seek to destroy our chances. You should consider who else might have a reason to keep us here."

The young man's face turned down, so he began again with a softer tone.

"All our men that night were accounted for. Only Private Rowe and Private Cambridge were on scouting duties but on that night and directly in view of *Viritus*. They said that they saw the flames start from the stern, which was facing away from their position. The flames enveloped the deck so quickly that a hastening substance must have been applied. They didn't see who did it, but they certainly didn't see anyone return to *this* shore afterwards. If I knew the damn ship was a target, I would've stationed people on the boat. It was a low tide, so we were able to make it to the vessel and put out the flames, but not before a lot more extensive damage was done. Since then, it's been difficult to maintain morale amongst the crew, and Smith is agitating, but we have been looking at building smaller vessels. Those we have already built are not exactly the height of British naval engineering. Still, they may allow for some medium range island hopping if it came to that."

"I didn't know," Abel said.

"There's something else. Horton's gone. He went missing not a week later. We haven't seen him since and while it's possible he drowned, both our ship and ship's master carpenter have been taken from us in mysterious circumstances."

"Nothing has made sense since I found the ship," Abel said. "It all seems like so much madness. Please listen, Vincent. The reason I'm here. It's because Chief Lokai has invited you and Doctor Wickman to the betrothal ceremony of his daughter. It's my friend, Mahina. She's to marry the son of another rival chief."

"An invitation? Then I guess I'll understand soon enough what this is all about. But Abel, you're going to have to tell me everything you know about this chief of yours and the one you call Marcello."

"I will. I promise I will. On the way, I'll tell you everything I know. There's some good news. Chief Lokai has sent with me supplies for your men. Baskets of yams, fresh fruit and dried fish have been stacked high on the kalia. It's a gift, to show he's peaceful. There are even a few live piglets for roasting."

The lieutenant was surprised by the gesture, and regardless of his misgivings, any extra food was welcome. This island was sizable, but so was the hunger of his men. Some stores had been damaged and perished as the hull of *Viritus* became compromised with sea water. Most of the remains saved from *Viritus* had already been consumed. They had taken many of the crops from the island but without replanting and with much of their nourishment coming from seafood and fruit, their diet was becoming limited. An attempt had been made to sow a crop of potatoes, but the soil was only producing a small crop and their other attempts at growing crops from other seeds bought across on *Viritus* were growing slowly.

"This is welcome. We'll accept this gratefully and hopefully I can thank Chief Lokai in person."

"You'll have your chance soon enough. We need to leave now," said Abel.

Several more sailors were sent for while Luther oversaw the unloading of the precious cargo.

"Mr Millstone," Luther shouted at the only remaining cook of *Viritus*. "Take care in unloading. I don't want any of it dropped into the sea. And I want every last shred of food accounted for and stored securely on the island."

With just one strong arm, Millstone could only supervise the crew unloading the parcels from the kalia. They had formed a human chain to pass the goods back to the beach, though they received no help from the Natui, as they refused to set foot on shore.

Worthstead had come to watch the operation and was sitting on the beach, rifle on his lap.

"You 'eard the man, fatty. Don't you drop a blimmin' morsel of that delicious fare or we'll cook your fat arse just like those fat piggies." He laughed at his own mockery, especially when Millstone shot him a look of disdain.

"I'm not fat anymore, bloody stinker. Nothing to eat but fish and more fish." Millstone had become slimmer over the months and had to tie up his oversized pants to keep them up.

"Oh, but you are still fat. That arse of yours is so enormously 'eavy that it's the only thing keeping this island from floating away and back to ol' Mother England." He writhed in hysterics at the expense of his friend.

"Enough. Hold yourself with pride in the face of the Natui," Luther cautioned. "If they think we're buffoons, then that's what will be reported back to their people."

"Yes sir, I'm sorry sir," Worthstead said, his grin still perched from ear to ear.

"What of Smith? What does he know?"

"Nothin' sir. When he demanded to know what was happening, I told him to 'fuck right off'. I told that hairy bastard that if I heard another question that I'd drown him in his own excrement … sir."

"Very well."

The doctor had been watching Abel as he helped to unload the food and livestock from the boat.

"He's changed, Doc," Luther said.

"Not so much. He was always of good heart and he remains so. I think he genuinely believes that there can be peace between us."

"I'm not saying that couldn't be. However, they have been spying on us. They burned down our ship, probably killed or captured Jack and have been keeping that young man captive on their mainland for almost half a year now. Does that seem like a peaceful relationship to you?"

Wickman frowned and wiped a bead of sweat from his brow. "This all started when we almost killed those poor children. *Whom,* I might point out, turned out to be the children of Chief Lokai. So you can be sure we would all be dead if they didn't survive. We have Abel to thank for selflessly, and at much peril to himself, taking them off this God-awful island and to safety."

"I haven't discounted that."

"So have some faith in the boy. He's still British. And he's still your family."

"Another family has adopted him," Luther countered.

"So what? He's alive and well fed. You could scarcely call him a boy anymore. By his grace it's perhaps that we're still left to our own devices. If you were the chief, would you also want to know what a group of strangers, arrived unannounced and unwanted were up to?"

A sudden warm breeze picked up and the dry sand billowed across the beach. The two men squinted before the breeze calmed again.

"Doctor, we're not far from the next hurricane season, so if we're taking that ship, we'll need a firm plan."

Wickman groaned and shook his head. "Take care of your ideas. We have no idea how they'll react if they believe we know of its existence. Perhaps let us discuss the follies of any such ideas on the way to this celebration."

"You won't be going, Doctor."

"But I thought ..."

"I need you here to provide reason and order if something goes wrong. We have loyal men, and Worthstead will take down anyone who causes trouble, but we are low on officers, and

Worthstead doesn't fully understand my wishes. You do. There are still men who plot against me for my actions against Larkin. I'll go alone, but I'll be taking Andrew Smith with me. Make preparations for a possible invasion in my absence. Also, we don't know if the food is poisoned so let the pigs eat some of the fare before our men ration it out."

"Ridiculous. I cannot prepare these men for battles. I'll be much more effective by your side. Worthstead is perfectly capable and with Cambridge and Rowe watching his back, your position here will be retained until we return. You shouldn't doubt the loyalty these men have for you. The men have accepted your rule. And I'm sorry but did you say you were taking Smith with you?"

Worthstead had overheard. His jaw visibly dropped at the news. "Why on earth would you take that fucking greasy swine, eh sir? Forgive me, sir, it just seems to be a dangerous prospect, given his history. Doesn't the boy hate his guts anyways?"

Luther ignored Worthstead and buttoned up his jacket. He had kept it clean and unused since their arrival. The heat of the day made its wearing unnecessary, but he decided to don the jacket for the occasion ahead. He withdrew and examined the blade of his military sabre. The bright steel reflected blindingly in the midday sunlight.

"I intend to present to the chief and his people with dignity and represent our England with the pride it deserves. Worthstead, I'm making it your responsibility to ensure Smith is presented equally with honour. Issue him with no weapon. You're correct, he cannot be trusted. On the other hand, I want my two pistols cleaned, shining and ready for battle in my hands within the hour. See to it, Private."

"Your wish is my command, sir." Worthstead saluted expeditiously and ran off to see to his mission, leaving the two to observe the movement of supplies to shore.

Wickman remained silent. Luther was relieved he didn't continue questioning his decisions. He wasn't in the mood to hear them. However, although Wickman wished to accompany Luther, he thought the doctor would have been grateful avoiding a dangerous journey. His words were persuasive. The crew of *Viritus* needed to band together regardless of whether he was present to keep control.

"Right then, Doctor Wickman. Pack your bag lightly and be ready to leave within the hour."

He couldn't tell if the twisted reaction on Wickman's face was fear or sheer excitement.

Luther had not always enjoyed the sea. Many years prior to serving on *The Victory* with Nelson, his first outing at sea was at an age not dissimilar to that of Abel's. He could only remember the feeling of the first days of that voyage; sickness, vertigo and the constant cold sweats. However, when that passed, and he was able to view the new world around him, he quickly developed a deep love of the ocean and its vastness. The freedom he felt at sea when the last vestiges of land were behind him lifted his soul. He felt the same upon returning; an intense satisfaction of an honest and successful voyage to serve King and Country. Luther had not taken a wife mostly due to this first love. Though he had occasionally bedded a willing young lady for relief and comfort during nights at port when he longed for a woman's company. He thought it for the best. A wife would spend her whole life waiting for him to return from his voyages.

Many of his journeys were as a junior marine in a time of constant war. Superiors were quick to discover his gift as a remarkably adept swordsman. Under Commodore Nelson he had fought the Spanish during the Battle of Cape Saint Vincent. That conflict was the most memorable for him. Memorable, but not by choice. The blood and guts of the day was a sight he had tried in vain to forget. In the eyes of every patriotic British subject, that battle signified a glorious victory over a Spanish enemy, who held superiority in size if not manoeuvre, and granted further glory to an impetuous Commodore. However, for the men present it was a day of terror during which over three hundred lives were taken by musket, sword and drowning. Battle worn already from previous voyages, his sword skills were put to use in the bloody wet work of a boarded vessel. Before boarding, it was the cannon which broadsided the San Nicolas that he remembered so vividly. Not for the deafening noise or terrible haze of smoke from the gun ports. It was the devastating effects on the human body from the thirty-two pound cannons fired from the gun deck.

During the first volleys, most strikes caused damage and mayhem to the hull of the enemy ship. A few struck above decks. Explosive devastation separated heads from bodies and ripped enemy sailors to pieces, leaving nothing but strewn body parts and bloodied organs spattered across the main deck. This he could not forget. No matter the distraction. He had learned to steel his mind against the emotions that stirred late at night when his mind would wander into past years, hardening himself for each battle and trial to be a consummate leader.

Watching young Abel on the kalia's deck, he wondered if he would become the same man, separated from his emotions and keeping his attachments light. They stood close to the mast, with Abel next to him and Andrew Smith opposite, keeping his eyes trained on Abel. The young man was less than pleased with his presence.

Abel had protested when he heard Smith was coming, but when Luther had demanded this as terms of his attending the event, Abel became resolved to the company he would need to keep and had not spoken to either man since. He had spoken with Doctor Wickman, who still had many questions about Abel's experiences since leaving the island so many months ago. Abel was not in the mood for much conversation.

The Natui were curious about the palangi guests onboard but they concentrated on their sailing and steering duties, allowing the four enough room on deck to make themselves comfortable once the goods had been unloaded and they had set sail.

"Thought you had perished," Smith taunted Abel. "I can't believe that you made it through alive. Seems you've grown a little taller. Certainly darker of complexion since living amongst the savages." He stroked his unkempt beard, looking thinner and more dishevelled since their arrival.

The days since the coup had not been kind to Smith. Although Luther had spared his life, he remained insolent and needed to be confined to small areas of the camp or kept at guard in the same cave he had imprisoned Mahina and Afah. "Treat me like an animal and I'll behave like an animal," he once said. So he had stopped grooming or trimming his beard and no longer washed the muck from his body or clothes. He had taken to picking fights with the marines. They beat him badly, but despite his insolence, he still retained loyalty from some members of the crew.

He scratched roughly at his behind and adjusted the clean red jacket, which was now ill fitting. His weight had diminished from the change in diet and he looked scruffy, even with the officer's uniform he had been forced to wear.

"So what did you have to do to survive, boy? Become the whore of some big cocked island brute did you, aye?"

"Ignore him," Wickman said. "Keep your eyes averted and heed nothing that comes from his poison lips."

"Ha! His silence is fine with me," he grunted before turning to Luther, who was squinting his eyes to make out the approaching shores of Natuini.

"I'm surprised you asked me to come to this primitive's party, but don't think that I'm inclined to be grateful. I suppose you've come to your senses and realise that these savages understand who's really in charge here and want to talk to the officer of rank. That's not you, by the way *Lieutenant*," Smith laughed and shook his head. "Mutineers don't hold rank."

Luther turned around. "Even here, on the ocean and surrounded by God's greatness, you cannot come to find humility in the face of adversity. We were once brothers. Of a different ilk but nonetheless we are Englishmen and with that comes a responsibility."

"What are you fucking talking about, you righteous cunt? We're stranded. There's no England here. Only a bunch of godless monkeys who need to be destroyed before they kill every one of us. You talk of being English, but you turned on your duty the moment one of these whelps needed saving. And for what? The death of your own kind. Our ship in flames. Horton probably being carved up for meat by your boys' new friends. But that's just dandy because we're going to tea with the fucking savage queen or king or whatever sub-human your boy Abel here has been turned into."

"That's well enough, Smith. Please leave Abel alone. He's been through so much already without your vulgar mouth flapping away," Wickman chastised the midshipman, but only earned himself a glare of disgust.

Smith continued, ignoring the interruption. "I mean, look at his arm and the devil's writing tattooed upon himself. You've all fallen low. You'll burn in hell, you will. You can drink some fucking tea with the fucking savage king of the monkeys for all eternity." By the end of his diatribe, Andrew Smith had formed a froth upon his lips and spat the mess upon the deck in front of Abel.

Abel clenched his fist and began to move forward, but with a quick hand Luther held him back.

"Abel, pay no attention," Luther said. "Come and speak with me, Smith. You need to understand our situation in perspective."

He moved to the port bow and stood on the edge, gazing at the large island ahead. They were halfway to their destination, and the Natui rowers were making quick progress with each stroke of a paddle.

Smith pulled himself around the mast and walked by Abel, who was still in a rage at the midshipman's insults. He joined Luther's side.

"In all seriousness, Vincent, what's your game here. Are we here to trade goods or have we found a way off the island? I'd like to not fucking die in this hole"

"I'm not sure. I don't really know what's going to happen when we step off this boat. I just know that you've proven yourself irredeemable and I couldn't leave you behind with the others, but I needed to leave so that's where we find ourselves now." Luther patted the midshipman on the back. "For now. Just for a moment. Look upon the beauty of this world and this place. There is a design to the place. You cannot deny the potential for God's hand in this paradise. The air so fresh, and the sea, it has always calmed me even at the worst of times." Luther closed his eyes for a moment and drew his breath deeply.

Smith laughed mirthlessly. "I see nothing but water and some pockets of land that are lucky not to be dragged to the bottom of the ocean. You witness a wonder of God. I see a desert fit only for the lowest form of beast. So fuck you and your opinion on who is irredeemable or not. We all know that no matter what you pretend to be, when we return to our beloved England you're going to be hung for your sins."

"It's a shame," Luther said. He opened his eyes.

"What's a shame?"

"That you couldn't find this moment to make peace. That in these moments you could not end with dignity."

Luther deftly drew a knife from his belt. It was so unexpected that Smith had little time to react and within moments the lieutenant had taken him in a headlock with his left arm and reached around with his right hand to his exposed throat. In a vain attempt to protect himself, he threw up his hand to his neck to stop the blade and struggled to break loose, but Luther thrust a powerful knee to the back of Smith's legs, and he sank to the deck. Only the tip of Smith's pinkie finger had intercepted between knife and flesh. The knife, well sharpened and oiled, neatly sliced through his finger which dropped with a small tap upon the timber decking whilst the rest of the blade cut the man's throat deeply, through to his windpipe.

Smith gagged and gasped. At first there was a small spurt of blood and then a flood of thick red liquid ran down his neck. Luther held his throat and quickly cut even deeper. Smith flailed, trying to break free from the torture.

The Natui crew stopped to watch the violent scene. Their hands dropped to their clubs but they made no moves to stop him. Abel and Wickman stood by each other, eyes and mouths wide open as blood splashed across the deck. Luther held the flailing man tightly as his life was ending.

When the doctor finally found his own voice to speak, he shouted, but it was all too late. "My God, what have you done. Vincent, stop!"

The dying man's body struggled and convulsed. Then after some time, the spasms slowed and stopped until he went limp. When there was no more life left in his victim, Luther let the body drop into the water and it floated adrift of the vessel, caught in a low wave. Face down and arms wide, Smith sank slowly beneath the waves, keeping just within sight of the surface until the tides dragged him further away from the kalia. Luther bent down, dipped the blade into the water and used his free hand to wash away the blood. He then sheathed the knife back into his belt.

Turning to face Abel, Wickman, and the crew, who were still watching in silence, he placed his hands in the air and gently nodded his head. "Now called upon eternal rest, I commit his body to the deep." He spoke this with a low and calming voice before moving back to the centre deck, holding onto a slack rope in the rigging.

The Natui sailors looked at each other. After a few words between them they returned to their sailing duties but kept a constant eye on Luther's movements. He knew that when they returned to their homes, they would tell their people about the merciless killer at sea, the palangi chief, to be feared. A man who took life as he saw fit.

Abel still could not speak except to mouth an inaudible, "Why?"

Luther didn't hesitate to answer. "If I left him behind, he would be certain to revolt and that would lead us only to more killing. If we landed with him, that would provide dire insult. He would surely be killed most brutally for the crimes he intended against your friends. So I chose to set him free. I gave him to the mercy of the sea, and an apology to the chief for the poor treatment of his children." He leaned forward and looked into Abel's eyes. "It's time to steel your wits, cousin. Make ready your courage. More terrible sights are in store for all of us I'm afraid."

TWELVE

Luther's arrival to the shores of Natuini was met with a show of strength. Twenty warriors led by Kalafa were waiting as the three Englishmen stepped from the kalia. They formed a line in front of the visitors and watched intently while they waded out of the water and onto dry land. Kalafa said nothing, but his face remained fierce, as if waking to an unwelcome intruder. Vincent stood tall and surveyed his surroundings. Each of the men was heavily armed and holding sturdy shields with frames fashioned of shaped timber and woven flax.

"Abel?" Luther raised his voice.

"I'm sorry, Luther. Ah … the man with the burnt spear shaft is Kalafa. He is the personal guard to Chief Lokai, and prime warrior of all the Natui tribes," Abel said.

The Natui sailors who brought them to shore took their leave but stopped in front of Kalafa, speaking to him briefly and gesturing back towards Luther. He guessed they had told the giant warrior about the incident, but if it meant something to Kalafa, he didn't show any signs of interest. Instead, he kept his cold eyes fixed upon Luther's. The crew of the vessel, however, avoided Luther as they moved on to shore. He was pleased. It meant they regarded him as dangerous. Almost alone, and surrounded, but a killer nonetheless who had ruthlessly put to death a supposed compatriot. He needed his people to be seen as strong and not to be trifled with. He wanted his arrival to be met with uncertainty. The desired affect seemed at least partly successful.

"Are you sure we're safe, lad?" Wickman said.

"Of course, Doctor. No one's going to eat you. They stopped such practices when Father Marcello made a convert of Chief Lokai. Anyway, they only ever devoured enemies fallen in battle."

Abel's explanation was meant to console but had the opposite effect on Wickman, who shook his head in wonderment at the prospect.

Another man walked towards the shore. Another European. Luther guessed this was Father Marcello. He was clinging to his robes as he stumbled through the sand in a hurry towards them.

"You and the priest must have attended the same athletics college," Luther said to Wickman, who grimaced at the joke.

"Ah, guests. I cannot believe my eyes. Welcome friends and pleased to meet you. Piasser de conosserte! It's a joy to me that I have other men of Europe to behold and converse. I am Father Marcello, a great friend to Abel. I'm sure he's told you all about me." He beamed with excitement and shook their hands vigorously.

"Yes, it's a wonderful occasion indeed to meet a man of God so far from home. Doctor Wickman, at your service, Father. And of course, this is Lieutenant Vincent Luther of the *Viritus*."

Luther seemed less impressed by the priest, but nodded politely, still observing his surroundings.

Suddenly, Kalafa stepped forward towards Luther and reached out, clasping both of Luther's shoulders. Then, leaning in, he pressed his right cheek against Luther's and let out a slight breath of air. Abel had prepared him for this common greeting but hadn't expected it from Kalafa. He had explained that in greeting him some of the Natui may "share their breath" with him; an exchange of trust and a gesture of friendship. This was a common method by which the Natui expressed their welcome and often also when bidding farewell to their kin.

Kalafa, still holding Luther close and pressing his muscular hands into the lieutenant's shoulders, offered a wry smile.

"Koe to'a koe 'i ho kakai, pea teu fakahaa'i aki, 'eku faka'ap'apa kiate koe. Lahi 'aupito 'ae kakai na'a ku tamate'i he faha'i 'ae fili. Kapau te ta fetaulaki 'i he mala'e tau he'ikai ha toe fakamolemole."

"Abel?" Luther looked at his cousin curiously.

"Ah, it's a little difficult but I think—"

"Let me translate for you," Marcello interrupted. "I'm entirely fluent in Natui, even though I speak it with a Venetian accent. Please forgive me if my English is poor." He cleared his throat before speaking again. "Kalafa bids you welcome and says, 'I know you are the greatest warrior of your people and so I offer you respect. I have killed many enemies also and so I look forward to crushing you without mercy in battle, if I am blessed with the opportunity.' In truth, he spoke his words with less finesse than my humble translation, but that was his meaning." Marcello held out his hand briefly. "And now my payment for services rendered." He laughed in jest.

"Hmm, and now you'll translate my words," Luther said.

"Indeed, please go ahead and I'll tell Kalafa as you wish."

Luther nodded at Kalafa and repeated the greeting, leaning in to share his breath against the other man's cheek. Luther was leaner than Kalafa but also well-muscled and just as imposing a figure in his red military dress with a sabre at his side.

"I'm glad for your welcome and will remain your gracious guest. I do not wish to battle with you, for I hope we'll be friends. However, if it comes to battle, I assure you that no number of blessings will save you from the swift death I would deal upon you."

Father Marcello was no longer smiling. "Good sir, I do not think it is wise to say this to Kalafa."

"Translate my words, Father, without adulteration."

Marcello shrugged, but reluctantly and with a slight tremor in his tone, he spoke the words in Natui.

It was with some surprise that as he finished, Kalafa's expression turned to mirth, and he let out a mighty bellow of laughter with his fellow warriors joining in with him. He nodded at Luther and gave him a friendly slap on the shoulder.

It seemed to please the Natui that their challenge was met with equal bravado, and Luther breathed a sigh of relief that the reaction was one of respect and not anger. Before departing with his men, Kalafa spoke briefly to Marcello and then left them alone. Two warriors remained behind. They stood at a distance but kept their eyes on the group.

Father Marcello sighed. "You 're lucky. The mighty Kalafa is in a fine mood today. He says that he'll keep these two men here to watch over you, but that as long as you don't leave Kahoua, you're free to walk as you please. He also says that as a representative of your king, you'll be as honoured guests during the betrothal feast tonight and will be given a rare privilege. You'll drink in the kava circle with the nobility of Natui and their allies. I am to sit behind you to translate and explain the night's events."

"Thank you, Father. We're grateful for your assistance here. And for helping to look after our good friend Abel since his arrival," Wickman said.

"A pleasure, really. But an equal pleasure to have a man of wisdom and knowledge in yourself to attend. I have many questions of news and politics of my homeland and Europe to discuss. I must say I'm beside myself with joy. This is to be a wondrous occasion. Please come with me and I'll show you the surrounds."

"Perhaps you can share with us some of your rum. Abel says you appear to have an unlimited supply of liquor despite having no still to make it with."

Marcello was taken aback by this jest and looked at Abel with a brief expression of annoyance.

"Yes, yes, of course. I was lucky enough to be left with a supply upon my stranding here. Abel would have told you of my most unfortunate circumstances. Please let us have a drink. It will prepare you for the dusty taste of the kava you'll be forced to endure."

They were led into the village by Marcello, who was obviously very excited to speak to the doctor and almost immediately began asking questions about England, the current state of war and if anything was known of his homeland in Venice. Luther sensed the man had spent too long away from his people and had developed an unsettled disposition. He felt a touch sorry for him, but kept in mind Abel's stories about the priest and the circumstances of his arrival that made little sense. He was hiding something, to be sure, and Luther didn't trust him. For now, however, he was an important information source and once the doctor had satisfied his curiosity, Luther would ask his own questions.

All the while they were followed by Kalafa's men who never interrupted them but also never let the strange group out of their sight. Luther was unsurprised to find that most of the men, women and children they encountered were curious about him, and he garnered many stares from all quarters of the village. The foreshore and village surrounds were bustling with people making temporary camps. Marcello explained many travellers had come from all over Natuini and even as far as Fiji, where Chief Lokai kept important trade links. An impressive number of people had come to witness this occasion of two great chiefly families uniting their children.

"The Fijians arrived some days ago. Marvellous ships they have. Unmatched in the Pacific. Lokai might even be jealous of their craftsmanship if he didn't believe them to be the worst sailors on earth. Can build some incredibly advanced vessels but then sail them about with the skill of a blind fruit bat. His words, not mine," Marcello said.

The cooking fires caused smoke to waft through the village, and the smell of food being prepared made Luther's stomach rumble. It was with some gratitude that as they passed by the camps of travellers, he found the Natui to be generous, and they offered him and his companions morsels of yam, fresh fish and dried sea-bird. Soon enough, he was well fed.

When Marcello had taken the group on the full tour of Kahoua, they stopped in front of Abel's abode. The priest scurried into his fale and when he emerged, he was grinning from ear to ear, holding two large bottles of rum, which he served to Luther and Wickman. Abel refused and instead gathered some fresh water for himself.

"The heat will give you a headache soon enough if you drink too much of that without some water," Abel said.

"The boy's a doctor now, it seems," Wickman said, patting Abel on the back.

Heeding Abel's word, Luther followed each gulp of liquor with a drink of water. He intended to keep his wits about him. They had long ago run out of alcohol on Pangai Si'i so he welcomed the drink. He picked up the bottle and examined its label as he listened to Marcello and Doctor Wickman discuss the nuances of the language spoken by the Natui, and how the priest, having no other choice, needed to learn the language quickly in his early days. Living amongst a people he could not understand would have made life unbearable.

"One day, I'll show you my chapel. I have almost completed the construction. There were, of course, some compromises with Masila. You see, Lokai said it must also be used for prayer to the heathen gods, and Masila must be able to perform his wicked rituals there. Beggars, as they say, cannot be choosers.

And so, I must share, placing my bible amongst his devilish totems and trinkets."

"A terrible sacrilege you must endure, no doubt," Wickman said.

"It's hard to complain too much. But I'm happy you and the lieutenant have come. I'm lucky that Lokai was interested in learning to speak English, otherwise I might have lost my own skills in the language. When Abel arrived, I was fortunate to have another English speaker to talk to and a good friend to converse with. We have become good friends now, I think. Is that not true, good Abel?" Marcello's eyes widened as he looked at Abel for an answer.

Abel had been quiet since their arrival and although he was paying attention to Marcello, only nodded gently and remained silent without changing his blank expression. Luther could see that Abel seemed only to tolerate the priest and was unimpressed by the overtures of comradery.

"Tell me, Father, how have the locals taken to Christianity? Abel says that you have brought light to the eyes of their leader. A truly remarkable feat, bringing God to the far reaches of the world has been a mission by our respective churches whether Protestant or Catholic. A noble pursuit."

"Well, Doctor. *That* has been a success not without hardship." Marcello scratched his salt and pepper-streaked beard. "Lokai has refused to let me teach reading and writing to anyone except for himself and some of his most trusted 'eiki. So I must hope the people remember the words I speak to them of the bible, since I cannot make copies of the scriptures. In fact, I feel that my efforts are sometimes in vain. Though now that you're here, I wonder if you have means to leave or if you have your fellow countrymen searching for you. If so, I would hope to leave with you, if you would allow."

"Of course. If we had the ability, we might have come to rescue Abel and set sail for home, but our ship is beyond repair. We've been slowly gathering materials for another vessel."

"Why haven't *you* left already?" Luther asked in a matter-of-fact voice.

"I'm sorry? I was marooned. I have no ship or crew." Marcello said with a forced smile.

"Yes, but you said before that Chief Lokai had a trade route through to Fiji. There would be a much greater chance of coming across European vessels there. Fiji has become a frequent port for American sandalwood merchants and even whalers for some years now. You could have left this place, surely?" Luther's eyes narrowed. "That was certainly our plan."

Marcello frowned. "I have a duty to God. I had a mission. To bring religion here and to convert these servants of nature to his worship."

"But that was not your original intention when you were on board the …?"

"*Tempesta*. I was chaplain on board the *Tempesta*."

Luther nodded. "Yes. Chaplain for a ship that cast you away. You didn't volunteer to be here, so why not try to leave when you had the opportunity on one of the trading vessels?"

For a short time, Marcello's frown deepened and his eyes flicked away towards the great speaking fale at the centre of the now busy village sprawling with people and preparations for the evening.

"Chief Lokai prefers that I remain here and tend to his educational and spiritual needs."

"It sounds very much so like you're a prisoner. Are you a prisoner?" Luther asked.

"No, I'm free to come and go as I please."

Marcello now cast a look of indignation.

"You mean you're allowed to leave the island," Wickman said, smiling and nodding at the question. "If they trust you and you have converted the chief, surely he has a Christian heart and has not held you here captive?"

The priest remained silent. Luther knew the answer already.

"Of course, he can't. He's shackled like the rest of us."

Marcello peered down at his bowl with a look of shame. His eyes glazed over with the effects of the rum and a glistening of water on his eyelids appeared. Luther felt embarrassed by the tears.

"Come now, let's toast to the chief's daughter. Let's hope that the occasion brings a favourable disposition to the Natui and they decide not to evict us from our little piece of 'paradise'," Luther said.

"Salute! That's the correct phrase in your lingo, yes?" Wickman said.

The priest nodded with a broad smile, and the four men raised their cups and drank. Abel had been distracted and his mood was overly sombre. Luther was unsure what Abel had gone through these many months. It was something he wanted to speak to him about alone when the time was right.

Luther accepted another pour of rum from Marcello before engaging with him again.

"When will we meet Lokai?"

"Not until this evening, when all the guests are present. He likes to play the suspenseful man. A man of drama and mystery until the very last moment when he will finally reveal himself."

Marcello smiled again when he saw Abel was distracted. The young man had been peering at the growing crowds.

"You won't see your friend until all the nobles are seated and young Malohi is present. For now, she is being prepared by her servants. I imagine they will be frantically applying their scented oils and hoping her skin will glisten for the rest of the night. The mark of a true virgin."

The others looked at Abel, who had turned crimson faced at the priest's presumption. His interest in the girl was more than mere friendship, and Luther reminded himself to ask his cousin about it later.

Their conversation was interrupted as a commotion arose from the village. A crowd of people were moving towards the impressive trilithon gateway. Marcello's eyes widened, and he rubbed his hands together gleefully.

"The blessed lady of Natui has returned. Glory be to God above."

❁

The grand procession moved lazily as it made its way from the south-eastern beaches towards the gates of Kahoua. Chief Doko and his son Malohi led their own entourage, returning alongside Ono Hiva's servants. Hiva had accomplished her mission. She should have felt happy to return to her own land, an arrival which marked a proud return to her people and an important step towards a longer lasting peace. Instead, her heart was torn in two directions. She revelled at the prospect of remaining with her daughter in Mo'unga Vela and had decided that living with the Grey Hair was a bearable sacrifice. But it would also mean spending a long time away from her home, and if her husband refused to allow the plan, it would be difficult to ignore his demands.

There was still much to be done before that subject was raised. To show courtesy and respect to the Chief of Kahoua, and allow the hosts to make preparation for their arrival, Doko had sent messages a few days prior. They had arrived on the beaches yesterday; a dozen ships carrying the fifty Natui and over one hundred people of Mo'unga Vela had landed during kind weather. A swift wind aiding their journey.

Hiva and Doko's servants had worked together to build crude shelters for just one night. That evening, a generous amount of gifts were carried to Kahoua. Baskets would have been counted and displayed for all to see to prepare for the feast that would be the pinnacle of the celebration.

The following day and as mid-afternoon approached, the visitors started their approach. Walking beside Doko, his son Malohi and trusted matapule kept close. Hiva was accompanied by her handmaidens and personal guardsmen. Ruaka was always just a few feet away. The procession sang a song well known to the Grey Hair. Its words told an ancient story originating from

Mo'unga Vela about two young lovers whose love was so intense, their bodies became one with fire and water, forming the smouldering lands of their home. The consummation of their love was the volcano at the centre of its island chain. The words were beautiful and held much meaning to all Natui people. Hiva always had a weakness for its melody and sang along. She had a voice made for singing, but it had been a long time since she had felt happy enough to use her talents. Handmaidens would shed a tear when on rare occasion she would sing for them as they often begged her to.

The slow pace was deliberate, and it suited Chief Doko. His legs were tired and at times, the taller and still strong Vai Nonga would take his arm and help to lead him forward. However, Doko was proud and determined, so pushed away his matapule's attempts to help.

It was during one of these moments that Hiva stopped singing and felt Ruaka's presence beside her. Without looking directly at her companion, she spoke softly enough so that only he could hear her above the song.

"Ruaka, will you be silent forever? You haven't spoken more than a few words of obedience to me in the last few weeks."

The warrior kept in stride with her, almost beside her, but never in front. It was her privilege to lead her people, and he was not to usurp that position. She could hear a low moan, but there was no more answer than that.

"Don't make me order you to speak."

He sighed and stepped closer. It was not unusual for the two to speak together on matters of her security. Chief Lokai had enemies. They were distant, but ever present, and there were times in the past when bandits had kidnapped chief's wives for ransom. For the ransom of land or simply to bring shame on an enemy.

"I have not spoken to you for I'm ashamed and unworthy," he said.

Hiva felt hurt. Not for anything her lover had done, but for not considering how Ruaka might have felt since the night he challenged Malohi. Her duties had meant she was expected to attend many ceremonies and discussions with Chief Doko and his advisers on the expected marriage protocols ahead. A marriage between high nobility was no trifling matter and there were a plethora of traditions that needed to be carefully seen to be in order for a legitimate marriage to take place, according to Natui traditions. If all these traditions were kept, the marriage would be blessed. The betrothal ceremony was only the first major event of many that would precede the marriage. She was tired from the days of endless talks on the subject and throughout she had missed her lover, more than she would have liked to admit. She had neglected him out of necessity and for fear of being caught being too familiar.

"Please speak to me. Why do you feel ashamed? You've done nothing wrong."

"You need not be soft on me, Ono Hiva. I dishonoured you when I lost my composure in front of everyone. Maybe you'll want nothing more to do with me after this. I can only beg your forgiveness. I failed you and placed you in an awkward position. That's not the action of a man who loves the Lady of Natuini as all should love you."

Hiva continued to walk with grace and tempo, keeping her eyes fixed forward. She thought carefully before she spoke and tears welled in her eyes at not having noticed his pain.

"Listen to me, warrior. I know why you did what you did. Listen carefully so that you may understand my heart. I have never been so proud of you. You will never again be a slave, and one day we will free all Natui slaves, if I have the power to make it so. I would do this for you." Hiva's tears ran down her face and she wished to embrace Ruaka, to provide him with comfort and love.

"As long as there are men like Malohi and your husband, all men will be slaves. But for you. My heart will always be a slave to yours."

"And mine to yours, my love. We will bide our time. We may be together sooner than you think." Hiva spoke swiftly but looked around to ensure no one had overheard. It relieved her that Chief Doko was still in deep conversation with his son, but when she turned to her handmaidens, she caught Pua watching them, but she looked away when Hiva caught her eye.

She is always watching, Hiva thought. *And I want to know which master you are watching for.*

"Ruaka, order one of your men to see who Pua talks to tonight; but not to get too close. Not one of your lumbering brutes, but a man of some stealth. A silent hunter. Perhaps Seletute?"

Ruaka nodded in agreement and walked back to speak to one of his trusted guardsmen. Seletute was a much slender warrior than Ruaka, but known for his extraordinary fitness and speed.

"I must say, Ono Hiva, that I did not think a day would come when your husband would take steps to bring our people together. He always seemed to envy my fertile lands. Now that I am here, I feel a surge of energy and I am excited by what the future will bring." Chief Doko patted his long white beard, which had been braided for the occasion. A puff of grey ash could be seen, but within his already white hair it was hard to distinguish the ash from the natural silver which arrived with age.

The men and women of Mo'unga Vela had prepared ash to be worn and had also made an ashen paste to draw intricate designs on their skin to represent their skill, background or most revered deity. Each was unique, and each held meaning for the wearer. It was for this reason that the Grey Hair also wore less tatau upon their bodies than others of the extended Natui tribal groups. They wanted to express their desires more often, and there was a recognition by their people what was important to them changed as one got older.

"There will be much time for excitement as two precious jewels are wed," Hiva said.

"It will also be a cause to celebrate when I'm gone to my father's house in the skies and my son and your lovely Mahina return to Mo'unga Vela as its rulers." The elderly chief smiled and sighed as he happily contemplated his ending.

"Please don't speak like that, Chief Doko. You will rule your people for many years to come, and guide Malohi towards the rulership. It's too early to speak of this. You're young yet."

She knew he was only being realistic. His time was near, and she could sense it. All around him could.

He extended his hand to touch her arm, but stopped before he made contact and withdrew his touch, wringing them together in front of him instead.

"Lady of Natuini. I know now, more than ever, why your people love you. You have the grace and beauty of Sina, the White Dolphin, and you are kind and intelligent. Kind even through your family's tragedy. The spirit and strength in you are strong. I would be a man of much greatness if at least one of my six wives had just one of the noble traits you possess. My cousin doesn't understand that you're his true power."

"You're cruel to say such things to your wives. They love you so much."

"Nonsense! Not one of them can wait until I'm dead so they can become ladies of leisure without any of the formality and responsibilities that come with being a chief's wife. My mistake was allowing my mother and father to choose all my six wives for me, and each one of them more useless than the other." He laughed, but it turned quickly into a violent cough.

Hiva reached her own hand out and took his arm, seeing that he was needing help to walk. She had begun to think of him like her own elderly grandfather.

"You see, Great Chief. Your wives are listening and they curse you with a cough for each prickly word. More kindness perhaps will make you healthier."

She gave him a broad smile, and he reciprocated.

"Oh Hiva, I believe, your offspring will heal all ills that have come between us. I promise I'll be kinder, since you've asked this of me. My wives will still be useless and lazy, but yes, I will be kinder to them. Before I'm gone."

The procession reached the trilithon that served as the great gateway to Kahoua. Beyond its stones it seemed if all of Natuini had come to witness this momentous occasion, with men, women and children waiting in anticipation of the triumphant return. An enormous area in the centre of the village and outside of Chief Lokai's meeting hall had been cleared for the Taumafa Kava, a ceremony of kava drinking involving the two chiefs, their families, and the lesser nobles of both lands. A feast would follow. They had constructed a great number of huts and sleeping canopies around the village to house the many visitors who had arrived from Mo'unga Vela and from their allied villages. Each would send honoured representatives led by the noble families and most important holy men and dignitaries. Each noble also had their own matapule, although none as influential as Chief Lokai's Masila or Chief Doko's Vai Nonga. Most had already arrived for the festivities, and when they saw the return of the Lady of Natuini accompanied by Chief Doko and his handsome son, there were many shouts of joy and more than a few tears flowed. Such outpouring of emotion deeply moved Hiva. The loud celebratory cheers of many hundreds, if not more than one thousand people were almost deafening, but brought smiles to the arrived guests. Stepping through the crowds came Chief Lokai and Masila both dressed in finely woven mats. Many layers of black dyed kafa rope held the chief's substantial girth. He walked with a great walking stick etched with the marks of his forebears, each vertical pattern representing his bloodline back six generations from his own. The symbol of the sun was at the zenith of the patterns marking his own heraldry. In front of him, Masila strode proudly forth towards Chief Doko. In his hand he held a freshly cut palm leaf.

He knelt and carefully placed the frond at the chief's feet. The village became silent. Lokai gestured forcibly towards the branch with the top edge of his walking stick. The old chief stood with confidence and renewed strength. Then, leaning forward while keeping his eyes on Masila, he placed his hand over the branch and, picking it up, clasped it across his heart.

Masila turned to Lokai and, facing the many faces of anticipation behind him, he made a proclamation of the visitor's intentions. "Oku nau ha'u moe loto melino."

The crowd erupted in a cheer of elation at the signal they had come with a peaceful heart. The celebration and ceremonies could begin.

Masila stepped in unnervingly close to Vai Nonga and looked him over before moving his face within inches of the rival matapule. He spoke in such a voice that only those close could hear over the din.

"A peaceful heart maybe. But hopefully not ugly and misshapen like the one who stands before me. I'll need to burn it far from the village to prevent whatever diseases you have brought to Natuini Lahi."

Vai Nonga held his ground and smiled. "I hear that your people now call you 'Seagulli', named after the intruder's word for a common seabird. I can see now that you are up close, that this is because your breath smells as a putrid belch from a Seagulli's arsehole."

Both men stood motionless. Vai Nonga retained his smile and Masila a look of fury. It was not until Chief Doko noticed the procession was halted that he spat out a hiss, short and sharp, and both of the matapule were snapped back to attention. Masila lowered his head to Chief Doko and gestured towards the camp with a polite bow.

Hiva expected this from the two. It wasn't clear where the animosity had come from, and perhaps the reasons for it had even been forgotten by the two men, but each time they met there was unpleasantries. It provided for an entertaining evening for spectators when they were forced to interact. However, it was to be a long afternoon and no one would be permitted to take their rest until very late so any interruption or delay to the night's events were unwelcome. She shot a glance of disapproval at Masila and though she was certain he had caught her eye, he seemed undeterred. Something that made her furious.

As she walked through the throbbing crowds of her people, they expressed their delight, shouting with joy at her return with the promise and union and strength between the two peoples. This made her happy, and she smiled at the villagers she recognised and the ones from far away villages she did not.

"Over there, Ono Hiva, look." One of her handmaidens pointed at a small group, who were also gaining much attention from those surrounding them.

The young palangi boy and Father Marcello stood far back from the crowds, looking on in quiet attention. However, beside them there were two more palangi men she didn't recognise and their presence surprised her. One of them, taller than his companions, stood out from the rest. He wore the strange clothing of the foreigners but seemed to stand with greater authority. His face was rigid, and he watched his surroundings with suspicious eyes like that of a warrior surveying his enemy. He was older than Abel and sported a short trimmed beard and moustache. This was the one called Lu'fa. Descriptions provided by Natui scouts left her in no doubt this was the leader of the intruders.

"Ruaka, keep an eye on those four, especially their leader. I don't trust any of the pale men. That warrior may be dangerous."

"Palangi can't hide here. They're like a blinding fire at night amongst us, lady, and they're surrounded. What trouble could they possibly cause?"

"Just do as I ask, Ruaka." She pressed her order.

"I'll try, my lady. As much as I can while I also watch you. You'll be seated amongst the wolves. The Natui ladies and wives of every noble and matapule in the land will be seated here tonight behind you in the tou'a. They'll be watching their men swing their sweaty manhood about, comparing the size of their 'lands' in boastful glory."

"The women are the same, you know?"

"Yes, and that's why I'll watch you ceaselessly. To ensure the wild boars don't pick you up in their dirty jealous tusks."

Hiva found herself distracted. She had not seen her daughter in the crowd. Ruaka noticed.

"You know you won't see her until she begins her duties in the taumafa kava. Even then you'll not have a chance to speak to her until the feast."

"I know. I've missed her. That's all. I'll watch for her from the tou'a."

Countless mats had been carefully arranged at the southern edge of the village centre and thatched shelters had been built to keep the sun away from the people seated underneath. It overlooked a much larger area in front of the chief's speaking hall that was also surrounded by dozens of mats forming an oval shape, where only male nobility and their matapule would be permitted to sit.

"Ono Hiva, please rest from your long journey. We've prepared a place for you in the tou'a."

Masila gestured towards the very front line of mats, and several servants were already present, having prepared a comfortable shelter with food and other refreshments ready for her arrival. It was the most luxurious of all shelters which would overlook the night's events. Other nobles of Natuini and Mo'unga Vela, including women and men of lesser nobility from the chiefdoms, were already seated behind and beside hers. When she approached, they stood to acknowledge her. Directly next to her shelter on the left was that of Lokai's aunt Siete. Ono Hiva walked to her, pressing each cheek against the lady's in greeting.

"Malo lelei Aunt Siete."

"Oh, my precious Hiva. It must've been awful for you. So many months away on that terrible volcano with those treacherous people. My nephew should've gone by himself. Of course, he's such a lazy puaka he can barely pace across the village clearing without breaking out in a sweat."

Hiva giggled. Siete spoke frankly about the world around her and was unafraid of Lokai. They had become close over the years, keeping each other's confidence in many important matters. As his eldest aunt, she outranked him in their family according to tradition. Siete was blunt and sometimes rude, but Hiva respected and loved her for her honesty and frequent irreverence towards the nobility.

"Siete, I'm afraid it's going to get much worse. There's more food here tonight than I've ever seen. You know my husband likes a magnificent feast."

"As does his other wife. He's fattened her up with child. Look at her over there. Gloating daily about how her child will be a boy and rule over these lands. I tell you, Hiva. I'm an old woman and I've seen Masila get his predictions wrong almost half the time over the years. But when he gets it right, everyone forgets about the dozens of times he was mistaken. That's the power of stupidity bestowed upon the people by the gods."

Lokai's third wife Becca was seated in her own shelter to the right of Hiva's. She was now very plump with child and her belly had dropped, meaning a child would be soon born and her husband would finally have his son. But only if Masila's premonitions were to be believed.

"If this is a boy child, he'll finally have his heir. Perhaps then his worries will be sated," Hiva said.

"That one will be lucky to make it through the birth. She's as small and thin as moko's broken tail. Lucky to have survived the consummation of the child with that humongous boar riding atop her!"

The two ladies laughed with each other for a moment before Hiva kissed Siete again and returned to her shelter, resting on the thick mats.

Ruaka was waiting for her.

"I'll need to remain here now in the tou'a. Where will you be?"

Ruaka pointed to a copse of trees just twenty paces from her shelter. "Hiva ..."

There was something wrong. The warrior's face scrunched and his eyes lowered.

"Speak. What is it, Ruaka? Is there something you need to tell me?"

His fists clenched. "If you need me, I am close."

Abruptly he bowed and led his men to an area where they would provide over-watch of the lady and ensure she was safe from any potential threats.

A tingling sensation trickled around her body. She knew Ruaka well. Danger was close.

THIRTEEN

After the procession arrived, Marcello became even more excited at the prospect of being able to tell the group about his vast knowledge of all things Natui and explained in great detail the significance of each tradition they witnessed. Luther was relieved when the strange white-haired people strode proudly through the trilithon, since it took away much of the curious looks and attention off them. Mobs of villagers were in a state of fervour over the return of Ono Hiva. As it was explained to Luther, her popularity had no equal in all the lands ruled over by the Natui chiefs, and the betrothal of her daughter was seen as a great step towards a lasting peace between two great rivals. The 'betrothal celebration' was as important as the actual wedding between the couple which would occur within ten days. It marked the beginning of marriage rituals, daily feasting and revelry between the families to bring a harmonious start to the wedded life of a couple. For nobility, it was also a period of negotiation over gifts and who had an order of precedence with the distribution of mats and other fine crafts. The eldest aunts on both sides were granted enormous respect, and it was usual for gifts to be provided to them as part of the celebrations. A wedding could turn sour and bring ill fortune to a couple if this was mismanaged. Fighting amongst families during the marriage was hard to avoid and grave threats would be thrown about, providing embarrassment to embattled parents. According to Marcello, this was strangely a common occurrence. Particularly when the complication of the status of aunts who were adopted themselves as children was often debated. As was how to meet the age-old gift giving expectation when certain parties were absent from the ceremony. Families that had estranged extended family would sometimes deliberately insult one another by changing the order of precedence or cutting out an aunt altogether. Marcello had seen blood spilled over these serious matters from commoners and nobles alike. But not today. Ono Hiva was a meticulous organiser and had decided many moons in advance on how these events would unfold; with honour upheld and strict adherence to protocol. For much of the afternoon it seemed to Luther that the lady's planning had been successful.

Luther and his companions were seated on the rim of the Taumafa Kava, a grand circle of nobles and matapule. He was fascinated by the discipline of the attendants and the obvious care that was taken to ensure each and every person was placed in exactly the right place. Marcello relayed the preparation of the ceremony and though the priest had barely stopped talking since their arrival, Luther was interested in understanding the event as it unfolded.

Before anyone sat to rest, Chief Lokai took his seat first at the head of the kava circle. Only when he was seated could others take their places. Lokai had appeared to a roar of approval from his people, emerging from the long meeting hall and accompanied by Kalafa and Masila. However, it was only Masila who sat beside him in the circle. The one Abel had called Seagulli.

Beside Chief Lokai and to his right was the leader of the Grey Hair, and his son who would marry Lokai's daughter. Malohi was a handsome young man whose long dark hair was intricately braided and reached close to the ground when seated. His features glistened with a thick oil which only enhanced his chiselled features, cold but striking all at once. Most young women of the village didn't hide their pleasure at his startling good looks, and even some of the Natui men were glaring hungrily at the noble's son.

On Lokai's left, Marcello pointed out Aunofo, his matapule, then at least three dozen nobles and some of the most powerful holy men from Natuini, Mo'unga Vela, Fisi and Natuini Si'i. Chief Maka of Natuini Si'i had sent his matapule to represent him. A tall and slender man with a weathered but gentle face was given a place to sit beside Luther's group. Their reasonable distance from the head of the kava circle was correct for their station as honoured guests but a deliberate slight towards the representative of a great chief of Ono Hiva's own blood. If it offended him, he kept a stony face and nodded politely to Wickman as he rested beside the group.

Beyond the opposite side of the circle in the tou'a, a much larger group of men and women had congregated, as if preparing for a large picnic whilst they watched the events of the ceremony. Amongst them were the wives and children of each noble present, high-ranking warriors, lesser holy men and artisans of wealth and repute. Beyond, the commoners. Bunched together and enjoying the afternoon celebrations and generous food and drink that came with it. The afternoon was sultry, but some relief came when some older boys and girls swept up the air at their backs with palm fronds, giggling at the sight of the strange men.

"There are no women in the circle?" Luther said.

"Correct, Lieutenant." Marcello nodded his head enthusiastically. "Only the males of the Natui may imbibe during the kava. Women may have their own kava ceremonies and may drink freely otherwise but not during a ceremony such as this."

"It's clearly a patriarchal society." Wickman drank another cup of rum.

"Yes and no. It depends, my friend."

Wickman's face scrunched with the strength of the spirit, and he coughed a little at its bite. "Depends on what?"

"On many things. On the occasion. And who is involved. Here, it's men who inherit land and title because it's men who must work that land and provide for their families with meat and crops. But it's women who are respected most. The eldest daughter is to be listened to by all other siblings, boys and girls. Also, the eldest aunt on the father's side, the fahu, outranks all others in the extended family. Confusing, yes? Chief Lokai may rule over these lands but his aunt, Siete, will still clap him on the ear for his rudeness. Women have much symbolic power. Men have material power. It creates a balance."

"That is complicated."

"It's also why today is so important. Lokai's daughter Mahina is his eldest daughter and her future will hold much responsibility as fahu to the future chief. That is, if Lokai leaves a boy. If not, she will rule and her children may one day rule over Mo'unga Vela and Natui."

When Chief Lokai arrived and stood in his place, Masila nodded, signalling for the circle to sit.

As silence fell, the matapule struck his staff into the hard soil with such force that dust and dirt flew from the blow. A rush of activity commenced. Servants carried three large carved bowls into the circle and spaced them out equally, with the largest at the other end of the circle from Lokai's seating place. The bowls were tremendous, with each at least five feet in diameter and perched on four ornately carved wooden legs.

"Kumete." Marcello whispered. "The bowls are called kumete. The kava ceremony has begun."

The Natui servants brought baskets filled to the brim with cool water and poured them into the kumete until each bowl was a quarter full. Then they placed several large kava roots beside the bowls, along with thick ropes of bast fibre from the hibiscus tree. Finally, tree branches the length of three hands with a thick blunted end was placed onto the rims. Three holy men from the tou'a stepped into the circle and each sat directly in front of each bowl, where they sat quietly for several moments, their eyes closed in contemplation. It was Masila who brought them to life once again with a clap of his hands, and, as he did, they each in unison picked up the kava roots, dropped them carefully into each kumete which they then rhythmically pounded and mixed with the thick branches.

The process was slow, and Luther felt weary just watching the kava being crushed and mixed. When the kava was sufficiently pounded, each man, again in perfect unison, picked up the bast fibre and began straining the now earthy coloured liquid. In the hot but gradually falling sun the kava looked thirst quenching. Luther's throat was parched from the day, and he felt suddenly thirsty.

By the time it was finished, daylight was fading. The three holy men rose together, bowed to the nobles within the taumafa kava, and stepped silently back into the tou'a. Luther noticed a change in everyone's posture. The 'eiki of the circle sat up and straightened their backs and looked around at each other in anticipation of something momentous.

"She arrives. Behold, Mahina," Marcello said, struggling to hold back his excitement.

From the tou'a, Mahina appeared and walked graciously into the circle. She was a beautiful young woman. It was without surprise that Abel was so enamoured by Mahina. Dressed modestly, she wore an ornately etched dress made from pressed pandanus leaves. Whilst it covered her from thigh to chest, her arms and legs were exposed, but glistened with oils which gave her a glowing appearance in the last rays of light. Mahina wore her hair in tight braids, with a pair of long pearl earrings and a perfectly symmetrical headdress decorated with brightly coloured feathers. In its centre sat a coral carving of a dainty seahorse. She was beautiful. An obvious strength permeated from her toned body. This was no fragile or helpless princess. Turning, Luther could see Abel's eyes gazing in wonderment. The look of longing and want in the young man was palpable. Even Wickman, in his now obviously inebriated state, had noticed and was nudging Luther with a knowing grin. On the opposite side of the circle from where she entered, Chief Lokai looked proud, peering at the reaction of his honoured guests, who were all transfixed by his attractive daughter.

As Mahina stopped by the closest kumete, she rubbed her hands together and kept the thick oils from dripping away with a movement up and around her wrists. With every moment, her audience would gasp and comment quietly to their neighbour on the astonishing beauty of Malohi's wife to be. Malohi was the only one present who seemed unaffected. Instead, he watched her without expression, and even when she finally stood directly in front of the kava bowl and offered a smile across the circle towards her betrothed, he simply nodded towards her, giving away no emotion. No one else seemed to notice, or if they did, were too polite to pay obvious attention. Especially Abel, who could not take his eyes off the young lady.

Lokai struck his hands together again. Taking a drinking bowl, Mahina scooped up a measure of kava, bringing it directly to her father. He took the bowl graciously, drinking it deeply before smiling at his daughter and beckoning her back to the kumete. Mahina repeated the offering of kava three times more; next for Chief Doko, and then for the most trusted of Lokai's nobles, Aunofo. Finally, the last offering was given to Malohi. Mahina stepped in close to him and bent her knees slightly, offering him a full cup of kava. He smiled back at her and drank it, finishing it with one gulp. Nothing was said between them.

There was an audible stir amongst the tou'a as the close encounter between the two occurred. Luther guessed they were gossiping. *Would it be a happy marriage? How long before the bride would bear children?* Much akin to a royal couple matched in England. There was little difference in this aspect between the two peoples; both served the greater political ambitions of a nation and the will of grand families rather than the needs or wants of those to be wed. Everyone, even the hardiest of Natui warrior, seemed to be pleased with the coupling. All except one. Abel. And that young man was looking distraught, trying to purge the events from his sight, if not from his mind.

Mahina stepped backwards five paces. She smiled gently and as she returned, she took her place again in front of the kumete. Malohi tossed the empty vessel unceremoniously to the side. Luther kept his eyes on the chiefs and their company. He was more interested in what politics were at play amongst the leadership than the fascinating but currently less pertinent nuances of Natui marriage. Because of his focus on the leadership rather than the beautiful bride to be, Luther was possibly the only one to notice Malohi's face change as soon as his bride walked away. It turned from one of kindness to disinterest, and perhaps even annoyance. He peered around bored, scratching the ground beneath him with a small stick. When his father leaned in and whispered a quick but clearly angry message into his ear, he dropped the twig and sat up straight. He ran his fingers through his hair and forced a smile.

Mahina sat down again. A group of young men and women entered the circle with large tapa cloth bags filled with kava. With great care they emptied the contents into the bowls and took up places beside each of the other two kumete. The nobles and holy men in the circle struck their own hands together, starting from either side of Chief Lokai, and as they did, a bowl was delivered to each of them.

When it was Luther's turn, he wolfed it down. Its taste was bitter and earthy but not completely unpleasant. They continued in strict order until each of the participants in the circle had been delivered their kava and drunk the contents. Masila stood up and took his own bowl in hand, lifting it to the sky.

"Ke tau inu eni, koe fakamanatu ki he ngaahi 'otua 'o Natuini. Pea ke faitapuekina mai mo tapuaki'i 'ae ongo me'a mali."

Then he also drank, with more than a few drops of the brownish liquid rushing down his cheeks.

"Malo." The gathered crowd announced in unison, expressing consent to the holy man's offering.

Then, as if by clockwork, more servants appeared and placed a variety of food held in flax baskets into the centre of the circle. They were filled with yams, seafood, fruit and other delicious assortments of food. At least forty roasted pigs, some no larger than a suckling, were placed around the circle and in front of each noble. Luther received his own and immediately felt hungry at the smell of the recently charred pork. However, no one ate. Instead, they looked at a particular roasted pig which sat directly at the centre of the feast in a basket. Kalafa entered the circle, and all eyes followed him. Luther was surprised he gestured for him to stand.

"Muimui mai."

Luther stood to face him. "What's going on here, Marcello?"

After a brief exchange with Kalafa, Marcello raised his eyebrows and looked at Chief Lokai.

"You are to present the chief his offering. It means that he considers no one of Natui blood to have higher rank than himself, and only someone of equal or higher rank amongst the Natui may accept this offering on his behalf. You are not Natui, and therefore you are an acceptable substitute. It's quite an honour really. But it's also a message to the other nobles present. Especially Doko and his son."

Luther took a deep breath and looked around. He didn't like the attention. He also didn't want to cause any unfavourable incidents. Stepping beside Kalafa, he let the warrior lead the way to the roasted pig. It was still steaming with heat from the cooking fires. He looked to Kalafa for guidance, but the tall Natui warrior simply gestured with his hand towards the pig. Luther picked up the package and proceeded towards the chief. Kalafa walked by his side, matching his steps. When he reached the head of the circle, Chief Lokai looked at Luther with a warm smile and lowered his eyes to an empty place in front of him, patting the ground twice and nodding once. Luther bent down and laid the basket in front of Lokai. He nodded to the chief and walking several small steps backwards he then crisply turned on his heel and made his way back to his companions.

"Well done, good man, well done." Wickman grinned. "You didn't trip up or drop that piggy upon their great leader's head. We get to live another day. Hoorah."

Luther didn't appreciate Wickman's joke very much and gave him a dark look of disapproval. The doctor had been drinking more than his fair share of rum and didn't seem to notice the scorn.

What Luther did notice was the fury on Malohi's face. He was looking directly at the lieutenant with the face of a killer. The young man began to rise to his feet, but a strong hand from his father on his shoulder and some whispered words into his ear were enough to quickly calm his mood. He remained sullen of expression, and when Chief Lokai carved a chunk of pork for himself, Malohi turned his concentration to eating and the feast began in earnest. Luther was famished as were his companions. They ate well. There was plentiful food to go around with all manner of Natui fare on offer. Servants served a special dish of raw mahimahi rested in lightly salted coconut cream with a dash of pomelo juice and zest. At first, the thought of raw fish seemed odd, but when he tasted its flavour Luther instantly enjoyed the taste. Wickman would have none of it and muttered something about the chef having forgotten how his cooking fire operated. The doctor was quite red faced from the rum. He poured another drink from Marcello's bottle and offered it around. They were having a merry time in conversation. Wickman was normally a conservative fellow but in a moment of unusual confidence turned to the matapule from Natuini Si'i and formally introduced himself. He took the bottle out of Marcello's hand and offered a drink to the man, grinning and poured a generous amount into his kava cup.

"I'm Robert. Ro–bert," he said, enunciating the syllables. "What's your name good fellow?"

The matapule pointed to himself and in a quiet voice provided an answer. "Paea." He took the kava bowl in his hands and smelled the scent of the foreign substance. Paea looked around with slight concern but, convinced no one was watching, he quickly drank the whole bowl in a single swig. His eyes grew wide then after a few moments, when a tear welled on his eyelid, he smiled and shook his head, chuckling to himself.

"More?" Robert showed him the bottle.

"Io, malo." He nodded, raising an eyebrow and, moving closer to Wickman, he held out his bowl.

"We're going to need more of that rum if you have it Father," Wickman insisted.

All the while, Abel remained quiet. Luther sensed he was still upset from what he had witnessed on the kalia, so placing down a chunk of pork he was chewing, he asked Abel to come closer to talk.

"I know you're upset, cousin. It's best that we come to an understanding so that we can move past this."

Abel looked down and poked at a piece of roasted sweet potato. "It's not at all a problem. I've seen men die before." Abel spoke without emotion.

"Yes, it's true. But you haven't seen me slaughter a man like that before. Perhaps you might call it murder?"

Abel gave no response.

"Look at me, Abel." Luther raised his voice.

This jarred Abel enough to sit up and pay attention.

"It seems if we're to move forward, you're going to have to deal with what has happened. This requires an explanation."

"Fine, then explain it to me. He was unarmed, Luther. You just cut his throat like a pig. Where's the honour in that? You taught me to face my enemy head on. That a moral, decent warrior attacks from the front and not like a miscreant highwayman from behind."

"I've always loved your spirit, Abel. And you've always shown your compass is pointed straight upon the righteous path. Much like you, we've endured much during our internment here. There's been much death. I've done what's needed to be done to prevent the rest of our men from falling to barbarity. Smith was going to be trouble for all of us. If he stayed with the men, I would've come home to insurrection. If I brought him here, he would've gotten us all killed for his contempt for the Natui people."

"I didn't care for him. But did he need to die?"

"The choice was his. Smith made it clear that he couldn't be trusted. There's another reason. He promised to take your life. I could see it in his face that he would've found an opportunity to kill you. I wasn't going to give him that chance."

"Did you also kill Master Larkin?"

"Yes, Abel. It was the only way to end the conflict."

There was pain in the young man's eyes. He was battling with himself, trying to reconcile his thoughts.

"How?"

"I shot him. Point blank in the head. And I'd do it one hundred times over. Listen, Abel. You must trust in me that my actions have been necessary for the good of the men. Smith and Larkin were embarking on a path which would lead us all to ruin. I would not – I *will not* – allow that. Sometimes, cousin, you must act against your better nature and do terrible things for the greater good. Do you understand what I'm saying?"

"Yes, Vincent. I do. I just … It's been difficult here. I missed you and the doctor. It was just a shock for me," Abel said. Tears welled in his eyes.

Luther turned away briefly from Abel to prevent his shame in crying, allowing himself a moment to wipe his eyes and take a deep breath.

They both looked around at the feasting and joyous mood of the Natui. Everybody was busy stuffing their mouths full of the year's bumper harvest.

"The girl who will marry the oiled fellow over there. You've become friendly?"

"Yes, we're friends. She's been kind to me. Her English is coming along really well, and she's taught me so much. I have loved …" Abel's expression began to fall again.

"And now I understand, cousin."

Abel didn't respond. His eyes swept up to Mahina. She was still smiling gently. Two of her female cousins has been chosen to provide comfort to her during the afternoon and they held palm fronds aloft to keep the sun from her face and bowls of water to quench her thirst. All around, the light of the day slowly left and torch lights sprung up all over the village, lighting the festivities into the evening. The feasting continued as more food was brought out to accompany the several rounds of kava drinking. The companions had drunk their fifth cup by the time darkness fell, and he could see and feel the liquid starting to take effect. The men of the circle looked very relaxed, talking amongst each other, their happy expressions broadening as the minute's passed. Even Wickman, who had been nervous since learning they would need to travel to Kahoua, was laughing uncontrollably alongside his new friend from Natui Si'i. They were drunk. The drug within the kava root they had consumed had also taken effect, with Wickman looking overly relaxed. Paea, who could not speak a word of English, and the doctor not a word of Natui, were shoulder to shoulder and singing a version of "The Coast of High Barbary" that the doctor had tried to teach him. It mattered not that Paea was only humming most of the chorus, since he had learned the last line of each verse and sang along with Robert. "Cruising down the coast of the High Barbaree ..." The sight was hilarious. Marcello joined in reluctantly at the doctor's insistence, and even Abel smiled at the conspicuous ruckus.

There was much revelry to be had amongst the nobles in the circle. They were all deep in friendly conversation. The tou'a and common areas to the south end of the kava circle were much louder with laughter, dancing and rhythmic drum beats throughout village where there was even less restraint on ceremony and people were able to enjoy themselves without the more subdued dignitaries nearby. Subdued, except for Wickman and Chief Maka's representative, who Luther had decided had both taken leave of their senses. Not that the nobles and holy men around them cared. In fact, it only brightened their spirits, with some ordering their servants to bring more kava to the foreigners to reward them for their entertainment. When it was becoming too much for Luther to bear, he pulled the bottle out of Wickman's hand and scolded him.

"Get yourself together man. You may need your wits about you yet."

Wickman and Paea provided a disingenuous look of shock and surprise, then a few moments later, burst into laughter once more. This brought the attention of Chief Lokai who had been speaking in a closer circle to Chief Doko and his son Malohi. Lokai looked over with a wry smile directly at Luther who stared back, unblinking.

"Tokoua. Ha'u ke tau inu kava," Lokai said.

Luther could hear Marcello take a sudden breath.

"Oh my God. Ah … ah," Marcello stuttered.

Luther turned to the priest and could see that he was horrified.

"What? What did he say?"

"He wants you to join him for kava. I am to accompany you." The priest stood and straightened his robes. "It's an honour. His intention is to show you off. But the invitation will not please Mo'unga Vela, as you are not of noble. You should not be seated amongst them."

Luther nodded. "Lead the way. I can play the prize pig for now. Doctor, pull yourself together." He stood and straightened his own uniform. "You're no good to me if you're without your senses."

Wickman wasn't listening. He had become distracted by Paea who had clasped him by the shoulder and was enthusiastically showing him each tatau inscribed on his body, likely telling the full tale of his ancestry entirely in Natui.

FOURTEEN

okai was pleased with himself. Every crucial chess piece was perfectly in place. As he had planned many moves in advance, the most influential of chiefs and nobles were present to witness this grand event. His game board had come to life. The queen sat dutifully in her place of honour in the tou'a. His bishop was taunting his rival's bishop with his usual venomous tongue. The pawns, the palangi men, were close and understood the power he wielded. The chief smiled at the approaching palangis. He gestured for them to sit to his right where mats had been laid, and his sub chief, Aunofo, was keeping a close eye on the mood of the evening. The one called Luther gave a crisp but respectful bow of his head as he sat, and this pleased him greatly. Even more so than seeing the look on the faces of his Grey Hair guests. They had baulked at his invitation to the palangi to join then in the circle. When he told Marcello to bring the foreign warrior to the inner circle of chiefs, the outrage smouldered like a forest fire. It was Vai Nonga who expressed his displeasure and directed it towards Masila, who dismissed the issue with a wave of his hand. This was how verbal arguments between powerful chiefs were fought, with their own matapules as proxies. The true heart of a chief could be heard through the mouth of his matapule. They were well versed in the day's politics and the wishes of their masters, who would ensure they were well prepared before any confrontation. Lokai and Masila had spent many months preparing for this night, and now that the evening had begun, Lokai was outwardly a man without worry. He drank and ate in copious amounts, praising the work of his people and glorifying the honour given to him by so many dignitaries coming to Kahoua to celebrate his good fortune. His rival, Doko, did not look half as comfortable.

"Seagulli, this seems a break in protocol. Does this foreign man have the blood of a great chief or king?" Vai Nonga quizzed, his voice smooth and unemotional.

Masila grunted and said, "He's a skilled warrior and a guest from a far-off land. And he's family to the adopted son of Aunofo. It's not strange for great warriors and craftsmen to be allowed a place in the circle if they prove themselves exceptional. Why does it matter to you, old man?" Masila chewed on a twig and cleaned a gap between his teeth to dislodge a thread of pork.

Vai Nonga shook his head and scoffed. "Exceptional? How is this man exceptional. He's simply a castaway. He and his men are stuck on our sacred island. I've heard many of our people have questioned the wisdom of allowing our sacred sites to be desecrated by their presence. It's forbidden, in fact, for anyone to live on that island. Only holy men and those of noble blood are allowed on Tapu Motu, and yet the island is overrun by these invaders."

"It's forbidden for Natui to occupy the island. There is no such rule for others of foreign blood." Masila dismissed his rival again.

"I guess you would forgive your wife for rutting another man, as long as that man was not of Natui blood? Perhaps we can invite one of the foreign men to Kahoua to provide her with the pleasure she has so long missed out on."

"Or perhaps your bulbous wives would benefit from such a union. Alas, they are absent. Such a shame you could not fit them on the kalia for fear of capsizing the entire fleet. Not to worry, though, my dear Vai Nonga. I have no doubt they're feasting right this very moment." Masila bristled in clear disgust.

"You men provide us with much entertainment!" Lokai bellowed in laughter, and even Chief Doko smiled at the exchange.

"Indeed, my matapule needs to drink more kava to calm his fiery tongue." The older chief laughed for a moment, but then caught something in his throat and began to cough.

"And perhaps for you also, my friend."

Lokai motioned to a servant for fresh kava to be brought to their mats for drinking. When Doko's cup was freshly filled, he drank a sip and his coughing stopped.

"You look a little tired, friend. The night is still a virgin, like our two younglings. You must remain at our side. Do you have the energy?"

"Yes. Thank you for your concern, but I'm fine."

The older chief wiped some spittle away from his mouth and Lokai could see a hint of blood on his hand, which he had tried to conceal. Lokai turned and considered the newcomers for a moment, motioning Luther and Marcello to move closer. He spoke to Marcello in Natui.

"God-man, I don't want to use my poor English to speak to Abel's cousin. Will you translate for us? I'm happy for you to convey to him what you hear tonight."

He gestured for Luther to drink, and then raised his cup. "I want us to drink together. A sign of friendship and strength as we join our families. A drink to celebrate our lovely children. And also, to our new palangi friends from far away."

Everyone raised their bowls to their lips and drank. Lokai nodded approvingly at Luther as he drank his bowl dry.

"Seems you like our kava, yes? Kafa e faifolau has become accustomed to its taste and can drink as well as the best of us," he said, using Abel's new Natui title.

Marcello quickly translated the exchange and after a pause, Luther put down his bowl to address his host.

"Aye. It's tolerable. Some of my men have taken to drinking it on our island. We English prefer ale but the kava is fine. One of our men has started mixing it with coconut water to smooth the bitter taste."

"Coconut water? I also enjoy that method. For our people, kava strained in coconut water is the gift a young nobleman must give to his beloved if they are to have a happy life. An old tradition. Is it not Masila?" he said.

Masila nodded. "Yes, Hou'eiki. An old tradition from the time of the first kings."

"The first kings? I thought there were no Natui kings?" Luther said.

"A long time ago, palangi, all Natuini was ruled by great kings. The 'Tu'i Natui' they were called."

"What happened to them?"

Lokai grinned and looked at Masila. A sign for his matapule that he wished him to speak about matters of social discomfort. It was well understood by Masila, who took the stick from his mouth and pointed it rudely at Vai Nonga.

"Perhaps the Grey Hair can tell you what happened. Yes, Vai Nonga? Tell the foreigner what happened to the last of the Tu'i Natui."

Vai Nonga shot back a baleful glance, but gestured towards Luther as he spoke.

"They grew too powerful. And led us to constant war with our peoples. The last Tu'i was named Taufa. He was infamous for his cruelty. He demanded that we worship only one god, Tangaloa. The 'eiki and their people rebelled."

"He means the Grey Hair 'eiki and their enemies in Natuini Si'i came together as one as they grew jealous and killed him, proclaiming there shall be no more kings. He was an ancestor of Chief Lokai," Masila said.

"It kept the balance."

"Why don't you go keep the balance with that lacky of Hou'eiki Maka, and drink with him."

Doko groaned. "Matapule, that's enough now. It's a happy occasion. Enough of the pointless banter. Lokai and I wish to speak on more pleasing topics. What of your wife, Ono Becca? Ono Hiva has told me you're expecting a son."

"She is at rest in the tou'a. But she will soon retire. I don't want her strained by the excitement. My son must be healthy."

"And what of your other wife?" This time it was Malohi who spoke.

"Yes, young man? What of Ono Hiva. She is seated in the tou'a as you can see."

"No. I mean, your second wife. The barren one you exiled in Hule." Malohi cocked his head to the side and straightened his long hair between his fingers.

"Son, you disrespect Hou'eiki Lokai." Doko raised his voice and for a moment shot a look of fury at his son.

Lokai waved his hand as if he were unconcerned, then sat up straight and looked at Malohi. "You're a curious little fish. Aren't you boy? Tihani holds a special place in my heart, as my second wife."

"But not a special place in your village. When Mahina is my wife, she'll be taken every night until she bears me six sons. I would not dare let her disobey me."

There was a moment of silence.

The chief suddenly felt hot. He wiped sweat from his forehead and raised his eyebrows, surprised by the sudden warmth. He was no longer smiling and balled his fist tightly for a moment, before releasing it and twisted his head from side to side. Two audible cracking sounds came from his neck. He could not hide that he was restraining himself from killing the boy, but feigned a smile anyway.

This time, he spoke louder. He wanted everyone to hear him. And many in the circle turned to pay attention to the conversation. "Be careful of your words, young man. You do not want to anger your future father-in-law, yes?"

"Why? You would challenge me? We could settle things with weapons. You'll find that your future son-in-law is a master of warfare and battle," Malohi said dismissively.

"A battle, one on one?" Lokai bellowed with a smile. "No, no, I wouldn't dare. I'm an old man and you're strong and quick. I've heard of your prowess with the weapon. I've been told that you dance with your starved opponents and slaughter them in droves. I'd like to see that one day. Let us see what my beautiful daughter thinks of your prowess."

Lokai summoned his daughter with a gesture of his hand. From her seated position she filled a bowl of kava and brought it over to stand in front of the hou'eiki.

"Daughter, please give kava to Malohi. He wishes to ask you a question."

Mahina obeyed and stepped in close, offering the bowl to him with both hands.

He took it and setting it to the side, Malohi took a deep breath and looked up. "Mahina, I am a warrior of great skill. I have killed dozens of my enemy, and amongst my warriors, I am the most feared. Does that not make the traits of a great husband?"

Mahina remained smiling, though it faded somewhat as she looked at her father.

"It's fine daughter, speak from your heart."

He watched as she turned to Malohi and considered the question. Then he awaited the answer he knew she would give. Mahina was his child. She had been raised by the gentle care of Ono Hiva, but she had his spirit and wit.

"No."

Malohi's eyes scrunched up in confusion. Masila chuckled at the answer.

"No? Did you not hear my question?"

"I heard your question. The answer is no. Having killed dozens of men makes you an adept killer. It does not make you a better husband than any other man."

"But a husband must protect his family and kill his family's enemies. It makes him virile. A great warrior can bear many children. You'll soon see ..."

Mahina was no longer smiling. She again looked at her father, who gave her an approving nod.

"No," she said again.

"What?" Malohi's voice was incredulous.

"You're right that a good husband must protect his family, as a good wife also must. I've also learned the arts of war so that I may protect mine. But slaughter for slaughter's sake is not righteous. Simply being a warrior does not mean you will have many children, and it doesn't make you *great*. I've witnessed farmers and artisans who have never picked up a pakipaki in their life have ten children that survived, and they're not warriors. It's the will of the god Tangaloa and nature which dictate the virility of a man and fertility of a woman. A good husband may have many traits, such as humility and kindness. To spill blood has nothing to do with greatness."

"Ha! What would you know. You can't compare me to a farmer, Mahina. When we are wed, you'll bear me children, and there will be no more need for you to learn the skills of a warrior. As a good wife your duty is to keep my wishes satisfied."

As Malohi finished, he tossed his bowl to the ground at her feet. She looked embarrassed, but she bent down to pick up the discarded bowl. Before she touched it, Doko stopped her.

"Please leave it, young Mahina. Please forgive my son. He's had a long journey and he's drunk too much kava. Now his mind's numb with stupidity. Please return to the tanoa and leave us old ones to bother you no more. He'll ask for your forgiveness later."

Mahina nodded and left.

As Lokai watched her leave, he looked sideways at Masila, giving him a knowing glance.

"Let us talk of the future, Chief Lokai. And how we secure peace." Doko spoke gently, trying to change the tone of the moment.

"But first let's talk about reparation." Masila said.

Silence. Confused expressions from everyone around him. Lokai was delighted.

Vai Nonga squinted his eyes and looked at his hou'eiki. Doko remained silent.

"Reparation for what?" said Vai Nonga.

"For the loss of trade with Ali'i Fetu of Ha'amoa."

"Explain what you're talking about. We have no relations with Ha'amoa." Vai Nonga shook his head slowly.

"That's because you murder their fishermen and take them as slaves. Some moons ago we met with Keola, the grandson of Ali'i Fetu and made peaceful words. We agreed to trade. When he left with his men, your "great husband" here brought the curse of the gods upon our agreement and took the grandson and his men as slaves."

Lokai was even more pleased to see the look of astonishment on their faces.

"There is some misunderstanding—" Vai Nonga began but was interrupted by Doko.

"This conversation is beyond our matapule, Lokai. What game are you playing? They were intruders, not the sons of Ha'amoa nobility who entered our waters. Malohi saw them hunt the sacred tofua'a and drive them to our beaches for sport. They know the punishment for this is enslavement."

"Lies," Chief Lokai said dispassionately.

"How dare you, Lokai? Hold your tongue. You dishonour me and my son," Doko said.

"Ask that prancing piglet of yours," Lokai said.

Doko was incensed. Every moment of his fury and confusion was a delight for Lokai.

"Son, what does he speak of. Tell us what you and your men saw. Tell Chief Lokai that he's mistaken."

Malohi shrugged. "He's not mistaken, Father. But it doesn't matter. They're our ancestral enemies and so I destroyed them."

Lokai could feel his heart beating. The board was open and pieces were about to fall in his favour. He gave a deep laugh. A mocking bellow. Then he leaned forward and slapped the dry ground to gain his guests attention.

"You see, my old friend Doko, some of the Ha'amoa men escaped and returned here to me. They told me they had been ambushed by your son as they sailed past Mo'unga Vela. They told me that Keola let it be known he was the grandson of a great chief. But your son, instead of using his brains, killed most of the Ha'amoa men and with a hot knife sliced away the noble tatau from the skin of Keola so no one would know his true heritage.

Then, as I am now told by my people who travelled home with you, your son killed them for sport."

The chief of the Grey Hair pushed himself to his feet. Vai Nonga tried to assist but was rebuffed by the ealdorman, who jabbed his finger towards his son.

"You did this?"

"Yes, Father, and I don't regret the slaughter of those kaka Ha'amoa. Now they know who holds power across Natuini and they'll fear another incursion into our waters. I'm the future Hou'eiki of Mo'unga Vela. I must have a name to be feared if I'm to rule our people."

The nobles from both sides began to stand to face each other. When Luther and Marcello rose to their feet, Lokai turned to the priest and spoke to him briefly in English.

"Tell the palangi everything you hear."

Then, facing the young man he began again, with a loud voice so that everyone in the Taumafa Kava could understand. "I will remind you that you are *not* Hou'eiki yet, so you will pay. Your dumb decision to put spear to flesh cost me good fishing waters and trade with Ha'amoa. This is a work I've been toiling for many a year to accomplish. Ali'i Fetu has demanded compensation from the Natui people which I'll be obliged to pay. So you'll pay in my place."

"What price do you ask of me on this day our children are betrothed?" Doko demanded.

"I will have from Mo'unga Vela, seventy-five pigs, three hundred baskets of yam, and you will build for Natuini Lokai five double-hulled kalia to hold fifty men each."

"That's outrageous. Today we brought great tribute. How can you insult us like this?"

"I am the aggrieved party, old man. Will you pay compensation?"

An eerie silence washed across the village. Every man and woman present were wide eyed. The danger was sensed throughout the circle and even beyond in the tou'a.

"Hou'eiki of Natui do not negotiate in this way. Why have you done this?" Doko was trying to keep his voice low and calm, but Lokai could hear the trembling. The shame in his voice was like sweet bird song for Lokai and he did not respond except to offer an angry scowl.

The chief of the Grey Hair peered around at the crowds of villagers, nobles and warriors of Natui, awaiting his answer.

"If my son has done this terrible thing, we'll make compensation. But we will not negotiate like this."

"Good, that brings joy to my fat heart. There's another thing I'll ask," Lokai said. "Your son. He's not a man. I have people tell me that he prefers to fuck his manservant more than he enjoys the sight of a good woman. So he'll need to cut off his balls. It's important to me that all know he's more a daughter than a son."

The outrage in the faces of father and son burned bright.

"You have gone too far—" Doko's words were interrupted by a fit of coughing and Vai Nonga came to his aid.

Lokai nodded. "My daughter does not need to take part in this game any longer."

With a gesture, two of the chief's servants approached Mahina. They ushered her to her feet, escorting her out of the kava circle and to her ladies-in-waiting before exiting from the celebration altogether.

Lokai turned his attention back to his guests.

"Old man, you're dying. Do me a favour and die now so I can throw your corpse into the 'umu tangata and eat your old arse for supper."

Malohi balled his fists and stepped forward. "I'll kill you, Lokai. I'll skin you alive like the Ha'amoa sailor and you'll beg for mercy. You'll beg to take back your insults."

Lokai threw back his head and laughed. His belly moved up and down rhythmically as he did, with tears running down his face. "You little shit! Where do you think you are? You're in the lands of Lokai. This is not your home. Even your home is not your home. It belonged to my wife and her lineage. You and your father are just dirty thieves who killed your rightful nobles in the middle of the night. So go back to your pit in the ground."

"You can keep your whore of a daughter. She's nothing. I cannot believe I agreed to marry that fat sow."

With Malohi's words an audible gasp of shock from the crowd was heard, and a number of nobles in the circle cursed angrily at the insult.

"You never *were* going to marry her, little boy. You think I would've entrusted the future of our lands to a cock-eater like you?" Lokai laughed again. "But thank you for the tribute you brought today. It's only right that you pay tribute, as you're just a lesser noble who occupies Mo'unga Vela at my pleasure."

By now, Doko had recovered and had breath enough to speak. "The Grey Hair will take our leave. I see now what you're about. You want to be the Tu'i Natui resurrected from the dead. I was foolish to have come here. But you'll see that you were foolish to believe you're like the shark god Tukuaka. You believe you'll destroy all the reef guardians and rule the sea. But the Grey Hair are the eight-armed feke, and we'll squeeze your bones from your fat flesh."

"Leave now to your volcano. But remember this little shit," Lokai said directly to Malohi, "For calling my daughter a whore I'll ensure your death will be excruciating."

The three men ignored his threat while they turned and took their leave, pushing their way back to their encampment. Other nobles and warriors loyal to Mo'unga Vela left with them, taking their possessions from Kahoua and began the march back to their kalia on the shore. Everyone else remained where they were seated, unsure of what to do next. As Lokai watched his new enemies leave the taumafa kava, Masila came to stand beside him.

"It is done, Tu'i Natui Lokai," Masila said, thumping his staff into the ground. "I'll make a sacrifice of a dozen pigs to Maui for good fortune and make blessings upon your great venture."

"Hmm. Yes. Make the sacrifices and appease the gods. We'll also make an offering to the palangi god. Ask, Marcello what would be appropriate."

He looked over at Luther. His guest was watching the situation as it unfurled and barely appeared to be flustered, as if watching the ongoings like a calm but deadly eagle, ready to swoop down and attack its prey.

"Look at those eyes. That man is as cold as an ancient weathered rock. Warriors like that are like a rare jewel. He'll be useful."

"As you wish, lord."

"Listen to me matapule. I'll meet with my chiefs. Have Aunofo tell them I'll speak to them in the morning when they've woken from their kava dreams. But tonight, I'll speak to the palangi. Bring him to the great hall and ensure Kalafa and his men are at my side. Tonight, there may be danger yet."

He strode towards Paea. Hou'eiki Maka's matapule had been drinking the powerful palangi water. Just moments ago, he had been in a state of revelry and had been communicating with the palangi healer. There was no such revelry in his face now as they stood, facing each other silently and without speaking. He did not need to say anything to Paea. He knew that soon his master would hear about what had transpired here and would know his intention. That was what he wanted. The matapule frowned and nodded. Before the man left, he turned to Wickman and smiled.

"Malo 'aupito, Lopeti," he said, leaning forward he grasped the doctor with both arms, and touched his cheeks against the doctor's in the Natui fashion of farewell. Then he was also gone, stepping out of the firelight and into the darkness beyond.

Lokai took his leave from the circle. With Kalafa and his men protecting his sides the chief entered his meeting hall. Warriors made a protective circle around the building. All the nobles loyal to Lokai flocked behind him requesting an audience. None was granted, except one whose powerful warriors pushed through the crowd. After a confrontation between guardsmen, she was eventually allowed to enter, Ruaka by her side.

FIFTEEN

Lokai had barely entered the pavilion and had not yet seated himself before Ono Hiva burst through a curtain entrance. He had expected his wife and had stationed Kalafa and his men at the door to prevent her entry. A completely futile decision. He laughed at his own foolishness as soon as she entered. No man could raise a hand to his first wife, and Kalafa would never physically stop her. It had almost come to blows between Kalafa and her guardsman. In the end, Ono Hiva had threatened to spear Kalafa through the eye for blocking her passage, and he capitulated, knowing that was a distinct possibility.

"What have you done to us, husband?" Her trembling voice was on the verge of shouting. The loyal sentinel, Ruaka, was at her side, but lowered his eyes and held one step back out of respect.

"Wife, I thought you would be pleased? You never wanted the match between Mahina and the boy."

Hiva's eyes were wide open.

"I know you, Lokai. You planned this all along. You never intended for a wedding and you used me to provoke war with Mo'unga Vela. You've shamed me and your eldest daughter."

"No," Lokai insisted. "I've saved our daughter from a life of servitude to a weak-blooded tit of a boy. And I intend to return your lands to you. That is the depth of my love for you, my loyal wife," he said with a sarcastic voice.

"I went there for nothing. I endured that shame for your petty designs just so that I could bring him here to be shamed as well. You're a monster."

"Your presence in Mo'unga Vela served a grand purpose, my love. Now I know the best landing places for my ships, the depth and height of their walls and gates. I know the lands around their village, and where crops and food grow for my soldiers' bellies. I know the numbers of warriors he has to spare, and I have a detailed understanding of where their defences are weakest." He smiled. Lokai could see her eyes light up, her mind racing to understand.

"But how …" She turned to Ruaka, tears welling up in her eyes. "You."

Her guardsman kept his eyes lowered. "It's true, my lady. I scouted the village and surrounds, at Hou'eiki Lokai's orders. When I returned, I reported what I saw."

"You betrayed me."

He looked up at her and shook his head. But it was Lokai who spoke.

"He did not betray you. He followed my orders, and very well, it seems. You needed to be my devoted wife, finding a match for Mahina. I didn't want to burden you with his scouting, or my designs."

"All the times you were missing. It was because of my husband's planning and scheming for this sickening treachery."

Ruaka shook his head again. "No, my lady. I did what must be done. For you. For your honour"

She wiped the tears from her face and turned back to her husband. "What poison have you whispered in his ears?"

"No poisons. Only truth. That I would kill you both if he were to speak my orders to you. And that when we have conquered all of Mo'unga Vela, you will be queen and these lands will be returned to you. My love, there is great benefit for us both. I know you loath the Grey Hair. I know you seek vengeance."

"Not like this!" she screamed. "We were meant to unite the two lands through our children. Through a lasting peace."

"And that would've taken too long. Many more years than I have left in this world. No, my plans are more urgent. And once we have conquered Mo'unga Vela, we'll turn northwards to the great cliffs of Natuini Si'i where I will spill the guts of Maka and hang them to dry on his village gates for all to see he is vanquished. Then, and only then, will I truly be Tu'i Natui and all of Natui will be reunited under the strength of my fist and spear."

"You're mad." His wife's face was drained of colour. Lokai watched her servant, Ruaka, and saw how his eyes looked upon her.

"Don't be saddened, love. When I've taken Mo'unga Vela in war, you'll be there to see their blood soak into the fertile soils of their island. And then you'll remain there and pay tribute to me. Queen of the Grey Hair. Queen of Mo'unga Vela." He stepped in closer to her and lowered his voice so only the three of them could hear. "When all is done you can take your man servant's cock in your mouth every night for all I care. Because you will never return to Kahoua again." His eyes darted to her guard. The warrior could barely restrain his rage.

Ruaka was about to speak; however, the chief placed his finger up to his own lips. "Shh, child, it's best you don't try to deny this. I've known for a long time."

His attentions were on Hiva again. "Some of your servants have tongues as loose as your fat cunt. I would've killed you both a long time ago, but you serve a purpose and so will stay alive for now. Anyway, you're popular with the people and you'll need some warm arms to console you on the cold nights in Mo'unga Vela, when you're exiled and I keep our daughter here in Kahoua. With her father where she belongs."

"You can't do this. Please, she needs to be with me."

Lokai shook his head. She was begging. A rush of exhilaration flowed through his body at her pathetic pleas.

"Take my loyal wife away now, Ruaka. She is distraught and needs to sleep after such a long journey."

He swept his head up in an arc towards the door, but noticed the look in Ruaka's eyes had turned from shame to something bestial. For a moment, he feared the warrior may have torn him to pieces with his bare hands.

"Take your eyes off me, son. Think of your queen. If you're stupid at this moment, I'll ensure the pain you both endure will be plentiful and long lasting." He bared his teeth at the younger man.

"You will not take my daughter from me. I will have my vengeance, husband. You will see who ends this world in pain." Hiva turned, leaving with Ruaka behind her.

Standing at the entrance of the pavilion, Lokai watched them leave. Hiva held her head high as the crowd of villagers congregated like a swarm of flies to witness the evening's drama. Awaiting Hiva were handmaidens who rushed to accompany her away from the throng of people. Pua was amongst them and was the first to meet her ward.

"Ono Hiva, we have prepared your sleeping fale—" Pua's word were cut short as Hiva let out a sickening scream and struck her servant across the face with the back of her hand. Pua fell backwards, shocked by the blow. She tried to stand up, but Hiva kicked her over again and she rolled in the dirt.

"No, my lady. I'm so sorry. I'm sorry. Please stop!"

Pua shrieked while Hiva rained down blows with her fists. Then, as she cowered, her hands over her face, Hiva began to kick her in the stomach and ribs. She rolled close to a cooking fire while her assailant continued to scream incoherently. Pua reached out to others for help in vain. No one would dare intervene. Spying a large piece of smouldering timber with one half inside the flames, the noble lady hefted the stick and thrust it into the girl's head, holding it in place. The flames quickly engulfed her hair with a burst of light, and Pua screamed in pain as the flames singed her scalp, but her shrill voice was quietened as the club smashed into her head. An audible crack was heard by the gathering crowd. Hiva did not stop. The club was held high and swung again and again at Pua's head, which soon became a bloody, broken pulp. Blood spattered into the campfire and sizzled on the hot rocks surrounding it. To the terror of witnesses, this horror continued without pause. Again and again the noblewomen smashed Pua's face and skull until her features were no longer recognisable.

Others may have attempted to stop it. But this was Ono Hiva. Commoners were forbidden to touch a noble without consent. It was only when Ruaka stepped in front of her and shouted at her to cease that she hesitated. The world spun around Hiva like a cyclone. She looked at her blood and brain-soaked hands, as if they were not even her own. Hiva dropped the smouldering club and peered at the pool of blood which was once her handmaiden. She had stopped screaming, but another wail from the crowd erupted as Pua's mother and aunt saw what had become of the young girl. They ran over and cried whilst they held the lifeless body. Hiva ran away towards her fale. Her handmaidens followed in her wake, their faces pale and tearful.

Lokai looked on with morbid curiosity. The scene pleased him. In just a few moments of fury, Hiva had undone a mystique so preciously held. The Great Lady of Natuini was once a flawless pearl in the eyes of their people. Now all the people of the land would tell stories of Hiva, the slayer of innocent girls. The handmaiden would be a loss to his spy network. But not irreplaceable. He would need to find another of Hiva's servants who was willing to share her secrets.

Abel witnessed the savage beating and then watched as most of the crowd quickly dispersed. Those visitors from closer villages packed their belongings and left as soon as they could, fearing to be caught in any further conflict, while Natui warriors doubled their guard surrounding the village with a ring of torchlight. The remaining dignitaries and nobles settled into huddles around their campfires to talk about what they had witnessed that night, and what it meant for their future. Some had already consumed too much kava and went to their sleeping fales to wait out the night knowing they would be summoned by Hou'eiki Lokai in the morning, when many suspected he would announce his plans for war.

Luther and Marcello had barely returned from the taumafa kava when they were both called away to meet with Chief Lokai. Luther looked worried. With the help of Marcello, he questioned Masila on why he was needed, but no answer was given. However, to ease Luther's concern, Masila placed his hands up as if to tell him not to worry.

"You are safe here. Lokai wishes you and your people no harm. But you will come and have audience with Lokai nonetheless. This, you have no choice in."

Only Doctor Wickman and Abel remained behind. Seeing that Wickman was accompanied by Abel and trusting that he appeared to be harmless, they were left alone. He was too drunk anyway to fully understand what had happened. He stumbled through the encampment as Abel led him outside the village where Marcello and Abel had sleeping fales, just beyond the edge of the torch light. He helped the doctor into his fale, and as soon as he saw Abel's sleeping mat, he lay down and passed out. Contrary to the doctor's own exhaustion, the night's events had shaken Abel awake, and he could not bear the thought of sleeping. Before he left he placed a bowl of water within reach. Wickman was going to wake with a pounding headache. Outside his abode, he was unsure what to do or where to go. His mind raced. What had he just seen? The day had started and finished with blood. None of it made any sense.

Sounds of breaking twigs under light feet nearby gave him a fright. A slender hand grabbed his wrist from behind and pulled him away. It was Mahina.

"I was worried that something was going to happen to you," he said.

She remained silent and pulled him away with even greater urgency towards the beach. When they reached the edge of the shore, she took him westward. They hurried away from the village until they could see no more campfires. Ahead was a rocky outcrop which divided this beach from the next. It was low tide. This was the only time a traveller along the shore could walk around, and even then, the cool water was up to their thighs as they waded through and onto the other side of the cove. When their feet touched the dry surface again, they stopped at a shallow depression in the dunes providing shelter from the wind. The surface was soft beneath their feet. As they stopped, Mahina dropped his wrist and stood before him. He could barely make out her face, though he could see she was still wearing the ornamental headdress, the fine feathers gently swaying in the wind.

"Why have you brought me here?" Abel said, but perhaps not loud enough for Mahina to hear over the breaking waves, the water's sound encompassing everything.

They had escaped away from the world around them. At that moment, they were completely and utterly alone. She reached out and pulled his waist close to hers. Then, holding him ever so tightly, she leaned in even closer and kissed him on the lips. And there, hidden by the elements, even if for only a brief time, they could share what they felt for each other. As they lay down together, Mahina pulled away her ta'ovala, her naked body pressed against his. He was terrified. Perhaps she was also scared. She trembled in his arms, but they couldn't restrain their passion. A myriad of senses overwhelmed them. The sea spray, the deafening ocean and the touch of the fine sand upon their bodies. They made love. Holding each other in blissful abandon, they forgot all about the world's pain. Just one night.

When heavy breathing gave way to a calm rhythm, they remained in each other's arms, keeping themselves warm against one another's firm bodies. She lay her head on his chest, listening to his beating heart. Then she wept, sobbing despairingly. His own eyes filled with tears and then exhaustion taking them both, they fell asleep, alone on the beach.

SIXTEEN

It had been less than two weeks since the drama that ensued at the taumafa kava, but the whole world had changed faster than Abel could comprehend. The cyclone season was over and as the seas became calmer, a warm breeze remained. The winds moved favourably for fishers and traders. Despite this, it was widely appreciated that the fate of a kalia fleet bringing warriors to war, was entirely up to the quick temperament of the god of sea and sky, Tangaloa, whose intentions were a mystery to mortals. If the correct sacrifices were made by the Natui holy men, the Natui may indeed survive a long journey with the lives of their greatest warriors intact; equally Tangaloa may decide that the evils of man needed to be punished and a reminder that no mortal is a greater master of the ocean than he. Abel had seen Marcello attempting to persuade Lokai there was only one god. However, when Lokai had come to believe the Christian god was only one of many powerful gods, Marcello compromised and accepted he may eventually convince the hou'eiki that the Christian god should be revered above all others, but to do so he would need to understand the likes of Maui, Tangaloa, Touia Fatuna and Siuelo. He had imparted the knowledge on his observations of the Natui pantheon to Abel reluctantly. Marcello considered spreading this knowledge as bordering on sacrilege, but eventually gave way to Abel's many persistent questions.

Now Abel had a rudimentary but growing understanding of the gods and goddesses. He remembered being told by Chief Lokai that the Christian god must be powerful if he had given such knowledge to the palangi. Otherwise, how would they have built such great ships and deadly weapons? The chief was hedging his bets and proclaimed a holy day before he launched the invasion. Masila and Marcello would hold a service to make offerings to the gods. Marcello was irritable. He had muttered curses to Abel in private, but chuckled at the thought Masila was likely equally enraged. He would be less than pleased his own influence with the gods needed to be shared with a foreigner. This would be a private affair held in the Red Grove, where Marcello's new church had been recently completed. Only the closest of Lokai's noble allies and the leaders of his army were to be invited as was Luther, who had just arrived to Natuini with the remaining marines and sailors of *Viritus*. They had set up a makeshift camp on the shore under the watchful eyes of Kalafa's own warriors.

After being called to an audience with Lokai the night of the betrothal ceremony, Luther hadn't returned until the following evening. When he did come back, he was so exhausted he went straight to sleep before telling them what he had learned. Abel had spent the night with Mahina, but she had left him on the beach, returning to the village before anyone found them. Since then, they had spent almost every night together, sneaking out when it was late and finding secluded places where they would not be seen, away from the eyes of anyone who would give away their secret. Her mother Hiva was only seen briefly. Abel felt terrible for her, and Mahina had been unable to console her mother. Some nights it was all that Mahina would speak about; that her mother's mood had become dark, and that Mahina was the only other soul that she would see. Even then, she would barely speak at all and only hold her daughter tight as if she was a young child in her arms. As for Mahina and Abel, they had found comfort in each other's. Mahina admitted she had never wanted to marry the boy from Mo'unga Vela and was relieved that it did not go through. The shame was not hers; in fact, the people of Kahoua had expressed anger on her behalf, and Chief Lokai had used this to his advantage, rallying the people together to avenge the slight upon his daughter. With each other they had found an escape from the world of politics and the will of their elders – an escape they were acutely aware may soon end.

The morning after Luther's return from the council with Lokai, he had a small breakfast of dried fish and fresh water before meeting with Wickman and Abel. Marcello was still sleeping, but Luther had deliberately left without telling him of their plans.

Only one of Kalafa's men was on duty to watch them, but the young warrior had been distracted by a pretty young servant girl from Fisi who had travelled to Natuini with a noble family. While the Englishmen spoke at a distance, he was trying desperately to convince her to come to his fale when the moon arose.

"Smart bastard, that chief of yours, Abel. Marcello taught him the art of chess a little too well, and now he's almost literally embarking on a life size interpretation of the fucking game. You can guess which piece we represent at your leisure."

Abel and Wickman were surprised at Luther's profanity, which they had only heard from him during times of high stress or after the occasional rum. Luther's debrief was succinct. He was on edge and wanted to return to Tapu Motu as soon as possible, but relayed what he could to Abel before he and Wickman left later at midday.

He had spoken directly to the chief, who lost no time in outlining the current position of his crew as guests in his lands. Their choices were limited. He had allowed them to live untouched by pirates or others seeking to extract them from the sacred island. It was only because of his goodwill and love for Abel they had intervened.

"At least that was the reason he claimed," Luther said.

Abel felt embarrassed. His cheeks turned a shade of crimson.

"Then he gave me two choices; we could join his invasion of Mo'unga Vela as an ally and help him defeat his enemies until he is king of all Natuini. Simply put, he wants our skills and experience with musket and cannon to tip the battle in his favour. If we comply, he will provide us with the goods and vessels to leave Natuini with all of our men and go home."

"And if we don't comply?" Wickman asked, grasping his cheeks with both hands in shock.

"Our second choice is to do nothing. Of course, that means he will also do nothing to assist us, and he'll let the Natui people know that his protection is rescinded. He'll also not give us a vessel or a means for escape. Not really a choice, as you can see, so I obviously agreed to his terms. However, when I did, I also requested immediate supplies for our men currently on Tapu

Motu. Blankets, cloth for bandages and tools for fishing and cutting lumber. I also asked for coconut oil to stop our weapons from rusting. Millstone has struggled to make it but has proposed its properties will work the same as tallow for lubricating the muskets."

"We also need some local medicines to relieve pain. I'm low on most supplies," Wickman added. "My dwindling supply of chloroform and laudanum is only for the most severe cases, and I'm worried we'll soon entirely run dry of any kind of analgesic."

Abel was now distracted. He could only think about the revelation that they could return home, and was suddenly overwhelmed with the possibility.

"The ship," Abel exclaimed. "He must be preparing the barque for the invasion. The chief must be relying on us to sail it to Mo'unga Vela. It's a mighty vessel of war and can hold hundreds of men if needs be, as well as supplies for the battle."

"Maybe. He didn't mention it, and I wasn't about to give away that we knew. Either way, I don't trust his word, and we need to be prepared for Lokai's men to turn on us at some point in the battle. If we survive, we're going to have to take the barque by force. There's nothing to be gained from Chief Lokai keeping his word."

This made Abel shudder. He suddenly understood his life here was coming to an end, and what that may mean for his relationship with Mahina and his Natui friends. Luther requested the use of a vaka, and he returned to Tapu Motu with the doctor. Despite the lieutenant raising the matter with Lokai, Abel returning with them was not up for negotiation.

After his cousin's return to the crew of *Viritus*, a number of vaka were loaded with supplies, and, true to his agreement, Lokai provided the Englishmen with the supplies that they asked for. Two weeks later, Lokai proclaimed the invasion was to begin and sent Marcello to bring Luther and his men back to the mainland. The Natui sent three large kalia for this purpose. Not only did they need to retrieve all forty-four marines and sailors but additionally their muskets, cannon and round-shot. The cannon had to be removed from the remains of a scorched vessel at low tide. It was not an easy feat but before he had disappeared, Jack Horton, the crew's shipwright, repaired their ship's pulley system which removed a number of cannon from the vessel. This was made difficult by the rough coral. It had significantly damaged the remains of *Viritus*. Most of the ship had either been scorched by fire or damaged by the storms since beaching. Horton had also cannibalised large parts of *Viritus* where the timber was undamaged to build shelter or to repair the smaller row boats that survived. The condition of the cannon was variable; some rusted from sea water spray, though only a small number was needed for the task ahead.

By the time Luther arrived with the crew of *Viritus*, Chief Lokai's call to arms had mustered over 1,200 fighting men. The army comprised of warriors of Kahoua and those men contributed from the lesser nobles who ruled over smaller villages across Natuini and the many outer islands under his influence. Only two lesser nobles, Lord Kakaea and Lord Ahomana who lorded over villages on the far eastern shores of Natuini had not responded to his demand for warriors to enter battle with Mo'unga Vela. This was not unexpected. Both lords had strong ties with Mo'unga Vela through trade and family alliances. The position of their bases on the far eastern shores of Natuini had made them difficult to control, and they had only ever paid respect to Lokai in word, not in material tribute, which was instead offered to Doko. Now, they had chosen a side, a dangerous proposition given their location, and Abel had been told that Chief Lokai would seek to punish those chiefs as a warning to others.

The encampments had turned Kahoua into a bustling town. Many of the warriors had brought their families with them. They would help the men prepare their weapons, armour and carry supplies to the kalia that would transport them across the waves. A fleet of forty double hulled kalia made an impressive sight in the shallows of the beach. Abel had seen them hold over fifty men at a time. Two of the kalias gifted by Lokai's trading allies from Fisi held more; these feats of engineering could hold around one hundred sailors, though for this voyage would transport much of the food and goods required by the army. Along the seashore and low grassy cliffs, men, women and children abounded. Luther's arrival with his men caused a stir as many pressed forward to see the faces of the Englishmen for the first time, whilst others kept a distance, fearful to approach after hearing rumours and stories about the palangis being sent by the gods of the underworld. There were those who believed they were the living ghosts of long dead warriors. However, Lokai had ensured that his people were very well aware that Luther's men were allies and as friends to Natuini, they were to be welcomed as brothers in arms. The crew were wary as they arrived at what they might encounter, but as the kalia slowed to a crawl and then stopped short of the beach, the crew who disembarked were met by half a dozen young smiling women who presented colourful leis, draping them around the necks of sailors and marines alike. Luther was the first to step onto shore and received the first lei, followed by Worthstead and the two scouts, Rowe and Cambridge.

"Oh brother, I think that one likes you, Cambridge. Maybe you'll find a nice lass here to marry you after all." Private Rowe smiled as he received the flowers around his neck from a young lady.

His fellow marksmen gave a polite nod and smile to the girl who had presented the lei.

"Aye, you two lover boys. Mind yourselves," Worthstead countered with a cheeky grin. "Get your hands on the wrong pair of 'cat heads' 'ere, and you might end up in a delicious pot o' sailor stew."

Rowe chuckled. "Yes, sir. We've heard the lieutenant's warning a few times already. We would still taste a far sight better than anything Cookie could whip up."

When Worthstead saw Abel, he gave him an enormous hug. "Good on ya boy. You get bloody bigger every time I see ya."

Abel couldn't help but smile. He had always liked the foulmouthed sailor. "You've gotten ruder," Abel said.

This earned him a friendly punch in the arm, which Abel took well.

"Hey, Worthstead, take a look at my tattoo. It's fully healed." Abel turned his shoulder and showed off the dark lines of his tattoo, which had taken on a much more dark and defined tone in the past weeks.

"Nice one, lad. Beautiful. Beats the poor attempt at drawing on ol' Buxley over there," he said, pointing at the enormous sailor pulling off supplies from a kalia. "He had one of his mates etch a mermaid into his back a while ago, and instead it turned out looking like a diseased wagtail. Funny as 'ell. Go take a look."

"I'd rather not …" Abel said quietly.

Worthstead nodded and frowned. 'Oh yeah. Bad 'istory. Don't worry. The boys were upset at first when they 'eard about Smith but when the boss let us know we might 'ave home ahead of us, they spun around. Not sure they're so keen to battle someone else's fight'n though."

Luther stepped forward and interrupted. "Worthstead, secure the camp site and make sure there's no trouble. They'll answer to me directly if trouble is caused with the locals."

"Apologies, Vincent, we're expected at the Red Grove shortly," Abel said.

"Excellent. Lead the way."

On the short distance they travelled to the sacred site, Abel asked Luther about the men's mood. He told Abel the task was no easy sell; the men had already seen enough conflict, but they understood that there were few choices. Luther hadn't shared his doubts Lokai would be true to his word, keeping hope alive if they survived the conflict, they could see Mother England again. There was also the matter of the ship that was being hidden on the north coast.

"Where is it? Has Lokai mentioned he expects us to sail the ship to Mo'unga Vela?"

"Nothing, Vincent. No mention at all, and there hasn't been any opportunity to scout the northern cove again to see what's happening. With so many Natui around since the Taumafa Kava I'm always watched."

When they entered the Red Grove, Luther's features gave away his surprise at the sight of a chapel with a small crucifix attached to the entrance's upper panel. Ruaka waited for them outside. Abel spoke to him in Natui. His mastery of the language was growing, and he also felt some pride in being able to show off his skills.

"Malo e lelei, Ruaka. Are we able to enter? Vincent was expected."

Ruaka's face was dark and unsmiling. He had the appearance of a man who had not slept.

"Malo e lelei, Abel. Your Natui grows stronger. Vincent may enter. You must remain outside."

Abel stopped and felt frustrated that despite living amongst the Natui and being accepted as part of a noble family, he was still not provided with the instant privilege that Luther had captured from Lokai. But he understood this was a matter of hierarchy and Luther's position amongst the palangi crew. Ruaka said nothing to Luther but nodded towards the entrance, which Luther stepped into without hesitation. From the door, he saw several others inside: Chief Lokai, Ono Hiva, Aunofo, Kalafa, Father Marcello and Masila. There were a dozen other nobles from the scattered villages of Natuini. Many of them were present at the failed betrothal ceremony, and all of them would sail alongside the armies of Lokai in the days to come. Everyone except Masila sat on crudely made benches facing the front where a roughly hewn stone altar sat above a layer of timber planks. Behind the altar both Marcello and Masila presided, and as Luther entered, Marcello motioned him to sit down. Marcello was sweating profusely in the intense heat of the day, so before he began, he took a damp cloth and wiped his forehead. Then, the priest made the sign of the cross.

"The grace of the Lord Jesus Christ, and the love of God, and the communion of the Holy Ghost, be with you all. Amen."

"Amen." The congregation replied in kind.

Lokai had insisted on his nobles paying homage to this new foreign god, and although Abel had been told there had been some whispered resentment, Lokai had not forced his subjects to abandon the ancient Natui gods, only to recognise an addition to their pantheon. They had done so, and now many commoners were following the lead of their 'eiki and offering prayers to a powerful but largely unknown entity. Marcello was busy these days, travelling from village to village and doing his best to preach Christianity with the blessing of their most powerful chief.

Marcello delivered his sermon in Natui; another reason he had taught the word of his god so successfully was because the man had painstakingly interpreted large parts of the scripture into the local tongue. The project had begun some years ago. Since then, Marcello had made significant headway towards completing a full translation of the Bible.

The priest spoke to the gathered party of the need for strength and faith in times of turmoil, that God would protect all those who repented their sins from harm. He pressed forward that this was a kind of holy conflict between those who had embraced the lord and those who were still held in the darkness, away from his light.

Abel listened from the entrance, but as Marcello started speaking, Ruaka pulled him away. They walked to a safe distance, out of earshot from the service. His face grew dark.

"You and I have not spoken often, but we have the same heart. I am Hiva's protector. Her daughter is important to me too. We have much in common."

"What is it you want, Ruaka? I know she loathes me. Probably because I'm palangi. I notice how she looks at me."

"No. You have mistaken the lady of Natui. She's worried for her people and worried for Mahina. Do you love her?"

The question took Abel by surprise.

"Why would you ask that question? She almost got married recently."

"Don't worry. I'll keep your secret. It's obvious to me the way you look upon the girl, but it's also the way she speaks of you. There's love between you, I know. I see it for there is a love that I too am forbidden." Ruaka lowered his head.

"I don't understand Ruaka."

"Hiva. She and I … we've held each other for many years now. There's nothing but bitterness between her and Lokai."

"Why are you telling me this?" Abel looked around to ensure that they were not being watched and his mind swam with the fear that if Ruaka knew of his feelings towards Mahina that others may have noticed.

Ruaka drew closer.

"I tell you this because now we share a common secret. Something that will never be accepted. A knowledge that may be of danger to both of our lives. So now we must have trust between us. Do you agree?"

"Please tell me what it is you want."

"I need your help. I need Lu'fa's help."

"Help from me and Vincent? What can we do? My cousin doesn't know you so he has no reason to want to listen."

"Lokai expects a boy to be born from the womb of his third wife, Becca. But it's uncertain if it's to be a boy. If we conquer Mo'unga Vela, I believe that Lokai will try to kill Ono Hiva."

"Why would he do that? How?"

"I don't know how he'll do this terrible thing, but I know his mind. She – we – have betrayed him, and he'll never forgive this. He also wishes to rule without question. Ono Hiva has a claim to Mo'unga Vela. She still has noble families there who would support her rule. You must understand that Lokai would expect her to be a subservient ruler, but I know her mind, and once she has her lands, she'll one day rise against him. So he will kill her to stop this."

Abel shook his head in disbelief. "I'm not sure that I can help you. I'd like to. No doubt I owe you. You didn't have to protect me from Kalafa, but you did, anyway. But I'm just one man, and I don't think we can convince Vincent to interfere."

"He must, and you must ask him. Please, Abel. I'll keep her safe as much as I can, but I need allies. Only my loyal men will turn upon Lokai. The others would be too fearful, even to save Ono Hiva. But you and I, we are brothers now. We know each other's secrets."

"I don't know what to do. Vincent won't agree to this."

"He will. Tell him that if he helps keep Ono Hiva safe, if he helps me, I'll be in his debt. My warriors will help the palangi to leave this place. Abel, the chief holds a secret, a way for the palangi to escape."

"We already know about Marcello's ship."

Ruaka held a look of surprise, but then nodded and clenched his fists. "Maybe so. But you must know that Lokai will never let you take the palangi ship. It's his greatest treasure. They'll never leave Natuini alive." His eyebrows narrowed, and he was clearly angry. But then his face softened with emotion. "Please, please tell Lu'fa of my pain. I'll give an offering to the gods for you. I'll give my spear and akatau to the palangi cause. You must! Please, Abel, if you love Mahina then you'll help us."

Abel brought his hands up in front of him and widened his eyes at the man's ever heightening voice.

"No more. Speak no more. I'll do what I can. But you must understand that Vincent will not endanger his men without just cause."

Both men returned to the entrance of the chapel. Marcello had finished his brief service with communion and had been ushered away with a 'hiss' by an impatient Masila who began his own blessings. Abel tried to listen; however, he found much of the narrative too difficult to understand. The language used by Masila was Natui, but the words spoken were an ancient form or he used concepts for complex words he had not yet learned. Later, Marcello explained some of Masila's service. Chief Lokai stood and handed his war spear to Masila. He accepted the weapon and placed it onto the altar. Masila, dressed in an ornate ta'ovala, lifted a cup made of woven banana leaves into the air. He was showing the sacred drink to the gods to thank them for the sustenance. Then he brought the cup down and took a sip of the contents. He looked to the skies and uttered his prayers. At first, he whispered, speaking secretly to the gods. When his personal pleas were done, he raised his voice for all to hear.

"We live upon the land, and our hearts turn to the goddess Lupe for her generosity. That our feet stand strong upon the earth and our bellies are full by the nourishment of her earthen womb." Masila put down the green bowl, and picked up a small piece of kava root, placed it into his mouth and chewed it with vigour. Once he had developed a mouth full of saliva, he spat the remains onto the floor. Then, picking up a handful of dirt, he slowly sprinkled the dirt upon the head and shaft of the weapon in front of him.

"We come from her earth, as do the instruments of the warrior. To her we ask for blessings upon this, the great spear of Hou'eiki Lokai, who seeks to unite her lands together as one great kingdom."

He poured the rest of the liquid from the banana leaf bowl on to the spear's pointed head.

"But it is mighty Hemoana whose ocean over which we must travel. To him we must ask for the blessings of swift journeys to our enemies' shores. And it is to him I offer the ocean of my body for his blessings. "

Masila took a small knife and ran the edge across his arm. A line of blood appeared, which he held over the spear, and the congregation watched as a few drops splashed against its wooden tip, making the crimson glisten in the bright sunlight of the midday sun.

He picked up the spear with both hands, handing it to Lokai. The chief turned to the gathering of his allies.

Masila's sermon raised to a shout. "Ke tapuaki'i mai 'ae me'a tau ni ke ngaue 'aki hotau 'eiki ke ne tau'i 'aki 'ae fili."

With his final words, Lokai raised the spear high above his head before bringing it down; the butt thrusted firmly to the ground with a 'thud'. The congregation rose to their feet and shouted the same words in unison. The blessing was over and Chief Lokai walked out of the chapel, spear in hand, with his nobles following in his wake. They had their heads raised, feeling ever powerful and confident. As he walked by Abel, he gave him a friendly slap on the back and smiled.

"The Gods are with me now. It will be a glorious victory."

"Maybe for him," Abel heard Luther say to himself as he left. "I'm not so sure about the rest of us."

SEVENTEEN

It wasn't until the next morning that the fleet sailed from Natuini Lahi carrying Lokai's army and the palangi mercenaries he had coerced into his cause. Lokai's captured barque was nowhere to be seen. The Englishmen were evenly split between two double hulled kalia. They also carried several Natui sailors and some supplies for the journey. The entire fleet comprised forty-two vessels. With sails unfurled they were a beautiful sight to behold as they left during the early hours of a pristine morning, the skies blue and cloudless. Onboard, a legion of warriors, ship carpenters, cooks, sailors and noblemen waved and shouted their goodbyes to their families who had lined up at the shore to see them off. Even the Englishmen were farewelled by the cheers of Natui visitors, who saw the addition of allies to Chief Lokai's army as a boon by the gods to secure his victory over Mo'unga Vela. This boosted the morale of the marines. They were relieved by the welcome they had received and the change from their isolation on Tapu Motu for more than half a year.

Mahina and Ono Hiva sailed together in the middle of the fleet and were protected on all sides by a dozen ships. Ruaka and his warriors were tasked with protecting them on this journey. Their presence was important since Chief Lokai had wanted his wife to persuade some of the elders in Mo'unga Vela who still recognised her family's rule to surrender. Also, if they were victorious, Lokai would not have to send for her before returning home and could leave her to rule over Mo'unga Vela in his name, a move that would quickly solidify his rule over a people Hiva better understood. Her presence would likely quell any further bloodshed. Besides the noble lady and her handmaidens, a handful of female warriors also rode along with the fleet. Marcello had explained that female warriors amongst the Natui were not unheard of, particularly those who protected noble ladies of the realm whose husbands or who themselves preferred a female to watch over them. Several noble women had offered their protectors to Lokai's army. He had called to all of his loyal 'eiki to submit soldiers to aid in his conquest. His second wife, Tihani, had sent Melino, a formidable fighter. She was often by her side and presented as a tall and strong-armed terror who wielded a short spear and shield. Maau had told Abel he was both terrified and transfixed by her and always had been. He and Afah had chosen to journey with Abel on the ship carrying Luther and most of his marines, and had spotted her ship from a distance. Melino's hulking figure was well known amongst the people of Natuini, and as they sailed, they could see her standing at the very forward bow of her kalia on which Aunofo and his warriors rode. It sailed close to Chief Lokai's flagship, a monstrous vessel made by Fisi boat builders and able to hold over one hundred warriors.

The three young men stared out towards her with Maau's arms wrapped around the shoulders of his friends.

"Look upon that woman, that goddess. She will one day be mine."

Afah raised one of his eyebrows "I thought you were always joking but now I think you really are in love with that beast."

Maau smacked the back of Afah's head. "Hey! You wait! I'll take that tongue from your mouth if you insult my woman again," Maau threatened.

Afah laughed and rubbed his sore head. "Save your anger for the Grey Hair." Afah picked up a pakipaki and pretended to swing it towards an invisible enemy.

"Melino has more than once threatened to cut me to pieces and feed me to the sharks but I know, deep within her heart, that she desires me."

"You're crazy. She's as old as your mother and would beat you with as much strength." Afah parried an imaginary strike. A large wave rocked the kalia, and he stumbled, almost clipping Private Millstone, who had been sitting nearby but avoided the wayward strike at the last minute.

"Aye lad, mind that club of yours. Abel, can you tell your friend that I don't want to be dead before we even get there? I'm not even supposed to be here. What good's a cook in the middle of a bloody battle?"

"Sorry, Millstone," Abel said.

Afah looked amused, not understanding the palangi man's words but understanding his protest.

"What did he say? He looks like he's been eating all the puaka on Tapu Motu. Is he a mighty warrior?"

Abel smiled. "No, not a warrior. He's just worried that you're going to knock him off the boat. He's the ship's cook. Not a bad one really."

The gods had been favourable to the crews, and with a moderate breeze blowing, by mid-morning the fleet had reached the eastern coast of Natuini, and Abel could see smoke billowing from several locations just inland from his view. These were the villages of Lord Kakaea and Lord Ahomana. A group of warriors from Kahoua had travelled by foot across the island to demand their contribution of men, but when they arrived, most of the inhabitants had left weeks ago when they allied with Chief Doko. Left with empty villages, Lokai had ordered them burned in punishment. From their vantage point at sea, Abel could see a number of warriors ashore. They were picked up by one of Kalafa's kalias and joined the fleet, sailing away from the island and towards the south-eastern ocean.

Luther was deep in conversation with Wickman and Worthstead. Abel had been surprised to hear that Worthstead had become Luther's second amongst the Englishmen and that despite his small stature and wiry appearance had shown himself to be an intimidating force, keeping others in line when things started to get chaotic. He could also be brutal. Not cruel, but certainly willing to lay down the law if threatened or if he thought that Luther's command was being challenged. For this reason, Luther had grown to trust him. He wasn't a marine, so was a popular choice amongst the seamen.

Once they boarded, Abel told his cousin about Ruaka's plea. As he suspected, Luther didn't take it well. He screwed up his face and told him in no uncertain terms he was not going to risk the men's lives getting involved in local politics.

"It's bad enough we're taking up arms against a people whom we have no quarrel with. It makes me ill that I have agreed to this alliance, but it's a necessity. Taking the word of a Natui who claims to be having an affair with Chief Lokai's wife? That's a dangerous prospect. I'm sorry, Abel, but it's not our business to interfere. Don't speak of this again."

Abel didn't blame him. He was under pressure and the crew of *Viritus* were being dragged into a war they wanted no part of. Most of them anyway; Buxley had loudly exclaimed that he welcomed the chance to break the boredom of the isolation and was looking forward to shooting some people. Now he spent his days sharpening his sabre and keeping his firearm well oiled. The crew still had an ample amount of weaponry and powder at their disposal. The remaining sailors and marines were each armed with a sheathed sabre, a pistol and a Brown Bess rifle. Luther had not removed all the weapons from their island. Most armaments were hidden the evening prior to their departure, to ensure they still had the ability to defend themselves if Chief Lokai decided he no longer wanted a foreign presence in his lands.

A strong, cool wind picked up at dusk. The men brought up their collars and huddled together to avoid the chill. Doctor Wickman was spying the distant horizon with his sextant whilst making notes in his journal. Throughout the day, both Luther and Wickman pored over a large map they had saved from the ship's wreckage. Wickman regularly stabbed at parts of the parchment and shook his head in frustration. Mo'unga Vela and its surroundings had not been previously charted, so Luther had asked him to keep a record of the navigation and chart any islands they spied. Lieutenant Page of *Viritus* had been their chief navigator, but had been killed by a stray piece of shrapnel during their fight with the French. Dried remnants of his blood were spattered over the northern seas of New Zealand, as he had been killed standing above his ocean survey. When night fell, Wickman put his sextant safely away in an oaken box and rubbed his eyes. Abel couldn't sleep. Afah and Maau lay beside him. They had both somehow found some comfort on the hard deck of the kalia and had long since drifted into slumber. But for Abel, he could find no respite. Instead, he stayed awake to watch the brilliant stars. The sky was clear. He had already counted seven shooting stars before the doctor noticed he was still awake.

"Get some sleep, dear boy. You'll need your rest for the days ahead. I'm told it will take us around four days to reach Mo'unga Vela. These voyages can be gruelling." He smiled warmly as he drew a blanket up around himself and turned off the small lantern perched at the side of the vessel.

Abel nodded, but it was not for a long time later that sleep finally took him.

The first encounter with the enemy ensued on the third day of their voyage. Abel had been watching Afah drag a small fish onto the boat using a short fishing line. They had been trying to decide what species they had caught when a number of shouts were heard from their far-left flank. Everyone stood and looked to the north where several allied kalia tacked into a defensive formation, drawing closer to each other and into protective line. It was Maau who spotted the enemy kalia first.

"There, to the north. Circling from those islands!" he shouted and pointed.

A dozen small but fast moving kalia and double outrigger canoes had appeared from the safety of an atoll where they had been hiding in wait for Lokai's fleet. Many of them were smaller but travelled at increasing speed, using favourable winds to close with them at a distance of less than one hundred and fifty yards. They sailed parallel to the line of kalia protecting the inner fleet which held most of the supplies upon the slower moving vessels.

"Abel, tell the Natui helmsman to take us to the northern line," Luther ordered.

"Sir?"

"Just do it, Abel."

Abel ran to the Natui crew, who had responsibility of the kalia's rudder and sails, to relay Luther's wish. They didn't hesitate and tacked into the wind, bringing them ever closer to the line of defence. Several Natui were drawing arrows into their kaufana. Natui long bowmen had already begun loosening towards the approaching kalia. The arrows were falling short and in the moderate winds were also falling away from their target. However, this served more as a warning. The deadliness of the arrows would be felt if the boats drew closer.

"It's Lord Kakaea's men. Doubt he's with them, but you can see it's his people by their lizard totem. It's etched on their sails," Afah said.

Maau agreed with a swift nod. "Very strong sailors. Kakaea's warriors sail in the most violent seas. They'll outpace the fleet."

"Surely they can't expect to destroy us with a dozen ships. They can't have more than one hundred men between them," Abel said.

Maau shook his head. "They're not trying to destroy us, just harass us. They want to slow us down. Head us away from our destination. They can attack and retreat all morning if they want."

Abel's kalia had drawn up into the northern defence line quickly and taken a place in between two other vessels when Luther ordered his men into firing position. Ten marines and eight sailors of *Viritus* were on Luther's kalia, and each moved at speed to secure their rifles. They crouched to one knee at the edge of the vessel side by side.

"You too, Abel. Get yourself on that line," the lieutenant ordered, and tossed him the long-barrelled weapon.

It has been some time since he had handled a Brown Bess, but he had been drilled so long and hard in its use that his muscle memory soon kicked in. Taking a position beside Private Cambridge, his breathing became quick and shallow.

The seasoned scout saw him and placed one hand on his arm. "Easy, son. Aim, shoot and let God decide the rest."

Cambridge opened the latch on his cartridge box, which hung across his shoulder, and took out a cartridge, tearing an opening with his teeth. Nodding at the box, he motioned for his companion to do the same. Abel also tore open a cartridge and poured some of the precious powder into the pan then closed it.

"Not too heavy handed on the black stuff," Cambridge warned. "Else it'll flash hot and your shot will be delayed."

Abel tipped the rest of the powder and ball into the muzzle and rammed the lot deep within the musket. The boat's movement made the task difficult.

"Take your time and listen to the lieutenant. He'll give the order. Don't pull your trigger before that. You'll be wasting your time at this distance. Aim higher than you think. Bess will always try to pull down your shot."

The crew loaded. Then they waited. Some arrows passed at a distance from Kakaea's canoes, a wide berth still held between the two fleets. Suddenly, Kakaea's vessels swept inwards into attack and dramatically shortened the distance between the two fleets. They were attempting to head off the army and force a direction change, which was a brave manoeuvre given the difference in numbers. The size of the enemy vessels allowed them to attack and retreat at a much faster pace than Lokai's fleet which need to avoid being drawn away and cut off from the rest of their allies. Arrows fired from both armies were now landing closer to their targets. As they swept closer, Abel counted thirteen ships in total. The men on those kalia hailed down arrows on the much larger vessels and although still at a distance, several struck the kalia directly in front of them. One Natui sailor was hit in the chest. He screamed and fell from the boat. The first kill of the battle caused outrage on the vessels ahead of them where sailors loosened dozens of arrows towards the double outrigger responsible for the fall of their brethren. None of them struck their target.

A larger canoe holding at least twenty men approached Abel's vessel at speed. When it reached the seventy-five-yard mark, several warriors loosened a few volleys of missiles in the kalia's direction. Some of the arrows struck the main deck, and one pierced a sail beside Afah.

"Make ready!" Luther shouted.

The Englishmen raised their guns. Each had already loaded a cartridge.

"Present!" Luther ordered louder, over the battle cries of the Natui.

Each man of the line lowered their weapons towards the enemy. They took aim as well as they could on the swaying deck.

"Wait … wait." Luther watched the kalia draw closer. He raised his own rifle and prepared to fire.

Fifty yards.

"Fire!"

A volley of shot, smoke and fire erupted from their rifles. The sound was like a clap of thunder on a sunny day, and it tore painfully through Abel's ears. The violence of the weapon pushed him back, his stance faltering with the recoil.

"Reload!" Luther shouted without hesitation between volleys.

The breeze hastened the smoke away, providing visibility once again.

As he took another cartridge from the scout's satchel, he looked at the vessel they had fired at. It was no longer moving towards them; the helmsman had steadied the boat and was looking around in confusion at what had caused such a noise. Two men had been hit. One had caught a ball in the temple and his blood had soaked the bark cloth sail so much that it was dripping red liquid wantonly upon the deck. Another had been struck in the chest and was lying on his back, holding the wound with his hands, screaming in pain.

"Make ready."

Lokai's warriors had been warned about the rifles. They winced at the sound, but continued to loosen arrows at the approaching vessels. The enemy had no such warning. They halted for a moment. Shocked by the horrendous noise that had trumpeted from the sky.

"Present."

Kakaea's men saw the Englishmen were preparing to use their sound weapons again. They had never encountered this before, so were paralysed with indecision on whether to retreat or continue their assault. Other vessels in the attacking line of boats had also stopped short.

"Fire!"

Another volley. This time three men were struck. Two fell from their boats and were taken under the waves, whilst another was caught in the hand, his fingers blown to pieces of flesh and splintered bone.

"At will gentlemen, at will."

By the third volley, Kakaea's vessels swept northwards again and disengaged. Their fear of the unknown weapons, employed by Lokai's palangi allies, had broken their courage and they retreated with haste. However, the third volley struck the vessel's helmsman, who had been perched at the steering paddle. The helmsman's leg was horribly wounded. He lost balance, steering the ship into a wide circle. Combined with a strong wind, it snapped crucial lines of rigging. The damage to the vessel made it easy pickings for Lokai's warriors. They caught the stricken vessel, boarded it and slaughtered any of the crew who tried to put up a fight. By the end of the encounter, only five of the twenty men remained alive on that vessel. They were taken prisoner and questioned for what they knew about Mo'unga Vela and the preparations for battle.

Only one allied Natui warrior had lost his life. His crewmen returned to retrieve his body so he could be buried on land. Abel's blood ran quickly through his veins. He could barely remember pulling the trigger and was still clutching his rifle with white knuckles, when Cambridge carefully prised it from his hands.

"Nice shooting, friend. You can let it go now."

When Abel finally stood and turned around, he could see that the crew of *Viritus* were celebrating, yelling out obscenities at the retreating vessels and patting each other on the back. Afah and Maau were still wide eyed, but they ran to Abel and smiled, shouting over each other as they demanded that Abel promise to teach them how to work the palangi weapon. The "Fire Spark" as they called it.

Over their shoulders, he could see Luther standing proudly with rifle still in hand, looking to the centre of the fleet where Lord Lokai also stood, watching the spectacle, but at this distance it was too far to discern his expression. It was clear that Luther had sent a message. The Englishmen would fight for the Natui. And now the Natui understood what they had unleashed.

EIGHTEEN

M o'unga Vela was the largest island at the far end of an archipelago, with a fair number of smaller but picturesque islands leading to its shores. On one such island that Abel estimated could be walked around in less than fifteen minutes, the fleet moored before nightfall and the army set camp. From here the army would launch its assault. It would also be the base where the army would fall back to regroup if the battle turned against them. A tiny group of fishermen lived there and were terrified senseless from the sudden arrival of a thousand men and women on their shores. Lokai ordered his men to leave the simple villagers alone, and once they had come out from hiding, they offered whatever meagre food they had to Lokai and his chiefs, which was politely declined. These people were not fighters, and the intruders meant them no harm.

Campfires were set and Luther's men enjoyed a tasty supper of fish and baked 'ufi, a yam which Millstone had learned to cook in many delicious ways. He complained about the lack of potatoes in the Pacific Islands, and although most of the men baulked at the floury root vegetable, Millstone had eventually discovered ways to add taste and prepare it in a method that was palatable to the Englishmen. Taking a wrapped cheese cloth bag out of his pack, he passed around a batch of sea salt that had taken some time to gather from drying sea water. It added much needed flavour and was one of the few spices available to the men on their island. He had added some dried and crushed lantana to the mix, which had not been received well by his diners.

"It's full of mould, you right twerp. You're gonna kill us all." Worthstead poked at the salt, fingering the green specks inside.

"It's not mould," Millstone countered in an offended tone. "It's a local herb. I dried it and added it to the salt. Now we 'ave herb salt. Like parsley salt. Except it's not parsley."

"That's right. It's clearly not parsley. I'll tell you what it is. It's mouldier than a witch's arsehole."

"It's not mould!"

"But it ain't fucking *parsley* either, is it? Why can't you just make normal salt ya daft bastard?"

Most of the men chuckled, but Abel wasn't feeling very mirthful. He sat alone and thought about Mahina. He had only seen her from a distance on the sea and not at all since landing. Now that they had settled to camp, servants had constructed makeshift bivouacs for each of the hou'eiki and 'eiki men and women. Mahina was amongst them, staying with her mother, so she was well protected and completely out of sight. When they finished their supper, the lieutenant set a watch. Kalafa had accepted Luther's offer of some of his own men to take guard duty at night; not that there was a lack of alert warriors. The lieutenant didn't trust anyone else but his own men, so he organised a roster and ensured there were always four men awake.

"Cousin." The lieutenant walked over to offer Abel a drink from his waterskin and then sat beside him.

He welcomed the offer. The salt air had dried his lips with the heat of the day, making him tremendously thirsty.

"You made me proud out there today. Cambridge said you aimed true and steady."

Abel shrugged but the compliment was welcome. "I don't know if I killed anyone."

"That's not the point. On the line, each man does his part. He listens to orders, keeps a cool head and stands by his brother. A disciplined army wins wars."

"Is this a disciplined army?" Abel asked.

Luther looked about. "It's a brave army. And most certainly experienced. In my time I've seen the skill of warriors from the Pacific and they are some of the bravest, dangerous fighters I've ever seen. There's a strength and experience in these people, and the Natui warriors are no exception. But disciplined? No, not from a marines' point of view."

"I can't see them running from battle, Vincent. You just said they were brave …"

"Brave doesn't mean disciplined. If the Natui fight like the Bati of Fiji or the Fitafita of Samoa, they will launch themselves into battle as they like. There are tactics employed in the field of battle but there is no unit cohesion and the concept of ranking officers is rudimentary. Basically, when the battle begins, it's every man for himself. I'm not sure, but I'm guessing it has something to do with each man wanting to become a warrior of renown. You can't stand out from the rest if you're stuck in the second rank of a shield wall, and yet that is the very thing that won battles for European armies before firearms became our mainstay."

"I'd say that one on one these Natui warriors would be more than an equal match for your marines," Abel said defensively. He also considered himself a warrior of Natui.

"That may be so." Vincent smiled. "But army to army? I don't believe so. Which is why I've persuaded Lokai to consider a change of tactics. He wanted to have us blast our way into the fortified village, then mass attack with his soldiers, but I counselled it would not be necessary. That the enemy would come to us and he should hold a line of shield men to meet them."

"What did he say?"

"Haha – what did he say? He told me to shut my mouth. That I had no idea how the Natui do battle. Or something like that. I think Marcello held back some of the stronger words used when he translated. I'm sure he called me a buffoon during his rant. It was late in the morning after the wedding feast, so tempers were frayed. I thought that may have been the end of me."

The two laughed. When they stopped, there was a time of silence. Abel felt there were many things to say to his cousin, but didn't know where to start. He had been away for six months and so much had changed.

"If you need to tell me something, then do it. I won't judge," Luther said.

He thought long and hard, not really sure where to begin or what he was really feeling. So, he began with what was most at the front of his mind. "Whatever happens, I'm not going to leave her. I love her."

Luther raised his eyebrows briefly and sighed.

"You said you wouldn't judge," Abel said.

"I'm not judging Abel, but please be honest with me. Have you bedded the girl?"

"That's not your concern."

"Normally, yes, you would be right. But if you have relations with the daughter of the very man who can order our deaths with impunity, then it becomes my concern. And what if she fell with child?"

"Fine. Yes, we are together in that way, but nobody knows it. We've been discreet. And she's not with child. We'll be careful."

"Discreet? It's openly clear you desire her, and likely the young lady will not be able to hide her emotions. The point is, there is nothing wrong with your love. But there are consequences for you – for both of you and also for your fellow crewmen."

"So we'll take her with us when we leave. Otherwise, I won't leave without her."

"Have you asked her what she wants?"

He hadn't. In fact, he had only just decided what he wanted. "She won't want to be without me or be married off to some other old man she's never met."

"Abel, you can't save every woman in Natuini. You won't leave Mahina behind. Fine. I'll support you in that if it comes down to it, whatever that looks like. But you also made a promise to the other wife of Lokai. What was her name? Tihani? And you just asked me to try and save Ono Hiva. Listen, you're not D'Artagnan and you can't sweep the world up over your shoulder to carry it all to safety."

Abel looked down, embarrassed by Luther's words. His cousin was right. He was all over the place with his thoughts, and now his plans seemed so childish.

"I'm sorry cousin. I didn't mean to berate you. It's possible that you're the bravest amongst us. Certainly, you have the biggest heart. If it's within my power to help you, I will. Just remember, I have a responsibility, to you and to the other men who have put their lives in my hands."

"I know. Thank you. It's just that I don't know what to do. I missed you. I was so alone. I am so alone …" Abel held back his tears as well as he could.

Luther looked into the fire light. "Not anymore, Abel. I'm here for you. We'll survive this together."

For a moment, Abel forgot about the impending danger and remembered the Luther he had always looked up to. The hero who fought for Admiral Nelson and the man he wanted to be. It strengthened his heart, and he felt better for telling his cousin about Mahina. For now, he could sleep, even if he knew it might be his last.

From a distance, even in the low light of dawn, Abel saw that Mo'unga Vela was entirely different from the landscape of Natuini Lahi. The lands of Hou'eiki Lokai had some raised plateaus and gently sloping hills, with a climate that seemed noticeably cooler than these waters. There were even several coastal cliff faces which had sheer drops to the shoals below, rising high above the seas. However, for the most part, Natuini was flat across much of the island. Mo'unga Vela was immensely hilly. In the centre of the large island a triangular volcanic peak rose over

4,000 feet into the air and dwarfed everything around it. A tiny trickle of vapour spread from the cone of the volcano, and it provided for an ominous sight as they approached. The mountainous centre had steep sides, surrounded by lush forest. As the volcano descended, it curved out into more gentle slopes and level areas all the way out to the ocean on every side of the island. The island was not as expansive as Natuini Lahi, but certainly much more visually striking. A flock of seabirds circled near the crater. He wondered if anyone lived near its peak and had the sudden urge to want to climb to the top and peer inside.

The fleet approached a circular bay. Its waters were peaceful and provided a safe harbour as they navigated through channels in the coral reef. The fleet's navigators knew the routes well, so they formed a line of vessels following one another into the bay and beyond the rough waves of the open ocean until all ships were safely accounted for. Paddlers slowly made their way towards the shallower water and avoided any sharp rocks or coral that might damage the hulls of the larger kalia. There was an unusual silence. The Natui warriors were clearly on edge, bow and spear in hand waiting for any sign of movement from the far tree line at the very edge of the white sand beaches where the eyes of the enemy may be watching, waiting to ambush the vulnerable landing party. As they finally reached the shore and the Natui scouts searched the dense woods beyond, it appeared that there was no enemy to be seen and that they were alone. This was not entirely unexpected. Luther had explained that one of the scenarios theorised by Ruaka during the planning of this invasion was that the Grey Hair would seek only to defend their fortified village. They had ample amounts of food and water stored and could hold out in a siege for a great length of time. Ruaka had spent a significant amount of time studying the island surrounds and understood the walled layout of Kolo Mo'unga. He had explored several possible marching routes for a large force of warriors. They had planned the invasion carefully and understood what steps were needed if Doko decided not to take a stand on shore as they landed. Lokai believed his own army had greater numbers to bring to bear in the fight, so it was likely they would need to besiege the main village.

Within an hour of landing, scouts returned from some of the smaller outlying villages and reported that they were bare, having being evacuated within the last day. All food, materials and weapons were also missing. They had left nothing. Farms and crops had been torn from the ground in a hasty attempt to prevent an enemy from engaging in a long siege. The army would need to eat so would be relying on what they had brought with them, what they could scavenge, and the efforts of their fishermen. With over one thousand men to feed, Lokai was aware he would need a swift victory. He intended the battle to begin as soon as possible. The village gates had been shut, strengthened with timber and a long trench dug around the walls, lined with rows of jagged spears to slow down would-be attackers. Warriors with bows and spears watched over the surrounding area from high platforms inside the village walls. The hurried movement within suggested they were aware the army had arrived. However, they were safely tucked inside the confines of their fortress and were prepared to defend themselves.

The beach was soon swarming with warriors, bringing smaller vaka up to shore and unloading supplies from the kalia.

With the help of several Natui, the Englishmen unloaded the heavy eight and a half feet long, twenty-four pounder cannons that had been spread evenly throughout the fleet due to their immense weight. After the cannons were unloaded onto dry land, each gun carriage was carried onto shore and the cannons lifted atop each wheeled construction. Transporting the guns into the hills would be a slow trudge. Unlike their field counterparts, ship's naval carriages were not designed to move long distances and each component would need to be painstakingly hauled. Ruaka had told them the forest surrounding the village walls was sparse but regular, except for the grassy fields directly in front of its main entrance. The forest had been cleared to only thirty yards around its flank and rear; however, the fields which led to the main entrance were wide, with almost one hundred yards of open space except for several heilala trees which had grown along a well-worn road leading to the village. With four cannons to bring to bear, one hundred yards was well within the range of effective battery. But it was too close to the fort, and Luther feared his men would be vulnerable to the Grey Hair bows which had an effective range of up to one hundred and fifty yards. He had convinced Lokai to clear a narrow fifty-yard swath of forest to provide enough distance for the cannon to be set and commence firing without risk of his men being hit. He had argued for more, but had been refused, mostly because the task would take time, whilst they used precious resources, and tire his men before battle. The Natui set to task as soon as evening fell. It would be too dangerous to begin during the daytime when archers could see them from the walls so their plan was to work at night, using axes and knives to clear trees and foliage under the cover of darkness.

Luther wanted to view the battlefield himself, so Ruaka and a small group of Natui scouts set off to view the village surrounds. He returned the same evening without incident, relaying to Abel and his men that the forest was still sparse up to where the cannon placement would need to sit, but that the task to clear the foliage would not be easy. The line of sight would be narrow with less than twelve feet between each long gun. Luther described what he had seen; an island surrounds which was a place of unusual beauty, carefully manicured and landscaped in part. Strangely surreal. He was impressed by the length and size of the walls around the village, which would have stopped Lokai's army from an easy siege. It would take a massive force without siege weapons to conquer its walls. The village was built strategically on a high plateaued hill as it gave defenders superior oversight of anyone approaching. However, his mood became dark when he described the material the wall was made of. This had also taken him by surprise. Abel had told him about Marcello's account of the walls built by Lokai's other rival, Hou'eiki Maka. He supposedly had seen the island fortress having been built out of thick basalt rocks.

Luther had drawn his marines and sailors close to him for a debrief on his mission.

"The wall surrounding their village is expansive, but it's mostly a design of woven flax and several tight rows of tall bamboo stakes."

"What 'bout the height? Can it be scaled?" Worthstead said.

"The wall was thick and tall but our cannonballs will pass through like it was hot butter. So the walls won't collapse easily.

Every cannon shot is going to penetrate entirely without much impact on the structure. It's going to be terrible for the defenders inside."

Most of the men simply shook their heads and grimaced.

At first Abel was unsure why they would be overly concerned for the defenders. Then it dawned on him. The surrounding villages were empty of men, women and children. Unless the unfortunate commoners had fled elsewhere, they were likely all holed up inside.

It took a further two nights and one hundred men to clear a deeper corridor into the forest. They started from the furthest point from where the cannon would sit and worked their way forward, quickly cutting down trees and bush to provide an uncompromised space where the guns could operate. It was not entirely successful. Some of the large banyan trees were too thick to fell with their limited time. However, the largest bushes, palm trees and other vegetation blocking their view were cut down. The defenders did not leave the safety of their walls but occasionally fired arrows towards any light or noise. By the end of the task, five of Lokai's men lay dead. This wasn't a committed attack and the Grey Hair probably feared the destruction of the foliage was a trick to draw them out or to cause confusion. The relentless sound of trees being hacked and felled until the early hours of the morning would have been unnerving for the inhabitants. A quick withdraw before sunrise each day avoided them being spotted by a well-aimed archer. On the morning of the third day, Lokai gave orders for the army to move.

Abel and the crew of *Viritus* collected their arms and equipment, then assisted with the transport of the cannon. He looked down the beach towards where Hou'eiki Lokai had camped, surrounded by the army on all sides, and witnessed Mahina and her mother preparing to leave. They were flanked by Ono's personal guard. Afah ran between a group of marines who were putting out the flames of the cooking fires and reached Abel, puffing with the effort.

"Come on, we're waiting for you."

"What do you mean?" Abel said. "I'm fighting alongside my crewmen."

"You're to fight alongside me and Maau. We're joining Ono Hiva's personal guard. We'll be led by Ruaka. Come. Our mission is to protect the Lady of Natuini. It's a great honour."

"That's right. It's been arranged." Luther stepped between them. He had a short white jacket in hand and put it on Abel. "Wear this during the battle. It won't stop a spear or musket shot but it will cushion a glancing cut from a spear or arrow."

Abel slipped on the jacket, and Luther secured its buttons.

"I don't understand, Vincent. I want to fight alongside you. Mahina will be behind the battle at a safe distance."

"I know. And it would be an honour to have you at my side. But this is my wish and my order. Now stand to attention, enslgn!"

Abel stiffened and stood straight.

"You are to protect the noble lady Hiva and her daughter, Mahina. I'm charging you with this mission. You are to do so with all of your skill and do so with all the courage you can muster. You are to honourably represent *Viritus* and your English brethren in the task. Is that clear?"

"Yes, sir." Abel saluted.

The lieutenant nodded. "Good. Just listen. You may not be in the front rank, but you may be in just as much danger as the rest of us, so keep your eyes open and stay close to your friends. Afah and Maau seem like good companions. There's another thing. I'm sending the scouts with you. Cambridge and Rowe will provide some additional eyes on the battlefield from the rear of the army. If your party is in danger, they'll warn me and if I'm able, I'll assist."

"Thank you, Vincent. I won't let you down," Abel said defiantly.

"You will if you get killed. Retreat if you must, but don't get yourself killed."

Luther regarded him one more time in silence, then walked away to gather the rest of his marines.

"I'm coming with you as well," Wickman said. "A doctor's place is not on the front line. I'll be able to help with the wounded once it's all done."

"It will be great to have you along, Doc."

Abel, Wickman and the scouts joined Afah and returned to the hou'eiki's campsite. Ruaka led a small force of twenty-five warriors who would protect Ono Hiva and other non-combatants at the rear of the army, distant enough that they would not be in danger of stray arrows, but close enough that they would be able to view the battle and make plans to retreat if it didn't go their way. It was too dangerous for Ono Hiva to remain on the shore since a smaller, hidden enemy force might attack when the bulk of the army had left, leaving her vulnerable to capture. In any case, Lokai had insisted on her presence so she could watch the defeat of their enemy and the reclamation of lands once controlled by her family. Some of the warriors, including Ono Hiva and Mahina, wore a light suit of armour made from thickly woven coconut fibres. It covered their torso and legs down to their knees, whilst reaching halfway up their arms to their elbows. It was thick enough to soften the blow from a club, but was hot to wear, so many Natui warriors preferred to protect themselves with only a small shield. Others did battle unencumbered with just weapon in hand and short ta'ovala to provide superior movement.

Abel and Mahina saw each other as they marched together alongside Lokai's army. He wanted to walk beside her and longed to hold her, but Ono Hiva kept her close as they walked in the centre of the ring of protective warriors, all with spear and pakipaki in hand. They began climbing the gentle slopes of the island's outer forest, and then slowed as the terrain became steeper. There was already a well-used path that had been carved from centuries of use by the denizens of Mo'unga Vela, and the village of Kolo Mo'unga was only one hour's walk for an unencumbered man. For an army of this size transporting cannon and watching for ambush, it took three times longer.

"There's the target," Rowe said to his companions, pointing to the top of a high hill where the village of Kolo Mo'unga was perched. The army was spread out, moving with confidence through the forest. Impressive work had been performed by the warriors who had worked ceaselessly through the evenings to cut down the foliage. The army stopped at a safe point. They could see the movement of dozens of men along the walls of Kolo

Mo'unga, waiting with bow and arrow in hand to strike down anyone who dared approach, confident in the strength of their walls. They were still too far to reach the army with arrows, but he saw a few stray shots launched from the walls. They fell harmlessly into a distant canopy of the trees. Ruaka moved his guard to the left flank of the army, behind a large contingent led by Lokai and Kalafa. The right flank of the army was headed by Aunofo, both forces a mixture of warriors contributed by nobles of Lokai's allies. The army was growing in fervour, with warriors singing or chanting battle cries. Abel could feel the warriors around him becoming tense with a sudden battle lust. He even felt a sense of excitement and dread. The pit of his stomach churned. Hairs on the back of his neck stood on end. He was sweating profusely. The jacket was stifling.

Their group found a high point in a small clearing. From here they could see the whole army as they brought the cannon into position under Luther's watchful eyes. A single frangipani tree was the only object of notice, so they stood near it to shade themselves from the sun, and waited. Cambridge and Rowe checked their equipment; armed with two rifles each, they prepared each weapon, holding one at the ready and one leaning against the tree.

"We'll be heading into the tree line. It's a distance but we'll be watching," said Rowe.

Abel nodded. "Watch each other's backs out there."

The two marksmen took their equipment and soon disappeared beyond the line of foliage to their left.

Abel had a pistol in his belt and his rifle and sabre by his side. The firearms were loaded, and he clutched the barrel of his

Brown Bess so hard that it hurt his knuckles. He took a moment trying to relax, releasing his hand slowly from the rifle and breathing deeply to slow down his heart. He could almost hear its rapid beating.

"Epeli."

He heard a voice from behind him. He turned and was surprised to see Ono Hiva looking at him, Mahina beside her.

"Epeli," Hiva said again, as if waiting for him to approach.

He did, cautiously, until he was close to both of them and outside of earshot of the others. Hiva had never spoken to him before. He bowed his head and spoke in Natui. "Ono Hiva."

"I haven't been kind to you," she said sternly.

Abel shrugged. "You haven't been cruel."

"But I haven't been kind, have I? Mahina has always spoken well of you. I know you've become good friends. I've watched you. I know you mean well for my daughter."

"I care for her very much. I would never hurt her ..."

"I know, young man. But my daughter has seen a change lately. A mother knows when her little girl has become a woman."

Mahina looked at her wide eyed. Her mouth fell open. "Mother ..."

"Shh, Mahina. Let me speak." The noble lady placed her finger upon her own lips. "I know you're the one. Now I recognise Lokai cultivated your union to shame me. I was so blind to it all but now I see it all so clearly." Tears welled in her eyes and she appeared to falter. But holding back her emotion she took a deep breath and continued. "Be assured you need not fear me. What you have both done, is out of love, and I know you would give your life for my daughter. Not even the gods can control our hearts. You must know that your world and our world are not the same. So your love can never be spoken of to others. You know it can never be as you wish. She has a great destiny before her. One that you'll have no part of. Do you understand?"

Abel looked at Mahina. Her face dropped with her mother's words.

He lifted his chin with courage and turned his attention back to Ono Hiva.

"My lady. I have the greatest respect for you. You're correct, I'll protect her with everything I have. I'll give everything for her. And you're also wrong. You'll never break our love. None of your words can undo this; whatever you think or what you may do. So kill me if you must. It matters not. We'll be together one day. We'll be wed and no god or Hou'eiki will stand in our way." He stood defiantly but spoke softly. A rush of relief overcame him as he revealed his feelings.

Hiva nodded slowly. "You're brave. I pray you last the battle."

He bowed again and walked back to his position beside Afah and Maau, who were practising with their spears in preparation for the fight.

Abel watched as another figure approached from the ranks of warriors taking formation on the battle field. Melino, the tall shield maiden sent as Tihani's representative, strode purposefully towards Hiva, and as she reached the hill, she bowed deeply, holding her long spear by her side.

"Ono Hiva. It is my honour to present myself to your disposal. Ono Tihani has ordered me to stay by your side and ensure your safety in the battle ahead."

Hiva regarded her with cold eyes. "Strange, she would care. Your lady never considered me as friend, even when I tried. But I bear her no ill will. She is a prisoner to my husband's conquests as much as we all are."

"None of that is any of my concern. My intention is only to serve, my lady. My shield will not break. And my spear will keep you from harm."

"Very well. But understand that Ruaka is chief amongst my personal guard and you will perform your duties as per his command."

"I will obey his words as if they have come directly from you, lady."

Ruaka watched from close by and motioned for Melino to join him. She stood almost to his height and her shoulder span equalled his.

"We haven't spoken before. But I've heard your reputation as a fierce fighter. Just stay in my warriors' battle line and listen to my orders."

Melino thumped her spear to the soft ground and raised her shield. "Understood, Ruaka. I have respect for you. I know you to be one of our bravest. Perhaps even as deadly as Kalafa. Certainly not as ugly." She scoffed and leered at him with a wry smile, which he returned briefly.

"Just tell your men to give me a wide space. I don't want to turn their wives into widows if they get too close to my kolo or spear."

"Very well." Ruaka nodded. "Prepare yourself. The bloodshed is almost upon us."

She was an impressive woman. Her face was handsomely chiselled and her hair was cropped short in the style of the Natui men. Up close, Abel could see the many scars she sported on her arms and legs; remnants of battle between the warriors in the north of Natui and the raiders who would harass the coast during the winter months. She wore a short tapa skirt and her legs were bare of any protection. A thick strip of interwoven bark and flax formed a suit of armour covering from her waist to above her breasts. She tugged at the cloth and grimaced when it moved too loosely.

"You there, boy. Come here and help me tighten this. She pointed her spear at Maau. His face darkened and he stood motionless.

"Go on, before she smacks you on the head with her kolo." Afah shoved him forward.

Melino turned around and fingered the thick threads of kafa rope at her back which kept the armour in place.

"Tighten these up, son of Aunofo. Make it real tight. I don't want to be dealing with a shifting cuirass when I'm slaughtering these Grey Hair pigs."

Maau was still wide eyed but feverishly set about unloosening the ropes.

"Don't pull the vest down! I don't want my tits flying out all over the place, boy."

"I wouldn't mind. I mean … I'm sure your tits are just fine even if the armour did fall. I mean …" He looked back at his friends and shrugged. Beads of sweat ran down his face.

"Shut your mouth, little man, and get it done."

He pulled the straps tightly and re-tied the armour. "Is that fine, Melino? Is it tight enough?"

She turned and pulled on the shoulder, giving a satisfied grunt at the attempt.

"Not bad. It will do." She looked at Maau. He was taller than many of the other Natui of his age, but Melino towered over him nonetheless. She grinned.

"Keep your head concentrating on your long spear during the battle, not your short one." Before she joined the front line of Ruaka's warriors she shoved him and he stumbled backwards towards Afah and Abel.

Maau turned to his friends with a look of indignation on his face, and Afah placed his hand on his shoulder with a broad smile.

"Your *short* spear?"

❌

Luther waited patiently for the petty officer's opinion, hoping he would not waste his time with his usual attempts at dark humour. Finally, Worthstead scratched his head.

"Dunno, boss. That's awfully close. Those bowmen aren't bad shots at all."

The two men surveyed the battlefield.

"No choice really. The Natui will hold shields to protect us from any stray arrows, but at that range they're not very effective, anyway. We just need to be quick about it. Once we fire, I suspect they'll have no choice but to attack," Luther answered.

"You lookin' to win yourself anuvva pin to put beside that one on your chest, boss?"

Luther looked down at the small decorative pin, won for his gallantry during the battle of Cape St Vincent, fought alongside Admiral Nelson.

"I'm not sure they're giving out prizes for this particular battle," he said.

The Englishmen were at the very centre of the army with two flanks of Natui on either side, who at the moment were preparing themselves for battle, but staying at a distance from the range of the Grey Hair arrows. On the edge and forward of each flank, fifty warriors on either side readied kaufana, the deadly long bows, planting the arrows into the ground beside them for quick access when they were needed. The Englishmen would fire their cannon until the walls came down or the defenders had no choice but to attack. Luther suspected the Grey Hair would leave their fortified town. Unlike the stone ramparts of Europe, these walls were made of light, porous materials meaning that the cannonballs would pass though quickly, leave a small hole but not do a tremendous amount of damage to the integrity of the palisade. The problem for the defenders, however, was that they had no answer to the cannon. They would have a hard choice to make. They could remain in their village until the ammunition was spent, or flee the village to attack Lokai's forces in the open field.

"Ready the men. We need to haul the carriages and guns into place under fire so we can't make any mistakes. As soon as they're up and prepared, we begin firing and we don't stop until either they emerge, or the walls come down and Lokai's men can enter. I'm desperately hoping they'll surrender."

"Surely they will. I wouldn't wanna be in the middle of the hell basket when the blasting begins."

"Nor would I. We also don't want to be unprepared if the Grey Hair decide to attack. If this happens, I'll give the order to form a firing line behind the cannon. Lokai's armies will advance. I reckon we will have one, maybe two rounds of fire before its pistols and sabres drawn. Then its close combat, but we're not to be on the front line of that, so we're to move to a defensive posture and let Lokai's men do the bulk of the wet work."

Luther finished, noticing a dozen men, including Kalafa and Marcello, approaching. Several of the Natui were carrying large planks, each holding several strangely shaped cannon balls.

Worthstead peered at the priest disdainfully. "Come to join us in the front ranks, aye?"

"Haha, no. I morti no i pol amar gnanca odiar, e 'no ghen'è laoro, gnanca progeto, gnanca cognossensa, gnanca sapiensa ntel Sepolcro. The dead cannot love or hate. There is none of God's good work to be done in the grave, so I will keep safe. I will remain with the soldiers protecting Ono Hiva."

"That's not what that means …" Worthstead scratched his beard.

"What?" Marcello replied incredulously.

"Your quote, Father. It's from Ecclesiastes. I know that verse real good. My pappy was a fire and brimstone preacher and used to quote it to me as he laid into me furious an all with the belt. I was a lazy bugger, and he used to quote that very verse while I turned black and blue. It means that if you do anything in your damned life, you best be doing it well, since you can't bloody well do nothin' well then you're dead as a donkey. Work hard."

The priest looked blankly at Worthstead for a moment, then smiled briefly and shrugged without a further word.

"Those are not our shot, priest," Luther said, looking at the planks, still being held by the men standing aside Marcello. "We already have an ample supply of munitions, as you can plainly see."

Luther pointed to piles of cannonballs neatly stacked into small pyramids. They had hauled the munitions from the beach using dozens of thick sacks.

"Blimey now, where did you get those? Pull them out from under your frock?" Worthstead joked, kneeling down to examine the ammunition still being held by the Natui.

"Ah, Vincent. Yes, I've made a recommendation to Chief Lokai that these may be more effective. He agrees and so you shall use these instead."

"You and Lokai must think us stupid, Marcello. We know where these have come from. What in God's name is going on here?" Luther looked at Kalafa, who was grinning ear to ear as if he enjoyed the confrontation.

"Take a look at this, boss." Worthstead picked up one of the balls with his hands. It split into two halves, but was joined in the middle by a five-foot-long chain.

"Chain shot?" Luther looked back at Marcello, gritting his teeth. "Chain shot is for crippling ships masts and ripping canvas to pieces. But do you know what this does to soldiers? It tears them limb from limb. It's a killer of men, not a means to collapse a palisade. These are a butcher's weapon, not for siege upon a village, populated by civilians. We're not using these."

"I apologise, friends. But Lokai insists these are used first and there will be no argument. That is, unless you want your alliance with the chief to be short-lived." He looked at Kalafa, who held up his ashen club.

"You son of a whore!" Luther launched himself forward and punched the priest in the face. The blow took everyone by surprise. Marcello fell backwards with a loud thud, but the assault continued when Luther leaped on top of him, pounding his face. Worthstead and some of the Marines dragged him off the priest, pulling him back to his feet.

"Let me go, you bastards." He struggled out of their grip and turned to Marcello who was struggling to get off the ground, his face bloodied and his clothes dirtied.

"You did this to seek favour with that cunt? There are people in there. Women and children. You call yourself a priest, a man of God, but there is nothing godly about you. Lies, you're full of damn lies. Traitor."

Marcello brushed off the dirt and stepped back behind Kalafa, who was now openly laughing at them both.

"Stronso! I am not English. I am Venetian. I do not answer to you, so I am no traitor. I answer only to God who has given me favour to convert Lokai and the Natui to his beloved teachings. The natives within that fort will feel God's wrath, and those who survive will beg to receive his mercy. It is for the greater good. You should be grateful for the opportunity to serve. Just like your carpenter. He learned quickly to obey his new masters without question once he understood his place. And so, shall you."

"Are you talking about Jack? Jack Horton? Where in hell is he?"

"Preparing a ship of war at the pleasure of our great chief. But it matters not. If you serve Lokai well, like all of us must, you'll see him again. But maybe you'll all perish here today."

"There is nothing good about you or any of this. Get from my sight, you stinking worm. And you tell Kalafa that one day I'll wipe that smile from his ugly face." Luther spat at the ground, barely missing Kalafa's feet.

Marcello translated Luther's threat purposefully. "'E 'iai pe taimi teu fakangata ai ho'o mo'ui."

Kalafa was no longer laughing and the look he gave the lieutenant was enough to show he understood, even without the priest's words.

Worthstead threw a small rock at Marcello. The priest dodged the throw as it harmlessly landed a few feet away.

"Get your fat arse out of the lieutenant's sight. The next one's gonna take your bloody eyeball, Venetian scum."

Both the priest and Kalafa turned and left. The men who carried the chain shot dropped the munitions roughly to the ground.

"God forgive us," Luther said. He turned around. The entire crew of *Viritus* was silent as they watched him, waiting for his orders.

"Before we all 'drop the perch' do ya mind addressing this worthless lot of rum gaggers?" Worthstead raised his eyebrows and motioned to the men, who were waiting patiently for orders.

Luther nodded and turned to his crew. He was sweating and swept away some moisture from his brow. This wasn't unusual given the heat of the day, but Luther was glad it was not a cooler climate, otherwise at that moment he would not have been able to hide his fear. Showing that fear would have been devastating for the courage of the crew. There was much more danger here than they had faced before. He knew not all these brave faces would survive the day, and he was uncertain anyone would escape what was to come. Noticing his breathing had become shallow, he took a few heaves of fresh air, calming himself before speaking.

"Be vigilant and fight with honour. It's been my privilege to lead you in this dark time. If we survive, it's possible we may get to see Mother England once more. This is not our war but we must fight it still. For each other, brothers."

NINETEEN

From his vantage point Abel had an impressive view of the battlefield. It was a shock to even the hardiest of Natui when the first barrage of cannon fire began, followed by a flash of white smoke. The cacophony of sound roaring from the cannon made everyone jump. Even Ruaka took a step back and held up his spear towards Luther's firing crew, as if warding off a charging boar. As soon as the first shots were fired from the cannon, manned by three sailors each, Luther's men cleared the cannon of debris and reloaded the powder charge. Everyone's eyes drifted towards the fort. The damage that appeared seemed limited. The cannon shot had made four elongated holes at different intervals along the wall, each no longer than the length of a man but the walls stayed upright. None of the hits had struck the main gate. At first there was silence from both the fort and allied armies. The men atop the high platforms inside the village wall were looking inwards, moving erratically. Some of them were looking back towards the cannon, confused by the destruction. There had been some arrow fire as the war machines had been set up; at least two Natui and one sailor from *Viritus* had been struck whilst preparing the cannon, which seemed a miracle given the plethora of arrows they had rained down. The warriors of Kolo Mo'unga did not know what the palangis had been preparing, though they sensed it was something terrible and had reacted by trying to kill those working the cannon. The bows and arrows they used mostly fell short. But not all. Natui warriors caught a number of arrows on their shields in defence of the Englishmen, but after the cannon fire the arrows stopped coming and the archers on the wall were looking about themselves, suddenly disoriented.

The silence didn't last. Abel heard screams from behind the walls. Hiva and her personal guard looked at each other and then towards Kolo Mo'ugna, trying to comprehend what this new weapon could have wrought. In the fright, Mahina stepped away from her mother and took hold of Abel's arm, not caring what the Natui maidens or men around her might say. He took hold of her hand, pulling her close.

The danger of these new weapons must have become clear to Doko's army since the number of archers upon the wall doubled and suddenly, arrows were loosened upon the Englishmen, this time with greater speed and urgency. Despite the air now filling with missiles, the arrows were being unloaded in panic, and not with any careful attempt to hit their target. Soon the battlefield was covered by arrow shafts sticking from the ground, like stalks of strange grass. Very few came close to the cannon crew. Three minutes after the first barrage, Luther gave the firing order, and another deafening blast was unleashed.

This time, three of the cannonballs struck the wall, one of them destroying a large upper portion of the main gate. The fourth struck not the wall but a group of three archers who stood side by side. The chain shot, fully outstretched upon impact, hit the poor men directly across their torsos, ripping their bodies apart. It caused a fountain of blood to spurt upwards and over the wall whilst their fellow warriors looked on in abject horror. The smoke from the cannons drifted over the battlefield towards the army's left flank, where Hou'eiki Lokai and Kalafa were preparing their men for battle. The initial fear of the cannon blasts was now subsiding, and the sight of the destruction on the enemy caused the army to cheer. Some warriors danced in joy at the sight of their enemy's blood drawn so dramatically. So wantonly. The screams from inside the village became louder. More blood curdling. By the time of the third barrage of cannon fire, Lokai's army was getting restless. A few men were running forward, closer to the wall to taunt the defenders, showing their buttocks and then running back to a safe distance before any more archers struck them. Of the allied archers, many were also running forward with bravado to loosen their own arrows at the wall before falling back again.

The cannons fired a third volley and soon after a fourth. The special cannonballs had been depleted. Luther called for the standard shot and once these were loaded, another barrage hit the village.

A shot struck the top of a banyan tree. It disintegrated the top part of the tree and caused the cannonball to fall short of its target, striking the ground some fifteen yards before the wall. The other three shots struck their targets, making a series of holes along the perimeter of the palisades, long pieces of bamboo exploding upwards and splintering mercilessly into the defender's faces. Some were blinded by the shrapnel, their heads and torsos turning into a bloody mess.

With each barrage, Lokai's army became more incensed. Their bloodlust reaching a height as Aunofo led his flank of men in song and a battle dance of old. He stepped to the fore of his frontline and threw a spear towards the gates of Kolo Mo'unga.

"The gods, they weep,
The gods, they shout,
Earth and wind become my spear,
Earth and wind become your death."

His voice roared even above the din of a thousand soldiers and some of the lesser 'eiki also stepped forward to accompany him in the challenge to their enemy behind the walls.

Each warrior hefted their weapons and slammed their feet with tremendous impact, following their own interpretation of the dance. Each movement was a message to their worthy opponents that they were here to fight and die with honour. When Aunofo chanted the second verse, the masses joined him in song.

"Every man will become life,
Every man has become a brother of blood,
The mourning of your children has come,
Give your final breath.
We die, we die!"

When the song was done, as if by providence, Luther's cannon crew opened fire once more and the army erupted into a state of unbridled mayhem. A surge of men moved forward and were barely stopped by the orders of their 'eiki and leaders amongst the throng, who were screaming at them to hold their ground.

When the fifth volley struck, it proved to be a breaking point for the occupants of Kolo Mo'unga. The main gates were thrown open, and the defenders poured out of the village. Hundreds of warriors swarmed from the entrance and ran chaotically towards Lokai's army. To Abel it was like an enormous termite mound had been poked too many times and cracked open to expose the angry defenders within. The cannon crews retreated from their positions and picked up their rifles in the second rank of two firing lines. At Luther's command, every man with a rifle fired at the warriors streaming towards them. It was an effective volley; the warriors had launched themselves from the fort at such ferocity that they were packed together, and with men all strewn over the battlefield, their bullets struck true. A dozen men fell. Luther's crew had another rifle prepared at the base of their feet, and they picked those up for a swift second volley.

Firing his own rifle, Luther screamed at the soldiers. "Fire at will! Watch your sides, boys!"

As the second volley of musket fire was let loose, another dozen Grey Hair fell. The army, flanked on either side of the riflemen, charged forward to meet their enemy, throwing spears into the oncoming horde and drawing pakipaki to strike down their opponents as they reached each other on the green fields of Mo'unga Vela. With no high ground, it became difficult for Luther's men to use their rifles without endangering their own forces, now that Lokai's forces had swept in front of their view. They placed their shots more carefully, aiming higher, whilst several sailors drew sabres and pistols, moving closer together in a protective line.

The first dozen warriors of Mo'unga Vela who reached the front line in disarray were quickly struck down by Lokai's forces. However, it was as if the entire population of Mo'unga Vela was streaming from those gates and the short distance they had to cover was quickly bridged by the hundreds that had emerged. Both sides flung spears at each other, striking down men on both lines. The two walls met, and a bloody melee ensued.

Doko's forces became a frightening array of ghostly figures, surging forward with screams of outrage and fierce battle cries, their hair covered in a white powder that billowed around them like a hazy cloud. As battle began, the powder became caked with viscous red blood which gave the impression of undead soldiers returning from the underworld.

Both sides were adept with the vicious pakipaki. Today, the weapon was employed in close combat to great effect as warriors from both sides struck hard, breaking bone and skulls with terrible ease. Arrows from Lokai's archers cut down a swathe of Grey Hair. The archers continued to fire arrows into the back of the army, to avoid hitting their own men. Soon a contingent of Mo'unga Vela warriors who had been manning the walls had also joined the army and were now firing arrows into both the left and right flank of Lokai's army, causing many of the warriors to push forward into battle to avoid being shot. The crew of *Viritus* were still holding their line, watching as Natui warriors rushed past, prepared to engage in battle.

Lokai and Kalafa stood in the front rank of the forces, and surrounded by the armies most skilled fighters, were now embroiled in a bloody battle, screams and cries punctuating the rhythmic snap of a bow strings and arrows singing in flight. If there had been a front line, it had quickly disappeared. Now warrior amongst warrior, the lines were blurred as swing upon swing of club quenched the soft ground with blood and strewn bodies. Some fighters stumbled over the dead and dying, only to be crushed in a charge of men.

The left flank was holding firm. Kalafa was surrounded by a pile of enemies who had dared challenged his immediate circle or attempted to attack Chief Lokai. Abel watched as he swung his long handled pakipaki in an arching fashion over his head and brought it down on the shoulder of a charging enemy, cutting one man down then thrusting the head of the weapon into the belly of another, throwing him backwards. As he fell, he brought the weapon down swiftly upon his face, causing his nose and forehead to implode with the force of his blow. Lokai 's weapon was a long spear. He stood behind a circle of alert guards, and as an enemy would come near, his men would part ever so slightly, allowing the chief to thrust out and puncture the torso or thigh of an unfortunate combatant. No more of the Grey Hair were exiting from the gates. Their numbers were sizable but did not match those of Lokai. The advantage they had was higher ground. Bowmen held a better view of Lokai's armies from their vantage point on the higher parts of the plateau, and as they fought, they came at speed from uphill, the force of momentum providing them with a superior position.

'Eiki Aunofo held command at the army's right flank. His forces had attempted to surround the oncoming defenders and had spread themselves too thinly. A large group of Grey Hair broke through the ranks of allied warriors and in their rage charged towards the battery of idle cannons. They found no crew but spied Luther's line of soldiers and sped past the war machines towards his row of awaiting men. Abel saw Luther react with an order to his men. As they received the charge, each aimed their weapon and with a puff of smoke, more than thirty rifles and pistols unleashed their load upon the enemy. Numerous warriors fell, but not enough to stop the charge. At once Luther and the crew of *Viritus* brandished their sabres and with a battle cry rushed into the oncoming warriors who had been momentarily shocked by the volley. Luther was the first to strike, cutting a man down, his sabre brought squarely upon the temple of his opponent. The Grey Hair swung their pakipaki and fought back, drawing the palangis into a desperate battle. Now they were committed, their encounter drawing them into a maelstrom of combat, sword against spear and club.

"Over there! Look." Maau cried out.

He was pointing to the forests on the far outskirts of Lokai's left flank. With alarming speed over two hundred warriors emerged, threw deadly spears into the fray and charged into the sides of his forces, killing many shocked Natui warriors who had just moments before been concentrating on an enemy to their front. The attack pushed deep into the side of the army and forced it to spread backwards. Ruaka's brows narrowed at the sight.

"That's much too close to Ono Hiva. I recognise those men. It's the two traitor chiefs, Lord Kakaea and Lord Ahomana," he said. "We'll move you back further to safety." Ruaka turned to Seletute, one of his most skilled warriors and a trusted friend. "Escort our lady and Mahina back to the shore. Take Epeli, Afah and Maau with you. I'll stay with the others and occupy the fleeing enemy."

"I don't want to leave your side, brother, but I'll take them to safety and return."

"We'll not retreat." Hiva was stoic in her reply.

"Ono Hiva, I must see to your safety."

"What you must do is remain here. They will not see me retreat from battle. I must rule here, and I will not be seen as weak, running from the slightest of danger."

Hiva held her position. Nothing was going to move her. Ruaka gritted his teeth and swore under his breath. He drew his warriors into a tight defensive line and told Abel, Afah and Maau to remain closer to Hiva and Mahina. Marcello was also standing behind them, nursing a bloodied nose and black eye.

Lokai's warriors were now facing two fronts. They were made to split their forces into two different directions, as they were still battling over control of the steep hill, with the defenders continuing to press downwards. Like an arrow, the traitor army seemed to be quickly piercing a corridor towards Chief Doko's personal guard with unusual speed and ferocity. It was then Abel spotted at its very tip a skilled fighter who was leaving a pile of bodies in his wake. Malohi whirled two pakipaki like a hurricane upon his enemies. His speed was unlike any he had even seen. His fighting style seemed to bewilder his enemies who would often appear more lumbering or traditional in battle technique. At one moment, three of Lokai's men were killed as Malohi leapt bodily into the air and brought down one pakipaki to crush the man's skull. He then landed deftly upon his feet, crouching like a panther, and swung his second pakipaki around his head, smashing the sharpened edge into one warrior's throat. Instantly he swung around in a circling fashion, caught another man in the belly with the club in his offhand, jerked it backwards and ripped out the man's stomach. This gruesome display of skill terrified

Lokai's men. The warriors surrounding Malohi were his own, fighting alongside him and bringing the enemy close enough for Malohi to swiftly end their lives. He swung again and again, each time stepping ever forward, sometimes during a leap, but always striking with deadly accuracy. He was a killing machine.

The two sides were for just a moment more evenly matched, the sudden appearance of a secondary force having provided Mo'unga Vela with a much-needed boost to morale and numbers to counter that of Lokai. Abel watched, his heart beating for every second that passed. The front lines were almost indistinguishable. Hardy warriors for both sides fought and moments later were dead or maimed, their limbs crushed or carved from their bodies, sacrificed to the field. The ebb and flow of battle dragged on. Neither side gained further ground for very long and when a few men would fall, they would be replaced by others with a renewed enemy who would push the balance of the battle in the other direction. He watched the crew of the *Viritus* hold their own, fighting tooth and nail to survive the onslaught of Doko's soldiers. They had been incensed by the use of cannon by the foreign fighters. Luther's men stayed close together, brother protecting brother, surrounded by the haze of gunpowder vapour.

However, Aunofo's right flank had closed the gap in their lines, making considerable ground and was pushing the Grey Hair forces back with every man felled. Mo'unga Vela was simply outnumbered and whilst they attacked with great ferocity, the bombardment of their walls had provided the attackers with a significant advantage. Arrows continued to rain down at the sides and rear of the Mo'unga Vela forces, who themselves had spent nearly all their ammunition in a futile attempt to bring down the distant cannon crew. With an aggressive push from the allies, the forces facing Aunofo and Luther's marines collapsed. They appeared to have no distinct leadership and were battling in random directions, not knowing where to run or engage. Before long, pockets of their men were being surrounded and speared to death. Coupled with the pistol fire from Luther's men not engaged in hand-to-hand combat, there reached a final breaking point for the entire Mo'unga Vela force facing Aunofo. They buckled and fell in droves. Some of the men, surrounded by overwhelming numbers, gave up and surrendered, with some being spared. Others continued to fight and were slaughtered whilst the remaining fled in any direction they could, whether it be into the forests or back towards the village. Aunofo, covered with a coat of gore, blew a conch that hung by his side, warning all warriors of Natui they must follow him into battle and rally together. He led his forces forwards to support Chief Lokai, bringing to bear almost five hundred men. This tipped the scale entirely. The combined forces of Mo'unga Vela and the traitor lords were halted in their advance and routed, with only pockets of trapped men holding their ground in futile defiance.

Malohi, fresh from killing another man, was hailed by his men as they surveyed the battlefield and realised it was lost. Much of the army turned. They fled erratically without any semblance of order. Most of the army turned to escape through the forest behind them, hoping it would shield them from pursuit, but not all could find a quick route. Malohi's warriors had penetrated Lokai's warrior ranks too far, and only a narrow corridor behind them remained. Another conch was blown, this time from the lips of Kalafa. Instead of pursuit, the Natui warriors surrounding a sizable contingent of Malohi's warriors withdrew slowly, bearing weapons at the Grey Hair to ward them off but allowing them a passage to retreat to the rear of the army. About one hundred men took advantage of this offer to escape and rushed upwards, directly towards the hill where Abel stood with Ono Hiva and Mahina in front of a tall frangipani tree.

Ruaka saw the danger, but it was too late to retreat. "Hold. Surround the lady. Do not let them through. Do not leave the circle and raise your shields!"

Abel thought Lokai's forces would pursue Malohi as he fled. However, as some of the Natui warriors ran towards the hill to assist them, Kalafa blew his conch again, and they halted their pursuit, conflicted by the scene but ultimately not moving.

"They've abandoned us. This is what he has desired. But I will not go softly." Hiva stood tall, gritting her teeth with determination.

Moments later, the first of the fleeing Grey Hair and men from the combined forces of Lords Kakaea and Ahomana reached their defensive line on the hill. It seemed at first that perhaps they would avoid conflict as the first group of men passed by the group, clearly fearful they would be pinned between two forces. However, as Malohi reached the small hill and saw who remained there, he ordered his men to halt their pace as they came within ten yards of Ruaka's shield wall. Only the men of Mo'unga Vela stayed with Malohi, the warriors of Kakaea and Ahomana disappearing in to the forest beyond. Fifty of Malohi's most skilled warriors, handpicked and trained by Malohi himself, faced just half their number of Hiva's personal guard. Ruaka stood before them, brandishing his favoured weapon, the multi-pronged long spear. He was stoic, ready and unmoving.

Malohi looked to his rear, towards the bulk of the Natuini forces. They were not pursuing his retreating forces.

"I see the rumours are true. You're not in favour, Ono Hiva. Your husband won't be helping you today." Malohi laughed, pacing in front of the line of men protecting her. He wiped a swath of blood and dirt off his brow with the back of his hand.

Hiva brandished her own spear and with eyes widened in rage she strode forward to attack when both Afah and Mahina pulled her backward.

Ruaka's face twisted in rage. "Speak to me only, worm. Ono Hiva would pluck out your eyes for your arrogance. You're lucky I stand between her and you otherwise you may already be dead."

Ruaka gritted his teeth, and although he spoke with bravado, Abel could see that he was counting his enemies.

"Maybe I should let the lady's handmaidens battle you, Malohi. From what I've seen, they can wield a cooking spoon as well as your men can wield a spear."

Behind them, Melino laughed loudly. She dug her heel into the ground and widened her stance, readying herself for a sudden attack.

Malohi ignored her and gave a brief smile. "You think you've won this battle? I'll return to reclaim my rightful lands. But first let me tell you, slave, when I'm done wiping your blood from my pakipaki I'm going to bash the brains from Hiva's pretty head.

As for her daughter, I'll take great joy in throwing her into the pools atop the great Mo'unga Vela and watch her boiled alive."

One of Ruaka's men screamed and charged out from his battle line. He brought his spear down to slice into Malohi's head. Malohi stepped back and to the side, dodging the blow. Then bringing the pakipaki up into a swift attack, he brutally smashed open the warrior's lower jaw; a burst of bright red spurted wildly onto the long grass. Stunned, he dropped his spear. Malohi hit him again with his offhand pakipaki, the sharp tip piercing his eye socket. Death came swiftly.

"Stand your ground, Natui!" Ruaka shouted.

His men moved nervously, their spears pointing towards the enemy, who seemed eager to continue their fight.

"A brave man. Dead. But braver than you. Let's fight Ruaka. You've tried to fight me once before, slave. Let's see who the mightiest Natui warrior is. My men will not interfere." Malohi taunted.

"Gladly." Ruaka's rage took hold, and he left his line amongst his guardsmen, facing off with Malohi.

Hiva looked on desperately. "No, Ruaka."

It was too late. As soon as Ruaka accepted the challenge, the Grey Hair stepped to the side and gave the two men room. He didn't hold back. With a leap, Ruaka tried to ram the spear into Malohi's bare chest. Both men preferred to fight unarmoured. Aside from their short ta'ovala, their bodies and limbs were exposed. This allowed for both of them to move at great speed and so the first thrust was brutally quick. Malohi expected it. He moved to the left. Ruaka did not falter, thrusting again but without success as Malohi dodged to the other side of the weapon.

Ruaka brought it backwards and swung in a short arc towards his opponent's head. This almost struck true and if it wasn't for the younger man's dexterous reflexes, may have shredded off parts of his face. Instead, he leaned back to avoid the strike. Then he counter-attacked. Using his off-hand weapon, Malohi bashed Ruaka's spear downwards and into the ground. He held it there, using the spear as leverage before cartwheeling towards Ruaka. With a deft kick, he bashed the sole of his foot into the warrior's face, making him fall back. Ruaka almost let go of his spear. He dragged it backwards with him and crouched into a defensive posture as Malohi swung his pakipaki. Ruaka brought his spear up and parried the blow. However, the two sharp-headed pakipaki did not stop as he swung again and again, each strike capable of killing a man.

Malohi was a fighter of immense speed and skill, relying not only on his light weapons but also his entire body to fight. He was lither than Ruaka and not as muscle bound, but his speed and skill were incredible to witness. He blocked each well-aimed strike as they rained down on his thighs, torso and head. Suddenly, Malohi threw his offhand pakipaki at Ruaka's face. It was unexpected. The veteran raised his spear and blocked the glancing blow, but his opponent ran in so close to the warrior his spear became difficult to wield. A pakipaki struck his side, puncturing the larger warrior's flesh, and then with his elbow, Malohi bashed him across the face. The warrior fell backwards and tripped over an exposed tree root. He hit the ground heavily. A smile broadened across Malohi's face.

"It's over for you now. Grey Hair brethren, kill the rest of them."

All fifty men attacked, charging towards the shield wall, and a bloody battle ensued once more. Seletute had prepared a line of throwing spears and quickly launched one into the chest of an incoming fighter, felling him before he could reach their line. Beside him, Melino drew a throwing kolo from her side and tossed it into the face of one of the approaching warriors. It smashed into his teeth. A mist of red and white exploded from his face. With a swift movement she brought her spear up and skewered him with a thrust to the belly.

Abel knew this could be his last stand. If the shield wall fell, he, Afah and Maau would be next. They were skilled for their age, but Malohi's warriors were seasoned veterans. They would soon be dead, but looking at one another they stood beside each other as friends, ready for whatever was to come.

"We fight together," Mahina said, stepping beside him. She was joined by her mother and the five of them formed their own wall.

Thinking his opponent stunned, Malohi bent forward to pick up his weapon but realised his mistake when Ruaka swept his spear into a low circle. It struck him across the ankles, tripping him. Both men scrambled back to their feet. Ruaka thrust his spear towards a Grey Hair warrior who had charged at him as he stood up. His spear struck him in the belly, stopping his charge, then bringing the butt of his spear around, Ruaka bashed him over the head, knocking him to the ground.

The screams of men in close combat were deafening. Ruaka's warriors were holding the wall as well as they could and only a few of them had fallen, taking as many enemies with them. But they were overwhelmed by numbers and Abel was fearful they would not hold. Several men took advantage of a shield warrior falling and shoulder charged their way past the wall. Two men were cut down before they could make it through the breach but a further three passed through and towards Abel and his companions. One of them threw his spear. It slashed across Afah's thigh. A thick red wound opened, followed by a gush of blood. He stumbled but held up despite the pain. The same warrior drew a pakipaki, charging forward at Abel as did his compatriot. Abel brought up his pistol at close range and shot the warrior in the stomach. He stopped running, the wound appearing in the middle of his open torso. Mahina stepped in and finished him off with a firm blow to the head with her spear. The accompanying warrior began his assault on Maau. Abel's friend was able to fend off the first blow but the second strike from the pakipaki bashed into his ribs, which gave off an audible cracking sound. He fell, clutching his chest. The next strike would have taken off the top of his head if both Hiva and Afah had not flanked him and, with their own spears, stabbed him from both sides, until he retreated, wailing in pain. He stumbled and fell, so Hiva pursued him and jabbed the spear into his belly, then his neck. The remaining man saw the noble lady was exposed. He swung his pakipaki with both hands above his head. Before he could bring it down, the side of his head exploded. Private Cambridge came running at speed towards them from a place of hiding behind a copse of trees, his smoking rifle by his side.

"Cambridge, with us!" Abel shouted.

The man she had struck was dying, so Hiva left him to bleed out and returned to their line. She gave a nod of thanks to the Englishman, who pretended to tip an invisible hat and took his place by their side. Cambridge started loading his rifle again with shot.

"Glad to be of service, ma'am."

Doctor Wickman had seen Maau fall and threatening Marcello with a swift death of his own if he didn't assist, ran up to pull Maau out of danger to the other side of the frangipani tree where he tended to his wounds.

Without Maau, it was the five of them now, side by side. The shield wall was beginning to falter, but Ruaka's men would not retreat. Melino looked backwards for just a moment and they could see the desperation on her bloodied face. They were fighting to the last man and woman as the Grey Hair continued to bash them backwards, each fallen Natui warrior, loyal to Hiva, taking a life of their own. The odds were against them. Simply, their opponents were equally skilled. There were also more of them.

The one-on-one contest of battle between the two Natui warriors continued. Malohi had the upper hand with Ruaka now sporting a bloody temple and several cuts along his side and arms. Malohi still seemed almost unharmed, his stamina unrelenting as his opponent's was waning. Strike after strike, Malohi continued his assault whilst the great spear would block each attack, an occasional thrust towards the Mo'unga Vela noble was easily dodged. Then, one glancing blow on the edge of Ruaka's temple and the battle appeared to be won. The mighty warrior of Natuini was dizzy from the strike, and his legs buckled. Malohi prepared to strike again, but before he could kill his enemy, fate changed its course once more. A loud blast from below the hill was followed by a shrill puff of wind. A jagged line of blood opened up on Malohi's right arm. He clutched it in pain. The shot only grazed him but the sting of the strike from a lead ball caused him to reel and turn in confusion. A Grey Hair warrior behind him was struck in the back of the head by another blast. He fell and died behind Malohi, who turned again to view the new threat.

Luther, with sabre drawn, was charging up the hill and towards Malohi. He had just discharged his pistol, throwing it to the ground. Behind him, almost half of *Viritus'* crew followed with their own knives and sabres drawn. His marines and a few of the sailors with him charged into the back of Malohi's men, taking them by surprise. Malohi tried to warn them, but the din of battle made it almost impossible to hear anything through the shouts and screams of dying men.

Luther stood in front of Malohi. "Come now, boy. Let's see what you have," he said.

Malohi charged forward again and attempted to kick the sabre out of Luther's hand. The Englishman withdrew, stepped back to avoid the strike, then bashed the hilt of the weapon into Malohi's face. The young nobleman stepped back and shook his head to break the shock of the blow. His nose was bleeding heavily.

"Kapau te ke fili ke ke mate fakataha moe kakai, teu 'ave koe ki he langi lau."

Abel understood. If they chose to die with these people, Malohi would help Luther to the afterlife with them.

Malohi brought his pakipaki up high like a snake moving with a hypnotic motion from side to side to draw Luther's gaze. Instead, Luther attacked, slashing at the younger man's head and then alternating strikes on either side of his torso. Malohi was quick to block the sword strikes, though seemed unused to defending against a blade. The two backed away from each other for a moment. Malohi considered Luther's movements, watching the way he stood, his posture, the way he held the weapon and studying his unfamiliar movements. Then he struck again, thrusting downwards upon the temple. Luther brought his sword up to parry the blow, which instead turned out to be a feint for the intended strike; a blow to the belly from the head of his offhand pakipaki. It landed and almost winded Luther, who stumbled back in pain. If not for Ruaka's recovery from the glancing blow to the head, he may have been struck again. Ruaka whipped his spear up and downwards towards Malohi who again avoided the strike with a few quick steps backwards.

The three men faced off. Luther thrust his sabre forward. Malohi parried again, but this time the blade sped up his arm and cut him deeply. He groaned in pain but threw his club at Luther. The sharp tipped pakipaki hit Luther hard in the right elbow, the sharp end biting deep, causing him to step back and drop his blade. Luther's face showed his agony. Kneeling, Luther tried to pick up the sword, but his arm was in such pain, he could barely grip the hilt. It slipped from his hand, so he swiftly picked up the blade with his left hand and stepped in to join the battle again, but was challenged by another of Malohi's men before he could move forward.

With the lieutenant occupied, Malohi turned to Ruaka and rushed at him, dodging past his spear, and thumped the sharp end of his remaining pakipaki into his stomach. It pierced deeply into his belly. He dropped his spear. Malohi smiled as they stood face to face. At first the mighty warrior appeared to falter, his face growing instantly pale, though no sound of pain came from his lips. His expression showed that he knew he was done. However, when Malohi tried to pull his pakipaki from his opponents' belly, it was stuck. Ruaka was holding on to it and would not let Malohi free his weapon, keeping the noble close.

"Let go, slave."

With what would have been an agonising feat of strength, Ruaka brought his knee up and smashed Malohi's groin with tremendous impact. The younger man groaned in pain and fell backwards, the large warrior collapsing on top of him. The warrior wrapped his hands around the noble's neck and with the rest of his strength he squeezed, strangling him with all the force he could muster, the eyes of his victim bulging in surprise as he tried to breathe. Malohi's hands struggled around him, and he struck at Ruaka's sides wildly without effect, not being able to move the weight off him from a much larger warrior.

His hands tightened around the nobleman's neck, resulting in a sickening gurgling sound as Malohi struggled in vain to escape and draw breath. With another squeeze, Malohi's windpipe was crushed. Ruaka sat up and plucked the pakipaki from his belly. Struggling to breathe, Malohi raised his hand as if to stop the attack. Ruaka brought the pakipaki down so heavily that Malohi's skull cracked, the sharp end of the club bashing a hole in his forehead. The young Grey Hair noble, and heir to Mo'unga Vela was dead.

Standing over his body, the injured warrior looked towards Hiva behind the maelstrom of battle and could see tears in her eyes. His eyes flicked upwards before he fell, broken and bloodied. Unmoving.

Without any hope of victory after the arrival of the Englishmen and seeing that their noblemen had perished, the remaining Grey Hair broke and fled. Luther had dispatched his own attacker with a few sword strikes and took the chance to regather his crew. They formed another defensive line in case of another attack.

Hiva ran to her lover, cradling his limp body. She wailed, a river of tears running down her cheeks whilst the remaining fighters saw to their dead and dying under the shade of the flowering frangipani tree.

The battle was over. The decisive victory on the side of Hou'eiki Lokai. The warriors of Lokai and his allies rounded up the remaining prisoners and confiscated their weapons, pushing them towards the village where they would be held while the victorious nobles of Natuini decided on their fate. They also counted their dead. One hundred of Lokai's men lay dead or dying. But their enemy had suffered greater losses with almost two hundred Grey Hair perishing on the battlefield. Countless others were wounded on both sides. One marine and three sailors had also died, including Rowe, who had been killed trying to alert Luther that Abel and his companions were in danger of being overrun. The scout was struck by a stray arrow through the chest and into his lungs. He bravely delivered the message but by the time the battle was done, he was found amongst the dead. His friend Cambridge was beside himself in sorrow and refused to leave the body. He could not be consoled. He remained on the field, cradling Rowe in his arms. His lifeless friend's eyes were wide open in horror, looking endlessly into the blue sky above.

Ruaka was barely alive. Doctor Wickman promised Ono Hiva he would do whatever he could to save him. Afah and three of Hiva's personal guard carried his body to a safer place, seeking shelter in the village. Lokai spared no time ordering his armies to occupy Kolo Mo'unga, so he summoned Ono Hiva, Mahina and his nobles to his side so that they could witness his entry to the fortification as a conquering ruler. The noble lady quickly composed herself and made her way towards where the Natuini nobles had gathered at the threshold of the town gates, which had been mangled in the cannon bombardment. Luther was also summoned. He was wounded, so Abel helped him up the hill, lending his shoulder to balance his cousin as he walked. When they reached the entrance, they could see Kalafa, Masila and Lokai standing together. Kalafa was covered from head to toe in bloody gore. When Ono Hiva arrived with Luther, Kalafa smirked at both of them. She took no notice. She stepped close to her husband, whose face was covered in the dirt of battle, and he beamed with a toothy smile.

"My beautiful wife. My heart flutters with joy that you're alive. I'm sorry. My army didn't know Malohi had caught up with you. He ran like a scared rat from my spear! Please forgive me. Any way, you look just radiant. How's your man servant?"

"He's alive. I'm alive. And now I wish to take my prize. My former home where my family's blood was spilt. The line of Kavelu has returned." She spoke loudly for all the nobles surrounding the entrance to hear.

Lokai frowned and looked at her emotionless face. Then, grunting, he turned and walked through the gateway.

"First, we need the current lord to yield his title to you. It's that or execution, but we'll give him the choice. I wish to be benevolent."

An elder noble of Mo'unga Vela greeted them at the gate and fell to his knees. He formally surrendered the village and asked for the inhabitants to be spared.

"Get up," Lokai shouted, kicking the man in the ribs. "Take us inside and if you please me, you might just live."

Abel walked beside Mahina. They held each other's hands. As they stepped inside, his stomach turned at the sight of devastation the chain shot had caused in its wake, having passed through the village walls with ease. Dozens of men and women were dead, struck by the cannonballs and cut in half by the chains which burst with incredible power through their fales. Homes where they thought they would be safe from the battle raging around. Blood, broken bones and body parts were scattered. Ruined buildings lay flat. The village had been packed with civilians from the surrounding smaller villages, and they had come here with the false pretence of safe haven. Huddled together, they could not have known the devastation that would befall them as the cannons were unleashed. There were screams of pain from all areas of the village, and the devastation on limb and property were incalculable. Even some of the hardiest of the invading soldiers emptied their bellies in sickness at the sight of the death they had wrought. Lokai's eyes widened, but he did not stop his march through to the great speaking hall of Kolo Mo'unga.

"Take me to Hou'eiki Doko. I want to see his face. I want him to beg for my mercy," he said, asking the prostrate nobleman to show them the way.

Masila glowed with pride. "Mighty Lokai. The gods favour you today. I will send messages to Maka in the north of your victory. He must know that he'll be next to feel your wrath. The kingship is close my lord."

The group walked into the meeting fale. This was the great hall where the village chief would entertain guests and hold council. However, as they arrived, instead of Hou'eiki Doko, they found all six of the chief's wives standing in a line to greet them. Beside them, Vai Nonga and Doko's two brothers waited silently with heads bowed. Each of the wives had recently had their hair cut, and they wore it unkept without ornament. Solemnly, they stood aside and allowed the party to pass.

"What's the meaning of this? Why are you wearing your hair in the fashion of mourners? Vai Nonga. Answer me, where's your master?"

Vai Nonga looked up at Lokai and then turned to face Ono Hiva. "As you see, he's inside." Vai Nonga pointed into the building.

He entered and gestured for them to follow. Inside, they saw a row of mats surrounded by bowls of frangipani flowers and of luscious fruit. Atop a high bed of mats, the lifeless body of Hou'eiki Doko lay. White of colour and covered in ash.

Vai Nonga turned to face them.

"Our great lord died five days ago, before your arrival from Natuini. We have been in mourning day and night, praying to the gods in thanks that he was not alive to see what you have done with his beloved Mo'unga Vela."

The venerable Doko, Chief of the Grey Hair, had already lost an unwinnable battle well before the first cries of war had sounded.

Epilogue

Tihani's near naked body glistened with freshly rubbed coconut oil. She knew well enough her guest, a Tongan snake handler called Kulapo, could not but gaze unashamedly upon her pleasing curves, covered only by a small, tightly worn mat around her waist. She sat with her legs together and comfortably by her side. Her beauty, as she discovered, could lower the guard of most men and even some women. She had been more careful over the years to wield this power as it sometimes attracted unwanted attention, mostly from persistent nobles who wished for more than the nourishment of her refreshments. However, when needed, secrets would flow from the mouths of those who were entranced by her deliberate seduction, and so with this tool, she learned of the goings-on around her. She applied this method so skilfully today.

"A strange profession. Snake handling," Tihani said curiously, sipping on a bowl of fresh coconut water.

"Yes. A dangerous profession indeed. It's been my calling, as was my father and his ancestors before him. For generations we have been masters of the serpent. Our techniques are the most efficacious, and so are our teachings."

Enjoying some light refreshment of fruit and coconut flesh, the strangely attired man sat cross legged across from Tihani within the cool confines of her expansive fale. As well as a traditional ta'ovala, the man wore a series of thick tapa cloth bandages around his arms and legs. But it was the torn palangi shirt and worn boots which caught her eye. He had explained that he had travelled to the far reaches of the Pacific and had met peoples from all over the world, boasting he may be the most travelled Tongan in all the ocean.

"Since last I saw you, my skills have been in much demand. I'm well received in the islands of Niue, where I saved two young brothers from the bite of the yellow-bellied sea snake. In honour of my service, they decorated me with this tatau."

He pointed to his arm where the inked image of a snake standing on his tail had been etched. His entire body was covered in tatau, each drawing a snake of various description and pose.

"Amazing." She feigned interest. Leaning forward, she touched his arm sensually and was pleased when he took a startled breath. She could almost see his heart beating out of his chest.

"Has your lord Finau claimed his empire?" she asked.

"Finau? No. He started a civil war that seems will last forever, but his control now extends from his lands in Vava'u to Ha'apai. So, for now, his raid on Nuku'alofa has quenched his thirst for blood and he's content to let Tongatapu alone. Maybe he's seen enough bloodshed. Though, like Finau I understand your husband also used palangi weapons to fight his enemy."

The man scratched his neck and winced as if he felt a twinge of pain.

"Lokai's last great rival, Maka. He prepares for war. He has heard of the massacre on Mo'unga Vela and has sought to strengthen his stone walls. What's more, he has sought to trade with palangi sailors, paying a high price for their weapons."

"What else have you heard since your arrival?" She smiled seductively, leaning forward and moving closer to him.

He was turning red and shifted uncomfortably.

"I've been told that three months on from the victory, Hiva now rules from Mo'unga Vela, and her daughter has returned to Kahoua with her father."

Kulapo drank from the bowl of coconut water. He spilled a portion onto his beard, which he wiped away with his free hand.

"I was told Hiva has taken Vai Nonga as her trusted adviser, sparing his life in exchange for his eternal loyalty. The mighty warrior Ruaka lives yet. Though it is said his body was badly broken. After he recovered, he disappeared. Rumours are he has fallen into a dark mood, exiling himself to one of the outer islands. His second in common, Seletute, now protects the noble lady."

"And what of the palangi? I have met the handsome young man, Epeli."

"Ah, yes. I saw him from a distance in my travels when I traded in Kahoua. He's strong and has gained favour with Lokai. I've also heard rumours about his friendship with the chief's pretty daughter ..."

"Are they true?" Tihani asked, motioning to Samena to pour another drink for the weary traveller. The older of the two servant girls, Lulu, bent down behind his back and massaged his shoulders, digging deeply into the knots of muscles.

"Oh, yes. Malo. So wonderfully good ...." He groaned and closed his eyes.

"Well?" she asked again.

His eyes flickered open. "I apologise, lady. The hands of your servants are lovely. Ah, perhaps the rumours are just mere gossip. I can't believe that Lokai would allow the boy to live if he had taken his daughter. It would be difficult to find a suitor, and it would bring shame to the girl's mother. The common people would blame her for a wayward upbringing. They would say that the morals of her mother have been passed to their daughter."

"Unless that's what Hou'eiki Lokai wants."

He considered her suggestion before speaking. "Possibly, but I wouldn't know the mind of the great Hou'eiki of Natuini." He shrugged and wiped away the sweat from his brow. "Forgive me, the ocean winds blow hot today, don't you think?"

"Lokai's mind is closed to me since I was banished to Hule. I'm not sure he cares for the commoner's opinions. He never did while I was his wife. In any case, it's up to every woman or man to decide who they'll love. It should never be something designed by what's convenient for the hou'eiki or the people. The commoners may sleep with whomever they choose, but they will spit upon their 'eiki for the same."

"Yes, that's always been the way of the Natui. My people as well."

Another female appeared at the entrance and stood to one corner of the fale. She was clearly a seasoned warrior given the scars on her arms and body, and sported two throwing kolo attached at her side by a leather belt.

Kulapo shifted uncomfortably when he saw the woman. She stood at a distance behind him but was watching him from the shadows.

"I didn't know our conversation would be attended by warriors. I'm a master of serpents, not a weapons trader."

"Do not fear Melino. She's my trusted shield maiden and fought in the battle of Mo'unga Vela." Tihani ran her fingers along his arm tatau. "Now tell me more. Tell me of the palangi."

He looked unconvinced by her assurance, but continued to converse. Samena poured another generous amount of coconut water into his cup. He took another long drink and coughed.

"It went down the wrong way," he said, whilst continuing to cough. When he had stopped and collected himself, he continued.

"The other palangi were told to return to their island. But they're not alone. Soon after, Lokai sent some of the captured Grey Hair women and their children with them. The widows and orphans of the fallen warriors. The palangi leader, Lu'fa, he did not want the Grey Hair to stay but Lokai left them on Tapu Motu anyway."

"He wants the foreigners to remain," she said, sitting back in a resting position.

"I'm sorry. Why?"

"Lokai betrayed the palangi. He promised they would be allowed to leave if they helped him win his war. What he didn't tell them was that the war is not won until Natuini Si'i is destroyed. Hou'eiki Maka will be his next conquest. So he sent them back to Tapu Motu to await his preparations for his next campaign against the north. Lokai expects the palangi leader to train Natui warriors to use the palangi weapons. The ones that kill with invisible fire. He sent women so they may form relations and bind the palangi to him further. It's very smart. Insidious, but smart."

Kulapo looked confused. "If you know all this, why did you ask me?" he asked with sudden irritation, gently pushing away Lulu's hands.

Tihani did not speak. She sat in silence and watched him without expression.

"My lady. Then you already know that the newborn son of Lokai and Becca, the heir to his lands, is dead. The poor boy, barely a month old, was found killed by a poisonous snake."

She remained silent.

"The strange thing is, my lady, with utmost discretion, I procured a deadly katuali sea snake for you on my last visit. There is no land serpent in all of Natuini that has such a deadly bite … and katuali virtually never bite without provocation."

"And I must thank you for your discretion in this matter."

Tihani nodded towards the towering female who had been standing at attention close by. Kulapo sensed the immediate danger and attempted to stand, dropping his drink to the ground in panic, but as he tried to escape, he immediately fell to his knees, overcome with fatigue and confusion. Looking at his now empty bowl, a fine silt remained at the bottom of the cup and he knew he had been poisoned.

Before he could speak, two hands reached around his head, and with a quick twist the strength of the warrior was enough to snap his neck. He died instantly.

"Melino, when it's dark, take his body and throw him to the sharks." Her order was dispassionate. He had served his purpose. Now he was an unnecessary witness.

Her personal guard and hero of the battle of Mo'unga Vela dragged the body away from the comfortable tapa mats whilst Samena picked up the cup, removing the evidence of his demise.

Tihani stood. A fire burned in her heart.

"I haven't finished with my husband. He's made me suffer this indignity too long, so before I return to Ha'amoa, I will become his great goddess of suffering and his dreams of an empire will be burned while I watch."

"Why not take what you have of the fleet now and flee? I would ensure your safety, lady. You know I'll go with you to the end of the earth." Melino bowed her head in respect.

"I know you would." Tihani gave her a brief smile. "I dream of leaving my husband's prison. I will. But not before I've spoiled his dreams."

Tihani stepped out of her fale and into the sunlight. Around her the people of Hule worked and toiled, preparing Lokai's great war fleet, building his weapons and gathering resources for what he believed would be his great victory over the whole of Natuini. Trusting her to faithfully see to this task was his mistake. She would ensure that all he had ordered would be ready for war once the next cyclone season was over, and she would also ensure her most loyal people were on those ships and would play a pivotal role in the days ahead.

As she emerged, those who saw her bowed deeply and averted their eyes. Her people loved her for her generosity and outward compassion, but those who understood were also terrified of their noble lady whom they knew wielded the power of the dark gods, and those who defied her died mysteriously or disappeared, never to be seen again. She enjoyed the feeling that fear provided her. Sometimes enjoying it more than the love of her people. Now it was that fear which gave her the energy she needed to take her vengeance. The oncoming war and the appearance of the foreign fighters gave her an opportunity she could not ignore. Lokai had used the palangi and their weapons as his instruments of death, but now she saw how she could turn them to her own advantage.

For now, it was a time to be patient. A time to prepare. A time to remind a brave young man to keep the promises he once made.

About The Author

J.M. Antony lives in New Zealand with his beloved wife, son and daughter. Throughout his career he has been lucky enough to travel to and live in some amazing places, including parts of Asia and the Pacific.

J.M. spent several years living in the Tonga islands where the journey towards writing *From The Sky* began. It was there, he learned incredible histories of ancient ocean empires spreading from Tonga to Samoa.

When he is not writing, J.M. is a medieval history enthusiast and has taken up various styles of sword martial arts over the years. He loves playing games with his children and possibly admits to being ever so slightly competitive over a good game of scrabble.